DARK DAYS OF THE 22ND CENTURY

First Published in Great Britain 2021 by Mirador Publishing

Copyright © 2021 by Bryan James Harris

All rights reserved. No part of this publication may be reproduced or transmitted, in any form or by any means, without permission of the publishers or author. Excepting brief quotes used in reviews.

First edition: 2021

Any reference to real names and places are purely fictional and are constructs of the author. Any offence the references produce is unintentional and in no way reflects the reality of any locations or people involved.

A copy of this work is available through the British Library.

ISBN: 978-1-914965-12-8

Mirador Publishing
10 Greenbrook Terrace
Taunton
Somerset
TA1 1UT
UK

DARK DAYS OF THE 22ND CENTURY

BY

BRYAN JAMES HARRIS

ALSO BY THE AUTHOR

Don't Let The Sun Go Brown
(As Bryan James)

DEDICATION

FOR SEVERAL REASONS I WANTED to dedicate this work to someone who helped make it possible to have it published, and whose friendship I value as well and as much as his generous spirit. Thank you, Lester. You have made a difference in being there for me. You do make a difference, and I hope you will continue to be you, promoting your own special thoughtfulness and kindness, day to day, for a very long time.

CONTENTS

CHAPTER

1. — ESCAPE	9
2. — SO THIS IS WHAT HAPPENED	54
3. — MORE PLACES TO HIDE	89
4. — TAKING CARE OF BUSINESS	120
5. — EXPANDING THE BUSINESS	169
6. — CONSOLIDATION	218
7. — SOMETHING MORE TO CELEBRATE	277
8. — REVERSAL OF PROSPECTS	338

CHAPTER 1

ESCAPE

IT WAS DARK FOR THAT time of year, or so it seemed. The stars were not as bright as they might have been. Trees and bushes rustled as though some unwanted creatures were pushing their way through. Wild dogs howled to intensify the feeling of loneliness, giving the late evening an even more sinister tone.

Robin snuggled deeper into the frayed material he'd found to help make his bed of leaves and earth just a little more cosy. The gouge on the top of his head still pained him after all this time, even though it had healed to a scar that felt huge to his fingers. It had been all of 20 days since the attack that had changed his life forever, and he wondered why he was still alive. In his misery he felt it would have been kinder to him if they had finished him off completely. Something told him he was due plenty more misery before the world was done with him.

He always called himself Robin, the name given to him by his father, even though his allotted personal id number was always fresh on his tongue. He preferred not to think of such things, mysterious though they were to him, as he slowly dropped into a troubled sleep, hoping for a restful night without his worst nightmares plaguing him.

The night gave him little rest though, thanks mainly to the yowling dogs. That noise somehow refreshed the memory of the Mo brothers kicking and beating him. Then the horror of the pain in his head as a sharp knife ripped into his skull. He heard again in his nightmare, the sound of wild dogs as his mind took him on a fearful journey of his life so far. His night drifted on with visions of one sad event after another.

He awoke, scared and trembling, not just because of the cool morning air, and he knew right then that he had to do something to put his nightmares to rest. He could always go back to the home he had shared with his uncle, aunt and young cousin Mark. His uncle would be angry at him, as he always seemed to be of late, not like the loving way he had accepted him in when his father had been taken away. Even if his uncle didn't make life hard for him, he knew the Mo brothers would, and they would surely beat him up worse next time.

Something strange had happened to him though, and he knew that this had changed his life forever. Perhaps the knife had damaged his brain, or something, for he was no longer recognised by the security post at the edge of the village. Whenever anyone went out hunting rabbits, they had to pass the posts which always showed their number on a tiny screen. If anybody wasn't back by nightfall they would be hunted down and punished. Ordinary villagers were not allowed to just wander away.

The security post south of the village, no longer knew him. Neither did the one to the west. He no longer existed, so it seemed, but if this was death then it was more painful than life. He could come and go as he pleased, but people still had eyes, so he had hidden away as his head had healed itself. He still needed food and felt as hungry as he usually did. He hadn't felt the comfortable feeling of a full belly for many years, not since his mother had cherished the family with her tasty rabbit stew. After his uncle had taken him in, he was only given enough to eat to give him energy to work in the fields. Now, in his isolation from the village, he kept traps for small rodents, catching the odd rabbit and roasting them over a small fire. Fruit grew on many bushes and trees, but his inner hunger never really faded. Could it be, he wondered, a hunger of a different kind than from food?

His thoughts wandered back to his immediate future, perplexing him, for he had no experience of life outside the village, and he was very afraid of what might be out there. He wondered if he could continue to survive. One thing he decided on though, was that he had to clear up his past, or it would haunt him forever. He had to deal with the Mo brothers, once and for all. Then he could move on. Perhaps the world outside the village was a better place.

He sought the high ground, a high, wooded hill that overlooked the village and much else, although for now his interest lay only in one direction. He needed to know what the Mo brothers did, for he was sure they never worked in the fields. As the sons of the village chief they had privileges and special duties. He climbed the tallest oak tree he could find. A giant of a tree and beautiful as trees went. It smelled good and felt good to Robin as he made his way up with ease to the highest big branch that would bear his weight. That's where he stayed throughout the day for seven days, making a mental note of everything that happened. He was surprised at the number of people, from outside, who came to do business with the chief.

Most of the men that had paid a visit to the chief came with a package of some sort, but it was the fact that they had all entered the village from the north which Robin found most interesting. Did this mean that there were a lot more people to the north compared to the south, or was it a case of the chief doing his own special kind of business with his own particular friends from the north? Sometimes the visitors took away some of the stored produce from the barn. Several callers brought handcarts on which to load the fresh vegetables.

Before climbing down and retreating some way into the thick part of the woods each evening, to seek some food and to sleep, he always took in the views from all around him. If he squinted, he imagined he could almost see movement towards the north, as though lots of people were milling around or walking in a certain direction. The way the dimming sunlight now shone on the surfaces suggested the paths were wide and smooth. Perhaps that was a river, he had heard about, in the distance? He knew he had many questions that could only be answered by investigation, but he was not ready for that yet. First things first, he'd already decided, to handle his nightmares, after which he must be ready to explore further afield.

His observations of the Mo brothers suggested that they were confined to their house at certain times of the day, when the whole family came together and went inside. He knew by the position of the sun when these times were, and these times suggested themselves as safe periods for him to be about. Towards dusk the three brothers joined together, walking around and looking for someone to bully. The rest of the time they were located in different areas, abusing particular women.

From his vantage point Robin saw everything there was to see of life in the village. His uncle looked even more broken and unhappy than usual. None of the people he observed, save for the Mo brothers and the chief, ever looked as though they were enjoying life. They were lugging heavy things around, bent double in the fields, or trying to avoid contact with anybody else.

On a Sunday afternoon, the chief had pulled out a group of youths, just starting to sprout hairs on their upper lip, and locked them into the barn. A short time later a group of five, rough looking men arrived to take them away, after first tying their hands and linking them all together with rope. The men were none too kind, and the youths looked frightened. He knew those that had been taken away, not as friends, but as co-sufferers, and he realised that without the attack from the Mo brothers he would almost certainly have been marched out of the village, that very same day, to a life even worse than what it had been before. This was all too obvious. He swore to himself that he would at least try to pay the hated brothers back in some way. He hadn't worked out how yet, but like the patience he had learned in trapping small game, he knew that by watching he would learn how. Patience had been one of the few things his uncle had taught him, how to bide his time and strike at the right opportunity.

Realising that he had to stay invisible, now that he was unknown and probably thought of as dead, he slept in different places, so as not to leave a trail or disturb the bushes and plants too much. In the wet ground, he always did something to disguise his footprints. He was relishing his freedom and had no intention of returning to the village to be beaten down like his uncle or taken away like the other youths had been to suffer some unknown fate. Why would they be tied up if it was going to be something good they were being taken to?

His sleep was still disturbed by his nightmares, but with each passing night they held less terror for him. He was able to see the Mo brothers for the cowards they were, and an idea was slowly building in his mind.

Ever since the chief had moved in there had been many changes, even Robin recalled them, and he was all but 4 and a half at the time. They were no longer allowed to keep dogs as pets for one thing. They were banished from the village, and a special kind of fence was installed at the very outer edge of the perimeter of the village. This was a metal fence which gave off sparks if you touched it, and then it hurt like hell.

One of the duties the Mo brothers had happily taken on was to kill any stray dogs getting too close to the external periphery. They took out some fouled meat to places where dogs came sometimes, to poison the dogs, and beat to death any that could still breathe, as well as any that were not able to.

Robin still missed the cute puppy he had helped to rear, a deep brown colour and a placid nature. His Digga would never hurt anyone, and he cried when his father was made to take it away. It wasn't long after that that his dad was taken away. He'd been talking with the chief and lost his temper. Robin never knew what the argument was all about, but that evening 4 of the chief's men came into their home which was just opposite the painted brick walls of the chief's villa. Robin and his mother were dragged out, along with his father. He watched as they took his dad away, never to see him again. Some friends of the chief took over their sturdy hut that had been built by Robin's grandfather, leaving his mother to find a hovel to rest in at night. Robin was always sad that his grandfather had died before he'd been born but felt so much worse when his father was taken.

For days his mother cried, then she seemed to have made up her mind about something. She kissed Robin tenderly then took him to her brother. She begged him to take Robin in. His uncle reluctantly agreed for he was another mouth to feed, and that meant more work for him and his wife.

Robin didn't know what was going on with his mother, but as he came out early the next morning a small crowd gathered looking at something. It was the body of his mother. She had been beaten and slashed with a knife.

Someone said she had taken a knife to the chief, and that was what she had got in return. Robin, shocked and numb, crept back to the rear of his uncle's home and cried in despair.

Too many bad memories hit Robin as he looked around the village from his vantage point in the tree, his anger rising, now with it a determination to settle some scores. He noticed his aunt taking water from the well. She had never shown him much kindness, but then again, kindness was a rare commodity it seemed.

*

One of the Mo brothers was in the habit of visiting a hut at the edge of the village, where a woman lived, with a daughter around Robin's age. He was the youngest of the trio and was called Abdul. The brothers were all bigger than Robin, but it seemed to him that he should be selective. Take the weakest and the closest first.

The idea that had formed in Robin's mind was to make use of the dogs to repay some of the harm done to him and his family. Firstly, he needed to make friends with some wild dogs. Walking well outside the village, away from the paths, where the trees and bushes grew close together, he made himself a den up inside a tall oak tree. The dogs would not be able to reach him there, and he was far enough away from the village so that his fires to cook meat would not be noticed. Already he felt stronger after having been able to have recently trapped more game, and the fruit bushes were more productive in this area, but he decided he would need to be as well fed as the Mo brothers before starting with his plan.

This tree was a good vantage point for it allowed him to see the very edge of the village as well as a path leading to it from the south. One clear, sunny day, he spotted a traveller with a small barrow approaching his old home. The man stopped to rest, but then did something rather odd, that took Robin all day to work out. The man dug his fingers into the roots of an old rotting tree, which came out dark with a fine brown debris. The man proceeded to rub his very pale face with this material he had excavated, until his face was much darker. Taking out a small glass mirror, the man investigated his face, and rubbed some more to make the colour even and smooth across his face. Satisfied with that he rubbed his arms and hands with the same material. After this the man walked on, pushing his almost empty barrow.

All that day, and well into the evening, Robin puzzled about what he had seen. "Why would someone darken their skin?" he asked himself.

The puzzle slowly solved itself when Robin realised that the traveller had become the same colour as the chief and his brood. Most people in the village had white skin. Perhaps that was why they were hated and abused. It seemed likely that being the same colour as the chief would bring some advantages. It was a lesson he kept in the front of his mind.

That very night Robin's plan started to evolve when a lone dog was attracted to his cooking fire. He encouraged the dog by throwing bits of meat its way. The dog wagged its tail in appreciation but wouldn't come within 5 feet of Robin. The next night the dog was back, and the next. On the fifth night it came level with Robin, and took a piece of meat from his hand, then allowed itself to be stroked for a few moments. It ate its fill then it was off straight away.

The next night the dog he had called Digga brought a friend with him. A large Alsatian with his ribs showing. He called the Alsatian, Chief as he snarled just like the village chief.

Soon the 2 dogs were regular visitors. They both became friendly, and even visited during the day, mooching around and watching Robin. Then they started to linger in the evening, stretching out and yawning, with food in their bellies, and the heat of the dying embers to give them some warmth. When Robin relaxed against the tree, Chief would turn his back to the fire, as though he were on guard duty. That made Robin smile. He still clambered to his den each night because he still wasn't sure he could trust the animals totally, but friendship grew from both sides.

The small game was plentiful away from the village, helping Robin to go from strong but scrawny to well fed with muscle. When the dogs were around, he called them to come along. He even got them to stay in position while he checked his traps. When he went to a small heath where rabbits often played in the open during the day, he taught the dogs how to trap a rabbit between them. They were really proud of themselves, wagging their tails like never before. They even brought the prize back to Robin, who had been watching, so that the kill could be roasted.

Aware that he had been making too many trails around his den, Robin reasoned that it was time to find a new location. He did his best to camouflage his little home in the tree but realised the ground below would be a dead giveaway, to anyone coming close, that someone had been there often. His instincts told him to be invisible. He used an old tree branch to rake away his footprints and fire ashes, making sure that leaves and dead wood covered as much as possible.

He made his way east, about 2 miles, where the undergrowth became even thicker. His 2 dogs followed him most places by now. Finding a suitable tree he could sleep in, Robin cut up twigs with his rusty penknife, wishing he had something stronger to work with.

Over his meal that evening, dogs in attendance, he realised that he was putting off what must be done. He would never be free of the past if he couldn't consolidate it somehow, and he knew that meant confronting his worst enemies.

The very next day, avoiding the path where possible, he made his way to the security gate on the south side of the village. The dogs were happy to stay outside the perimeter, while Robin hid in the bushes outside the hut where Abdul frequently came to rape the woman and intimidate the girl. This day he was later than usual, but Robin was glad he'd taken the time to smear the brown substance over his face. It would mean that nobody would easily recognise him.

Abdul wasn't too interested in the woman that day. Robin heard him screaming at her, "You filthy whore. Don't just lie there. Clean up that blood." Then he left abruptly, but not back towards the village, instead he headed out towards the security post. Robin trailed some way behind.

The youngest Mo brother inspected the post. Robin watched as Abdul inserted a sliver of metal into a tiny slot and turned it around. Abruptly the lights on the post went out, and Abdul was able to walk past it without any signal from the post. Robin quickly realised that that tiny piece of metal was a valuable tool. Once he was the other side of the post Abdul reached backwards to turn the lights back on again and put the tool safely into an inside pocket.

Ah, so that's one of his little tricks, thought Robin, still wondering what his purpose might be.

Robin didn't need to worry about the post recognising him any more, so he continued to follow his enemy who was now confronted by 2 savage dogs. Abdul took out his long knife, slashing at the dogs, backing away towards safety. That is when Robin moved forward to take advantage of the situation. He quickly looked behind him to make sure nobody was coming, he found his penknife and readied it.

Looking behind himself Abdul spotted Robin only a few paces behind. "Hey, careful there," shouted Robin, those dogs look fierce.

"Yes," agreed the Mo brother, happy to see someone else that could distract the dogs from him, but that wasn't what Robin had in mind. With the blade of his penknife pointing down, he raised his hand, as if trying to scare off the dogs. Higher went the knife until it glinted in the evening sunshine. Suddenly Abdul looked worried, but far too late. The blade smashed into the top of his skull, causing him to drop like a stone.

Robin retrieved the long knife Abdul had been carrying, then he searched his pockets to see if he had anything of value. There were several things, including a wallet, that Robin kept for himself. He was mostly interested in the small metal tool that turned off the security post. The penknife was hard to remove. He tilted it back and forth making the hole bigger, producing more blood. At last it came out, very red and covered in gore. He let the dogs lick it clean.

Picking up his victim under the arms, Robin dragged his corpse up the path as far as he could, careful not to leave any obvious drag marks. Resting up for a few minutes, Robin was surprised at how well it had gone. Rather than any feeling of remorse, he actually felt stronger.

With the dogs sniffing around him, Robin pushed and pulled his victim off into the undergrowth where he had spotted a pit in the ground. He threw the corpse down there and started to wonder how he could get the dogs to eat the flesh of Abdul to make it look like he had a fight with them and came off the worse.

He made a little fire to make the flesh burn, and sure enough this smell got the dogs excited, but not just Digga and Chief. On the other side of the cavity 3 snarling pit bull terriers arrived and soon were laying claim to the body and eager to get down to it. Robin, not unhappy about this, backed away slowly, content for the savage dogs to have their way. Chief and Digga snarled back, but everyone knew they were no match for the ferociousness in front of them. One of the fierce dogs slid down into the pit, sniffing the body while still looking ominously at Robin. Still moving backwards, Robin's 2 dogs watched as hunger pangs overcame the inhibitions of the 3 savage dogs, who started to attack Abdul's remains, ripping his clothes quickly to shreds. That was the thing Robin had been waiting for. He took off like a flash, getting back to the path and running like a madman with his dogs panting behind him.

He ran up to where his traps had been set, picking up 2 fat rabbits, then scurried some more until he was out of breath. Finding a place where the foliage was thick, he led the dogs quickly into the darkness of the undergrowth, looking for a place deep inside to cook his rabbits and spend the night.

The triumphant feeling lasted well into the night, after he and the dogs had had their fill of meat, and he was too tired to climb anywhere. He snuggled up with Digga, with Chief at his back. He suddenly stared into the darkness and realised what he had done. He had taken a man's life. He was not sorry about who it was, rather it was the deed. He consoled himself saying it had to be done, but the fear and the shivering he suffered that night was nothing to do with the cool darkness surrounding him.

He barely sank into unawareness, as he lay there, watching in his mind's eye as the savage dogs ripped at the dead body. As much as he had hated Abdul, and the rest, his conscience troubled him badly, feeling himself to be not much better than a wild animal. In a lucid moment he asked himself, "What other way could I have removed this horrible creature from this

Earth?" Now he almost felt satisfied that he had achieved something good, especially for that poor woman that Abdul kept on hurting. Still he kept awaking in a cold sweat, fearing they would be searching for him, but after lifting his ears to the wind, and hearing no sign of hunters coming for him, he drifted back to his uneasy sleep.

It was almost morning, and the sky was beginning to lighten, when he forced himself to consider other ideas for dealing with bad people. He felt so alone, and unable to confront the chief's family directly. He recalled how a spike from some tree root had pierced the body of Abdul and wondered if this might be a better way to kill people or even protect himself from anyone looking for him. He saw it in his mind, a pit with sharp spikes, covered over with something soft, so that someone could easily fall down and impale himself. He told himself that he would have to mark them in a special way, so he didn't fall victim to such a fate. Then he forgot all about spikes and pits and relaxed into a brief, solid sleep.

Digga nudged Robin awake. It was still early, but the sun was bright, and the day called for some action to stop his mind working overtime. His first rational thought was that he should go and remove any trace of his involvement with Abdul's death. He decided that it must look like only the dogs were involved, if of course his body was ever found. They would know naturally that he, Abdul, had turned off the security post for a short time, so would suspect he could have gone beyond the perimeter fence. They would surely widen the search, meaning he had to act quickly.

Making his way cautiously to the scene of the crime, he nearly retched up the few berries he'd eaten for breakfast on the way. There was hardly any flesh left on the bones. The clothes Abdul had been wearing were torn and scattered, some even were dragged away. He could see no evidence of his own involvement. Even the hole he had made in the top of his victim's head had been well disguised by the dogs' activities. To make the scene complete, the dogs had left their turds close by. His 2 dogs had followed him, and even they showed no sign that they wanted to linger. Chief seemed to turn his nose up at the scene, now facing away from it.

As Robin turned away from the carnage, he noticed how both dogs suddenly became attentive. Their ears went up and they sniffed the air, whining. He knew it was time to get out of there. Someone was approaching.

Skirting around the pit, he headed deeper into the bush, away from the path where people could be. Running as fast as he was able through the overgrown bushes and brambles, he headed south, only stopping once to drink from a small pond.

As he continued, he came to a path, which clearly joined up with the southern path from the village, but now the path was going left around a mound. Not wanting to be found on an open path, he crossed it quickly and walked up the steep hill leading to the mound, his dogs still eagerly accompanying him.

The slope was heavy going and the trees grew close together, but there was plenty of greenery to hide him. Even when he climbed a tree at the top, he realised he could not be seen from any direction. To the south he saw the land drop away beyond the mound he was on. Several paths were visible that way, and he thought he saw evidence of a small fire close to what could be another village. His eyes strained to get more detail, but the distance and the bright sun got in the way of that. To the north he could just make out his village, for it was almost on a level with the mound, but not quite. In between, the land dipped down a little. He wondered what the dogs might have heard that had sent them all scurrying away, for there were no people visible on the path close to the pit of death, as he now thought of it. "Of course," he told himself, quietly, "it is always possible that the body had already been found, if not recovered."

He continued to survey the area for landmarks and places that could offer a safe refuge. There seemed to be greenery wherever he looked. The occasional glint of something bright reflecting the sun caught his eye, suggesting people in that area. Standing tall it seemed that everything to the far north glinted. "Too many people there," he suggested to himself, "more people means more danger." After his experiences in his village he certainly considered dogs to be better companions than people.

Chief's barking sent him sliding quickly down the tree. The last thing he wanted was for the dogs to attract attention. Digga was living up to his name, having scraped out a small hole in the ground. Chief was still barking excitedly. He had to check out what they had found and stop the barking.

He pushed Digga out of the way to look at what he'd found. At first, he saw nothing except that there was an open space beyond where the hole had been extended. He pushed his head in, only to be surprised that it wasn't dark inside. In fact he could make out what appeared to be steps going down. Thinking this could make an ideal place to call home, or at least hide out in, Robin used his hands to scrape away the soil. Chief being the impatient type worked out the hole was now big enough for him and brushed past Robin to descend easily down the hole. Digga quickly followed.

It was a few minutes later that Robin had improved on the size of the opening and followed on. It seemed odd that he could still see where his feet were treading. Perhaps it was the power of sunlight, he thought, followed by the notion that he shouldn't stay too long if he was to be dependent on the sun for light. The steps carried straight on down for about 20 steps. They appeared to be made of metal, quite strong, but showing plenty of rust in places. "They must have been there a long time," he told himself.

The dogs had disappeared through some foliage at the bottom of the metal stairway, but he could hear Chief barking for him to get a move on. He reached the bottom which seemed to be fairly solid. It was a surface similar to the paths, his mother had called it tarmac. Pushing aside a very heavily leafed tree branch, he found himself inside a large building. It was much bigger than the village hall, which only had 3 sides. This not only had 4 sides, but a proper roof as well. It felt strange to be in such a large covered space, and for a second he panicked, felt himself wanting to flee. The dogs broke his thoughts, sniffing about, tails wagging, clearly enjoying the new experience.

There was light coming from the ceiling, but it couldn't be sunlight because there was no hole. He stared at this and wondered. It was a long thin container close to the roof that gave out the light, and he recalled how the village chief had one like it in his house. He had seen it that time he had squeezed in between the walls between the chief's house and a neighbour's. That was when he was nearly 6 and the chief had taken his 10-year-old sister as a bride, even though he already had a wife.

What Robin had witnessed through the cracks in the wall horrified him. He could still hear his sister scream out in agony as the man who was in charge of the village entered and penetrated her deep inside, thrusting and crying out thanks to God. His sister had fallen to the floor sobbing hysterically and bleeding. It was 2 days later that she was buried. With such thoughts coming to the surface, Robin reminded himself that he had scores to settle, yet.

The room he now found himself in was full of dust, but there were still wooden tables there that his family would have been proud to have owned. On a counter were metal implements, knives and forks, and some real plates stacked on each other. He counted 15. His mother had only ever had 3 dishes.

A tap was noisily dripping some water into a large metal container. He tasted it and found it good and fresh, so he turned the tap on more to collect more water in his mouth, then closed it so it didn't drip. Next to that tap was another, identical. "Now why would there be 2 taps?" he asked Digga who had come up to see why Robin was being so slow.

He couldn't resist trying the other tap, and was amazed, and shocked even, when the water became warm, then hot. "This is truly a magical place," he mentioned to Digga. "Well done for finding it."

"Yelp, you're welcome," Digga replied.

The next thing to take his attention was a door. There were no real doors in his village, that swung back and forth like this one did, except in the chief's villa. The only way to close an entrance was to put something solid in the way, but there was never enough hard material to keep out the bad people or the bad weather.

Inside the door were several things of interest. More taps along one wall, and some odd-looking devices attached to the wall. They looked like they were for collecting water, but if that was the case, "Why do they have a little drain hole at the bottom?" he asked Digga. Several old metal signs were still visible around the room. The one above the water collecting devices said, 'PLEASE STAND CLOSE WHEN USING URINAL'. He stood close to one and peered closely inside it. He smelled some foul odour which suggested to him what it was possibly for. "It must once have been a wonderful world if everything was so well organised," he told himself.

A small room with the door hanging loose had a container attached to the floor, with a tiny amount of water in it. He guessed it might be connected with urinals.

Another door in that room looked interesting. It was quite solid and hard to open. Inside he spotted a pair of taps, but didn't see where the water came out. That was until he turned on one tap. He was suddenly hit with a flow of water from above his head, and that made him laugh out loud. A memory came up immediately, of his mother showing him pictures from a book she kept hidden from all but her family. She was showing how people used to keep themselves clean. She called it a shower. He also recalled how nice it had been those times when, as a small boy, he had been sat in a metal bath and washed all over. That gave him a nice warm, comfortable feeling, and he longed to be clean like that again. He told himself he would come back here and make himself fresh, but first there was more exploring to do.

He hadn't expected to find anyone else inside this place, and indeed had not seen nor heard any sign of anyone else, but when he walked past a shiny wall, he had assumed to be solid, he got quite a shock. There was someone there, through the wall. Robin stepped back immediately, wondering if he had been seen. Then he peered slowly into the shiny surface. As he did so a very dirty face looked back at him. Robin withdrew in alarm, a little afraid of the fierce looking face that had been watching him. He wondered why the dogs had not barked at this intruder.

Plucking up more courage, Robin jumped in front of the wall. The strange looking individual behind the wall did the same, at exactly the same moment, but this time they stood looking at each other for a while. When Robin raised his hand to touch his face, the other guy did the same. He moved closer, as did the other guy. It was only when Digga came into the room, and he saw its reflection in the shiny wall, that the penny started to drop.

Now making silly movements to amuse himself, he finally got a good look at the image he presented to the world. "What a horribly dirty monster I am," he told Digga who acknowledged that by wagging his tail hard.

Robin looked at where the water had hit his head, making his hair wet, and dripping down over his face to leave dark and light streaks. The brown stain he had used on his face was not in the least bit smooth. It looked like the Mo brothers had rubbed his face in the mud, and he'd cried all the way home. He laughed loudly at this thought. *Not any more*, he thought with determination.

"Look at those clothes," he said, assuming his mother's valence, admonishing himself. "There are bits of twig and leaves all over you, and you're bursting out of your top and trousers. I don't know where I'm going to get more material to make new garments. Have you been eating too much food lately? Just look at your hair. Anybody would think I never combed it for you." He laughed again at this, admitting to himself that his hair really was out of control, but really wishing his mother was there to tell him such things, then sobbed to himself at his loss.

He ran out of the big room feeling gloomy, straight towards a stairway, stopping just at the edge because it was mostly dark. Although he could see reflected light from below, he was initially reluctant to descend. Digga didn't allow him to contemplate for too long, brushing hard against Robin's legs, they both found themselves walking down stairs that had seen better days. The steps creaked but held their weight easily.

Dog and human made it to the bottom of the stairs safely, which opened up to a room so vast it made the big room upstairs look tiny. Lights were on in most of this area, and he could hear the buzz of something he assumed was electricity. "What have we got here, Digga?"

The dog kept silent, allowing Robin to find out for himself. Along the wall to his left a sign said, 'Chilled'. Remnants of some containers sat there. Some small plastic ones were called, 'milk', but when Robin touched one it broke open, spilling a foul liquid on to his fingers and on the floor. Looking closer, he noticed a date was printed on the package, just readable. He knew what year and approximately what month it was now, "May of 2119," he said, having no idea what the current day number was. The label said, 'BBF

03.01.2038.'

"Oh my, that's 81 years ago." His mum had always been so proud of his early skill with numbers. She knew it would help him to have that ability to read and use numbers and letters. He had been a natural student, but it was her patience that made him understand their value. Even when others couldn't count above 10, he fully understood about thousands and even millions.

Going further, there were more shelves on the left which were mainly covered in dusty fragments. The same applied to the wall that met him, causing him to turn right. There was a sign for, 'Eggs', and he knew what they were but had only seen the Mo brothers with some that had been cooked hard. He decided not to investigate the eggs, as they would also certainly be rather old by now and would smell worse than the urinals.

Walking on to some cabinets against the wall he noticed it became colder. There was ice inside these compartments. Across from these were other cabinets with doors on, some with ice protruding. He decided to remove an item to see what was inside. Some had interesting pictures. It took the use of his big knife, the one he had taken from Abdul, to prise one of the packets free. When some of the ice melted off, he was able to read most of the words on the box. It had in big letters, 'Chicken Pizza'. He had no idea what a pizza was, but he did like the image on the front of the container. Turning the box over, he was able to read how to cook it, but he didn't have an oven and 180 degrees seemed like a very hot temperature. He put the box back and investigated other cabinets.

"This is all food put into ice to keep from going off," he told himself. "There are carrots, and cuts of meat, and even things called fish. I'm sure nobody would mind if I tried some, but I need a way to be able to cook it." Suddenly, a brainwave. A label on the wall upstairs had something about turning off the power of the oven after use. He grabbed his pizza and went charging back upstairs.

There was indeed an oven. He clicked the switch next to the label he had remembered, and it all lit up. Reading the instructions again, he wondered what kind of thing he would put the pizza on, because the bottom inside the oven was grim and dusty. He decided the metal slide tray would be far better than putting the pizza in with the dirt, but with his mother again reminding him of some basic hygiene, he washed the oven tray under the hot water tap to make it a little cleaner.

Now he was confused with how he would set the temperature properly. He twiddled all the knobs he could find until the oven lit up. Also a number lit up which looked like the temperature setting to him. It showed 190, so he twiddled it some more to bring it down to 180. With that he put the pizza on the tray and put them both in the oven, wondering how he could estimate the time. He didn't see any clocks on the wall. Robin decided he could work out a way to time it. If he counted to 100 very quickly, he thought that would be one minute. So he proceeded to do that 20 times, checking frequently to make sure nothing was burning.

The smell from the oven told him the pizza was probably ready before he'd got past counting 100, 17 times. Strangely the dogs appeared from nowhere at this time and stood eyeing the cooked food still in the oven, through a glass window. He hadn't worked out how he was going to extract the pizza from the still very hot oven, meaning improvisation was required. Taking a plate, he washed it, then tried to slide it under the pizza. It wouldn't budge. So he tried that again with a fork in his other hand. He managed to get a grip, and all of a sudden, the pizza plopped onto the plate.

For a moment he stood there staring at it, then sniffed it. It really smelled good, and the dogs thought so too, but it was still hot. He used a silver knife with the fork to cut off some thin slices and threw each dog one. It was a while before they managed to eat their portion as they were still hot. The slices cooled rapidly on the floor, and the dogs finally wolfed their treat down, and were back looking for more, but the next slice was for Robin.

As he put the warm food into his mouth, careful not to burn himself, his taste buds went into overdrive as the cheese and tiny chicken pieces melted on his tongue. He threw the dogs another piece each, looked up to where he knew the sky to be, and said out loud, "Oh my God, that was good. If only my family could see me now, cooking food, and eating with real metal knives and forks. I feel like a lord." With that he wolfed down the rest of his meal, feeling happier than he'd ever done in his whole life.

*

The prospect of what else might be found in the cavern below prompted a determined effort to explore further. By his own reckoning he'd only walked less than a sixteenth of the floor space, and there was likely more that was hidden. Running down the stairs with renewed excitement, he took a right at the bottom, and systematically went along each lane, mentally noting anything he found that was still looking solid. He discovered a whole bunch of things he recognised, as well as many he didn't. When he found a large bag, he went back and started to pile treasures into it. Apart from clothes and shoes, there were towels, a thousand types of soap and shampoo, as well as practical things like scissors and combs. Robin decided that he had enough for his immediate needs and went back to make use of the shower.

He found the shampoo bottle fiddly, then managed to tip a quarter of its contents over his unruly hair. It was barely enough to create a good lather, his hair nor his body having seen soap for some years. It all made a difference though as he relished the warm water washing away accumulated grime. His feet, if cleaner, were rough, but he'd found something that might help that too, a cream to soften hard skin. It took a long time to wash away all the soap he'd used, but eventually having dried himself and stopped his hair dripping, he stood to admire himself in the shiny wall. Having never seen himself naked it came as quite a shock, especially as he was so pale, so pink.

Running a comb through his hair was a major difficulty, as it had become so entangled. "It is time for a cut," he told himself. That was easier said than done, but he chopped off strands here and there until he could at least push the comb through without obstructions. The only trouble was that there were big holes. He did his best to cut around the gaps to even it up, until eventually he convinced himself that it was pretty well perfect.

Stepping around the pile of damp hair on the floor, he combed his hair all the way back and caught the long hair into a clasp. Another interesting item he'd come across. "Now I look like my dad," he told the mirror.

"You'd better get a broom to clear up that mess," his mother's voice scolded, "but for goodness' sake get dressed first."

He did as instructed and marvelled at the softness and comfort of his new shirt and trousers against his skin, and loved the way the shoes enveloped and held his feet so firmly, even if walking seemed odd at first. It took a while to find a broom, but in the process a whole new category of cleaning soaps and devices had shown themselves to him. "I am really going to make this place shine," he told his mother, and he did, but wasn't sure where to throw the rubbish.

By this time, his stomach told him it was due to be delighted with some exciting new meal. Taking himself back downstairs, Robin scanned the cabinets with the frozen food inside. Feeling especially hungry he chose a couple of things, burgers and lasagne, to take up and cook. That was another success, with the dogs really enjoying the burgers.

He wondered where he could sleep that night. In the end he found a small space downstairs. It was cosy and there were plenty of garments to keep him warm, but it would have been nice to be able to stretch out his legs.

*

"Another day of freedom," he told himself on waking, deciding that he would find a better place to sleep at night. He did. There was a door upstairs that he hadn't been through. The floor was soft, a window looked out onto an overgrown patchwork of red brick and foliage, while a big wooden unit meant he would be able to stay hidden if anyone came through the door. With that settled he went outside to pick some berries for breakfast. A garden would be required where he could grow carrots and potatoes, which meant a sunny place out of the wind.

At the top of the tallest tree on the mound, Robin surveyed all around, looking for any sign of trouble or indeed any activity at all. The day was bright, with little sign that anyone lived on this world. He'd found some binoculars and used them now to scan activity in his old village. Everything looked normal there. To the south where he had previously seen smoke, he was just able to pick out details of another village. It was much like his, with 3 roads dissecting it, and people with glum faces working the fields.

Any growing field would have to be under the mound, he thought, providing there was enough sun. He knew where he could get seeded potatoes, for he saw some old sprouted ones below. Perhaps there were seeds for other things, as this place appeared to have everything he could ever need. He considered himself to be extremely lucky and hoped his luck would continue. "What about my uncle and aunty?" he asked. "They surely deserve some luck."

Thinking about his relations some more, he made up his mind to go and rescue them. He would do that tomorrow, Friday, right after weekly prayers when everyone returned to their homes. Robin still wondered what the whole thing was all about, as the chief only ever used words nobody understood at these meetings. They were made to rest on their knees, then stretch their arms forward with their faces in the dirt. The chief would always be at the front as though he was the one being worshipped, playing recorded sounds at different times, while they were all supposed to chant some unknown phrases back. It was all very tiresome, and nobody wanted to attend. Absentees were punished severely, with either a beating or being whipped.

*

On Friday morning Robin found a place to start cultivating his vegetables, and as he wandered the aisles of the cavern, there were even some seeds, which he planted. He made a pizza for lunch, giving a good half of it to the dogs so that he wouldn't be too full when he went to the village.

He used the sun to help him work his way towards the camp through the thicker part of the overgrown area leading to the village perimeter, with dogs in tow. He brought one long knife and the metal sliver that deactivated the security post. He wanted his dogs to come along with him, which he decided could cause some confusion if he was cornered.

He noticed how wary the dogs were of the gate and fence, so he gently lifted them over the little gate, then headed for some green cover just inside the village. The prayers were over now, but he could still hear the video show, which all kids had to watch. He'd seen the programmes so many times, he could almost recite them word for word. 'We must look after the planet. It is the only one we have. Nobody is allowed to use oil, or we will make the climate too hot and be flooded by the seas'. It went on and on, though he never found out what oil was, and he was a bit vague about the seas.

His intention had been to go directly to his uncle's home but hadn't expected anyone to be using the path. It was the 2 Mo brothers, he saw, and slipping past them would be hard. He decided to wait them out. They went to the small cottage a dozen or so yards ahead. It was the last home before the security post. He wondered why they couldn't leave that poor woman, and her daughter, alone.

The dogs placidly followed him behind a large bush to conceal himself from most directions. Chief and Digga had an instinct of keeping quiet when necessary. Robin touched their noses gently, to reassure them and himself.

A lot of shouting was coming from inside the small home. As usual the Mo brothers were accusing someone of being a vile whore for not attending prayers. Robin crept closer, wondering if he could use this situation to sneak past, but the abuse was getting worse. More shouting at the woman, followed by a scream. Robin was now in the open doorway, watching. Hafiz, the middle brother was standing over the woman lying in her bed, with a knife to her throat. Samar, the elder brother held the daughter by the wrist, restraining her.

"Do it," shouted Samar, as Hafiz's knife cut into the woman's neck producing a trickle of blood. The woman was clearly too weak to resist. The young girl tried to pull away, but she was held firm. She received a solid fist to the head from Samar, making her crumple to the floor.

"How dare you insult our God," screamed Hafiz, his knife sinking deeper into the woman's throat. There was already blood soaking her dress around her stomach area. She didn't look like she had much to lose, nor the strength to even protest, but still she tried to beseech them. "Please don't hurt my daughter," she croaked.

"Be quiet, whore of Satan. She will get her punishment as well," screamed Hafiz. With this, he pushed the knife deep into the flesh and across the woman's larynx. Her breath escaped in a rush, her eyes darkened, and her head fell to the side. Robin was frozen in place, unable to accept such barbaric treatment, but also unable to act, even though his hand was on the handle of his long knife.

"Now for this whore," shouted Samar, pulling the girl up and grabbing her dress to expose her. "You go first, little brother," he smiled.

Hafiz dropped the knife on the dead woman, preparing himself to inflict the required punishment on the girl.

It took a very hard nudge from Digga before Robin's frozen state melted somewhat. He knew what they intended to do, and saw red, still recalling how his sister had died. With Hafiz now approaching the girl, Robin could no longer restrain his anger. He took his knife, turned it upside down so that the blade was up. Samar saw him as he entered the small room but was unable to do anything before Robin had smashed the blunt part of the knife into Hafiz's head. He could never understand later why he didn't use the blade to kill this foul enemy directly, but he was acting on instincts which had taken over.

As Hafiz sank to the ground without a sound, Samar threw the girl aside and came at Robin with a knife in his hand and venom in his eyes. His upper lip curled upwards reflecting the hatred in his heart.

Unused to such fighting, Robin almost froze again, but Chief didn't. The dog hurled himself at Samar who was inches away from slashing Robin's face. Samar saw the dog and changed tactics, bringing his arm back and then when the dog was almost on him, he brought the knife across the dog's snout, gouging deeply. The force of the dog's leap pushed Samar to the ground, but not before the knife had been twisted around to be plunged into the dog's chest.

Now with a greater fury overwhelming him, Robin slashed at Samar as he tried to get up. First his blade went across Samar's chest, ripping his shirt, not penetrating deeply, but the scar would be a good one. Samar started to push himself up, his knife poised to cut into Robin's lower leg. Robin, now acting on furious instinct, saw that attack coming and slashed at Samar's wrist with brutal force. He watched the scene, frozen for a second, as blood spurted from the stump, with Samar's hand still holding the knife falling heavily to the ground.

Samar screamed out in pain as Robin kicked the knife well out of harm's way. He would have been content to let this awful excuse for a human being bleed to death slowly, and indeed watched him for a few moments relishing the pain he had inflicted. Robin knew that he had to end this completely. These 2 couldn't live to tell any tales.

The girl was still where she had fallen, watching in dread, wondering what would happen next. Robin decided to put on airs and graces to match his smart new clothes. He wasn't sure where his words came from, but they seemed appropriate. "As the server of justice, I pronounce you unfit to live." He slashed at Samar's good wrist to make it bleed, and further disable him. "You are going to hell," he said in Samar's face, remembering that phrase the chief had cursed so many with.

"You will not escape. I will find and torture you. You will die a horrible death," Samar spat out.

"Not a chance," said Robin, his own compassion now at a very low level. He put his small pocket knife against Samar's tongue so that he couldn't talk any more, then pushed the blade down to secure it firmly. All that Samar could do was groan and shake his head wildly in agony.

Looking at the girl Robin said, "We have to end this now. Unless we make it look like a fire killed these 2, they will come searching for us. Help me get that foul beast across your mother." She did as she was told. As they lifted Hafiz he started to groan. They got his torso so that it was partially across the dead woman. Robin lifted his head up by the hair, and for Samar's benefit, making sure he was watching, drove the long knife into his brother's throat, in a similar way to how Hafiz had murdered that poor woman. The hate in Samar's eyes was palpable, but Robin only gave him the evillest smile he could muster.

"You are next, pig's carcass," Robin spat out in Samar's face. "Oh, and when you get to hell, say hello to Abdul, because I sent him there as well." Feeling really evil now, Robin laughed again in Samar's face, and thrust the blade deep into his heart.

He knew that there was little time to cover his tracks. "Do you have anything that will burn and make a fire?" he asked the girl. "We are going to escape now that we have punished these 2, but we are going to live. I know a way out. We must burn this place down."

While the girl hunted for something to help start a good fire, Robin turned his attention to Chief who was still lying where he had fallen, still breathing. "Thank you, good friend," he said. "You saved me. You will go to heaven." Chief's watery eyes blinked, and beamed back, as if to say no thanks necessary. Again it was Digga that knew what to do, yelping gently, first touching noses with Chief, as if to say goodbye, he then picked up the knife and dropped it in Robin's hand. Robin knew what he was being urged to do and ended Chief's life as gently as he could.

The girl came back with a can. Robin wasn't sure what it was, as it smelled like rancid butter, but he wasn't inclined to be particular, as long as it would react to a flame. He poured some over Samar. The girl made a spark from 2 flints, and the man was alight almost instantly. Quickly moving to the woman's bed Robin doused the whole area well with the liquid, throwing some around the room. Very soon the flames were beginning to take over. He grabbed the girl's wrists, just to make sure she had no other ideas, got to the entrance to look out for anybody coming up the path, then with Digga at their heels they ran for the security post.

It was important that they didn't know the girl was outside the fence, so he turned off the security while they all walked through the small gateway. He used the small metal key to bring the security first down then back up. The girl blinked unhappily at this but questioned nothing. She was compliant, for now, but he suspected she would have a louder voice when the shock of everything that had happened began to wear off.

He took the usual route off the path, left into the deep undergrowth close to where Abdul had met his end. Carrying on some way until he felt reasonably safe, they stopped by a small stream to drink some water.

As they sat on the edge of a fallen tree, she turned to him, her eyes dull and devoid of any sparkle, "Thank you." She looked down for a second, then looked closely at him, noticing his clean clothes, "are you really the server of justice?" she asked weakly.

Robin smiled, "only as far as those evil Mo brothers are concerned. My name is Robin, and I used to live in the village before I escaped."

This caused her to look closely at his face, with slow recognition producing a ghost of a smile from her. "I know you," she exclaimed quietly, "and you helped me to escape as well. My name is Lucy. You look so like a lord," she continued, with admiration, unable to make longer sentences for now.

"When I escaped, I came to a safe place, where there are many good things. I will take you there, but we must keep it secret. We have to be very careful in how we move around."

She nodded gently, taking this all in.

"Today," continued Robin, "I was going to help my uncle to escape, but I saw what was happening in your home, and I couldn't ignore it. I am so sorry about your mother."

Her tears fell, and she looked away, then remembering something, she said in her stilted manner, "Your uncle is gone. His wife too. They took a lot of people. The chief said they were lazy."

Robin frowned. "At least I know not to come back here looking."

Digga decided at that point to come to get some attention and solace. "This is my dog. He is very smart. It was he that discovered our safe place." Speaking directly to Digga, he said, "Digga my good friend, please meet Lucy. She is coming to live with us."

Digga turned to Lucy, gave her a good sniff plus a little yelp of acceptance, knowing that it was too early to be friends or to get too close yet. He returned his snout to Robin's knees, still in need of more comforting after the loss of his good friend.

*

They waited behind the tree line until it was dusk to get across the path and not be too visible to anyone that might be about. There was nobody, but looking up at the empty greying sky, Robin felt some eyes watching him. "That can't be possible, surely?" he told himself, but his thinking turned to all of the amazing things that had been created by those that went before, and suddenly felt very exposed.

On the way to the stairway, Robin told Lucy about how he escaped. Explaining that a small electronic device had been gouged out when the Mo brothers attacked him. "It seemed to me that this tiny device is what knows our id numbers and tells the chief where we are. If we come through a security gate, it reports us. Without such a device we can go anywhere."

She blinked, saying nothing, getting the gist of what he had told her, but not understanding the implications.

"We must remove yours."

With great pride, Robin showed Lucy around the upper room. Her eyes went wide at the fact that there was light from the ceiling, but when she saw the oven, and felt warm water coming from a tap, she actually laughed in amazement. "This is like magic," she managed. He laughed too, in agreement.

"The first thing we need to do is to make you clean. You are simply too grubby to be in this clean place." She frowned at this but accepted his comment. He showed her the shower, and how to mix the hot and cold water to get the right temperature. "That is the soap for your body. The green bottle is to wash your hair. Wet it very well then use plenty of that liquid and rub it in well," he said. He opened the shampoo bottle because it was easy now he knew how, but suspected she would struggle with it.

"When you feel very clean, you can wrap that big towel around you to make you dry."

She smiled briefly and started to remove her clothes. "Don't leave me alone, please. I'm frightened."

So he waited and watched while she washed off a great deal of grime, and her long brown hair became softer. He saw how skinny she was. Her ribs had very little flesh on them, while bruises covered much of her body. Once again, he thanked the gods above for being able to save her. As she finished, he held the big towel up for her to wrap around her, then rubbed her hair dry with a smaller towel. "That was so nice," she smiled. "I must wash my clothes too."

"Don't bother with those, we will find you something better to wear," he said as he ran the comb through her hair, which surprisingly was not knotted up. "You do look so much better after that shower." For this he received another wholesome smile.

He took her down the stairs, to where the clothes were. She picked up some things that immediately crumbled in her hands, but beamed when Robin showed her a dress still in one piece and attractively green. The towel fell to the floor, to be replaced quickly by the dress. "You look like a princess now," said Robin beaming.

When she looked into a mirror and saw herself, she started to cry with happiness. "This is too wonderful."

"There are plenty of other things you can take to try on. You could have a new outfit every day." She tutted at the very absurdity of that, but still retained a half smile. She was still in wonderland.

"Look around here some more, while I go and get something for us to eat. Digga, please stay with Lucy." Taking silence as agreement from both parties, Robin went and selected firstly a bag, and then some frozen meals. Coming back he spotted some bottled drinks, so he took one called beer to go with their food.

"So, that is all that I've found so far," admitted Robin, to a young girl still fascinated at the number of clothing styles. "Come on back upstairs, these have to go into the oven. You can help me with the instructions."

*

While the food was in the oven, Robin said, "I want to go and have a look at that fire we started. Wait here, I won't be long. Digga, please stay with Lucy." He took the binoculars and headed for the big tree on top of the mound. Once he had reached a good vantage point, he trained the glasses in the direction of the village. The area just inside the perimeter was dark black, and the small home had been reduced to ashes. Several men were poking at the embers, but he was glad to see the fire had not spread further.

When he got back, he found that Lucy had been making her own discoveries. She had found many cupboards and drawers with interesting things inside and had pulled out a whole bunch of things including a huge stew pot.

*

They both enjoyed the dinner, although they couldn't say what it was exactly, the front label had come off. The beer, something neither had touched nor heard of before, made them sleepy, encouraging them to seek their beds in the other little room. He set out separate under covers and blankets for them both, next to each other, but Lucy, still feeling unsafe, snuggled close to her saviour under his blanket. He didn't object at all. The feeling of someone soft and warm against him seemed to satisfy a need he hadn't been aware of. Digga kept his feet warm.

*

He awoke with a start, something was wrong, but he didn't know what. He did know, however, that he badly needed to go and relieve himself, which was the first priority. Lucy had turned over in her sleep, and was now watching the ceiling, contentedly. "Good morning," he said politely, throwing off his covers and heading for the roof.

It was still very early, the morning was cloudy, cool, and uninviting. Once he'd performed his toilet and covered over the evidence, he felt a strong desire to look at the world from the top of the tallest tree. His first observation up there proved him right, it was a chilly morning. He shivered as he looked around. Looking to the east he saw lots of mist over damp ground. To the north, where his village lay, was something much more disturbing.

He could just see the entrance, the security post, that led to the village, but now there was something happening. A group of people were stood around. He went down to fetch his binoculars to get a better look but shouted a warning to Lucy to be ready to leave. Returning to the tree top he scanned the path he was all too familiar with of late. There was a dozen or so men with dogs now close to Abdul's pit. This didn't look good at all, but when he swung his glasses around, he was even more worried to see men and dogs approaching from the south.

"Lucy, we have to leave now. There are men with dogs looking for us." He grabbed a backpack, throwing what he considered his most important finds into it, then dashed back up, through the small entrance, waiting for Digga and Lucy to catch up. Placing some twigs and loose material over their escape hole, he disguised it as best he could. "We have to move fast," he told them both.

Getting onto the path, they turned right, following it until it started to bear right around the mound. Instead of staying on the path they plunged into the undergrowth, quickly passed the tree line and headed Northeast. Compass settings was one thing Robin's father had passed onto him, which was why he had taken a small compass with him. He kept a direct line, considering that even if it were possible for the hunters to know their exact position, they could still put some distance between them. "It's most likely that the hunters from our village will follow our trail, or they might just follow the path, but we have to confuse them and their sniffer dogs in any way we can."

Up to this time Lucy had said nothing, but now she had something to say. "If we go through water the dogs can't sniff us," she said with no further detail. It made sense to Robin, he nodded, and headed further east to where he had seen marshy ground.

An hour later, they had waded through, up and down several streams. Their legs were wet and muddy from the marshy ground they had deliberately passed through, and with some high ground in front of them, Robin decided it was time for a rest. Climbing the closest tall tree with his glasses around his neck, he sought out the 2 sets of people stalking them. He saw evidence of both, quickly. Even though they were in the rough growth they left quite a trail. They both, however, were walking exactly in their direction. He slid down the tree, worried and thinking hard.

"They know where we are," he said. "It must be because of that security thing in your head. They can track us with that, somehow."

"Take it out," Lucy insisted. "Now, do it quick."

He wanted to argue. He was no doctor. He could hurt her, but the urgency of the situation overcame his concerns. He sat down, with Lucy placing her head on his lap so that he could feel for the evil thing they had put in her.

Just beyond the hairline he felt something under her skin. "That must be it," he said.

"Be quick," Lucy insisted again.

"This will hurt like hell," Robin told her, as he reached for the small scissors he'd found in a first aid kit.

"I won't scream," she told him, still feeling brave.

The scissors broke the skin, and a little blood seeped out. Lucy went rigid for a moment, then as he dug deeper, she passed out. He knew he had to continue. The sharp blade probed further until a tiny device came into view. Without damaging her head more, he used some tweezers to pull out the offending object. He was about to throw it into the bushes when he had a better idea. He wiped away the blood, sprayed something called disinfectant on the wound, then covered it with a plaster. She awoke slowly, groaning and feeling her head with both hands.

"It is done," he said, showing her the tiny item. She blinked and started to stand up. "Take it slow," he said, supporting her. "You may get dizzy."

She took a few deep breaths, shook her head, then said, "I'm OK, let's go on."

As they walked, due east now, Robin kept an eye open for some small game, but it was a while before he spotted something suitable. As they pushed through some thick bushes, they spotted a bird's nest. There were several small blackbirds inside, who looked like they were ready to leave the nest. They shook their feathers at him as he came close. He grabbed the biggest bird by the body, with his finger and thumb keeping the beak open. The beak opening and gullet were large enough to accept the electronic device, in fact it slipped in easily. That done, he encouraged the bird to fly by throwing it into the air. It got the idea quickly and flew off in a northerly direction. "Track that," he said. If the hunters were following them by tracking that thing, then he hoped that it just got a little harder for them.

Taking a different route, they headed due south, and scurried on for a good hour. Lucy was bearing up, but clearly was getting tired. They finally stopped under an apple tree, which provided them with breakfast, and a good rest. Digga was not his normal boisterous self through missing Chief. He was content just to follow on, but seemed to welcome the rest, although he was not so keen on apples.

It was time to check if their pursuers were getting close. With no large oak trees close by they made their way to a hill that had some smaller trees. Taking the sturdiest, Robin made it up as far as he could, then scanned the area around him. The party from the south had almost caught up with the party from his village. He judged they were about 2 hours from his position. He watched for a few minutes to confirm his initial thoughts. Yes, they were going away from where he and Lucy were, and in a northerly direction. He said a few words of gratitude to the small bird that had taken on their burden, then slipped easily down the tree.

"It looks good," he said, "they seem to be going away from us."

She smiled at this, and it was a smile that awakened something inside of Robin. She was quite beautiful when she smiled, like his mother had been.

*

They rested for a while. The sun was still strong when they started off again, carrying a few apples with them. This time they took it easier. Every so often Robin would climb a tree to watch for the hunters as well as any other danger. Additionally, he wanted to avoid other villages and paths. There was a meadow ahead which looked like it might be a good place to stay the night. It seemed strange that there had been no wild animals around as they had walked through the woods and overgrown areas.

Perhaps the dogs prefer to be close to human camps, he thought.

The meadow was pleasant enough when they reached it. A series of big oak trees and several wild fruit trees surrounded what had once been an attractive house. It had no glass in the windows, and the doors were all weathered away, but it made a cosy place to settle down for the night. Lucy's head was giving her plenty of pain. She mentioned it but once, although her grimace was enough to tell the story. He collected some soft grass, made a comfortable corner inside the house away from any draughts, then had her relax there until she fell asleep. His mother had always told him that, "sleep cures so many things." Digga decided he'd done enough exploring and walking for the day. He snuggled close up to the girl and pretended to also be asleep when Robin called him.

*

While the pair slept, he looked out for any game he could make dinner out of. Despite seeing several rabbit holes, there was no evidence they were still in use, and he had no luck elsewhere. There was a nice cool fresh stream nearby. He filled his flask so that they'd have something to drink. Otherwise he returned empty-handed.

Just as it was getting dusk, he climbed a nearby tree for the last time that day to see where their hunters had gotten to. From the patterns they had left in the undergrowth, it would seem they had walked in circles mostly, but now were headed north. He collected some fruit and went back inside the house, to find Lucy was awake and stroking Digga. They were friends now. After eating a little they settled down together, cuddled up, with Digga lying across their feet, and slept the night through.

*

Morning came with a sharp reminder to Robin that they could so easily be found by those looking for them. His first act was to clamber up the tallest tree just outside the house to see what dangers lurked for them today. Digga was still not himself and stayed close to Lucy who was still dreaming.

The 2 hunt parties had joined together and camped overnight. Their fires were still burning, probably cooking breakfast, or perhaps it was to keep wild dogs at bay. He spent a good deal of time looking at every possible area, for potential dangers, wondering if it would be safe to spend another night where they were. He decided it would be a good idea to stay, to allow Lucy to recover. He recalled the pains he had suffered and how long it had been before they dispersed.

As he approached the house Lucy met him at the entrance, not quite bright eyed, but with a tiny smile on her lips in greeting. "I should take a look at your head," he said, "to make sure it is healing OK."

She lay down on his lap while he stroked her soft hair to one side, gently removing the blood-soaked plaster. "It has stopped bleeding, but I can see how tender it is. Does your head still give you pain?"

She thought for a second, "Not so much. I notice it when I touch it."

"As it is a nice warm day, I feel it would be best if we didn't cover it up. We should let the sun mend it." She didn't disagree.

*

Breakfast was apples and fruit harvested locally. "My tummy doesn't like so much fruit," she said, wandering off to seek out something more substantial.

Robin was concerned that he had nothing solid to give Digga, but game was scarce for some reason, and anyway, lighting a fire would attract the hunters.

Lucy came back 20 minutes later with a pile of root vegetables resting in the skirt of her dress with her holding up the hemline to stop her crop falling out. "Come on," he said, "hold them in your dress, we will need to wash them fully before we can eat them." He showed her the way to the stream, where they washed the mud off the parsnips and carrots, then left them on the grassy bank to dry.

"I haven't been able to find any small game around here," he admitted, "but these will help to fill our stomachs." He continued, wanting to please her, but not sure how. He relished that bright smile she kept for special times. "The hunters seem to be where they were yesterday, so we should be able to stay here tonight. In the morning we should go somewhere else, but even if we had some game, I fear any fire we made would attract those chasing us."

"That is sensible," she said quietly, not wishing to judge against her rescuer, her eyes still on the job of washing mud from their next meal. "Poor Digga will have to hunt for his own meat."

Digga was still lying where he had been left inside the house, certainly not full of the joys of spring. Robin wished he had something to give the dog to eat, but there was nothing. He lay down next to the dog, stroking his head gently. After a few minutes, Digga raised his head, tilting it, to look at Robin, his eyes blinked some form of greeting, then he gave a very quiet yelp. His snout went back to the floor, this time his eyes were open, though not focused. He stared against a dark wall.

"I know we had a hard day yesterday," Robin said to his dog, "but if you are going to rest all day why don't you at least do it in the warm sunshine? You'll feel better."

Digga responded with a groan, as if to say, "No, leave me be." His eyes looked at Robin, seeking something. Robin stroked the dog's head again, then his back, noticing for the first time how matted his fur was.

"You know," Robin smiled, "when we get back to our home, I'm going to wash you and cut off that horrible matted fur." At this Digga groaned loudly, moved onto his back as if to protect his fur, then wiggled to satisfy some itch. "That's better, at least your tail is working now," laughed Robin.

"Narrghhhh," groaned Digga, as if to say, "no peace for the wicked." He stood up, licked the hands of his friend then walked towards the doorway. He stopped, looking back towards Robin who was still sat where he had been, with a look that said, "well! Are you coming or not?" Robin laughed loudly and followed his 4-legged friend out into the sunshine.

*

Lucy had several naps that day, to make up for the heavy walking of late, but also for the stress of what had happened to her to sit better in her mind. She was no longer in a village where everyone seemed to hate each other, but relatively safe, and food had been regular if sparse. Here she was being pursued, was getting hungry after the physical effort, but she was only here because those evil people had killed her mother, and her fate would likely have been worse. It all took some digesting for a girl who had always been made to do as she was told and to hide what she may have felt.

*

Halfway through the afternoon, Robin was round the back of the house where Lucy had discovered the root vegetables, pulling out weeds, watering the vegetables already growing, and generally encouraging more growth. Lucy was inside, with Digga sunning himself in the front. A sharp, single yelp from Digga penetrated everything to reach Robin, who dropped what he was doing and came around the side of the house, knife in hand.

A man was approaching with 3 dogs held tightly on leads. They were not overly dangerous looking dogs, but clearly good sniffers. The dogs led the way but stopped in front of Digga, who was standing there as if guarding the entrance to the house, his eyes estimating the strength of the opposition. His hackles rose, and he stood tall, eyeing each dog in turn.

Surprisingly, the 3 new dogs did nothing but yelp gently, lowered themselves to the floor in a pacifying manner, and looked pleadingly at Digga. Robin watched, fascinated. He knew it was the man they'd have to worry about.

"Nice dog," said the man in greeting and nodding towards Robin.

Robin had no desire for fancy chitchat. "Are you hunting us?"

"Yes," said the man without a doubt and plenty of confidence. "I live in the village to the south. I was told to get my dogs out and go find some evil murderer. We've been walking around in circles looking for you, but this morning the search party leader decided that you were dead and told us to go home. I came this way because this is where I would have come after playing that great trick you did. I'm still not sure how you did it, but it worked. They really think you lost your life in the marsh."

Robin was in no mood to give anything away. "Are you going to take us back?"

"No, never," said the man, pausing and looking hard at Digga. "You can tell a lot about a man by how his dog behaves, and you have got a real spirited one there."

They both considered Digga for a moment, who stood even taller with the admiration, and wagged his tail hard.

The man dropped the leads to the floor and walked across to Robin offering his hand. He grabbed hold of Robin's reluctant hand and shook it warmly. "My name is Tom Springer, and I hear you sent 2 evil devils to meet their maker. Congratulations. I like your style."

Robin was in shock at this sudden turn around. He'd been expecting the man to turn on him. "I don't get it," said Robin, his hand still in the grip of the other man's hand.

"Oh, I can see that, but you have nothing to worry about from me. In fact, you are a bloody hero. I can't wait to hear what happened. First off though, where can I get some clean water for me and my hounds?"

Robin showed Tom where the stream was, still feeling perplexed. "If you found us, could the others?"

"Not likely," said Tom, wiping his lips after swallowing some refreshing water. "They haven't much of a clue about hunting. If it hadn't been for the help they received about where you were, they'd have never gotten close to you."

"What kind of help was that?" inquired Robin, still feeling that there were spies in the sky.

"Can't say really, but the lead hunters had something called radios which spoke to them. They kept getting told which direction to turn."

Robin had no idea what a radio was. "Wouldn't you get some reward if you took us back?" insisted Robin, still trying to make up his mind about this stranger.

"Reward? Ha! They'd probably give me a good citizen's medal I could hang on the wall of my falling down home, but otherwise no. Life would carry on in the same painful style, treated like slaves, worked until we died, or shipped off somewhere even worse than that. I was only in the search party because of my dogs, and I was told to be part of it."

"Let's go inside," suggested Robin, warming to Tom. Lucy had been lying down, but had heard the voices, and was now standing against the wall, literally shaking with fear. "This is Lucy." He went across to put his arm around Lucy. "It's OK, he's a friend. This is Tom. He has good news for us."

Tom sat down, with Lucy and Robin following his action. "I'm eager to know exactly what happened with that fire. I've met the sons of that cheating treacherous chief several times, and I liked none of them."

Robin wasn't sure where to start, but with the dogs outside now sniffing each other and getting friendly, that seemed like a good prompt. "I lost one great dog due to the vicious brothers. He saved my life and made everything else possible." He went on to explain the full story, watching Tom's jaw drop several times as details were related to him.

"I had a sister in that village. Not seen her for a while. What was the name of your mother, Lucy?"

"Ingrid Brewster," replied Lucy in her quiet voice, still uncertain that she should be talking to anyone.

They thought Tom was going to explode. He went deep red, from his forehead down to his spiky chin, while his nose flared in a violent fashion. Tears rolled down his face and he cried into his hands. Lucy and Robin watched him quietly, not sure what to say or make of this.

With a tear-stained face Tom looked at them both. "Ingrid was my sister. She was granted special permission to marry a bloke from that village and live there. This is what became of her." He paused to recover himself.

A few moments passed in silence. Tom put his hand on Robin's shoulder. "Son, I can't thank you enough for what you did. At the least you avenged the foul murder of my sister, but you also rescued my niece. Reducing the size of that evil family deserves 2 gold coins I wish I had to give you. You deserve more than a medal though. If I can ever do anything to help you, ever, just let me know."

"You've done plenty already," said Robin. "Your information was very useful."

Robin stood up and felt the side of Tom's head. "That device in your head has sunk in quite low. It will be hard to get out, but if you ever want to become invisible just say."

"Look," said Lucy, offering some berries and apples to Tom. "We only have fruit here. Please take some."

Tom took some berries with a nod of thanks. "I won't be able to linger very long, or I won't get inside the village until after dusk, then they'll have a party out looking for me."

"We should keep in touch, somehow," Robin said.

"Well, I am allowed out once a week, on a Sunday, to hunt for game. I will try and pass by here whenever I can. Where will you be?"

"We've got a hideaway not far from the road where it bends after coming from our village," Robin said, smiling. "I will return here occasionally to keep the garden going that Lucy found. Please let us be friends."

They all stood, Tom walked towards the sunshine, turned around and clasped 2 pairs of hands in his, smiling. "You know you were wrong about your dog. It's not a he, it's a she." He stood aside so that they could see how his dogs had taken advantage of Digga's hidden feminine virtue. One dog was still mounted, and they had to wait while it and Digga took their pleasure. The other 2 dogs were lying down panting, looking well pleased with themselves.

When satisfied, Digga came slowly to stand in front of Robin, with a double yelp, "Was I a good dog, eh, was I?" Robin could only stroke his dog's head hard as if to agree.

Tom said his final goodbyes, the dogs touched noses and swore to stay in touch, then the excitement was over for the day. The house suddenly was very empty.

*

"We can go home tomorrow," Robin announced. "It will be good to eat cooked food again, but that was a fine garden you found, and I would like to keep it going. Perhaps we can make this our second home?"

"Yes," she agreed. "We will both make the garden productive."

*

They set out at dawn, Lucy's head was feeling much better, walking purposefully towards the place of plenty. "You know, eventually the clothes and food will run out. We will have to find a way to produce a supply of meat and vegetables, and other things," Robin noted as they came close to the path. Their direction had taken them a little too far south, so it was necessary to go back behind the tree line, to keep out of sight and to get closer to the entrance to their home. Still wary of being seen, they didn't want anybody to become aware of them.

"Yes," agreed Lucy. "We must find out about material for clothes, too. Maybe it is made somewhere, otherwise we will become naked." She smiled in a way she'd not done before, in quite a suggestive way. Robin liked it but wasn't sure what to make of it. He of course smiled back in the same fashion.

Dinner that night was a frozen pizza, but while that was cooking he showed Lucy the range of food available. She, being a woman, would know how to make best use of them, especially now that she had a big cooking pot.

*

They fell into a routine easily enough. Robin would climb the big oak tree several times a day to watch for trouble. Mostly they went exploring within the mound, as there was still so much to know about in there. They discovered another kitchen area on the lower level, which was more compact. It had a stove, and everything required to make food with. Lucy made it her special area, marvelling at the appliances and cooking devices still in good condition that she could use. She was never happier than when she was preparing something to eat, and Robin quickly began to appreciate her skills.

There seemed to be a limit to the size of the downstairs cavern, as greenery pressed hard against the glass sides. "There must be more things under the mound to discover," he said one sunny day, pushing against what looked like a door to the outside. He worked his way around a corner, finding a break in the wall. Squeezing through to the outside of the cavern wasn't easy, but he saw it was still well inside the mound. There was plenty to inspect just there, although it was hard to know what he was looking at as trees and bushes grew everywhere. Digga naturally followed him through to this new world.

Making sure he could find his way back to the hole, and recognise it, Robin took careful steps while Lucy watched him anxiously. He came to a brick wall on his left, about as high as his hips, and followed it until it became nothing. Looking to his left, he saw a brick building, and further to his left another one. The closest building was not high, most of its roof was missing, but like everywhere else trees grew through it. It still had a big sign over some big entrances. The sign said, 'FIRE', although it looked like some letters were missing.

Careful to avoid crumbling brickwork, he peeped inside the fire building. A large metal contraption sat on 4 metal wheels, with many controls and attachments he didn't understand. It looked fascinating and he promised himself to spend time investigating it properly some time. Not today, because this was only supposed to be a short exploration.

He left that building and noticed opposite a tall metal tower that seemed to touch the top of the inside of the mound. He wondered if this could be another way in and out. It would be nice to have a second exit in case someone broke in. Justifying his actions in this way, to climb the rusting tower. It held his weight without any problems, and appeared to be solid and sturdy enough, so he clambered to the top, leaving Digga complaining below.

It wasn't hard to break through the thin layer of debris that had closed off the fresh air from above the tower. Using tree roots and dangling branches he heaved himself up to stand on the top of the mound, still hidden from the outside world by bushes and trees.

"Hmm," he said, used to expressing his ideas aloud, "it's not ideal. Good that it offers an alternative way in if we need it, but maybe I can make it better. I could cut some wood and make a little stairway." With that thought in mind he fought his way through the close-fitting foliage, looking for the normal entrance. His direction was a bit off, and nearly found himself on the path. He quickly turned to the right and found the usual entrance. He reminded himself that he still needed to disguise it better. When the winter came it would be easier to see from outside without so many leaves covering it.

Going quickly down from the mound top, he ran across the top level, skidded down the stairs, then ran towards where he had left Lucy. She was still there, sat on the floor, looking through the hole. He resisted the urge to tickle her, still not sure their friendship was up to him being so personal with her. Instead he gently tapped her shoulder.

"Arrgghhhhhhhhh," Lucy screamed, frightened out of her wits, fearing she had been found by the hunters after all. When she turned around and saw it was just Robin, her normally placid eyes became furious. Standing up she beat her fists against his chest, knocking him over. Unable to express her horror, she ran off crying, refusing to talk to Robin for most of the day.

He searched everywhere for her and spent hours looking. Digga was no help at all, and also seemed to have an upset for having been left behind in a strange place. She refused to join him, sulking under a pile of clothing. Finally he found Lucy inside a cupboard in the small kitchen area. Still she wouldn't talk to him, no matter how many times he told her he was sorry. "I didn't mean to scare you."

Approaching dinner time, Lucy came out and started to make something to eat. Digga stayed close to Lucy, sharing their dwindling distress. Robin could only mope around, offering to help and not getting any response. They had a very quiet meal, after which Lucy went to her bed early, keeping well to her side of the under-blanket.

In the morning, happily, Lucy was over it. He realised this when she gave him one of her tiny smiles in return for his, "good morning." She was still quiet generally though, making him very careful of what he did and what he said. Digga finally accepted a tickle under the chin, then she licked his hand, gave a brief yelp, and lay down at his feet as if to say, "it's all settled now."

After their breakfast of fruit, Robin was keen to tell her what he had found. He mentioned the fire building and the tower. "The tower can be a new way in here if we ever need it. I have some work to do to make it easier to climb onto the top of the tower, and I have to find a way to cover up the holes."

Lucy nodded, thought for a moment, then rushed off. She came back a few minutes later, struggling with 2 big pots. "These are for plants," she managed, a little out of breath. "Put spiky evergreens inside with soil. They will cover the hole."

"What a brilliant idea," Robin agreed, smiling with enthusiasm. They spent the next few hours finding some good soil and appropriate evergreens. The plants were quite tiny compared to the huge green pots. It was only when they'd added in more soil, more plants, and watered them, that Robin realised what a task it would be to get them into place. Lucy burst out laughing, further relieving the tension between them, when she saw his perplexed face, realising what he was thinking.

They struggled with the first pot, getting it to the top of the metal steps, but couldn't lift it higher out of the hole. "I will have to go up there and pull it," Robin announced. "I think we'll need to make a sling of some sort for it to sit in." Then he sat thinking. "If it goes through the hole now, it will just fall back down when we put it over the hole. I'm going to have to work out something smarter. The top of the pot needs to be level with the mound, but to use the hole we will have to be able to lift it out and back in again. Did you find anything that could be used as rope?"

She shook her head. "Let's go find something together. It will need to be strong." They went off to search the whole cavern, and it wasn't until they went to a darkened space they hadn't really looked at closely before, that they found some heavy-duty ropes residing on another metallic contraption sitting on metal wheels.

"That should do it," said Robin smiling. He'd already decided he should smile more to encourage Lucy to do the same. He clambered outside, made a little platform on which to raise and lower the first pot into position, then cutting the ropes he attached them securely, making sure they were well disguised under leaves and roots.

Leaving it in position after climbing down he said, "You try it to make sure it works for you. I'll check it from the top to make sure it's all well concealed." She did as instructed. He was pleased to see that it all worked perfectly. Without knowing how to lift the evergreens out of the way it was impossible to get inside that way.

"Well done," said Lucy, now smiling. "Only one more entrance to go."

He spent the rest of the daylight hours that day putting the ropes in place, and so forth, but it was the cutting of wood, and creating a stable walkway from the tower that took the time. He finally completed it, having Lucy walk up the tower to make sure she could cope with it. Her tiny nod and smile made his day. He had pleased her.

*

The metal tower outside the fire building gave Robin some concerns. The rust was quite substantial in places and could easily make the whole thing collapse. It was vital they had secure and safe exits otherwise they would live in constant fear. There were plenty of small trees that he could cut down in the area around the tower, so he made good use of them. He encouraged some trees to grow against each side of the tower to gently support it, but his major effort involved a solid wooden base around the tower. Where rust was most obvious within the tower, he strapped several cut branches to enforce the strength of it. He also made it easier to climb up and down. It took him a total of 10 days to complete, with Digga looking on with approval and some useful suggestive yelps from time to time. Lucy rewarded him with one of her brilliant smiles.

*

The next Sunday, they decided to go and see how their second garden was doing. They had hoped to meet up with Tom, but he wasn't there. Clearly, he had paid a visit as the garden had been watered, more weeds had been removed, and 2 rabbits had been hung up for them. They took the rabbits, leaving a smile carved into the wood where they had been, and loaded a few vegetables into Robin's backpack.

On the following Sunday Robin was up his tree looking for any sign of Tom moving towards the house. His glasses allowed him to zoom in on an area very well which helped him to scan for any strangers wandering the paths. He finally spotted Tom who had stopped for a breather. His face was so clear when he turned towards the tree, it seemed like Tom could actually see him as well. Hurrying back downstairs, he called to Lucy, "Tom is on his way to our house. We can go and meet him." Lucy was ready and enthusiastic to go, as was Digga, but as always proceeded with caution, taking time to disguise their actions and direction of travel.

As they approached the house, Digga became all excited, wagging her tail in a delighted way. The 3 dogs came to meet the newcomers, sniffing Digga, wondering if there was a chance for some more fun, like last time. While Digga was pleased to see the boys, she kept her rear end firmly on the floor, giving the message out that she was not currently available for that kind of fun.

"Hello," said Tom, with a big smile of greeting, as he came out of the house. "I've just hung up 2 more rabbits for you. My traps are so good these days I'm getting a lot more than I can eat." They shook hands warmly, and Robin thanked him.

Robin was keen to know if any more search parties were planned to look for them, "Have you heard any more rumours about us?" he asked.

"Nothing of any substance," replied Tom. "I did hear that the chief of your village was livid with rage that you'd apparently drowned in the bog. He had wanted you alive to punish you for the rest of your short life."

Lucy blanched at this, "Will he come looking again?"

"Not from what I heard. He's had some men brought in to make the perimeter fence and gate more secure. There is now a camera at the gate that starts up when someone with one of those things in his head goes by. I imagine though that if you've lost your device then the camera won't see anything."

"That's a relief," smiled Robin. "We are planning to be very quiet for the time being anyway. We need to make our little home better and more secure." Robin was still reluctant to share everything, for he feared Tom could be made to talk, and expose them.

"I see you've been working with wood," said Tom, "you've still got a few wooden splinters in there. You need to soak your hands in hot water, and pull them things out if you can, or they will get real painful."

They talked on for a while until Tom told them he'd best be getting back, or he'd have some trouble. Tom's 3 dogs had to be content with a lick each from Digga as he left, while Lucy and Robin made their way back to their residence as well.

As the summer bloomed, Lucy and Robin were able to stock up on some food, and freeze plenty of rabbit meat for a later time. They met up with Tom every so often to exchange greetings and share their friendship, and enquire about any news, but otherwise it was a quiet time of year with nothing drastic happening.

CHAPTER 2

SO THIS IS WHAT HAPPENED

IT SEEMED THAT THERE WAS always something more to discover in the cavern that they now called home. Robin had created a better place to sleep where they could hang several layers of heavy material up to act as doorways to keep them warm when the winter came. It was also well hidden. A basic requirement for any bolthole. They kept in touch with Tom, always enjoying his enthusiastic approach to life, but as the days moved through July, they found something that totally absorbed their thoughts.

Just beyond the fire building was another brick building that had taken Robin's interest. It had been securely sealed up, with no broken doors or windows to climb through. A big sign at the front declared it to be a library, although that didn't mean much to Robin. He had even gotten onto the roof, which was still all in place, seeking an entry point, but without success. He finally found a door towards the back of the building that eventually surrendered to his efforts to force entry. As he pushed at the door, it seemed like a whoosh of stale air hit him. That halted his progress for a moment, but seeing nor hearing anything else, he continued inside.

He saw rows and rows of books in shelves, and his eyes went wide. He knew very well what a book was. His mother had passed onto her son a love of the printed word, and he suddenly felt like he was in heaven. As he pulled out a few books to inspect them, careful to treat them with great care, he was even more enthused to see so many subjects covered. He immediately ran to fetch Lucy who had been doing some gardening.

"Come see what I've found," he said, making sure she had clean hands, before pulling her towards his greatest discovery.

She had of course seen books before but didn't have the love for them that Robin had. He started to change that, pulling out books he knew would interest her on growing vegetables and cookery. Those alone fascinated her, especially the pictures. "These are good," she smiled. "Perhaps I will make more different meals."

Robin was more interested in the geography of the land as well as trying to understand what had happened to what must have been a civilised world. Several large atlases helped to satisfy his curiosity on the whole world. Maps showed every country and what part of the world they belonged to. He still wasn't sure what country he was in but showed Lucy the images. His eyes almost popped when the atlas started to talk about outer space and other planets. "These pictures are so amazing, and people used to go there," he insisted, "or how could they have such detailed pictures?" Lucy agreed they were fantastic, but still her attention fell back to pictures of cakes and roast dinners.

They now spent most of their time looking through books. Even Lucy had become a convert to the printed word. The more she read the more she liked it. While Robin recognised many words, there were so many new ones that he at first had trouble with. Lucy had more trouble but looked at the pictures to work out what the words meant. "Look at this," Robin said one day, hauling over an enormous book that declared itself to be a dictionary. "Every word we will ever read is in here, so we can find out what they mean."

"How clever," smiled Lucy. Robin wasn't sure if she meant him or the book but smiled back anyway.

After exhausting what he could absorb from the geography books, Robin started next on the history section. This was huge, causing him to spend many days grasping the significance of how society had evolved from a stone age culture to one where men could visit other worlds. "It seems that we have been reduced back to a stone age society, almost," he told Lucy. "Certainly, our village is little better, except that stone age people were free of tyranny." He was proud of knowing that last word, which he'd found in several books. "It seems like the world fell to those that would use tyranny against us all, but how that happened is still a mystery."

No matter how much Robin learned, it seemed there was so much more to read about. There were so many sections in the library, and while the titles intrigued him, he knew he had to be very precise in how he acquired the knowledge before the books began to deteriorate. Realising what a massive task he had set himself to read all possible books, he sighed at the thought. "It will take me 10 years to read all these books. There is so much to know. So much gets repeated in different books, while some books describe things in so much detail it is hard to grasp the concept," he admitted to Lucy one cool August day.

"Do you have to read every single book of every section?" she asked.

"Maybe not."

"Perhaps, you can make a mark where important books are. Then you can find it again. There is so much to read your head will burst if you are not more selective."

A little stunned by what Lucy had said, as well as the amount, all in one go, Robin sat back for a moment and considered his approach. Just what was he trying to achieve? He couldn't possibly understand everything that had gone on before, but he could grasp the essential elements, the overall idea of what went before. "You are right. I need to be more discerning. Anyway, the books do not cover past the year we know things went bad, so there must be some information missing."

He started to pick books at random but avoided those labelled as fiction. He wanted facts only. A couple of books under the category of classics interested him, as they seemed to fall halfway between fact and fiction and filled in some of the gaps left by the actual history book. Too much unfortunately seemed to be made up stories, although he did take a fancy for science fiction novels, which increased his yearning to know more about outer space.

Lucy had picked up a story about an enchanted castle and a princess who was made to sleep until a real brave prince kissed her on the lips. She couldn't put it down, reading it over and over, captivated by this mystery land, wondering, if it could be a true tale, hoping it was. The whole story took over her waking and sleeping times. She tried to dress like a princess, from pictures she had seen of beautiful princesses. She searched in vain for fancy clothes that would make her a real-life princess.

As for Robin, he became totally entranced with the adventures of Robin Hood. The idea of helping the poor people and rescuing damsels from those in authority appealed greatly, especially when Robin Hood was rewarded with a kiss or a beatific smile. The archery competitions where Robin Hood always won seemed like a great game, and he wondered how he could make a long bow. Searching through many books, he finally found a book called an encyclopaedia, which had detailed drawings of a bow, and what the arrows were made of. He even took the book with him while he was cutting a suitable supple cutting that could be used as a bow. Making a string for the bow was much more difficult, as was attaching it. Using a variety of taut fibres and experimenting with different materials, it took quite a while before he had a bow that would function without falling apart. He was persistent, thinking that Robin Hood would have nothing ready-made in Sherwood Forest, so he tried to emulate what his thought process might have been.

The garden suffered a little while the 2 inhabitants pursued their interests, but meals were never skipped, and indeed Lucy's skill continued to increase with the things she had read. Digga was totally content, eating better than she ever had in her early life, and here she was safe while growing fat. "Digga, you are eating enough for Chief as well as you," Robin scolded one day. "You will have trouble fitting through that hole to the outside."

Digga was having none of that, 2 short sharp yelps told Robin she was still hungry, and to stop being less than generous with the rabbit.

*

It was well into September, with Robin almost abandoning the library to work on making arrows that flew straight. Cutting wood precisely was a challenge, as he didn't have any real tools, but it was the arrow heads that were most difficult to shape properly, with enough weight to hit something. After a great deal of experimentation, he finally had 5 working arrows, which he practised with constantly. At first the arrows only went 10 feet, but as he learned to lean into the bow, he taught himself to shoot 30 yards, sometimes he even hit the thing he was aiming at. "I'm sure this will come in useful sometime," he told Digga who was dozing happily in a ray of late warm sunshine that had somehow made its way through the thick foliage above. He wasn't satisfied though until he had a lot more arrows and was able to hit his target more often. He sewed on a strap for his backpack to hold some arrows. "I might even hit some game, you never know," he said to Digga. The dog had clearly got bored and gone off for a more comfy pre-dinner sleep.

Dinner came and went with no sign of Digga, which was very unusual. Lucy had made rabbit stew, adding in some herbs she had identified from a cookery book to make it even tastier than usual. "Hmm, that was superb," Robin said. "By far and above the best meal I've ever had. You are an amazing chef. Even Robin Hood would not have eaten as well as I do now."

Lucy smiled, "I may be better than Robin Hood's cook, but I want to be able to impress a prince and a princess." Her use of words had expanded greatly since reading so many books and learning the power of words.

"No prince could have eaten better than that meal," Robin asserted. "You deserve a big kiss." She presented her right cheek, and he gave her a sisterly kiss. "Now I'm too full to do anything else. I must rest, then I will go and search for Digga. I wonder where she got to?"

"I hope she didn't get stuck somewhere, with her getting so fat these days."

"Yes," Robin agreed. "Last time I saw her she was intent on having a good doze. I'll go look outside. Hope my belly doesn't get too big. Perhaps I should go now?"

They called the dog's name as they looked everywhere inside and outside the cavern, without any sign of her. Piles of clothing and other soft material was turned upside down in their search. Robin even went up top, but there was still no evidence of the dog's presence. A little worried, they went to their beds, recalling that Digga had gone missing twice before overnight. "She will be back in the morning," Lucy said hopefully, knowing how much Robin liked his dog.

They breakfasted on berries and nuts the next morning, with still no sign of Digga. "I hope she isn't hurt or has fallen down a hole or anything," Robin said, wondering how to extend the search. "If she was hurt, she could still bark. It doesn't make sense."

Just as Robin was about to take up his glasses to better look everywhere, they heard a familiar yelp, and a happy but tired looking mongrel came into view, wagging her tail, clearly pleased with herself. Lucy sliced the dog some meat, which she ate ravenously, while Robin stroked her head.

"What happened to you?" Robin asked. "We were worried."

Digga barked loudly in reply, turning on her heels, looking excitedly at them both. This was followed by 2 specific yelps, which they both knew meant something different each time, even if it sounded the same. Then she backed out of the small kitchen, stood wagging her tail, and yelped some more.

"She wants to show us something," said Lucy. "Well, you did ask her where she had been." At this the dog took off, with her 2 human friends following behind.

Outside the cavern they went, into the fire building, with Digga walking to the far side of the metal contraption that Robin had never fully explored. Suddenly Digga leaped up into a small recess and seemed to disappear. Robin clambered up to see where Digga had gone. "Digga was always good at finding interesting things," said Robin. "Perhaps she has found a secret entrance to an enchanted castle."

Lucy poked him in the ribs as she climbed level with Robin. It was too dark to see where Digga had gone. "Let me push that heavy sheet out of the way," Robin said. As he did so, and a little light came in they saw Digga, along with the reason for her excitement. Nestling against Digga were 5 tiny puppies being licked ferociously.

Digga looked so happy, her tail wagged incessantly, and she yelped at

Robin until he stroked her warmly, "Wasn't I a good dog, eh, wasn't I?"

*

They carried the puppies into the kitchen to wash them, while Digga watched the process very closely. The little cupboard, outside the kitchen had been given over to Digga, so it was just a case of cleaning that out again, to make it comfortable for dog and pups. After they were dried off and wobbling on the draining board the small ones were placed in the warm space, well away from draughts. Digga joined them immediately she had eaten, to feed and lick them.

The novelty of having 5 extra excited and excitable little bodies around took a good time to wear down, but it certainly increased the randomness. Initially it would be Lucy or Robin peeking in at the little family or cuddling a pup. As they started to get around the small dogs went everywhere. One fell into the soup as Lucy was busy adding potatoes but got rescued before being boiled.

They took the pups in Robin's backpack to meet up with Tom, and he was not surprised at the outcome of their first meeting. Tom's 3 dogs were very excited to see the little ones, each claiming to be the father. "Hope you have enough meat dried and ready for the coming winter," said Tom. "Rabbits get a little scarce after October. Your brood will be taking more than you expect."

"We have a good supply, thanks to you," said Robin, showing Tom his bow and how it worked. "What do you think of that?"

"Impressive," said Tom, smiling. "Let me know if you ever kill anything with it."

"Something I do miss from the village, although we didn't get much of it very often, was milk," said Robin. "I don't suppose you know how we could get a cow, do you?"

Tom laughed loudly. "A cow you say, no. We have 2 in our village, but they are overworked, poor things. They have to be taken to another village down south and reintroduced to a bull there every so often, but still they yield little milk. I'm told that bull lives like a king. Best straw and food, and as many females as he could ever want. That's the life, eh? I think I'll come back as a bull next time."

"Just a thought," said Robin, a little more quietly.

"A goat might suit you better," said Tom. "Still not sure where you'd get one though."

Changing the subject, Robin said, "I suppose you know most of the villages around here. Maybe sometime you can tell us about them, if they are friendly or might trade for something? Not sure what they would need though."

"I'll draw you a little map for next time," agreed Tom. "Some villages are quite friendly, but it depends on the time of year, and who is in charge. If you see someone blacking their face to get into a village then pass it by. Then again, you would need a special pass to trade. Those passes are like gold dust, and hard to come by."

"What is gold dust?" asked Robin.

"Never seen it, but it is pretty rare I heard," answered Tom.

*

By the next Sunday, the pups were too big and too active to fit inside Robin's backpack, so they decided to leave the dogs at home until the puppies could walk to the house on their own. "I hope they will be OK on their own," said Lucy, anxiously. "We've never left Digga alone before now."

"I'll explain it to Digga," Robin said, "she will understand, and keep her brood in line." Digga wasn't too unhappy about not going for a walk. Being a mother was tiring, and she agreed that she did need a good rest.

Tom was waiting for them just inside the house. It was overcast, with some light rain, meaning they didn't stay too long, but long enough for Tom to show Robin his map he had hacked out of an animal skin. "This is not very accurate in terms of distance. I copied the outlines from a very old map. Your village is there," he indicated a dark spot.

"So many spots," said Robin. "Are they all villages like ours?"

"Yes," agreed Tom, "over the years I've been sent out with others to deliver or pick up things. Those are all the villages I know about, and you'll see the lines, those are the paths."

"I think I'd want to avoid villages, if possible, but it is good to know where they are, and that there are so many of them. What is that area where that big black mark is? That would be a huge village."

"It is not a village as we know them," answered Tom. "I only saw it from a great distance once, but it is big. The paths are wide, and there are many people working there. There are big metal things that run on wheels. Nobody pushes them, and nothing pulls them. They run on their own power."

"That sounds like magic," said Lucy, with a frown.

"Not magic," suggested Robin, "but maybe it was something left over from before, when we didn't live like this."

"You could be right," agreed Tom, "but it is a place to avoid. I heard the people have to work machinery, that's more of the mechanical devices from before, and they have to work in horrible smoke and dirty places. No wonder they keep stealing people from the villages to work there. People die early."

"What an awful time and place we were born into," remarked Robin. "We know there was a much better way of life before all this, but what happened to make us all into slaves, and who are our masters?"

"The lords and gods are our masters," said Lucy solemnly.

"Is that place where our masters live?" asked Robin.

"Oh no," said Tom, "I heard they have palaces near the coast. You see the blue line that goes all around? That is called the coast, where the land meets the water."

For a minute or 2 Lucy and Robin were silent, taking in all of this strange new information.

"Do any of these places have names?" Robin wanted to know.

"Well, as you probably know, the villages are called UKS with a number attached. Your village was UKS56. The S stands for the south, so your village is number 56 in the south of the UK, ours is 60. I think 'UK' stands for the general area."

"So many villages, like ours," said an amazed Lucy.

"Many more than 60," Tom exclaimed. "I heard there were many hundred towards the north, all with about 1,000 people in, all living like slaves."

Lucy started to cry, "Why? Why can't we just be free?"

"I don't know," said Tom. "There are so many things that we never get to know about."

An angry frown crossed Robin's face, not just because Lucy was upset, but because he had realised that there was so much injustice imposed upon them. "I swear before my life is over that I will find out the truth, and I will make sure everyone knows why we have become slaves to the lords and gods," he said quietly but with steel in his voice.

"Just be careful," Tom pleaded. "You know how hard they were on people in your village if they didn't like someone. If they find you without that thing in your head, they will hurt you without mercy. Stay well hidden, and do not fall into their hands. Above all else, do not trust anybody you meet. Make them earn that trust. So many people have just fallen in with the line of command and will gladly hand over their own mother to be punished if told to do so for whatever reason."

"I promise," agreed Robin, recalling the stories of Robin Hood's adventures that he had read, now thinking of him as a distant ancestor and role model. "I will carry your words with me."

*

When they got back, Robin went straight to the library to see if any maps in the atlases he had found would match the rough one Tom had given them. Straight away he came across one designated as the United Kingdom, or UK for short. "That's where we live, Lucy. We are on a large island."

"Look," she said, pointing to something that coincided with the big black mark on Tom's map. "That horrible place has a name also. It is called London."

"Yes," smiled Robin. "Well spotted. Around the edges of the UK is the water. That water is called the English Channel. So we are English," confirmed Robin, "just like Robin Hood."

"Look at the bottom of the map," said Lucy pointing. "It shows how much a mile is on this map. We can work out how far it is to London, or to the coasts where the lords live."

"Yes, some coasts are not so far away, and with this map we can investigate many places while we stay hidden. Before we do that though, we must learn all we can about our UK." They went to work pulling out any factual details of the UK they could find, consolidating it all in their minds, until they knew its physical attributes.

"It's just a shame we do not know the name of the place where we are yet," said Robin. "I'm sure we will soon though."

*

They were so long and so often in the library now, that Digga was feeling lonely. They didn't want the dogs to be in such an important place in case they damaged something, but also, they would be a distraction. They agreed to set time aside throughout the day to be with Digga and her puppies. Once they were fully grown the small dogs would become better controlled, but for now accumulating knowledge was not just vital, it was a total necessity. If they were to live their lives without knowing what a real society should be like, then they would have failed to take advantage of what fate had given them. When they came across words they didn't understand, they really made sure they got them defined through the dictionary. This way they knew they could add to their education and knowledge of the world before. A little game was played between them whereby they would share any new words and use them in funny and correct ways to get familiar with them and to make them stick in their memories.

They even missed the odd Sunday meet-up with Tom, they were so engrossed in grabbing any last bit of data they could consume, about anything. Lucy sometimes got distracted with less serious subjects. "Did you say you found some bottled liquids labelled as 'whiskey'?"

"I did, as well as different coloured wines, and there was also something without colour called vodka, why?"

"It says here," said Lucy, "that they are called alcohol. They can make you very sleepy, and if you have too much you can pass out. Even, they can be used as medicines. Whiskey can also help to make wounds clean."

"Sounds like something we should remember," said Robin.

*

The days went by as they slowly began to understand what life had been like before. They became familiar with many of the things that had been a part of daily life, from trains and shops to money and holidays. Yet they could still find no clue as to what happened to wipe out a perfectly good society and way of life.

As the year stretched into November, they found extra things to wear to keep warmer, but as December passed into January, the snows came, and they both shivered a little more. The puppies were just big enough to take on the Sunday jaunt to the house, and to catch up with any news Tom might have. Digga kept the 5 small dogs moving after Robin. As one of the smallest fell below the snow, Digga picked it up and carried it in her mouth, while Robin and Lucy each took 2 puppies in their arms, but the young dogs had done well, for they were almost at the house.

When Digga and her brood met up with the fathers, there was total mayhem. Dogs were yelping, sniffing and running around each other, all so excited. Tom was in a good mood, having had a happy festive time, one time in the year where bellies had been filled, but his face had a worried look.

"That will probably be the last year end feast we will get," Tom announced. "The old village chief died a few days ago, and already they've replaced him with someone of the other faith. Now we all have to go and pray to their god, every Friday, with our noses to the ground."

"Just like we had to in our village," agreed Robin. "We hated that!"

"A few of our blokes objected," continued Tom. "They were knocked to the ground before they could even say what they didn't like. Just disagreeing with the chief is a crime now. It didn't stop there. The chief's 6 henchmen just kept hitting these poor blokes with metal batons until they stopped moving. All bloodied and battered they were. Everyone, including me, was too scared to do anything. We just did as we were told."

"You have to leave," insisted Lucy. "Those of the other faith are truly evil. Come and live with us."

Tom frowned, and thanked Lucy. "I will see what happens over the next few days. It could be the new chief was just trying to make an impression."

"Don't leave yourself in danger," said Robin. "We cannot lose you. You are our only friend."

Tom smiled at this and just nodded.

*

After the early cold and snow of January, when 2 heads had already become very full of facts and subjective information on the society that had been there less than 100 years ago, the weather calmed down to generally mild. Each time they went to the house Tom had not been there, and they began to worry about him. This prompted them to keep even busier, consuming every last piece of worthwhile data they could find.

*

One bright Sunday afternoon, after returning from their walk, with still no sign of Tom, Robin came across a book called, 'Idiot's guide to using a personal computer'.

"What's a personal computer?" he asked aloud, reaching for the dictionary. He proceeded to clear the word and read the book. It was quite informative, so he quickly picked up the terms used, and it all made perfect sense, as though he had known about it in a previous life.

"If only we had a computer, it seems that you could access many huge pieces of data from there, much more than we have found in our library. It is possible, that whatever happened did so very quickly, that connections were left in place. It's like we get electricity here for the lights and the shower, or the oven. Nobody had time to turn it all off. The greenery just overgrew it all. So if we can find a personal computer, we may just be lucky enough to get it working."

"What does it look like?" Lucy asked.

He showed her a picture. "A square screen, all lit up where the data and images were shown. Then they have this thing called a keyboard that has all the letters of the alphabet. You use that to ask questions. The book said there is a small object you move around on the table to position the cursor. I'm still not sure what a cursor is or how that would be used, but it seems important."

"Hmm," said Lucy, with a smile. "Perhaps we should get Digga in here to help. She was always good at finding things. I remember seeing something like this screen around the front. It was buried under a lot of dust."

They went searching.

An old stiff broom had been used several times to brush away dirt on the library floor, and this came in handy to work through several layers of dust and cobwebs that all but hid a wall on the other side of the library. "I really should clean this place up," said Lucy. "We never used to have cobwebs in our house."

"Perhaps when we have completed our task," suggested Robin, which he meant the finding out of how a rich society collapsed. She was thinking just about the locating of this personal computer.

"Found something with a light on," announced Lucy, as she wiped away the thick strands of spider webbing. It still took some unearthing, but when it was all uncovered it resembled the pictures in Robin's latest book completely.

"Well done," said Robin, smiling brightly. "You found that even better than Digga could have."

The personal computer or PC as it was abbreviated in the book was showing an image of the blue sky and soft white clouds. Finding something to sit on that wasn't too dirty, Robin touched the keyboard keys. Nothing really happened. He saw something that looked like the mouse in the book. On the screen was a little arrow that wandered around when the mouse was moved. "Ah, that must be the cursor." When he held the mouse too tight one of the buttons clicked open a dialogue on the screen, which disappeared when the other button was pressed. None of what had shown up made any sense to Robin.

"It says to open the browser if you want to search for a subject," Lucy said, having found the right page for using the internet. "Can you see some small figures at the bottom? They are called icons."

"Yes," Robin said excitedly. "There are several of them."

"Right click the mouse on the icon to the right," Lucy instructed.

Robin did so, and the screen changed immediately to a blank page, all white with a faint border. After some experimentation he found he could write words in there. "Look, Lucy, this will be useful. We can keep notes of important things we find out."

"Great, so see what the next icon does." It turned out to be a card game, which they loved after they had clicked everything and found out the rules. "That was fun, but let's move to the next icon."

Robin did as he was told. A strange looking screen came up. "What is this all about?" he wondered aloud while Lucy consulted the book.

"That is what you want," Lucy smiled. "This is what they call the browser. You can use this to find out anything. Do you see where it says, 'Search the Web'? Poke it with the mouse, and type in a question." Robin typed in, with some difficulty in finding the right keys, 'What happened in 2038'?

"Wow, it has found lots of information," said Lucy. There were headings for people who had died, as well as news about weather, but nothing that specifically answered the questions they had.

"Wasn't I right that they'd left it all connected?" said Robin, too pleased with himself.

"Yes," agreed Lucy, "you were a very good boy." Her big smile made that more of a fun compliment than a sarcastic comment.

Robin clicked on several entries, most of which related to stories of people, and statistics, but none really honed-in on the exact information they wanted. "Maybe it wasn't just one thing, but several all coming together."

"Yes, and if it hit quickly would they have had enough time to write about it?" she asked.

"True," he said, a little deflated. "Perhaps I need to ask the question in a different way?"

"Makes sense," she said. "You should use that first icon to copy in all that you find out. I'd best go and start dinner and chase the puppies around."

"OK, yes. I'll experiment with all of this for a while. It is too exciting now that we have found it."

*

After looking through the book a few more times Robin worked out a few more ways that he could do other things with the PC. He typed in, '2036', to see what he could get. Again, more important sounding people had died, with something about China having invaded the USA, but the only china he knew about was related to plates. He typed in, '2037', and this time there were no important people dying. Instead, one announcement talked about Europe being in the top league for coronavirus deaths. He made a note of that name in the writing page, then did a search on, '2039'. Some very odd things came up which made no sense, and certainly were not related to the year 2039.

He was just about to enter the word he had found related to many deaths, 'coronavirus', when he heard a yapping outside. It was Digga, and her message was urgent. He raced outside, wondering if they had been discovered by someone, wondering if he should grab his bow and arrows or follow Digga. He followed Digga who was as frantic as he'd ever seen her.

Digga led him to the lower kitchen area. Lucy was face down on the floor, with the puppies walking all around her. Digga licked her face to wake her up, then stood looking at Robin as if to say, "I've licked her all I can. You need to do something," but Robin was stunned, not quite believing for a moment that something bad could have happened to Lucy.

Something was boiling on the stove which smelled a little overcooked. He turned that off and stooped to look closer at Lucy. Her eyes were closed and her face was pale except for the part that had been pressed against the floor. She was breathing, but as he tried to turn her, he spotted a gash on her forehead. "She must have fallen against something hard," he told Digga, as he lifted her up and carried her to her bed. He noticed how she was much bigger, heavier even, than when they had first met.

He lay her down gently, making her comfortable, looking for any other areas of damage. He stroked her cheeks gently, but she gave no sign of waking up. He decided he should treat and examine the injury she had. Rushing out to where the alcohol was racked, he grabbed a bottle of whiskey and his first aid kit, thinking the smell of whiskey might wake her up.

After washing around the injury to clean it, he wiped it with a little whiskey, realising that the wound was not too deep, but that the fall could have damaged her brain. She stirred a little when he put the top of the whiskey bottle under her nose, but still didn't wake up. He felt so helpless and hadn't felt this miserable since he had lost his mother. He made her warm, and gently put a plaster over the cut on her head. He touched the area and noticed it had started to swell. That worried him again, and he didn't know what to do.

"Digga," he said, "watch over her," as he raced off to the library to see if he could find something there, some guidance on how to help her. He typed in several phrases on the PC keyboard until he got something that talked about head injury and concussion. He had to look in his dictionary to find out what concussion meant, and he didn't like the sound of that at all. The article gave a list of symptoms for which he was supposed to call 999 but had no idea how. The response to typing in 999 on the PC produced nothing understandable, and he had no clue what A&E meant, so he skipped on, looking for something tangible he could do to help Lucy.

At last he found something about holding ice to the injury to help with the swelling. "I've no idea what paracetamol is," he grumbled at the screen, now feeling desperate. His anger suddenly welled up inside of him, and fully realised how important Lucy was to him. Tears filled his eyes as his mind linked the idea that he could lose Lucy, then feel so terribly alone as he had done when his mother was killed.

*

On his way back to Lucy, Robin grabbed something frozen and wrapped it in a clean cloth, after which he pressed it against the swelling on Lucy's head. He wondered if some food would help her. Whatever she had been making was like a very thick soup now, but still had a nice aroma. He grabbed 2 bowls, filled them up and took them to Lucy. He took a spoon to the soup, half filling it, then tried to ease it past her lips. He noticed how firm and full bodied her lips were now. Not like before when they had been so thin. He looked at her, now seeing her in a new light, for she had become a woman. His tears welled up again as the soup dribbled down the side of her face, so he gave up on that for the time being.

*

Throughout the night Robin made sure Lucy was warm. He checked her breathing often, as well as applying something frozen to her head. He lay next to her watching in the half light, wishing he could do more. Finally, he fell asleep.

*

The early brightness of the morning crept uncomfortably into his eyes, as he awoke with a start, looking towards Lucy, and making sure she was still there, still alive. Her breathing seemed to be more normal now, and her cheeks had a little colour. He breathed a little easier as he watched her intently, willing her to wake up and be alright. He couldn't move, even though his bladder was complaining urgently that it was full.

It seemed like half an eternity, but it was probably just one hour before Lucy began to stir, and when she finally opened her eyes, the relief flooded through Robin that she might be OK. She looked at him with a question in her eyes as he smiled warmly at her. Before she could even do so much as smile back, she grimaced with pain, and her hand went up to where she had hurt herself. "Ow," she cried.

"Try not to move, it looks like you had a bad fall and banged your head."

"Ow," she said again, feeling the plaster on her head. "That hurts."

"Did you hurt any other part of you?"

"Don't think so," she mumbled, stretching her legs. She raised herself on her elbows then fell back down again, "Dizzy."

"Take it slowly. I will help you to stand when you are ready," said Robin.

"Oh," she said sadly, her face going beetroot red, her eyes turning away from Robin's face.

"What happened?" he said, concerned.

Realising that he would find out as soon as she stood up, she said in almost a whisper, "I've wet myself."

Robin smiled with sympathy. "That's not the end of the world," then thinking that would be a good phrase to search with on the browser. "You were out cold for more than 12 hours. I'm just so glad you are awake now. It would be too horrible to lose you."

She smiled at this, knowing it came from his heart.

Robin stood up and offered Lucy some whiskey medicine or some cold soup. She wrinkled her nose at both. "How is the head now?"

"Seems better," she managed. "Help me stand up." While she used some strut attached to the wall to pull herself up, he took her under the arms. She wobbled but didn't fall down due to Robin's strong grip. "I'm a little dizzy, let me stand for a minute." If she'd been expecting to see a puddle in the blanket she had wet, she didn't say, but her accident had soaked well into it. "Oops," she smiled. "That will need a good wash."

Gingerly she moved across the small room, without mishap, to look directly into the big mirror on the wall. "Oh no, my good dress," she frowned. "I should never sleep in a good dress if I'm unwell. Now you will have to find me a new one."

"I can do that," Robin smiled, "now don't worry. Are your legs feeling stronger?"

"I think so, but please keep holding me." That was something Robin found he rather enjoyed.

"Put your arm around my neck and we'll walk you upstairs to the shower."

They'd long since discovered that the purpose of the china bowl on the floor with water in was where they could do their toilet, and that was where she headed first.

"Help me get my dress off," she pleaded. Robin did so then helped her to balance over the bowl.

They threw the spoiled dress into the shower, Lucy walked in, slowly, placed her hands against the wall, her feet balanced apart, and her head under where the water would come. "Turn it on please." He did so, drowning her in a flurry of warm water.

Robin's bladder had got beyond urgent, so he had no option but to also use the toilet or he'd be spoiling his trousers.

She hadn't fallen when he got back to her, she was still in the same position, enjoying the rush of water over her head. He turned the flow off a little and washed her shoulders with the bottled soap, then saw it flow over the rest of her once the water was turned on again. He felt a little coy, feeling unable to touch more than her naked shoulders. He concluded that she wasn't like his mother. Yes, she had the shape and fullness he associated with her, but there was something more beguiling about watching Lucy, seeing her flesh.

She stepped out of the shower under her own power, walking into a large towel that Robin wrapped all around her, then he used a smaller towel to dry her hair. He combed her hair, as he had done that first time, even more sensitive to the feelings growing inside of him, for her hair was still so soft, so enticing, to the touch.

*

He walked her gently downstairs, but by then she was able to move unattended. "What about this red and gold dress for a beautiful princess?"

"Very nice," she smiled widely, "but I will need something warmer for the winter." She chose a heavier woven blue dress and slipped it on.

"Now I'm thirsty, and hungry. What shall we have for breakfast?"

*

Robin didn't leave her side for the rest of the day. He insisted she rested. "You've still got a bit of a bump, and your head feels a bit hot. You should lie down as much as possible and rest."

"Yes, Doctor," she smiled. "I remember now what happened. The little dogs were running around my feet. I only noticed that one of them had done their business on the floor as I stepped into it and went skidding. The next thing I knew was waking up this morning."

"That was a pretty nasty fall you had. We will have to train the dogs to do their business outside. I'm surprised Digga hasn't taught them that. We can't let them cause problems, and I never want to come in and see you lying on the floor like that, ever again."

"I promise to be more careful, but yes, let's make a special space for the dogs the other side of the glass. From now on they will eat outside."

*

They didn't go out on their Sunday walk to catch up with Tom. Robin had decided that Lucy should take it easy for a few days. He made the dinners from frozen packets, although they often didn't know what they were eating. Some cans, that they'd found in a different location added variety to their meals. They simply didn't know what they would find inside. Sometimes it was soggy fruit, sometimes beans, or even with some small cans they found something fishy, which they turned their noses up at, but Digga loved it.

By the Tuesday, Robin relaxed his concern over Lucy, and they went back to their library studies. "Look at this," Robin announced as he sat in front of the PC. "We know whatever happened did so around year 2038. Now if I enter a search for 2038 or 2037 the information looks normal, compared to other years, about people passing away, that sort of thing. For year 2039 it changes totally as though nothing new was reported. I can't believe that no important people died that year."

"Could it mean something else, that people were too busy fighting off whatever the problem was?"

"That's a fair point," agreed Robin. "I want to search on some terms I saw previously. For example, there was a report about something called coronavirus, with people dying of it in Europe." He entered the word. The screen came back with thousands and thousands of entries found.

After reading through several reports, Lucy summed up their feelings, "It looks like some nasty disease killed so many people. That must have been terrible."

"I think it was more than that," admitted Robin. "Let's see what happens when I enter a year with that name." He entered, 'coronavirus 2039'. Some entries came up, but nothing related to that year. He tried 'coronavirus 2038', and received many pages of information. "People were certainly dying from this thing, but their society was still functioning, just. Something else was happening, I'm sure of it. But look at this one."

Lucy read out the text, "The reason so many people are dying is because vaccinations given to people to prevent them catching the virus are killing them."

"Treachery," Robin shouted, taking note of the comments and its web address.

"What happens if you search on news for 2038?" He tried, adding in UK to make it more specific.

"Wow, that looks very interesting," said Lucy. "Those are the newspapers we have heard about." Online news lined up before their eyes to be read. Each newspaper was filled with many articles. "It's a shame we don't have 2 PC's. We could split up the articles between us."

*

They ploughed through the online news and made a summary of the most often repeated items. These included: immigration; coronavirus; the economy; climate change; child abuse; people trafficking; sex change; BLM; Racism; BREXIT. They reviewed all of these, noting what they were about, but it wasn't until they used the browser to search these terms individually that things got interesting. "We seem to have started with the official views first," said Robin. "They sounded just like the things we were told, as though there could be no doubt. Now it seems we also have the counter views, and these are much more interesting, and get more instant, more clear as time goes by." There was a great deal of counter views, and more kept coming up through links. They began to understand that the previous society was full of corruption, misinformation and outright lies.

"We were told," spluttered Lucy, "that Man had ruined the planet. That we were not to use energy. We were limited to what we could burn for warmth or cooking. Yet here are these so-called leaders, who said these lies to us, flying all around the world using engines that burn so much more fuel than we ever could."

"Exactly," agreed Robin. "The more we read of this, the worse it gets." They read some more reports that linked to the UN site, where it was clearly written that there were too many people in the world, and they had to be reduced. "The other article said it was something to do with a UN agenda. They called it the new world order."

"So this is the new world order, is it?" Lucy cried. "This is what those fancy politicians and big organisations were planning for us all along. It truly stinks, and I'd love to tell them that if I could go back in time, because we are now living like slaves because of their corruption!"

Robin was astounded at her lashing out like that but couldn't disagree with her. He did wonder though if the fall had loosened her tongue.

They read and they searched, and they read some more, doing nothing else for several days, barely stopping to eat or sleep, but finally they felt they understood what had happened. They were both livid with the results of what had come up. They could hardly sleep for the anger they felt. The virus had been just one more tool of the top politicians and others who ran the world, to suppress and subdue everyone. Television programmes had been a tool to make people think in a special way and ignore what was really going on. They now understood what brainwashing meant. Climate change was one of the biggest lies, to make people poorer and frighten them, similar to how they frightened them with the virus.

Robin found a short article that someone had written in despair at the way that thinking had become so perverted. He printed it out so that Tom could see it, but first he read it out to Lucy who was still flushed with anger. 'Mother Nature is amazing. She provides for us, creates a marvellous world to be lived in. There are beautiful unimagined sights that thrill the soul encouraging us to explore and be part of something greater than mere randomity.

Nature's forces create mountains and turn boulders into fine sand that line exotic shores. Ocean water is purified in the sky to make it taste good and free of salt, filtered to quench our thirst. Trees, fruit and many foods grow for our use and to nourish us.

Nature provides for us in every possible way.

The great oceans and wild areas are full of life; the skies often fill with birds and insects that stretch the dreams of us all as we wonder about their basic nature.

Precious metals lie within the crust of our planet gold, iron, silver. Many others are there, created in the vast furnaces of long dead stars. They were created to enhance the natural beauty and functionality of sentient life running at the peak of high survival potential.

With all of this, the store of inherent wealth available to mankind, it is not possible that it was created to go to waste, for fruit to rot on branches, for heat giving fuel to remain locked underground. SURELY Nature would not want it all to go unused? SURELY Nature would insist that all the hard-won resources now available, fashioned over thousands of years, to create a vast plethora of natural reserves, should be known about and utilised fully?

To leave a huge supply of wealth in the ground, as some want, is worse than irrational. The world has been manipulated by its very own laws to make these treasures available to enhance life, to make intelligent living more extensive, more rewarding. It would surely go against every natural *rule this universe has ever known to leave it untouched, unused.*

I don't think we should be offending Mother Nature by ignoring this wealth, do you?

It was carbon, in the form of coal, that dragged millions out of poverty and servitude during the Industrial Revolution. Now they want us to revert to that earlier state, with all the hardships, impositions, injustices and perverse rules they can think of, not to mention being forced into a very low quality of life'. Lucy and Robin sighed heavily together.

*

Suddenly it was Sunday, and they felt the urge to get out to walk and meet Tom, to help relieve the fuming anger they felt inside at the loss of their future and loved ones to a vile new world order that served only those that already had everything.

*

The pups followed happily after Robin as he grabbed his backpack and headed for the tower exit with Lucy. They crossed the road quickly after making sure no other travellers were in sight and made their way through the undergrowth to the house. Digga was the first to spot that something was not right. She ran around looking for Tom's dogs, then gave out a cry when they were not there. They found Tom inside the small house, shivering, wary and bleeding.

"What happened?" asked Lucy.

"Horrible things," admitted Tom, sighing heavily.

"You're hurt," said Lucy, again trying to illicit a real response from Tom.

Robin and Lucy sat either side of him, looking him over. Tom looked exhausted, but he didn't seem to have any severe injuries, plenty of scratches to his arms and face, but nothing that couldn't be washed away with good clean water.

They waited while he gained the will to speak and raised his head. "I've run away."

Tom leaned back, sighed again then continued, "The new chief is the worst ever kind of nightmare. You get beaten up for nothing. Too slow, they say, or not doing enough work. I couldn't take any more."

"What about your dogs?" asked Robin, knowing too well that Tom would not have willingly left his dogs behind.

Tom turned his head, and his eyes overflowed with tears. He could barely speak, but when he did it came out as a hoarse whisper, but an angry one. "They took them away and butchered them." The tears flowed down his cheeks as he looked Robin in the eye. "Those damned ignorant savages just cut them down and ripped them open, with a machete while 2 of the chief's bully boys held me down."

"That nightmare is over now," said Lucy. "You are going to come and live with us." She looked at Robin for agreement.

"You clearly can't go back, and we have plenty of space. But when will they come looking for you? How much time have we got?"

"I still have my pass to hunt for game outside the village. If I don't get back by dusk, they will send out searchers."

"We have a little time then," said Robin. "Firstly, we have to remove that damned thing from your head so that they cannot find you from the sky." He took out the whiskey bottle and asked Tom to adjust his position so that the chip was easier to get at. Scissors were removed from the first aid kit, which Robin hoped would be enough to dig out the evil device. "Drink as much of this as you can, it will make you sleepy," Robin said as he kneeled with Tom's head resting at an angle.

Tom took a good swig from the bottle, then almost coughed it back up again. "What the hell was that?"

"Medicine," insisted Robin, "now have at least 2 more sips." Tom complied and handed the bottle back. Robin splashed some of the liquid liberally over the area on Tom's head that he would have to dig into.

"Let me do this," Lucy said, taking the scissors from Robin's hand. Robin nodded, grateful. He really didn't like the idea of digging into Tom's skull.

Lucy's movements were concise, and having found the chip using her fingers, she cut into the flesh, in a line, right next to the device. Tom suppressed a scream, cursing under his breath with words that Lucy had never come across in their dictionary. As the scissor's point touched the chip, Tom gasped, suddenly relaxed before going unconscious. Lifting the flap of skin, Lucy then used some tweezers to grip and pull out the offending item, dropping it into Robin's hand.

They cleaned up the wound with some more whiskey, then attached a plaster to hold the skin in place. It was a couple of hours later that Tom finally awoke, groaning and holding his head. Robin hadn't been idle while Lucy was holding Tom's hand and watching over him.

Just like he had done with Lucy's chip, he wanted to add some confusion to those tracking Tom. So, keeping the device safe, he set out with Digga and her little hunters. He'd previously noticed a group of squirrels in amongst a group of oak trees. Before they got too close Robin had a word with Digga, indicating 3 squirrels playing together, clearly not hibernating as it wasn't that cold any more. "You see them?" he asked Digga. She looked, then turned back to Robin, licking his nose in acknowledgement. "I want you to catch one for me." Digga, still looking at Robin, gave a very small yelp in response. "Don't kill it," insisted Robin in a firm voice. "Bring it to me alive." Digga lifted her snout as if asking if that was it. Robin nodded.

Quietly, Digga went to each of her pups that had been smelling something very interesting under a yew tree, touching noses, and issuing a soft kind of barking noise, then she sent them off to surround the squirrels and cut off their escape back to the trees.

With the small dogs in place, Digga crept forward on her belly, then just a few feet away from the small, red, bushy-tailed mammal, she pounced. The squirrels ran in all directions, one even leaped as far as the nearest tree to safety, but the rest suddenly became statues as they spotted the puppies creeping up on them. That was all the time Digga needed. She grabbed the closest one in her teeth firmly without damaging it. She'd had plenty of practice doing that with her young.

Running quickly back to Robin, Digga allowed him to take the worried animal out of her jaws. Robin pushed the squirrel into a pocket of his backpack and sealed the creature inside, with just enough air coming in to keep it alive.

Robin made a big fuss of Digga, telling her what a great hunter she was. She wagged her tail effusively as if to say, "do I get my reward from the other dogs now? Where are they?"

Picking up on this Robin had to tell her the 3 dogs that had fathered her puppies had been killed. Digga lay down mournfully with her tail still, eyes watery, crying to herself. It took the combined effort of all 5 pups jumping all over her, nipping her gently, to become less desolate. Robin also helped by telling her what a good dog she was.

*

Tom managed to stand but was groggy from both the medicine and the surgery, but he was able to focus well enough on the electronic device Robin showed him, that had been taken from his head. "That's what they put inside us to make sure we remain under their control as slave workers?" grumbled Tom.

"Yes," agreed Robin. "That though is only a small part of the treachery. Not so long ago we were a free people. Then those that ran the world decided we had too much freedom and enjoyment. They put a stop to all of that!"

Not quite getting his head around what Robin had said, Tom looked a little dazed, then asked, "What are you going to do with that chip?"

Robin smiled, taking the small animal from his bag, he said, "I'm going to help confuse those that will come searching for you." With that he gently made the squirrel open its mouth wide and dropped the chip fully down its throat. "I'll not let this creature go just yet. I'd rather they didn't come and find our little house and garden. Let's go back a little way in the direction you came to see if we can find some other trees for our furry friend to escape into."

"Yes," agreed Tom, "I came past quite a few oaks on the way. Let's go that way," he pointed in the general direction of his village.

It was only after they had passed the third group of oak trees that Robin released the animal, unharmed and still with plenty of bounce. It leapt quickly out of Robin's open hands, circled the nearest tree and poked its nose around a branch to keep a close eye on its captors for a moment, before disappearing into the upper branches.

Even Tom had to smile at all of this.

"Time we got you to safety," said Robin. "How are you holding up? I know from experience that having your head cut open can be a real stress to the body."

"Got an awful headache," admitted Tom.

"That will pass," said Lucy. "We'll find you a nice warm place to recover."

"We will also leave the medicine with you so that it will help you to sleep," smiled Robin.

*

They got Tom through their secret hole although the dogs wanted to go first. He was groggier now, meaning Robin was almost carrying him down the steps. Once down to the first level Tom could walk a little. Robin pointed out the toilet, then guided Tom into one of the cosy rooms at the back with not so much light coming in. Lucy ran down to select some blankets and a floor covering, then made a cosy nest for Tom. They settled Tom down, giving him 2 more swigs of whiskey, then he was suddenly asleep.

Robin checked on Tom several times, but always found him fast asleep, with indications he'd had more swigs of whiskey. "You're getting a taste for that vile medicine I see," said Robin.

Lucy was up very early, sitting in the corner watching Tom who slept in until nearly midday when Robin and the dogs joined them.

"How does it feel to have survived your first night of freedom?" Robin asked with a smile. "You are safe here; nobody has ever found us."

"Feels strange," admitted Tom. "That bed was so comfortable and warm.

Nothing like my old hovel."

"You'll have to get used to a little comfort here," Robin announced as Digga jumped across and welcomed Tom back to the living with a big wet lick.

"Well thank you, Digga, that's a great welcome."

"You must be hungry," stated Lucy. "I heard your stomach rumbling many times."

"I'm always hungry, that's the nature of life now, but I'll take anything you have. My stomach thinks that my throat has been cut."

"No," smiled Robin, as Lucy went downstairs. "We didn't cut your throat, just your head. How is it now?"

"Just a kind of a dull ache," admitted Tom, "but I'm hoping that will fade away."

"It will be better with some food inside you. Lucy is bringing you some leftover soup from last night, but she does make tasty food."

A few moments later Lucy reappeared with hot soup. Tom sat up eagerly and wolfed it down. "This is rather a luxury. A clean, nice looking bowl, and a real spoon."

"Sorry we don't have any bread to go with it," admitted Lucy.

"Not to worry," said Tom. "That was fabulous. I feel like a new man."

Lucy took the bowl away, as Robin showed Tom where he could clean himself up. "That's where you can do your toilet," said Robin. "Just push that lever when you are done, and it will be washed away."

Tom looked at Robin with amazed eyes. "What is this place? You never told me you were living in a luxury palace."

"All will become clear when I show you around," smiled Robin. "Now just stay here while I fetch something for you. You are really filthy."

"Oh, sorry," said Tom, half frowning, "am I messing up your palace?"

Robin smiled weakly then ran downstairs while Tom relieved himself.

Returning with towels and clothing, Robin found Tom admiring the toilet. "You know," said Tom, "I've heard of these things, but I never thought I'd use one. They used to be called water closets. It needs a wooden seat on so you don't have to stoop, and for a bit of privacy we should be fitting a door..."

"Whenever you feel up to it," said Robin. "Right now we are going to get you clean. That," he said, indicating the shower, "is the most marvellous machine known to Man. You will need to remove those rags that pass for clothes, then I'll show you how it works." Tom complied and shortly was getting more luxury than he'd ever imagined. His hair got shampooed and his pale, skinny body washed, and he marvelled at the hot water washing all over him, making him warm, but also making him think he was in a dream.

Robin showed him how to wrap the large towel around himself and dry off, after which Tom was introduced to some new clothes, of a synthetic nature, that had already survived many years. "The green trousers look good on you, and that red top makes you look like a prince."

"I'm still in shock," Tom stated. "I feel like I'm in a dream world, so, seriously, tell me what is this place?"

Robin explained that this was some kind of store where people had exchanged money for food and clothes in the old days. "It was buried totally until Digga found it for me. I was just looking for a hole in the ground. Discovering this has really changed everything. There is so much to show you."

Tom stood looking at himself in the mirror. "My God, I do look a bloody prince, a lord even."

*

In time Robin introduced Tom to all of the features of their little home, followed by what had been discovered in the library. Tom had a natural affinity for books, and often spent hours in the library. Tom was amazed at the notes Robin had made that described how the past had fallen apart, and was just as angry when he realised it had all been done by a privileged few that didn't want to share any luxuries with riff-raff like him.

*

Tom soon got the toilet sorted and took over the training of the puppies. He split them up so that 3 of the puppies would get used to being with him, while Whiskey and Groaner stayed with Digga, Lucy and Robin.

*

They all 3 spent much of January and February researching the links about how society had collapsed, especially the ones that described in some detail how things really were, as opposed to how lies were spread that didn't match any evidence. "Climate change was supposed to make the sea rise," announced Robin, "but it didn't rise an inch! Polar bears were also said to be an effect of the changing climate, but in fact polar bears were thriving. It was all done as a control mechanism to make people believe authority and to do as they were instructed. Some called it brainwashing."

"Yes," complained Tom, "I get most of that but how could that virus thing keep killing people for so long? It started in 2020, they had several complete lockdowns after that, and I can understand that the people couldn't go out to earn money to buy things, but by 2024 you would have thought it would have all been over, but no. The virus came back in waves, so it seems to me, until all countries were bankrupt, with societies degenerating into chaos and riots. Finally, somebody must have introduced a more powerful virus that killed not thousands, but hundreds of thousands, but somehow everything came back to almost normal by 2031. What people were left had work, and stores had things to sell. It doesn't quite add up, if the world collapsed at the end of 2038?"

"Don't forget the crucial aspect of the result of the virus," answered Robin, "it was to get people to accept to have those chips put into their heads. By 2033 everyone was so scared that they agreed to have the chips and be tracked in everything they did and where ever they went."

"That makes some sense," agreed Tom, "but where does this new world order come into it all?"

"The new world order required that everyone be compliant, and scared," said Robin. "Then they could do what they wanted, slaughter, traffic people, abuse kids. With a police force and military working against the people there was no justice for the average person. Gradually things appeared to get better in the 2030's briefly, but that was only because the new world order was getting its final plans ready. Come 2038 they knew where everyone was. Infants were chipped at birth. They must have used the military to round everyone up, from stores, from homes, from wherever they worked. People were put into camps which eventually became the villages we know, and forced to slave for those that run the new world order."

"So it wasn't another virus that killed so many after the initial outbreak, there were other factors involved," Tom groaned.

"Move slowly, impose your will a little at a time, seems to have been their way of working. The powerful group that ran the world before the virus had always said the population should be reduced, and from what I've seen, it was the drugs, the vaccines they insisted people have to allegedly protect against the virus that killed far more than the virus ever did."

"Ah," said Tom in distress. "How could anybody be that evil?"

"Evil is a total understatement," said Lucy. "I've read report after report, from different writers, about children being abused in every possible way, tortured and killed. As far as I can see the whole thing was done to provide our masters with all the slaves they could want, and the means to kill children so that they could drink their blood."

"Yes," agreed Robin. "By torturing the children that caused their bodies to introduce a special kind of hormone into their blood, which was what these disgusting people craved. No, I'm not completely sure what a hormone is either, except that it is a natural body response to physical stress."

"These masters are not people, they are monsters," cried Lucy.

"It looks like this was all planned for decades, at least," Robin stated. "As they moved closer to their goals, they became careless and let more of the truth slip out, which is why we can see it now. People began to understand. I've read many articles from numerous people who knew what was being set up, but most people just wouldn't believe it."

"Yes," agreed Lucy, "that ranger chap who was talking about natural remedies and warned about the deep state. He was good."

"One of many that were ignored until it was too late," said Robin. "When the vast majority finally understood, it was too late. The new world order was powerful and had almost total control. People did riot, but against the army they stood no chance. They were often butchered in the streets, sometimes even in their homes."

"I'm not sure I can stand any more horrors," said Tom. "This is all so awful."

"We have to know the truth so that we can tell everyone what happened," said Robin. "I get sick in my stomach when I think about some of this stuff, but somehow we must find a way to break free of this slavery."

"You're right, Robin, but we are but 3, how can we change anything?" Digga never liked being left out and gave a yelp to let them know about her and her brood. "Oh, alright then, what can we 8 do to change anything? I don't see a way."

"Neither do I," Robin admitted, "but we are free, and we can change things by understanding fully what happened and passing that information on."

"So we are 8 against how many?" Tom asked. "Before it all collapsed there were millions of people to oppose the tyranny. How far did they get?"

"Actually, the good guys did achieve some notable successes before they were finally crushed around the world," Robin insisted. "In Germany they shot the prime minister for working so hard and so long against the German people, from flooding the country with immigrants to deceit and corruption in allowing the new world order to take over. The French president along with quite a few of his predecessors met a similar fate."

"Good for them," smiled Tom, "but what happened here, in our United Kingdom?"

"There was a massive uprising led by people who had been complaining about immigration and child abuse for many years," replied Robin. "They started a march from the north towards London, picking up people as they went. Well over 2 million reached the seat of government, but they were under-fed and tired. Those in charge of the country were well protected, mainly, so they waited out the marchers who became more desperate."

"That sounds like another sad tale," frowned Tom.

"It was," agreed Robin, "but not before they had punished a good number of politicians that had allowed the country to slip into the hands of the masters. A despicable UK prime minister who was elected in 1997 was taken from his home which was burned down. He introduced so many laws that paved the way for anarchy as well as filling the country with unwanted immigrants, so he was towards the top of the wanted list. He was also a new world order supporter. They cut off his head and placed it on a pole close to the parliament building."

"I don't imagine that the rioters got away with that for long?"

"Long enough to have killed others in their home who were complicit with the treachery, along with several other ex-prime ministers who had clearly been working against the best interests of the UK people. One was a woman who had deceived the country over leaving the EU. She was hung from a lamp post. Their bodies were all then displayed prominently. A very rich fellow who had been promoting the deadly vaccines and chips was caught out as he tried to leave London. They injected him with various poisons and hung him up. Somehow, he caught his feet in something supporting himself until he could be rescued, but it was as he was being lowered that his feet slipped and the rope bit into his neck, fatally."

"Oh my, they were angry, almost as much as we are."

"Their reign didn't last too long unfortunately, and they achieved nothing more than making those in charge even more vicious. The army came in and slaughtered many of them."

"Not a good end," Tom said very sadly.

"No, but it has to be a lesson to us, so that we can remember, so that we can never underestimate these foul monsters ever again. They have to be wiped out. If only we knew how!"

"It's a hopeless task, but hey, I wasn't planning to do anything special this lifetime," said Tom, cheerfully.

CHAPTER 3

MORE PLACES TO HIDE IN

Several more weeks passed as Tom got used to his freedom, Lucy and Robin became closer, and Digga's pups grew into small dogs. They'd worked their way systematically through all the books, picking out anything that could enhance their knowledge, generally. They now had various maps as they had learned how to print images from the PC. They shared and discussed everything they found, but still had no idea of how they should proceed.

"This map of the Swanley area, where we are, shows a supermarket right here," stated Robin. "That must be the cavern where we found all of that food. I'm just wondering if any more supermarkets survived." He typed into search for supermarkets. "Ah, that's interesting." He showed the others. "Look, some of them are quite close. We should investigate."

"I agree," said Tom. "No telling what useful things we might be able to find, but I'm also thinking we should have alternative places we could hide in if anybody ever finds us here."

"Oh please," Lucy said, pained. "Don't say that we would be hunted down here."

"It makes sense," said Robin. "If we established bases in different places, it would mean we could explore more of the country we are in."

"Hmm, OK," agreed Lucy quietly.

"Yes, now that the weather is getting better, we should get out more and find our way around," Tom said. "Time we found some fresh rabbit as well."

"Yelp," agreed Digga, licking her lips at the prospect.

*

"This feels a bit strange," said Tom as he emerged from the main exit point from the cavern into overgrowth above. It was damp after an early morning shower, making them all wet as they pushed their way towards the path. Robin clambered up a tree to make sure it was safe before they exited the greenery.

"All clear," announced Robin, "and it looks like it will be a nice sunny day once the wind blows the rain clouds away."

They had already decided that there were 2 supermarkets, as they were called on the internet, that looked promising. The places had names of Crayford and Gravesend, but that was only useful when looking at maps. It was doubtful that they would have signposts. "The one almost due north looks interesting," said Tom. "It doesn't seem to be close to any villages, but we need to keep a look out so that we don't barge into anything. By my estimate, I put it at about a 2 hour walk as long as the brambles don't get too thick."

Robin had brought his backpack along as usual, with everything he considered useful for exploring. Lucy was travelling light, with just a small bag over her back with some dried meat to keep them going. Tom had adopted a bag and contents similar to what Robin had, his motto was to be prepared.

After crossing the path, they headed at an angle of about 45 degrees to where the village would be and headed in to the thick foliage. Every so often Robin would find a tree to climb up to make sure they were not being noticed or likely to run into any trouble. They avoided the marshy ground but kept a good direction towards the north.

"How will we know when we get to this Crayford place?" asked Lucy.

"It won't be easy," admitted Robin. "We need to keep our eyes open for overgrown big structures." Then looking towards Digga, "That includes noses as well. I'm hopeful you will sniff us out something good today,

Digga." The dog wagged its tail, pressing her nose close to the ground searching for clues.

"When I looked at a different map," said Tom, "it showed a railway station close to where we are heading."

"Is that one of those places where people used to get on or off those long carriages that ran on metal lines?" Lucy wanted to know.

"That's what I understand," answered Tom.

They walked on in silence for some time, crossing relatively flat land which wasn't too overground and didn't have too many thorns to rip them with. They passed the remnants of what had been a house, but now was barely a shell, with its front all tumbled down. Shortly after that the land started to slope downwards, but it was taking them away from due north.

"We need to find a way to the left that isn't too rough to walk on," said Tom, "that should put us back on course." They found a path and walked that way until it ended near to a partially eroded building with some fancy metal work, that was still standing, more or less.

"That must have been an impressive building," said Robin.

"It might be that station we were talking about," suggested Lucy. "Shall we investigate?"

They passed through the wide entrance; the wooden floor was rotting away but stable enough to take their weight.

"Just a second," said Tom. "Look at the dusty floor. Something has been dragged in here."

"You're right," agreed Robin, examining the skid marks, "and it wasn't more than a few days ago."

"Wait!" shouted Lucy. "What is that noise?"

They listened. "It's getting louder," said Tom, "and it's making things shake. It must be a big mechanical thing. We must hide."

There was a dusty entrance at the side, dark and filled with cobwebs. "Quick," said Robin, "get the dogs in here."

They'd just got hidden when a big shadow fell over the doorway opposite to the one they'd come in by. Nobody said a word, but they shared the same thoughts, making themselves as tiny as they could.

They could hear things happening but were not entirely sure what they were. Tom was in the best position to watch and not be seen, being totally in the gloomy dark and resting on something that gave him some height. He saved his words for later. There were sounds like doors closing, and things being lifted. Tom counted 5 men who mostly stood by the gurgling mechanical hissing engine. A moment later the shadows of 2 men darkened the floor further as they passed by the hiding place, dragging huge sacks of something. Tom risked peeking at where the sacks were taken, which seemed to be just across the path, into a metal container of sorts.

After 10 journeys by the 2 men, the small dogs were getting restless, and didn't want to rest any more. The men returned for the last time, just as Whiskey wandered towards the open space. The second man almost caught the small dog in the corner of his eye, but before he could react an order was barked from one of the other men, and he hurried onwards.

More sounds like doors closing, and the mechanical gurgle machine began to move away. Still worried that some men might have stayed behind, they remained still and quiet, with just Whiskey brave enough to go see what adventure he could find. Eventually they followed Whiskey to where the 3 men had been standing.

"Yes," said Tom, quietly, "that was a train, look at those shiny metal rails down there."

"It sounded horrible," said Lucy. "If that was a train, I don't ever want to see anything like it again."

"Don't worry," said Tom, soothingly. "We came out to explore, and it seems we have found something we didn't know about before, so that's good. Knowledge is power."

"Let's get on with what we came for," suggested Robin, but no sooner had the words left his mouth than they heard something almost as loud as the train. Robin looked up the path to see some mechanical vehicle on wheels coming quickly towards them. "Quick, back into the dusty hole." They all moved quickly, with Robin taking a firm hold on Whiskey this time. He could see them approaching through a hole where the wood had cracked.

After the thing screeched to a halt, Robin whispered, "That must be a car." He watched as 2 men got out right next to the round metallic object where the sacks had been taken. The sacks were moved to the back of the car, which was turned around, then driven off at speed. Too fast in fact for one of the sacks which having been badly positioned, fell onto the pathway.

Once it was all quiet, they emerged from hiding, even dustier than they previously were. They listened anxiously as they walked gently forward, hoping that all the men had gone and there would be no more surprises. The path was clear except that the car had left a putrid fog of smoke in its wake. Robin immediately went to investigate the sack, with Whiskey yelping happily beside him. Tom went to inspect the round container.

"That sack is full of grains," Robin stated. "This would make a great addition to our diet if we could get it home."

"It would," smiled Lucy, "but it looks awfully heavy. Can we carry it all that way?"

"We should at least try," suggested Robin.

"This must be how they get things moved around, from village to London, or whatever, and from London to village," Tom said. "This could be profitable for us. There's nothing left in that container but a few barley grains, but I think you are right, Robin. We should get this little present home before anyone comes looking for it."

Lucy carried Robin's backpack while Tom helped Robin heft the sack across his shoulders. "Don't get too brave," said Tom, "rest when you need to, and I will take a turn."

Between them they got the grains home, even though the journey took twice as long, and both men had to lay down to ease their back muscles afterwards.

As they were eating their dinner that night, which had a good helping of barley, Tom spoke up cheerfully. "It seems our plans didn't quite go right, but we have gained some very useful knowledge, and we have a great addition to what we eat. Very nicely cooked, Lucy. It's been a very long time since I chewed cooked barley."

"Let's give it a few days, and we can go to that supermarket," suggested Robin.

"Agreed," said Tom. "A few days rest won't hurt, but there is something I want to do on my own, without the dogs. I want to rest my bones tomorrow and start out very early the next day. I want to see what schedule they keep and what things are moved, where to and when. It will be more knowledge that we can make use of. It will be safer if I go alone."

Nobody argued with him, but Lucy gave him a stern look, warning him to be careful.

*

It was still dark as Tom made his way back to the railway, but the morning was dry. Lucy had prepared him some food to last for 2 days, as he wanted to see how often the drop off point was used, as well as anything that might prove useful regarding the train. He arrived at the end of the tarmac path in front of the railway building about the time he would have normally been dragging himself off to work in the fields, back in the village. That brought a gentle satisfaction to his demeanour, and a bit of an ironic smile.

Inspecting the large round metal container, he found it to be empty. There was nothing else of interest in this cul-de-sac, so he walked to, and through the building to look down at metal rails that guided the train. The rails were overgrown in places with weeds, and some of the wood on which the rails rested was cracked, but that was as far as his observation went in that direction.

There weren't many structures still standing, except for the building he had entered through. At some point a bridge of metal had spanned the rails, but now, having rusted through, it lay dangerously across the double set of lines, blocking access to the south.

With nothing more to take his interest Tom looked for somewhere to get cosy where he could see what was going on when it happened. A thick bushy oak tree right next to the north side of the building met his favour. Just halfway up he was able to see where the train came from as well as having a good view of the path.

The broad oak was most comfortable and wide enough that he could lay down, with no danger that he could roll off or slip down. He made sure he was secure from other eyes then made himself comfortable, eyes closed, awaiting some disturbance.

It was probably about one hour later that the car arrived with huge amounts of green produce and early potatoes. The men didn't hang around and were gone in a very short time. Tom was tempted to steal some of the food, but his instincts told him to stay where he was. Another hour went by, the car arrived back, this time with eggs that were stacked gently outside the metal container in stiff paper containers. This was too much for Tom to resist. "I can't remember the last time I had an egg," he told the tree as he scrambled quickly down the tree, after making sure the train was not yet coming.

Taking 2 whole cartons to hide in the bushes, he cracked one egg and popped the contents into his mouth, "Hmm," he said.

Tempted further, he stole another carton, which slipped out of his hand as he heard the train approach. "Oops," he said, almost apologetic towards the eggs. With little time to spare he put the carton back with eggs oozing out of it, ran to his tree and clambered up just as the train came to a halt.

It seemed that there was one man that drove the train, 2 slaves and 2 burly men to guard the slaves. Tom watched the 2 slaves approach the container and heard them shouting back to the guards. They'd clearly spotted the broken eggs and didn't want to be blamed for that.

The guard took the damaged carton back to share the good eggs with his comrades while the slaves carried everything else into a wagon at the end of the train. There were 3 carriages to the train, 2 of which were already pretty full of grown things. A small carriage next to the engine was where the 4 men, slaves and guards, sat during the journey. Again, they didn't waste time, and were gone, back to the north, before the taste of the egg he had swallowed had totally left his mouth. This time the train left nothing behind.

With nothing else to take his attention, Tom dozed on and off, luxuriating in the feeling of freedom, now able to do what he wanted without some bully imposing his will on him. It was maybe 3 hours later that the car came back with lettuce, spring onions, and more early potatoes. Tom knew all this because he went to look after the car left. Then he went back into hiding after selecting a few choice items.

The car came back once more, but this time without any produce. Their cargo instead was 2 girls of about 14, dirty, dishevelled and broken of spirit. With their hands already fastened tightly behind their backs they were made to stand up next to the handle of the metal container. More twine was used to hold them close to the container, such that they couldn't sit down. For however long they were there they would not be able to move more than half an inch or so in any direction. Tom fumed when he saw this. More innocent girls being sent to the lords for abuse and an early death.

Tom was so agitated he couldn't keep still, thinking that the train would return at any time. He waited, watching. If the train was not due back until tomorrow that was an ugly trick to leave the girls there like that all night. With careful scrutiny of the rail line, Tom made a decision.

The girls didn't even flinch when he approached them, thinking it was someone else come to mistreat or grope them. "Hey," Tom said, "I want to help you get away. Will you promise to follow me, to keep quiet, and to do as I ask you?"

The girls looked at him with alarm, yet with a tiny amount of twinkle. They nodded, reluctantly, being used to being controlled by others, knowing that any help would require something in exchange. Sensing this Tom said, "I don't want anything from you. I have only recently gained my freedom. I just want to help you." One of the girls nodded with almost a smile on her lips.

"Here is the plan," Tom stated. "I will cut you free and we are going to carry some food away with us and run in that direction. There is a problem though. There is a device in your heads that will tell the masters where you are. I need to cut that out. It will hurt, but it's the only chance of freedom you have. Mine was cut out for me, so I know."

A half nod by way of acceptance was all he received, but it was enough. Using his sharp knife he cut through the bonds. It was hard to do so for there was metal in the twine, but he had them free and went to collect his packages. He gave a box of eggs each for the girls to carry, then picking up what else he could carry he started for the way home, encouraging the girls to hurry.

They made it OK to where the path joined with another. No sign of the train coming nor the car, but they couldn't rest, not yet.

The incline on the next path was quite steep which slowed them down. Tom continually looked for places to hide in case the car returned, but all was quiet for now, except for the wind whispering in the trees. The flat ground came not a minute too soon for Tom's nerves, but it was a welcome sight. They fled into the greenery, Tom looking for a place to hide and do his work. Finally, there was a dry ditch that suited his purpose.

"I will have to do something about those devices now or we will not escape," he said. "It will be painful, so please don't scream."

"Ha, we are used to pain," grumbled one girl, in a pitiful voice.

"You look starving," said Tom. "You'd better eat something." He broke open 2 eggs and had each girl swallow the contents. "That will help you, but you will need to chew on this meat while I am cutting into you. I must do it while there is still some sunlight."

There was nothing to disinfect the area where the wounds would be. Tom wiped away the dirt from each girl's head as well as he could, then felt for the device just below the surface of their heads. Fortunately not much skin had grown over the chip on either girl, so it was just a short nick and Tom could see the chip. Pulling them out was more painful to the girls as they had attached themselves to the skin well. The girls never complained but did gasp as the chips were finally taken away.

"There you are," said Tom, showing the girls the chips with their blood still on them. "This is how they always knew where you were. Now you will be dead to them."

"But where can we go now?" cried the girl with very dark hair.

"We have somewhere safe. I will explain more but I need to feed these to the fish." The girls had no idea what he was talking about, wondering if he were a madman. "I have to get a fish to eat these so that it looks like you fell into a pond. Stay here, do not move. I will not be long." He gave the girls some more meat to chew on after taking 2 small pieces to embed the chips inside.

He'd seen a pond on the earlier trip, which wasn't far, so he was back in less than 5 minutes, just as the sky was getting darker. The fish bait was now floating on the surface of the water in the middle of the pond, awaiting a hungry fish. The girls were still chewing on their food as he got back, although they still looked as miserable as ever.

"Are you going to sell us to somebody?" asked one girl.

"Never in a million years," said Tom. "I saw how they had tied you up and I just couldn't live with myself if you had been taken away for more abuse. What are your names?"

"I am 7..."

"No, your names," interrupted Tom. "You are no longer a number."

"Jane," said one, almost smiling for the first time.

"Anne," said the other, with some reluctance.

"My name is Tom. I escaped from my village when they killed my pets and kept beating me for no reason. I have friends. We have a safe place to sleep, and without those things in your heads you are free."

The girls were still reluctant that any of this wouldn't come without a price, so were unable to give a thanks, but they were looking more alive than they had been.

Tom thought he heard the car on the path, now several hundred feet away, which worried him. "Come," he said, "we cannot stay here. Can you carry those cartons?" The girls nodded and they took off for Swanley.

*

It was dark when they reached the safety of the entrance into the top of the cavern. Digga announced their arrival even before they'd made it down the stairs. The girls stood petrified as Digga kept her distance, but nonetheless looked menacing to the girls who clung to each other. "This dog won't hurt you," Tom shouted. "She is a pet."

As Tom made it down with his bundle, Robin and Lucy appeared, with surprise on their faces. "Come here, Digga, you are frightening them," Robin shouted. Digga obeyed and sat down between him and Lucy.

For a moment nobody said anything as they all looked at each other. Robin broke the silence with, "did you get the chips out?"

"Yes," smiled Tom, "fed them to the fish. Sorry I am back early to disturb you, but this was a bit of an emergency. I found these 2 tied up ready to be transported away on the train for more abuse. This is Jane and Anne."

Recalling how scared she had been when Robin had rescued her, Lucy smiled at the girls, and gently walked towards them. "You don't need to be frightened. We have all gone through similar things to you, so we know how it feels, but this is our home, and you are safe here." She took their hands and led them forward.

"What's that light?" asked Anne, with some alarm.

"Oh," answered Robin, "that is something our ancestors left for us. They have been very good to us in providing for our needs." The girls were perplexed but said no more.

As the girls moved more into the light Lucy, who never missed a day without a shower now, said, "I will help you to wash. Robin and Tom, take those boxes downstairs, and find some clothes for these girls."

The men did as they were told, while Lucy got Anne and then Jane washed and thoroughly clean all over. Meanwhile Tom was telling Robin what had occurred.

"I stole what I thought I could carry, then that car brought those girls. I couldn't leave them there," insisted Tom.

"You were right to rescue them," agreed Robin.

"It seems the train comes once a day, but the car seems to get produce from different villages, which then gets transported to the lords on the train. The train must stop at other places because some carriages were full of food, no doubt stolen from hard working slaves."

"I'm not sure how we can use what you've learned, Tom, but I will add the details to our note keeping. Certainly we can go back there occasionally and get some more fresh eggs, and we might even find more people to rescue."

"Let's give it a week," said Tom, "for things to settle down, and we can go looking for that supermarket as well. We still need to have different safe places to hide out in."

*

The next morning, Lucy, having spent the night with the girls in the room next to Tom, began to explain about the cavern and how they had frozen food to cook and eat. The girls, while clean of body, were still very shy, still carrying with them the fears they had always had. It would be some time before they were able to fully explain all that had happened to them.

For the first week the girls did as they were told or spent the time huddled together. The cavern was almost too much to take in, and with every loud noise they flinched, expecting a beating, or worse. Digga did her best to help. She brought her brood along, lay down in front of where the girls were sitting, laid her snout on her outstretched paws and did her best to smile. This was repeated for several days before any progress was made. Whiskey, being the cheeky one was the first to get a response from the girls. Bored of just watching, Whiskey stood up and walked quickly towards Anne, nudged her leg until she reached down to touch the dog. Soon she was stroking his head and looking a little happier. It took a while for Jane to do the same, but by now the rest of the small dogs had moved forward for some love, nudging the girls' legs, and bringing traces of smiles to their lips. Digga watched happily.

*

While Tom and Robin discussed how they might learn more about how the masters and lords had organised everything, Lucy had plans to get Anne and Jane into a better frame of mind. "They need to be doing something," she told Digga, who heartily agreed.

Taking the girls into the lower cavern, where clothes and other materials still sat, Lucy had decided that it was time it was organised better, with all the old dust and rotting fabric removed. "I could really do with some help,"

Lucy said to the girls. "I've been meaning to tidy this all up for a long time. Will you help me?" The girls agreed that they would. There were many racks of clothing of all types that were still in good condition. With assistance, Lucy moved these all to the far side of the cavern, close to where they went out to the library, but arranging it so that the flat back of the racking acted as a barrier. She organised it in logical rows, with male and female attire in different rows. She had wanted to make it a contained area, to stop the cold wind coming in directly, but also to separate it from other things. Having achieved that, there were several piles of rubbish, bits of this and that, as well as plenty of dust that had to go. Once that was all cleared away outside, they had a large area with nothing in it. "I will find something to fill that space," Lucy said.

That night as the girls were doing better, Lucy went back to her usual sleeping area with Robin. "Oh," he said, pleased. "I was afraid you would be sleeping with the girls from now on."

"No," she said, kissing his cheek warmly, and snuggling closer. "I don't ever want to have us separated."

*

Lucy was in the habit of sending the pups to wake everyone up for breakfast. Robin was an early riser, but Tom, Anne and Jane had gotten used to having a long lie in and their faces washed for them while they were still dozing.

*

Walking around the very empty space in the cavern, Lucy wondered what she was going to do with it, and indeed, what else she could get better organised, when she heard giggling. She followed the happy sound to find Anne and Jane standing in front of a mirror, holding up fancy tops to see how they would suit them. Lucy smiled. "Try a few on, see what you like yourselves dressed in. The boys are outside planning a trip, so they won't disturb you." Jane blushed, but Anne just grabbed a red blouse to try on.

Lucy walked away to further her contemplations, happy that the girls were coming out of their shell.

*

"I suspect," said Tom, "that if we carry on that slope, past the path to the railway, and then bear left, our supermarket will be on the left."

"If we do find it, and it has useful things," said Robin, "it is a long way to carry it all back."

"Agreed," said Tom. "We just have to remember our purpose. It is to find a fully stocked hideout. We can still check for eggs or anything the car has dropped off though."

"Yes," smiled Robin, who now enjoyed cooked eggs at any time of the day.

*

They reached the bottom of the slope after the railway turn-off without any problems, and did a left turn. The tarmac path, what there was left of it, seemed to be in several different places, while to the right a whole row of old buildings, overgrown with huge bushes and trees looked interesting.

Looking around, Tom pointed at a very large mound just beyond some small damaged buildings. "Let's follow that path around. That could be what we are looking for."

They kept to the path which seemed to be going in the right direction. The greenery came thick and firm up to where they were walking, but there was nothing solid to climb on.

The path now curled back on itself. "Let's see if we can make an entrance through here," suggested Robin, "it's far enough from the railway so it won't be noticed, and that is the direction we need to go." Digga agreed with that, disappearing between 2 bushes, and yelping for them to follow. It was a squeeze, but they made it through there.

It was quite dark initially as they appeared to have entered the forest of bushes and trees at a place where everything was dense. They followed

Digga through, and soon made it out to a less populated part of the greenery. "Now that is a secure entrance," said Tom.

The canopy above them seemed to lift, giving them more space to stand upright, but clearly now resting on the roof of the building they now saw in front of them. A part of the structure extended out a little, suggesting there might be a door there. There was, or at least it appeared to be a double glass door, but it wouldn't budge when they tried to open it.

"Need something very slim," said Tom, searching in his bag for a small knife. He poked it into the narrow gap but the thing wouldn't budge.

Robin meanwhile sought another way to open the doors. Very clearly it would have used electricity to open, so that would mean a switch or something. On the left side, sitting in the wall was a button of sorts, with a key dangling just below. "This has to be it," he said, pushing the key into its slot, and hitting the button.

"Well done," said Tom, frustrated at getting nowhere. "We must remember to close these doors and take that key with us."

*

Inside, the place seemed to be a lot bigger than the Swanley cavern, and yes there was a foul smell of much rotting produce. Walking around they found most of the shelves contained dust or decomposed material. There were several rows of frozen food cabinets, which pleased Robin, but right at the end they found many glass bottles of drinking water. "Excellent," said Tom. There was several rows of beer and wine.

In the middle, opposite where they had come in a strange kind of stairway met them. It went up to the level above, but it had no steps, The broken rubberised tread was flat, and not that easy to walk on. Upstairs they found a vast array of clothes. A brightly coloured dress took Robin's eye. "Lucy would love that." It went into his bag.

"You'd better find something for the girls as well, or they may be upset," said Tom.

"Good idea," agreed Robin, grabbing 2 pretty, but different, dresses.

There was even a good-sized kitchen. There were several places where they could make snug places to sleep.

Back downstairs, they looked at the shelves to the right of the straight stairway, but no food was there. They did find some electric devices, and there were even folding personal computers. Robin couldn't keep his fingers away from a black model, found that it was working, and decided he couldn't live without it. He disconnected it, then grabbed a similar one for Lucy. He made sure the power cables and mice were in his bag. Tom wasn't that interested.

"OK," said Robin, "we've found this. Do we need to do anything else?"

"I don't think so," said Tom. "It will be enough to know that this refuge is here."

Digga followed them out, happy to have had a new place to sniff around. They closed the doors with a whoosh, and Robin put one of the keys back where it was, the second went into his pack, which was quite heavy with 2 laptops inside.

Tom wanted to look at the back of the building. "I suspect the railway is just over there. Let's see how close we can get." There were a few rusting vehicles to skirt around, then they were right up against a metal fence, beyond which they saw the rails. They were the other side of the broken bridge, but the view towards the north was clear. "Look, the train is coming in."

Their view was restricted because of the train, but they heard a lot more people get off than usual. "I think the car has just arrived as well," said Robin. They listened, straining to hear what was being said, but it was mostly inaudible until the men from the car walked close to where the train was parked. Then they heard some angry shouting.

There was something about, "quotas," and "returns," then, "missing juveniles." Some other muffled anger was expressed, then they heard a loud bang. All was silent for a long moment until the noise of the car was heard driving away. The train also started to pull away, while Tom and Robin tried to grasp what had just occurred. As the train slowly moved back up the line, they saw a man lying face down, with a pool of blood forming around him.

"Looks like they killed one of the car men," said Tom. "I hope it wasn't because of us, but then again those thugs don't need an excuse to be brutal. We should definitely avoid the railway for a while."

*

The trip home was uneventful. Lucy and the girls were thrilled with the dresses. Robin received a cheek kiss from Lucy, and a nice smile from the girls, both of whom now had a bit of sparkle in their eyes.

*

"We need another safe place that isn't so close to any railway, I feel," Tom said. "Shall we try that one further west next time?"

Robin agreed, "let's give it a couple of days."

*

They did locate the next supermarket on their list, as well as one a bit further north. That made 4 places they could escape to in the event of a problem. Robin made sure Lucy would be able to find them even if she hadn't been there. He had marked them on a special map he had created.

*

While not hunting for supermarkets Robin spent many hours, days in fact, understanding how to plug in his laptop and make it work on the internet. Finally, he had it working to his satisfaction except that he couldn't find a way to transfer data from the library PC onto his laptop. That took a whole 3 weeks of fiddling and frustration before he worked out how to do that, then he discovered that there were 3 other PCs attached to the local internet. He hunted these down, mostly being in upstairs rooms. They all had passwords which he couldn't guess at, so reluctantly abandoned them, feeling that they might have held key data. Lucy wasn't so entranced with her PC. She found out how to play card games, how to download recipes, amongst other things, but had little interest in the mechanics of how they worked.

*

"With the summer ahead of us," Tom told Robin, "we really should make plans for where we want to explore."

"I'm keen to get a look at the coast, perhaps around London," agreed Robin. "That is the shortest journey we can make to get close to the sea or at least to the big River Thames."

"I'm happy with that," said Tom, "let's get to work with maps and identify the compass headings we need to follow, as well as any landmarks." They did that over the next week. They each took all the useful things they had accumulated, tools, knives, binoculars, with enough food to last a week at a stretch. Lucy told them to be very careful, while the girls just gave them a sad look. Digga of course went along, while Whiskey was left in charge of protecting the girls.

*

The plan was to avoid any camps or railway lines. That meant initially heading east, towards a place called Gravesend, where they knew another supermarket was situated, but they feared that would be harder to find. If they could get to it then that would act as another refuge, but their main intention was to get to the edge of the land and follow it towards London. A secondary objective was to identify locations where the lords had settled with their palaces.

They reached the area they thought was Gravesend by late afternoon. There were no signs of any camps or well used paths, and no obvious hillocks that might hide a supermarket. After a short rest for their tired legs, they pushed on until they could see and smell the River Thames as it moved towards the ocean.

"That's what you call a wide stream," smiled Tom. "I wouldn't want to wade across that."

"Me neither," said Robin, "lucky we aren't going that way. It looks terrifying."

There were walls that they could sit behind to get away from the cool breeze blowing from the river if they sat down. They found a sheltered corner and decided to rest there. It was certainly time to eat.

Lucy had prepared some meat and vegetables that had had the juices drained out of them. It was delicious even if it was cold. The sky darkened somewhat as they looked around, wondering if there was a more sheltered place in case it rained.

A very loud toot almost took their breath away. It was so close, and they immediately ducked lower behind the wall. More toots and whistles came, prompting them to think they might have been found, but with no other indication they slowly raised their heads to peep over the wall and look in the direction of the discordant sounds. Their eyes nearly popped out at what they observed. A heavy silver vessel was floating in the water. It was moving away from the ocean, and there were lots of people on it.

"My god!" exclaimed Tom. "That must be a floating palace that keeps the lords happy."

"It's enormous," managed Robin, "even longer than that train we saw."

"Much much longer," corrected Tom, "and there is much below the water that we cannot see. There must be 3 stories above the water, and it is so bright and sparkly, inviting somehow."

"Look towards the front," said Robin, who had retrieved his binoculars. "There are people playing some sort of game."

With his glasses trained on the front of the ship, Tom agreed, "you can certainly tell who the slaves are. There are about 10 men with weapons, those must be masters to look after the slaves in rags."

"Just look at how glamorous the lords are dressed, and that table of food is so tempting even from this distance," said Robin. "Some of the slaves look like they have trouble standing. They are so thin."

They watched as a lord, not the grandest, noticed one of the starving slaves looking at the table, drooling. He smiled. "Do you think they will give some crumbs to that poor guy?" asked Robin.

"Unlikely," said Tom, "look at how that lord is smirking. He is having fun with him."

"He is offering the slave something to eat," said Robin. "See how he pushes it towards him."

"This is not going to end well," Tom stated, having witnessed many such games played by masters and others.

Still drooling, the slave reached for the morsel of food offered, only to see it pulled away out of reach. The lord grabbed his arm though and pulled him forward, causing the slave to tumble to the ground. The crowd laughed at this but cheered louder as the lord kicked the slave in the stomach, then there was another kick to the head.

"The poor slave is unable to get up even, he is so weak," Robin said.

"That could so easily be you or me there," Tom said, as the lord lifted the frail, almost unconscious victim up with one foot and threw him towards the masters who continued the punishment with their own weapons, pummelling the poor soul until he seemed as good as dead.

"I truly wish I had my bow and arrows here," said Robin through gritted teeth.

"Just as well you don't," answered Tom. "Even if you could hit him, that action would be the end of us. They'd hunt us down and torture us until we told them about the girls. They would not hold back if they thought we were even a small threat to them. Best we work in secret, for now, if only for the girls' sake."

"I would never tell them anything," stated Robin with bitterness.

"Eventually you would," said Tom. "A few years back there was a man, with a good wife. He would have died to save her, but they smashed him up so badly he made lies up about his wife to stop his punishment. That is how easily they can break someone. If brutality doesn't get the desired result, they fill you with disgusting drugs that turn you into an animal, all too ready to answer any questions truthfully or otherwise."

For a full minute Robin was silent, then gasped as a frail body was tossed off the vessel into the deep water, accompanied by laughter.

"I will kill that man one day," promised Robin.

"Don't just aim for one lord, there are thousands like him. Aim to kill them all," insisted Tom.

They sank back behind the wall, shocked into silence as the silver vessel passed them by, moving closer to the dreaded London.

*

They dozed the night away fitfully, still astounded at the outright brutality they had witnessed. When morning came, they were stiff and aching, but promised each other they'd find somewhere better to sleep in future.

*

It was generally easy to follow the coast, but sometimes they had to go inland to avoid marshy ground or areas where wrecks of buildings made it impossible to get through. In one place their progress was curtailed by a strong metal fence, so they had to retrace their steps and go around this obstacle. They always tried to keep the water in sight, if possible, and mostly this meant going through what might have been some industrial workings of some sort or even docks where heavy materials had been stored. In some places tall cranes used to shift heavy items, still stood, if weakened by time. This was all heavy going.

Walking through one old factory there were still some stores that attracted attention. "What the heck are corrosive acids?" Tom asked after seeing a warning sign about it.

"No idea," admitted Robin, "but if it might be useful, we could investigate it. We can spare a few minutes."

"It does sound interesting," Tom said, "and I'm seriously wondering if it could damage that silver vessel. Shall we see what happens when we pour it over that metal strip?"

The acid didn't disappoint, it ate into the metal and made it bubble up.

"That might just do the job," Robin smiled, "if we ever get a chance to get close to their vessel. Just make sure it doesn't touch your skin. If it does that to metal, imagine what it could do to us." They found several small containers that contained the acid, made sure they could be opened but were otherwise secure. "I don't think we should take more than one each, otherwise it could get tricky." They walked on, taking extra precautions with their find.

After a good 2 hours of hard slog they came to a place where the land seemed to jut out into the river. They had originally wanted to avoid this area as being unimportant, but when they saw that the silver watercraft had parked itself right next to the head of this land, they felt that they had to get closer to whatever was there.

As they were considering how to proceed, a very loud whirring noise distracted their attention. "Ye gods, there's a flying machine up there," Robin said with awe. "How do they make it stay up there? It has no wings."

"Technology still in use from the time before," Tom answered wisely. "You can bet they burn oil with that thing while we were always denied it."

"This surely must be a place where important lords live then, if they use flying machines and water vessels to get here," stated Robin. "I was hoping we'd find such a place as it will be useful to see if I can get onto their internet, and perhaps borrow some of their files. That was the main reason I brought the PC along."

Tom was more interested in surviving this trip, but he didn't want to discourage Robin from getting more information. "I see a gate over there, that has to be our way in."

They passed through another gate. They resembled those that gave access to the village camps they were so familiar with, except that they could walk through these without being recognised by any computer systems, nor even noticed. They were going in the direction of a good-sized villa. It also sparkled. Another shiny vessel, almost as big as the silver one was parked close by the first boat. This other water vessel was golden in colour and shone brightly with the sun on it. The villa was mostly quiet, but if all of the people from the boats were inside then the house must hold several dozen people easily, at least that was their estimate.

Reaching a group of trees they agreed to use a big oak tree as a means of spying on the side and front of the house, while still keeping the watercraft's visible. They could also make sure they were able to keep a check on their escape route.

The sun was above and behind them, the time being just after midday. They settled comfortably into the branches to spy on what their lords were doing. Digga knew it was time for a rest and found a cosy spot out of sight under a big blooming bush. Robin climbed up to where 4 broad branches came together, making a comfortable work space, where he could put his back against the main part of the tree, while stretching out his legs with the PC resting on his lap.

There was a strong internet signal coming from the huge house. Several other PCs were linked in, so it didn't take much time to see the files available. He browsed a few which didn't mean very much to him, so instead of reviewing everything, he just copied the whole lot onto his PC. He could see that there were plenty of program files that had an identifier of .EXE, but their names didn't mean anything. It took about 2 hours to complete the transfer, by which time there was a big party happening at the front of the house facing the river.

Tom was planning ahead, "when it gets dark, I will try and sneak onto the vessels. If I can get to the lower level, I'm hoping I can just drop the acid to rot away the bottom, and with any luck they will sink in deep water when it is full of lords."

"I haven't seen anybody moving about on the vessels. They must all be at the house, so that will make that task easier," said Robin.

The party was producing a lot more noise as music blared and people shouted. The lords were mostly dancing or something like it. They all seemed to be drunk and enjoying themselves, except for the young slaves that had been made to stand against a wall contemplating their fate.

Robin's heart soured when he saw how beaten, and yet how young the girls and boys were. They were mostly around 9 years of age, so it seemed, but they were skinny, with plenty of bruises clearly visible from where

Robin sat with his glasses. They were naked and were hosed down with cold water every time they soiled themselves.

The music was turned off with the lords also going quiet, and someone shouted, "time for the first one, and who will be master?"

A tall, rather gangly individual stepped forward, looking very fanciful in his deep blue velvet outfit, with beads around his neck. "My turn I feel." He went along the line of desperate children each trying to become invisible. He selected a lad, taller than most, grabbed him by the throat and took him over for a thorough hosing down. The lad had tears rolling down his cheeks, and his eyes were wide and frightened. When the lord saw the boy was crying, he slapped him across the head to cheers. "I'm not going to hurt you," the lord said in a strained voice, mocking sympathy. The crowd roared approval.

Both Robin and Tom were already disgusted and fuming, unwilling to watch, but their eyes were drawn to the scene ahead of them anyway. Disrobing, the lord, with practised moves, entered and sodomised the lad, leaving the boy bleeding and in pain but too frightened to even cry out. "Oh no," said Tom, in anguish. "This is pure torture," but the lord was not done with his abuse of his victim, which was about to get worse.

The lord, still unadorned, walked over to a table that had previously been in shadow, dragging the lad with him. There were 6 men sat around the table whose features were visible as the nearby lights came on. The 6 were clearly not lords, but still they were stocky and well dressed. They all had long straggly beards, except for one who had stubble on his face and his head. He also had a zigzag mark, from an old wound, across his forehead that made it look like his head was loose.

"Ye gods," exclaimed Tom, fit to burst. "That fat swine sitting facing us on that table is the chief from my old village." Waves of hatred and fear washed over Tom, who would have loved to have run at the fiend with a large knife. His fear of what would happen next and his responsibility for others stopped him. He gripped a small branch with white hands straining at the effort, the anger boiling still within him.

"Here," said the naked lord to Tom's ex-chief, holding the lad out. "This came from your village. You know what to do."

While the lord held the boy by both arms, the chief rose up smiling at the honour. Yanking his short knife out, he cut deeply into the lad's throat. Blood spurted out, but the intent was not to kill the victim outright. Dropping the knife, the chief took hold of the boy now slumping, unconscious, and put his mouth over the wound, drinking deeply of the blood that came out. The lords and everyone else, except for the petrified slaves, roared with encouragement.

Now the lord took the dying boy to another area, holding him over a silver tray where his lifeblood drained away. Even before all the blood had come out, the lords were queuing up to dip small golden cups into the silver tray, to collect a large mouthful of blood to drink. The corpse was thrown on to the table where the other chiefs sat. They in turn greedily sucked at the wound to gather just a little of the drug they all sought so badly.

As the loud music started up again, Robin saw that Tom was crying, with his face turned towards the bulk of the tree, away from the scenes of horror they had both witnessed. Robin was feeling solid with his own anger and could think of nothing to say.

The music and the shouting continued. Neither Tom nor Robin felt like moving, and it was becoming dark before Tom at last was able to stop sobbing and face his friend.

"This has to stop," pleaded Tom.

"Yes, it must," Robin whispered back, his voice frail. "Let us not forget this dreadful torture and abuse we have seen today. Every time we think we cannot fight against these evil devils, we will remember this, and renew our will to change it."

Tom looked up, his face wet, "oh, yes, I will never forget this day."

"And remember this," Robin continued, with anger impinging on every word, "what went before, the deceit, the drugging of children, the forced poisonous vaccinations, the chips, the ruination of society," his voice rose in strength as he let all of his anger pour out, "it was all for this, so that these diseased perverts could take their pleasures with us, time and time again."

*

Unable and unwilling to move, they both sat still as the darkness enveloped them, feeling totally drained. A light yelp from below reminded them that it was well past time they ate something, and poor Digga was also hungry. Coming slowly down from the tree, Robin fed his dog and himself. Tom also tucked into something.

"If we are going to pour that acid into their water vessels, now seems like a good time," said Robin.

"Yes," agreed Tom.

Digga followed as they made their way to the shiny looking ships, first was the silver one, then the golden one. "Remember," said Tom, "don't take any risks. If there is any danger, or anyone aboard, just pour that stuff where it could do some damage, ideally close to the water line, so that these things eventually sink."

"OK," said Robin, then he spoke to Digga. "Stay out of sight. Warn us if someone comes." Digga yelped gently in response.

*

Gangplanks gave access to both ships, and they found nobody guarding either vessel. Inside the golden ship, Robin dropped some acid around the steering apparatus, but saved the rest for the bottom of the boat, which he eventually came to after going down 5 sets of stairs. He didn't want to make it too obvious, so he poured the acid directly into a small cupboard built into the side of the hull. With that act of sabotage done, he was back on land and meeting up with Tom and Digga in a very short space of time. They took their acid containers away with them, with the intention of hiding them some place else.

Reaching the group of trees where they had been hiding, Digga alerted them to someone coming their way. All 3 quickly hid behind a bush, to see that a lord was dragging a boy of about 8 behind him. Reaching the area mostly enclosed by bushes, the unclothed boy was tied by the wrist to a small tree. The boy was wide-eyed and terrified, but so accustomed to brutality that he couldn't even think of resisting it. He stood there just awaiting his destiny to overtake him as the lord took off his jacket then his trousers. Both Robin and Tom knew where this was heading and had no intention of watching it nor allowing it to happen. They had hatched a plan in a second without even speaking.

The lord approached the boy, a sickly smile on his face, "I'm not going to hurt you."

"No?" demanded Robin, standing now to the lord's left with his sharpest knife in his hand.

The lord turned to face Robin. He was athletic, and taller than Robin, confident that he could easily take the knife from this upstart. That was when Tom hit the lord on the back of the head with the acid container he'd been carrying, allowing a dribble of acid to fall on his back. The lord, now very angry and screaming in great pain, turned around snarling. Fortunately, the music from the house drowned out the screams. In any case, the other lords were used to victims suddenly finding their voice as their peers took delight in hurting their victims.

Robin now poked his knife, not too gently, into the left shoulder of the lord, to make the lord turn around to face him again. The lord was now feeling fear, and worried that he might not be able to fight off 2 assailants. "What do you want?" The lord challenged, looking for an escape route. That was when Tom grabbed both of his arms and held him firm. For the first time in his life this lord was truly afraid. His eyes darted back and forth, looking for a way out of this.

"It's your turn to be scared now, you filthy, disgusting excuse for a human being," Robin shouted into the man's ear, as his knife moved closer to its target. The lord tried to call out, but his mouth was too dry.

Contemplating what he was about to do, years of accumulated horrors rushed back on him. The loss of his father. How his mother had been savagely beaten and killed. How his dog had been killed. All of these sad memories, and many others, flashed by in a split second, fuelling his anger beyond boiling point and energising the power in his arms.

Robin's knife plunged deeply into the lord's groin, producing a loud gasp of pain and confusion. The lord was pleading now, his eyes more frightened than his potential target. With all of his strength Robin lifted the blade upwards, now using both hands to bury it deeply within the lord's guts. Upwards went the knife, towards his heart, through the ribcage. The man was dead before he hit the floor, blood seeping out of him, as his lungs expelled his last breath.

Tom and Robin acted as one, knowing full well that they could be caught at any time. They picked up the dead lord by his wrists and ankles, carried him to a nearby seawall and threw him over.

"Quick, the boy," whispered Tom. "Can you hold him still?"

Tom felt for the chip in the boy's head, telling him, "this will hurt, but not as much as that beast would have hurt you. We have to remove something bad. Try to be still. Try not to scream." Something of this got through to the lad who was still wrapped up in terror. He nodded.

Happily the device was close to the surface of the skin, which meant Tom had but to make a small cut, and it all but fell out. Tom showed the thing to the boy, "This allowed them to track and find you. Now you are free." With that he cut the bonds holding the boy to the tree, wrapped the lord's jacket around the boy, and looked at Robin, "have we forgotten anything?"

"No," said Robin, still in some shock even though he'd cleaned his knife and wiped the blood away. "We must go now." He grabbed his bag and made for the exit.

"Come with us," Tom said to the boy, gently taking his hand and picking up his bag with his free hand.

*

They kept stopping and listening to see if they were being hunted, but there was no sign of any pursuers. The music and shouting from the house got gradually quieter as they walked further on. They made it through the old factories, getting breathless but too afraid to stop. Soon the wall where they had first seen the silver ship came into sight. It was reached with some relief. They slumped down, worn out with the excitement and exertion.

The boy had said nothing up to this point, still wearing his terrified look, he obeyed instantly when Tom asked him to run or to stop. Now he just looked up at Tom with wonder in his eyes, not knowing what he should do or what to expect of these strangers.

Taking some dried meat from his pack, Tom chewed a piece, then placed a similar piece into the boy's hand. The boy was all too aware of the game the lords had played with food, and initially was reluctant to play. Tom moved away, and encouraged him to eat, "When did you last have food?"

The boy shook his head. He just couldn't remember.

"Eat that," said Robin, very gently, very quietly. "We were slaves like you, but not so badly off. Eat that and feel better. We know how difficult this is for you."

The boy took the meat, chewed it and swallowed. Tom gave him more and was rewarded with a tiny smile. "What is your name?" Tom asked gently.

"Mickee," said a sweet voice.

"I am Tom, this is Robin. We must go on some more tonight, then we will rest." Tom shared some water with the boy before they started off again.

*

They found shelter a couple of hours later. It was too dark to travel without bumping into things. The sign said, 'BUS STOP', but it made a cosy place to settle down for a few hours, with only a small entrance open to the elements. It was cool, but somehow they all welcomed that. Their insides were still fuming.

*

Dawn came creeping in to their haven to awaken them. They didn't wait around. They swallowed a little food and water, then dashed for home, their feelings numb.

*

It was about midday when the 4 of them squeezed down the cavern entrance to be met by the dogs. Digga was pleased to greet them all, wagging her tail and sniffing them in turn. Lucy was right behind the dogs, with a concerned expression, as she realised from the look on Robin's and Tom's faces that they had experienced something terrible.

Lucy took Robin's hand in hers. He squeezed her hand in acknowledgement but was unable to say anything or even look at her. He just allowed her to lead him downstairs to their own sleeping area. Washing his filthy arms and hands Robin briefly looked at Lucy with eyes that had seen too much. His tongue was still, his mind numb. He wanted to be with her, but couldn't, he felt so solid, so distant from life. He clambered back outside to sit at the top of his favourite tree, surveying the landscape, not even thinking but seeing things in his mind that he'd rather not.

Tom had taken Mickee under his wing. Clothes to fit the boy were a bit of a problem but with help from Lucy they managed to find a short top with half sleeves, then some men's short trousers that almost fitted as long as the elastic holding them up was tight enough.

Anne and Jane hid away in their room, too worried to meet anybody new. Lucy actually took the boy in to see the girls, but they just looked at each other, without words.

The lord's jacket Mickee had been wearing was too much of a reminder for Tom. He took it outside the cavern and burned it.

Lucy was getting anxious by now, with no word from Tom or Robin about what had transpired. She stopped Tom, as he came back inside, with Mickee trailing him. "What happened, Tom?"

"It's too horrible to talk about," Tom answered, but Lucy wanted more. "We found where some lords live. We saw how they live and what they do to boys like Mickee. They live a great life, every luxury, even a flying machine. They are flesh and blood, but they are not human." That was all Tom could say. He gently slid past Lucy.

Retreating to the library to settle his mind, Tom picked up some children's book, to just look at the pictures. He gave one to Mickee and showed him how to turn the pages. They both sat there glued to the images for most of the day.

*

Lucy made dinner as usual and made sure everyone gathered around the kitchen area to eat, all except Robin who was still up his tree. She was becoming a little angry so went to find Robin with Digga. Despite calling up to him, Robin stayed where he was, so Lucy left Digga to get him down, "Digga, you get him down here and into the kitchen immediately."

Digga yelped and looked up at her as if to say, "now how the heck am I supposed to do that?" She stayed anyway, and made the effort, yelping gently but persuasively until she finally got Robin's attention. He was stiff and cold after so long straddling the tree branch, so it took a while to climb down. Digga jumped straight at him, licking his face profusely, "where have you been. We were worried." She led him downstairs. As they passed the shower room she yelped at him, "don't forget to wash your hands and be tidy for dinner." Robin of course obeyed.

*

Dinner was a very quiet affair. Nobody spoke. Afterwards, Robin was about to go back outside when Lucy grabbed his arm and took him somewhere else, asking the girls to wash the dinner things. She had a more important task.

Lucy had made their bed space extra comfortable with a new blanket underneath. She pulled Robin down, her hand resting on his arm, but he was still feeling so mentally solid and unable to talk. She looked him dead in the face, and with a certain amount of rare steel, told him, "I know you had a really horrible experience. Won't you tell me? We can make things better, together."

That seemed to reach him. He reached for her, holding her tight, his whole body rigid against hers, then with a sob said, "The lords, they killed a boy and drank his blood. Then a lord had Mickee, he was going to rape him." He stopped unable to say more. Lucy held him tight and pushed her mouth in close to his neck.

"Go on," she murmured, kissing him gently below his chin.

"I killed a very bad man," cried Robin. "My knife. Hated him with all my heart. I killed a lord." He sobbed again, then some more, clinging on to Lucy, who had the patience to say nothing more. She knew the details would come out at some time, but for now she was happy that Robin was releasing his sadness and anger as tears. She was well aware that the tears were not for the dead lord, but for everything that had happened, especially the sad things that had happened to Robin. Her lips continued to try and kiss away the hurt. Her lips brushed over his fuzzy chin, his lips. She tasted the tears falling down the side of his nose. His lips tasted better, her lips lingering there until he finally responded. That very night they became joined to each other, as man and wife, from there on out.

CHAPTER 4

TAKING CARE OF BUSINESS

SEVERAL DAYS AFTER THE INCIDENT involving the lords, Robin was discussing with Tom some of the details. "Will you remember the faces of those 6 that sat at the chief's table?"

"Remember them?" snapped Tom. "They are imprinted in my mind's eye. In particular my old chief, then there was that guy covered in beard stubble with that zigzag cut on the top of his brow. Those and the other 4 I promise to catch up with at some point. They were just as vile as the lords."

Out of the blue, Jane spoke up. She had barely said any words at all, apart from showing her good manners, with a whispered, "thank you." She just wasn't in the habit of having something to say. "That sounds like my father, with the zigzag cut. My mother did that to him."

Robin and Tom looked at her with surprise. "Was he the village chief?" asked Tom.

"I don't know," Jane managed, a little flustered. "He was friends with the chief. The chief was old and sick. Perhaps my father was made chief after I was sent away by the old chief."

"You have to understand what power village chiefs have," stated Tom. "If your father is a chief, then he is a bad man. They send children away to the lords to be hurt, abused and killed. Is your father a bad man?"

Jane stood up, her eyes flashing. "My father is a very bad man. My mother was sick. He lay on me, hurt me here," she indicated her groin. "Mother so angry when she saw. She fought him; she was too weak from fever. She held blade to his head, scratched it deep, several times, then he hit her hard. She died."

Lucy and Tom went to Jane, to hold her, to comfort her, but having started it seemed she had more to say. "He took me to other men. Made to lie still. Hurt me again and again, down here. Many times he took me to other men, and also to chief. Then one day he had new wife. They took me away and you find me."

"Your father is not just a bad man; he is a criminal. He must be punished," said Robin.

"No," said Jane. "It should not be you that punishes him. I will kill him, for mother." With that she fell to the floor crying.

"Tears are good," said Lucy, "they help to take some of the pain away."

*

Jane recovered, and even smiled, but Anne seemed to be constantly about to cry. Later that day, Robin said to Tom, "we must find out more about how the village system works."

Tom agreed, "we seem to be the only people left in the world who knows what happened, and can do something, even if it is slight compared to the power of the lords."

"We must tell everyone what has happened," insisted Robin, "as well as taking away the evil chiefs."

Tom called Jane over to join them. "Do you recall the name of your father or if the village had a name?"

"He had 2 names. Vick and Keating. Village name I don't know, it was more than 30 minutes in car away."

"Thank you, Jane," Robin said, "that will help us find him. Tom, do you know how many thugs your chiefs had?"

"Varies," said Tom, "between 4 and 6 usually I'd say."

"Yes," stated Jane. "The bullies always hung around close to the chief. Sometimes 10 or more, but the chief only gave privileges to about 5 at a time."

"Interesting," said Tom, smiling at Jane. "That means we would have to be prepared to handle at least 6 mean bullies if we were to attack a village. We would need a very good plan. Perhaps we should work out how to send some of the men away somewhere?"

"A wild goose chase," said Jane, imagining it, now smiling like she never smiled before.

Robin went off to look at the data he had taken from the lords to see if it could help, passing by Lucy holding Anne's hand. He kissed her cheek and squeezed her shoulder lovingly.

*

Lucy had worked out that Anne was also having difficulties speaking about what had happened to her. "Come," she said, "let us go somewhere quiet." They went outside the cavern, into the fire building. It was shaded, making Lucy think that this would make it easier for the girl to get things off her chest. She sat them both down and cuddled Anne, "Now, I want to hear all about your village."

It took a while, with several prompts before Anne managed to say anything. "I was in Jane's village," she revealed. "It was always pain from someone."

Lucy squeezed her shoulder, encouraging her to tell more. "Who hurt you, Anne, was it your father?"

"Father dead, mother dead. Lived with Aunt Jo. Always work, always she beat me."

"I do understand," said Lucy. "We all came from dreadful villages. Always hurt and work."

"Always hungry," said Anne, "hands red and sore."

"Yes," agreed Lucy starting to feel overwhelmed by it all, "bad men would hit me for no reason. Touch me."

"Oh," exclaimed Anne, "and more hurting by them," she cried.

With tears welling up, Lucy continued, "a bad man kept coming to hurt mother. She was sick, still he hurt her, beat her, and me sometimes."

"Too many bad men," said Anne, squeezing and comforting Lucy now.

Their tears mingled as they cuddled closer and relived some of the terrors they had experienced. "Bad man raped mother. She was very sick."

They both sobbed as Anne spoke about the men. "They would smell of nasty things. Always putting their mouth close. Made me sick, couldn't breathe, men so heavy. Always hurt me inside, bleeding."

"When my mother was too sick, bad man killed her with his knife. Then he and brother were going to rape me."

"Horrible nasty men," cried Anne. "Always they hit me when they had done with me."

"Horrible nasty men must be punished," said Lucy. "At the last moment Robin rescued me and punished 2 bad men. I love him so much now."

"Robin is good husband for you," smiled Anne, "you should keep him."

Lucy smiled deeply, tears drying up a little, "I will."

"Everyone here so kind to me and Jane. I think someone will beat me, but no.

"Nobody will ever beat any of us again," insisted Lucy. "Here we are safe."

They sat there together sharing tears and past history until at last their eyes were dry, and their past troubles had been partly exorcised.

*

Initially nothing made sense from what Robin had copied down from the lords' PCs. Much of the content of files was in strange characters he couldn't make anything of. He tried to run some of the .EXE programs, and found that they were reading the data files, and some of it started to become clearer.

After being at it for some hours, he found a list of id numbers. Sometimes they had a name as well, but they always had a village identifier as well. Against his old id he found a status of dead, with a village identifier of GBSE05. He worked out that meant village number 5 in the Southeast of Great Britain, which he knew was another name for the UK. He checked for the name of Jane's father. It showed him as a chief in village GBSE08. There was a link to a map that showed exactly where the location was, but just as interesting was the data supplied about the village. It showed every person in it, as well as quotas for foodstuffs they were supposed to provide.

Robin was wondering how he could make use of this information, and indeed if he could alter any of it. As he was on the internet, it was just possible that he could reduce some quotas with the changes getting posted on all PCs. He tried altering the number of pounds of carrots to 20 instead of 60. It blinked as it updated, the 20 remained but there was no way to know if it had been replicated around the system of lords' PCs.

He sent a copy of the map showing the village locations in the Southeast to the printer and searched for more usable data. Another execution module showed a map of the whole country, with coloured images in different locations. It wasn't until he enlarged the map that he realised each dot was a location of importance to the lords. The villa where he had killed a lord showed up as a golden dot. When he clicked on it many details were shown, including the layout, and the fact that it belonged to the high lord of the south east.

Another program was a live view from up above of the ground. He could control the view to look anywhere at any magnification. Robin moved it over the villa to see if anything had happened there. The flying machine was still sitting on the roof, but he didn't see any sign of people anywhere. Wondering if they had found the lord's body, he searched close to the sea wall. There it was, clearly, it was still there where they had left it. The water vessels were gone, and even after searching the river and the open sea he saw no sign of them. He was still hopeful that their dangerous stunt had been worthwhile and would bring a result.

He spent 2 complete hours looking at the palaces, stores, homes and factories that were marked. He noticed that there were big palaces on some islands to the south, but these were owned by a king lord, and absolutely huge, with enough rooms for an army of people.

There was so much detail that he couldn't absorb, so he tried to look at the overall concept of what was in front of him. The area in London and around was a vast panoply of buildings and proper roads, with many factories and stores making or holding every possible material and food item that Robin had ever heard of as well as a load he couldn't even guess at. His head began to spin with the words that meant nothing to him, so he switched views.

An option he liked was to highlight the positions of different things, be it mansions, palaces, factories or prison camps. There were 3 prisons just in the Southeast alone. He zoomed down to get a closer look at the closest, perhaps 15 miles away to the west. It was a similar view to what he saw in his village, except with people chained together, and made to work at something.

The cavern was easy enough to find, so he focused on it for a short time to see if there was any evidence that might betray them, from above, that they lived here. Nothing untoward took his eye, so he moved onto his old village. He saw the people working the fields, with several mean-looking guards watching over them. *Wouldn't it be wonderful*, he thought, *if it were possible to focus on someone then send a beam down to hurt them.* He looked around for some such options. Below the main screen were several choices including ACTIONS and HISTORY. He clicked on ACTIONS which took him into a screen that gave an explanation, 'To shift to a target, click the word TARGET below, then click on the actual target'. Robin couldn't resist clicking on TARGET, them zoomed in to where the chief had his house. He clicked the mouse button on his house. More instructions followed, 'choose severity of punishment, ANNIHILATE, BURN, SUN-TAN, BRIGHT-LIGHT'. Without a second thought he hit ANNIHILATE, and watched, not really expecting anything to happen. A bright light rested on the chief's house for a moment, then intensified. Suddenly the roof melted, the walls fell down and all that was left was a smouldering ruin.

"Oh my GOD," screamed Robin. "I've really done it now."

Tom came running when he heard Robin screaming. "What happened?" he demanded.

"I've just destroyed the chief's house, and most likely him and his whole family as well," cried Robin. He showed Tom the image.

"Do you think that anyone can trace the fact that you did this from the cavern?" asked Tom.

"I really don't know," answered Robin, now very frightened. "They can target a single person to be killed if they want to. I didn't think it would do anything like that. I guess everything depends on how closely they monitor the spies in the sky as to whether they will or could trace where this was done from."

"I think you'd better turn that off for now," said Tom, with a degree of anger in his voice.

Robin complied, and disconnected the PC from the internet as well, as Tom walked away in a huff. "I'm going to climb up my tree to make sure they are not sending their army after us."

*

A week passed very slowly, while Robin spent all of his time up a tree searching everywhere to make sure they were not about to be hunted down. He hadn't touched the PC at all in that time, but now that Tom had cooled down, they were able to laugh at what had occurred. "It couldn't have happened to a nicer man, and he probably thinks it came from a lord for missing some quota."

"Now that would worry him," agreed Tom, "but it looks like you have discovered something fantastic, if we can use their resources against them, it will be most useful. You'd better tell me all about it."

Robin described everything he'd found so far. Tom had his mouth open at the amount of information. "That is just so incredible. I'm not sure I want you to go back in from here. I'd prefer it if we could find another place with internet."

"Good idea, perhaps close to the village?"

*

That very day Tom and Robin made their way towards Robin's old village, going directly across the path through the trees and bushes that were thick enough to hide an army. Digga of course went along to protect them. They found a dell that had a soft layer of grass to sit on. Robin turned on the PC, connected to the nearest internet, executed the program to look down from the sky and sat back to watch.

"My god, that house does look a mess," said Tom, when Robin had zoomed in. "You really do a good job when you zap houses." The house which had been the best in the village was almost all rubble.

Robin showed Tom the keywords at the bottom of the screen, ACTIONS and HISTORY. "I went in through ACTIONS to zap this place, but I'm hoping I can see what happened by going into HISTORY." Several confusing options came up on the screen which still showed the destroyed house.

"What does it mean 'day minus count'?" asked Tom.

"Where is that?" asked Robin, his eyes still confused with too much detail.

"Just there," Tom pointed it out.

"Ah, yes, I'll set it at minus 5." He did that but the image remained the same. He tried 7, and the image showed the house as it used to be, in good condition. "There must be a way to roll it forward."

"Perhaps that option called 'forward'?" suggested Tom, now feeling like he knew something about PCs.

Hitting the 'forward' icon had the effect of moving the image on by 10 minutes every 5 seconds. "That's it," said Robin, as it got to the point where the beam did its work.

Another 2 frames further on, saw a whole bunch of people crowding around the rubble.

"Do you recognise anybody?"

"Some of the people look familiar. Hey there he is. That's our chief, standing in a space on his own. Look how angry he is," said Robin.

"He's not just angry. He is really scared," said Tom. "Let's see if anything interesting happens."

The only thing that happened was that the angry chief hurled abuse at everyone to go back to work. This was clear from his behaviour, and no talent at lip reading was required.

The chief went to the very back of the building where one wall still stood, partially. He dragged away some of the mess until he unearthed something. He hadn't been looking for any family members, he had been searching for a terminal. It was still lit up, but now standing at a funny angle, so that the chief had to stoop to key in whatever he was trying to do.

"He's probably asking the lords why they tried to kill him," smiled Robin.

"They will probably laugh at him, but I somehow doubt they will take his problem very seriously," said Tom. "OK, enough of this evil toad. Show me what else you discovered."

They went through all of the programs Robin had run before, which took several hours to wade through, as there was so much data there. "Look," said Robin, showing the registry entry for Tom, "I'm happy to say that you are dead to their system."

"Never felt better," said Tom. "Can we print off the maps that show all of the places where the lords have some kind of building or establishment, and get a detailed map of London?"

"Yes, we can do that, but we will have to be on the library internet to do that. I'll do that later. There are still some programs I didn't try out yet, like this one called 'memo'." Robin ran that. The screen lit up with a list of locations broken down by countries, with a title called WORLD WIDE MEMOS. Robin clicked on GB, which showed another map of locations and villages. "I'm thinking this must be where terminals are located."

"Click on your old village. Perhaps we can see what that mad toad sent."

A list of memos was shown, with a date on the left side, and a subject in the middle. A simple click on the subject of the topmost entry opened the memo.

Tom started to read it. "Oh yes, I like it. So nobody saw the beam strike. He's asking for material to build a new house; he said an earthquake demolished his old one." They both laughed loudly at this until Digga frowned at them and yelped for them to keep the noise down.

*

There were other memos connected to the village, mainly about quotas, or special requests to send specific young people to London for processing and reassignment. Robin noted his name in one note. It seems the Mo brothers had done him a favour after all, or he could now be slaving in some awful place, still unaware of what was going on.

They chose the memos for the lord's palace they had visited, and that was a bit more interesting. The first note was from someone called the third lord of the west. It listed lords from the Southeast of England that were invited to an international gathering to celebrate summer in Miami, USA. There was a reminder that each lord must provide 3 young slaves under the age of 8 years.

"Oh no," said Tom, "that will be an even bigger party of abuse than we saw before. I feel sick."

"I'm not sure we can do anything to stop that abuse, other than to blow it up," said Robin, but maybe we can do something important if all of the lords are going to be away."

"Blow them up, yes I'd welcome that," said Tom still disgusted.

"Is there a date for this get-together?"

"Yes, look," said Tom, "they leave the UK in 7 weeks' time, a total of 92 lords and their ladies. They come back after 5 weeks of debauchery."

"We have to make plans, most certainly so that we can celebrate with them," Robin said with a crooked smile.

They found another note that cheered them up. It seemed that 2 ships had sunk for no obvious reason, and several lords were drowned. It didn't mention if any slaves also drowned.

"Look at this note," said Robin, smiling. "Seems they still haven't found the body of the lord that we killed. He is listed as missing, but they don't sound at all worried."

"Great. I think that's about all I can take for now," said Tom, "there is only so much good news I can digest. Let's go home now and work out how we can use what we have learned."

*

"There's no doubt," Robin said, when they sat around in the cavern with Lucy, after returning, "that we have to take advantage of this situation. Just imagine if we could kill a lot of lords from around the world. Wouldn't that help to change things?"

"It might," agreed Lucy, "it could also kick over a wasps' nest. It could make things worse."

"Yes, I agree, Lucy," Tom said, "there could be bad repercussions. But I feel we have to make the attempt. Even if we don't wipe out the system, because others will be there to walk into the roles currently held, it will weaken it. What we do have to consider though is how we can prepare for the kick-back, when they come looking for answers."

"The palace we visited may just be empty while this gathering is going on. If we are going to blast anything we should do it from there."

"Good idea, Robin," said Tom. "I'm trying to work out how we can get some people on our side. How can we get rid of the village chiefs?"

"Send them a note," suggested Lucy, who really had no love of chiefs. "Meet outside their villages and zap them." She smiled at the prospect.

"Yes, that might work," said Robin, "if we could get rid of say 5 chiefs, and have someone sensible stand in for the role in those villages, we could also get people to help us, but we would still have to deal with the bullies each chief takes with him."

"Let's face it," said Tom, "whatever we do will involve danger. We have to be prepared to do what is required for the greater number of people held as slaves."

"Don't forget the people locked in that metal camp," Robin said. "Perhaps we can make use of them to create some chaos?"

"Perhaps," said Tom, "or maybe we keep them in reserve. Our plans need to keep us all safe, or this rebellion is over. Let's do what we can control, without making the lords too suspicious."

"Indeed," agreed Robin, "but won't they be suspicious if their leaders all get blown up?"

"Probably," Tom agreed, "but if we activate that beam from one of their palaces, they just might think a lord who didn't get invited had done it."

They continued to go over how they could use the technology they now had available to them to make an impact, realising they had to act soon, and do a lot within 7 weeks prior to the gathering.

*

The next day Tom took his 3 dogs out hunting, leaving Whiskey, Groaner and Digga with Robin. "It's time we stocked up on rabbit meat, and anything else I can find."

Robin spent his time printing out useful maps and digging further into the programs he already knew quite well. "Look," he said to Lucy, zooming in on what he assumed to be a prison camp, "they keep all of these people locked up for some reason. I wonder why?" Lucy was getting bored with the PC. She was keen to get the girls and Mickee helping with weeding the vegetable garden. She also had plans to reorganise the layout of the shelves and cabinets within the cavern. She just wanted it to look nice and be cosy.

*

A few days went by, where the big plan was neither formulated nor talked about, then one bright sunny day, Tom came out with, "It's no use us ignoring what we need to do. I propose we start with my old village. There are a few good people we could possibly get to help us, but we need a way to eliminate the bullies and a way to capture the chief. The chief will know things that keep things running. Without his knowledge we might just do something silly and bring a reprisal from the lords."

"I can see that," said Robin, "but at the end of the day, we might just have to trust to our luck. If there is a new chief that would be the excuse for messing some things up or missing deadlines."

"What about," suggested Lucy, "if we send a note to this chief to say that an inspector is coming to find out why their quotas are not satisfactory."

"I like that, but as soon as he saw me, he would recognise me," Tom said. "How about if I went in late in the day and spoke to my ex-friends, to support us?"

"It's a tough call," said Robin, "but we should make use of a note certainly, and perhaps if I'm watching what's going on I can strike down the chief and his bullies. Do you think you could get to talk with your friends easily, Tom?"

"I've got an idea," Tom smiled broadly. "I go in and warn 2 guys that something is going to happen on the next Sunday. They can spread the word. Then we send the chief a message that he is to get everyone to come and listen to a message he and his trusted helpers must read out. Then you zap them, Robin."

Lucy started to laugh. "Yes, but it must be something that will make people laugh at him, like a nursery rhyme. Tell him if anybody doesn't smile at the words, which are really a code to encourage dissent, then they should be locked up for the lords to question."

"You have a wicked sense of humour, Lucy." Robin kissed her cheek.

"That might just work," said Tom. "That means I have 4 days to get into the village and warn them that something is going to happen, and that they should all smile at what the chief and his bullies read out."

*

Getting into the village was easy for Tom, locating his contacts was not so easy. They were living in different places to before. They both were shocked but happy to see him alive. He explained briefly how he had a friend that had removed the tracking device from his head, and so had escaped his life as a slave. They were reluctant to believe that the chief could be taken out and replaced by a good man, but they promised to spread the word about Sunday. Robin watched for any sign of trouble using the spy in the sky, but Tom's mission went off successfully.

On the Friday a memo was sent to the chief, telling him to deliver a special message to everyone in his village at midday on this Sunday. He would start, then each of his helpers would read the next line in turn. If somebody couldn't read then they would have to learn the words from somebody that could read, remember them and say them at the appropriate time. He was told it was important that everyone got the message as there could be heretics around, and any such people would react to the coded words. The memo included the full text of the message, which went along the lines of, 'Little Bo-Peep has lost her sheep, and can't tell where to find them...'

Sunday came quickly enough. Robin found himself a comfortable tree just on the outskirts of the village, and connected to the local internet, while Tom went inside but stayed out of sight until it got close to the designated time. Digga found herself a nice cosy spot to lie in out of sight of everyone.

Robin watched as the chief came out of his house, calling his helpers to him, and telling them something. Without being able to lip read, Robin guessed it was to get all the villagers from the fields. That's what happened. The chief and his 8 bruisers stood on the little hill in the centre of the village, ready to start.

Tom had moved up to stand just behind his friends, gave them a friendly nudge and a smile of welcome which they returned, clearly wanting to interrogate Tom, hoping they would have a chance later.

The chief started with a brief introduction. "The lords have sent us a very important message. Everyone must learn this by heart. Everyone." He started off with the first sentence, "Little Bo-Peep has lost her sheep, and doesn't know where to find them."

The crowd were open-mouthed, for most of them knew this nursery rhyme, even if the chief didn't. They wondered what this message could possibly be about.

Mack, the chief's biggest bruiser, carried on in a very gruff solemn voice, "Leave them alone, and they'll come home, dragging their tails behind them." Some of the older girls began to sing along.

Everyone watching burst out laughing, for this was the funniest thing they'd ever seen, their chief and his louts reciting a nursery rhyme to them.

Robin saw that it was time to throw some light on the announcers. He clicked the bright-light option, causing those reading, or about to read, to be illuminated in a ray of brightness from above. Certain that the lords were really paying attention and were supporting his role in getting this message out, the chief stood up very straight and proud.

"Little Bo-Peep fell fast asleep," the next gruff voice started, but didn't get any further, for Robin had changed the option to annihilate. A broad flash of light covering just the area where the chief and his brutes stood reduced them all and everything on it to ashes. The crowd of villagers gasped and stepped backwards, amazed and in awe.

Tom stepped towards the front but couldn't stand on the hill as it was still smouldering. His friends helped him by lifting him onto their shoulders, "Tom has something to say."

Tom looked around at the familiar faces, now strained and wretched, ill fed and poorly clothed. "That's what we think of the chief and his bully boys," he shouted. "With the help of friends I found a way to escape, and I've come back to tell you that you can live better lives. I am sick of seeing good people like you treated as slaves and worse."

He had their attention. "The lords treat us all like playthings, theirs to do with us as they will. The chief was working for the lords, sending not just most of the food you produce to sit on the lords' tables, but also your children. A very short time ago I was able to witness the evil depravity of the lords, and also our ex-chief. What I saw turned my stomach and made me very sick. If you knew what they do to our children, how they treat them, you'd feel sick, too. We cannot let more children leave this camp. No more, not one more."

Some of the people were getting his message, a man old before his time said, "We were told they were going to serve the lords, like servants."

"Not like privileged servants, for the lords do not believe in rewarding us slaves in any way. That's what we are, slaves. I saw..." tears started to flow down his face as he recalled the horrific scenes he had witnessed at the palace. "I saw," he tried to carry on, caught his breath, then wiped the tears away. "Small boys of 8 or 9 sodomised and killed. The lords were having a party." He paused, breathing heavily, "Those evil swine then drank the boy's blood. It was an awful thing to watch. I knew I had to come and tell you. We are all slaves, and worth nothing to the lords."

Now many were visibly angry, shouting and throwing their fists at the sky. He let them vent their disgust and wrath, realising that he could have overdone things. He needed to rein everyone back in again.

"I know exactly how you feel," Tom continued, "but we do have to be extremely careful. If we were to run amok, they would slaughter us all where we stood. We mean nothing to them. They have no conscience, but there are a great many of them, and they have powerful weapons."

This seemed to settle them down a little, but voices were raised, "Well what can we do? It's no use telling us all this if we can't fight back."

"Here is the plan," Tom shouted once more, "this is how we are going to win our lives back. First, we get rid of the chief. He was the first," he said, indicating the brown hill. "There are many more like him, mistreating our people. We will take the villages back one at a time, and we will build our strength. For now though we must act in secret. We must pretend that nothing has changed. Can you do that?"

A loud roar of agreement met Tom's words, and he was relieved that he had gotten that point over. "We start off by putting in our own chief, someone who will not beat anybody, someone who will resist the demands of the lords for ever more and larger quotas. Who will you trust to do this?"

"You," demanded several voices.

"Not me," pleaded Tom, "for I have other villages to free. Choose someone who is literate and can communicate properly with the lords and others. Whoever you choose you must support him, for it is a terrible responsibility, trust him, but make sure he is not corrupted by the power or concedes all to the lords. Who will you appoint?"

Someone was being pushed forward to stand at the front of the crowd, it was the weathered, grey-haired man who had asked that first question.

"What is your name? We do not deal in numbers any more."

"My name is Richard," said the man. "If I have the trust of the village people, I will do all I can to be a decent chief."

"Everyone will be watching, Richard, but I know your character from years back. You have my blessing."

Richard smiled.

"Your first task will be to increase the food rations. Get more people out catching rabbits and so on. Just don't do anything unusual. The fields will need to be worked still, but not as slaves, as free men."

"I can organise that, and each family will benefit by what they produce," Richard stated.

"You will have to be careful about the agents of the lords that pass through. You must deceive them. You must have good reasons why you can't send people or as much food. You won't be able to get away with sending no food, but include a lot of leaves and so on. I'm sure you can find ways to bulk up the sacks."

"We can probably blame a lot on the old chief," Richard suggested. "Something like he gave so much away to someone else, from the south."

"I think you are going to do very well," said Tom, climbing down. Everyone wanted to speak with Tom, but he just said, "I will be around overnight, so we can talk further. I just need to go and do something." He walked out of the village to where Robin was. "Mission accomplished. Excellent light show, by the way," he said, with a huge smile. "You should be getting off home. I will join you tomorrow. There are still things I need to get across to these good people." They shook hands and went in opposite directions.

*

Not one person spoke to Tom about how the chief and his bullies had died from an angle of sympathy towards them. They were all universally loathed. He did get plenty of questions though about how he had made it happen. He was vague with his replies, because he didn't understand it either. It still bordered on the magical, that Robin could click some things on his PC and people could go up in smoke. He mainly told people, "It was from the spy in the sky. We found out how to use the lords' technology."

They had a big feast that night, with the best stew possible. A large cooking pot had been brought out to feed a good number, but never enough to feed the whole village. Instead people separated into groups, each with their own food. Tom was the celebrity, with everyone hanging on his every word. They talked late into the night, with Tom making suggestions to Richard on how to manage things. At this point Richard was still in shock about the whole thing, but quickly grasped the opportunities ahead.

In the morning Richard wasted no time. He knew the farming land within the village so well he could actually easily visualise it in his mind, which helped him to partition up the land into family groups. "Each family group will be comprised of 10 families, who will work the plot together to feed themselves," Richard said. "But don't forget we will have to send produce off to the lords to keep all of this secret, so we all need to be productive."

Tom could see his presence was not required here, but one of his objectives had been to free up his 2 buddies from being tracked. "Let's go somewhere quiet," Tom said, "because I don't want to alarm everyone." They went to where Tom's old house had stood before the old chief had had it pulled down. There was at least somewhere to sit down with a degree of comfort.

"Johnny and Andy, I am going to let you in on a secret. You know that every time you go through the gate your id numbers show up on the post?"

"Yes, I've always wondered about that," said Andy.

"It's because you have an electronic device in your heads," Tom informed them. "I used to have one, but my good friend Robin took it out for me. It hurt like hell, but it means I can go anywhere, and the lords will not know where I am. Let me see your heads, to see if I can feel these things." They leaned forward, with Tom probing with his fingers. "Do you feel that?" he said to Johnny.

"Yes, it's like a knot in my head."

"As we get older, the thing seems to sink deeper into our heads. Yours, Johnny, is just behind the hairline, so we will have to shave that away first if we go ahead."

Tom inspected Andy, "That's good, as you are balding yours will be easier to get at. In any case they are both quite deep. I can cut them out if you want me to."

"Oh yes," both agreed, saying they wanted to be free of this tracking device.

"Just one thing," said Andy. "I know from experience that you don't have any knowledge of healing or surgery. My nan always taught me that if you are going to cut into someone that you have to make the knife sterile."

"Oh, OK," said Tom, "tell me more."

"It's not complicated," said Andy, "we just need to make a fire and burn off anything that could cause an infection. Where's your knife?"

Johnny was told to go and find something to cut the hairs away on his head, while Andy got a small fire going, and Tom took out his small sharp knife.

Johnny came back with more of his scalp exposed, just as Andy had finished bathing the knife in the flame of the fire. "I know you've probably done this before," said Andy, "but would you mind if I did this for Johnny?"

"Not at all," smiled Tom. "I might learn something. Before you start though I have something else that needs doing." He took out the whiskey bottle he'd brought along. He poured some into 2 pairs of hands. "This is alcohol. It will help to clean your hands of germs. Here, let me wipe your head."

"Can we start now?" asked Andy.

"Just as soon as Johnny has had 2 long swallows of this stuff. It tastes awful but will dull the pain."

Johnny took the bottle and swallowed the biting liquid twice, pulling a face and gasping at the same time. Then he lay down.

Andy didn't waste any time. "Tom, hold his head steady." The knife went into Johnny's head, blood spurted, but Andy quickly located the offending object and had it in his fingers, covered in blood, before the pain fully registered for Johnny.

"So, these perishing little things are what made us slaves to their lordships," snapped Andy. "What evil villains they are."

"That's only a tiny part of what they did to us," said Tom. "My anger has boiled over many times as I learned more of the deceit and horrors they piled on us, but it's coming to an end, I swear it. Now, Andy, your turn, swallow the medicine then lay down, try not to move."

Andy complied and barely gasped as the knife cut into him, not as quick and as smoothly as Andy had done for Johnny, but professional enough. Andy sat up, holding a whiskey-soaked cloth to his wound, smiling at Tom.

"You will need to rest well for 2 days, but then I will be back, for I need you to come on an adventure with me. You will think those wounds worthwhile and of no consequence when you find out what has been discovered. Now remember, everything has to appear normal. Don't attract attention. Don't mention the devices to others, just yet, or we will certainly get found out if a lot of people suddenly appear to die."

"We understand," said Johnny, smiling broadly. "Can't wait for these adventures." Tom said his goodbyes and left for the Swanley cavern.

*

"Do you think it will work out?" asked Robin when Tom made it back.

"I really hope so. Richard, our chief seems to have the right ideas. I did warn them several times to keep things looking normal, but human nature being what it is someone will mess things up. Richard understands the issues, and I do believe he will be able to handle most situations."

"So, we just sit back and watch what happens."

*

Tom returned to the village 2 days later, with Robin and Digga. The changes were already showing. People were no longer downcast, some actually smiled at Tom and children came to stroke Digga. As well as working the fields, men were improving their homes. They found Richard digging out the little hill that sat in front of his new house. It was mostly black but easy to slice into with the tools found in the chief's house. "I want to plant an apple tree here and put a bench all the way around."

"That will look nice," said Tom.

Richard stopped his work and invited the 2 inside his house. "Do you know I've found so many luxury things in this house. Look at that stove, and a real kettle. I want all the villagers to have such basic things. There are cups, and real plates, even a supply of tea. I hadn't tasted that for over 20 years. See if you have a taste for it."

While Richard prepared the drink, Tom said, "I wanted you to meet Robin. He is the reason that all of this has been possible. He was the first to escape, and he's found out so much about what life was like before, and how the lords made us their slaves."

"Happy to know you, Robin," said Richard, shaking his hand warmly. "Even if this lasts for just a short time, I will be ever grateful for this taste of freedom. Thank you for starting this."

"I had no choice at the time, but I was lucky," admitted Robin. "I have my dog here to thank for a lot of my good fortune. Digga, say hello to the best chief in England."

Digga complied with a short yelp, and wagged her tail at the man, then licked his hand.

"Hello, Digga, so nice to meet you as well. Would you like some water?"

Another yelp sent Richard off to get a small bowl with water in, which Digga lapped at happily.

A knock at the door brought Johnny and Andy to the meeting. "We saw you come in," said Andy.

"How are your wounds?" asked Tom.

"Fine," said Johnny. "That whiskey really helped. I actually feel better with that thing out."

"Nice one," said Tom, smiling. "I've brought Robin here to meet you. He can tell you so much about what has been happening. It was Robin that found out how to send that beam down to kill the chief."

"Impressive," said Andy. "How on earth did you gain that knowledge?"

"A little at a time," replied Robin. "It slowly built up, but it helped that so much of the old society, like electrical power, was left in place."

"Robin is not just a great explorer, he is also an investigator, and he reads a lot," Tom interrupted. "He was the first to realise that we all had these devices in our heads that the lords used to track us."

"I discovered a whole library of books, that put me on the right track to finding out how the lords had destroyed the old world," admitted Robin. "It's so nice to be with you all, to have real friends."

Andy and Johnny shook Robin's hand warmly. "They say from small acorns great oaks grow, but it sounds like we are well on our way to many great oak trees," Johnny smiled.

"Yelp," went Digga, feeling left out.

"Oh, and none of this would have been possible without my good friend Digga," said Robin. More head stroking and licking of hands followed, then Digga lay down on a nice soft rug.

"This is very nice in here," insisted Andy. "Looks like that mean chief kept all the luxuries to himself."

"Yes," agreed Richard. "I'll be sharing some of this stuff around when the homes are a bit more decent for living in. I've already sent a memo request for building materials and rugs to the lords. I got a reply back saying it would need approval from the lords after they adjusted our quotas. So, we'll see what the lords have to say."

"Oh gosh," said Tom, alarmed. "That was perhaps too brave."

Richard went a little red in the face, "Have I overreached myself already?" he asked.

"We will see," said Robin. "I'll see if I can intercept any notes on this subject. I might be able to get the lords to approve it."

The new chief smiled at this, "That would be wonderful."

"Let's see how we can use their game against them," said Robin. "I enjoy doing whatever I can to cause them problems. The don't seem to care much about what happens, as long as they can have their parties and abuse children. Which leads me on to the next part of the plan."

The 3 locals looked blank, not aware that there was a plan.

"This village was just the first we had to reclaim," said Robin. "There are about a dozen in this area that we need to get chiefs removed from and replaced with a decent human being, like Richard." Richard blushed hard.

"Things are hard to do when there are so few of us, so we must have more free people, because at some stage there will be a fight between us and the lords. For now we want to reorganise villages, but we do know that the lords are having a big party in the USA, and all high-ranking lords from here are being invited. We have something in mind to make that go with a bang. In the meantime, we need support from you all with the villages, plus we want to explore one of the lord's palaces."

"That's a lot we want to achieve," put in Tom, "the lords are off in 6 weeks' time. We have to free up as many villages before that and prepare for any assault they make on us afterwards."

"It's also vital that we pass on all that we know," said Robin. "Tom and I are not invincible, and something could happen to us. I want to provide each new chief with an education so that he can pass it on to his people. That's another thing that you, Johnny and Andy could help us with. I will start with you 2, and you can help with the education, if you are willing?"

"That sounds like a hell of an adventure," said Andy, "count us in, and thanks for the invitation."

*

They finally got to drink their tea which they all enjoyed, then Tom and Robin made to leave. "I'll be back in a couple of days to have you help me with the next village," said Tom.

"Before you go," said Richard, "there was a word you mentioned earlier, what does 'England' mean?"

"Ah," said Robin, "that will have to be a part of your education. Just consider it to be the land you live in. I'll create something for you to understand more when Tom comes back." With that they all said their goodbyes, the 2 men and their dog left, while the 3 men remaining still feeling excited at the news, sat down on a comfortable floor to go over and over what they had just learned, and wondered how the future would pan out.

*

The attack on the second chief, the one that Robin knew all too well, didn't go quite as easy as the first. The chief hadn't seen his personal memo due to the work going on to rebuild his little mansion. Tom, Andy and Johnny had gone in to the village on the Wednesday before the Sunday, to get some support and to warn them that something was going to happen. That was when they realised the chief couldn't get into his console which was boarded up to protect it from harm while the new structure evolved. It was of course top priority within the village. Men had been pulled away from the fields to labour on the new building. It goes without saying that the chief was determined to make his new house even more luxurious than the old one.

"We will have to come back when he can access his terminal," said Tom, "but that may be some weeks away." They left even more quietly than they had arrived, all travelling back to the cavern to discuss options.

*

"Let's go for Vick Keating's village. We can still do it this Sunday if you 3 are up to travelling straight there?" said Robin.

"Yes, we're fit enough for that," replied Andy. "Let's go for it."

Jane had overheard this, "If you are going to deal with my father, I want to be there," she insisted.

"OK," said Robin. "You will be with me then on Sunday. We will deal with him together."

*

Tom, Andy and Johnny, did their deed to alert the villagers and gather some potential friends, while Robin sent a memo to Keating, which he acknowledged. Keating was all too aware of how the lords liked little games, so the rhyme came as no surprise, in fact he expected it to herald some interesting development.

This village was about 12 miles away from the cavern, meaning Robin, Tom, Jane and Digga had to start out at dawn, meeting up with Johnny and Andy on the way. As before, Robin found a comfortable place to sit, well hidden, and logged onto the local internet. Jane sat next to him, while Digga found a nice bush to settle under.

It was well before midday when the 3 other men walked past the fields towards the village centre. They split up to look for the men they had befriended a few days back. That was when Johnny ran into a spot of trouble. "I don't know you," a Keating thug screamed. Before Johnny could escape, the thug had him tied up and marched towards the village centre. "I'll deal with you after the lord's message is read out."

The time came for the presentation, Keating stood tall and straight, realising his stock was on the rise with the lords. He would do them proud. "Little Bo-Peep has lost her sheep and doesn't know where to find them," he began. Again the crowd started to laugh at the chief giving this odd message out, then the next thug started, "Little Bo-Peep fell fast asleep..." That was the signal for Robin to prompt Jane to hit the button. The venom in Jane's eyes would have turned a man to stone at that point. Never more determined had she been to wipe the evil past away. Down went her finger, her eyes watching intently for the desired effect.

It seemed to those watching from the crowd that a bright ray of sunshine had struck the ground where the chief and his men stood. Those with good eyes would have seen the men getting very hot as their hair started to smoke or the tops of their heads became fluid. It was but a moment later that they had all been reduced to ashes to cheers and applause from those watching who would remember this theatre for a very long time.

Tom gave his speech as Johnny was untied, then they went through a process to find a suitable new chief. Johnny spoke up about the opportunities a decent chief could give the village, describing the difference his own new chief had made in a very short time. The crowd liked all of that, especially the way the farming land was shared amongst family groups.

The new chief, a slightly reluctant Benny, was voted in, and gave his own little speech to say how he would make everyone proud of him. There were several able men that could have become the Andy and Johnny of this village, but Tom warned against too many. "Let us keep our activities to a minimum, so that we do not draw attention to what we are doing." They selected Paul and David to have their chips removed. Like before, Tom and his 2 helpers stayed overnight to encourage and point the way forward.

*

On the Monday, Robin was busy getting information ready to give to the villagers, to educate them on the lords and generally what they had done to impoverish them all and make them into slaves. He had some very specific data taken from the internet, but for a start he wanted to provide maps of villages within the country, so that they would know they were not alone, as well as showing them where friends were located.

"Are we up for another village this week, or should we wait for my old chief to rebuild his house?" Robin asked Tom.

"I suggest we aim for another village, as that house will take a while to complete. The one to the west of us would be appropriate," answered Tom. "I feel we need as many troops as we can get, before we visit that palace. An extra 6 good men should be about right."

"OK," said Robin, locating the view of the mentioned village on his PC. "Let's see if there will be any surprises there." The view showed an extensive farming area with crops of wheat and barley, with limited space for vegetables. It was easy to spot the chief, he was stood in front of the best house issuing orders and being demonstrative. "He looks like a suitable candidate for roasting."

*

"We need a better way to keep in touch with each other," said Tom. "I'm thinking of training the dogs to take messages. Do you think it would work?"

"A great idea," Robin agreed, "but don't start doing too much. If we overstretch ourselves physically, things could go wrong."

"Good point, I will start on that after we have the next village on our side, and they've all seen the basic information you are preparing. I'll do my village first with Johnny and Andy, then they can do Benny's village next, and David and Paul can do the third village. That will give me time to work on the dogs before we go visiting the palace."

*

The third village fell to Tom, Andy and Johnny, only after they convinced some sceptics that they really were not working for the lords to trick them, and it took much of Sunday afternoon. The villagers had no love for their chief and his enforcers but were reluctant to take 3 strangers at face value, even if they had magically disposed of their tormentors without any fuss.

"You say that you are helping to free us from the hardships imposed by a nasty chief on behalf of the lords," said a tall, elderly woman who had clearly seen more than her share of beatings and abuse. "How do we know that this is true, and what price will we pay for accepting your word?"

Tom replied, "You are clearly a survivor. You must have worked out by now whether you could trust someone by their attitude, and how they speak. As for what we want. We ask nothing of you in return. If you wish to join with us to help free other villages from anarchy, then that help would be welcome. Otherwise we would just be happy to have given you a small taste of the freedom that every man, woman and child should be enjoying. We do this out of love for our fellows, because we have all suffered awfully, and others continue to suffer. We are not lords. We are ordinary people who saw an opportunity to change things for the better."

The crowd was coming around, but the thing that finally convinced them was Tom's anguished account of what had happened at the palace.

*

Their new chief was called Bruno, a giant of a man, with great passion, but an inherent kind persona. They selected 2 men to be the helpers for Tom and Robin, called George and Harry. Staying overnight, Tom went over all the things Bruno needed to be aware of and told Harry and George that with their chips removed they would be able to move around freely, and most importantly they would be needed to help support Robin and Tom when they raided the palace of the lords. Andy and Johnny had the job of spreading the information Robin had collated, and that all went down fine. Tom, Johnny and Andy left the next morning after telling their 2 new recruits to be ready for action in about 8 days' time.

*

Robin prepared backpacks like his own, full of the things he had found useful. While the villagers settled into their new lives, Tom took all of the dogs to each village in turn so that they could sniff it out and become familiar with each chief, such that all Tom had to do was to attach a note to the dogs, whisper a chief's name, and the dogs would deliver the message to the right person. It meant making a hole next to each gate to allow the dogs to get in and out, but it was agreed that was a small price to pay to be able to keep in touch.

*

Counting down the days until the lords would go off on their travels, Robin kept a close eye on activity at the palace, and there were plenty of comings and goings. Many trips were made by the flying machine, but Robin found it hard to track where they went. He was more interested though in how many people, slaves, masters or lords would remain at the palace, and that wouldn't be certain until the get-together in America had started. He had identified the exact location of the American venue, a huge building, by searching the maps in a browser, then using the coordinates to pin it down. It was an easy matter to have the spy in the sky zoom in on it. Robin felt he was as ready as he'd ever be.

*

It seemed that the final departure had been made from the palace, and at most Robin only saw 4 people left behind, but it was impossible to know how many were inside. He saw the people start to arrive at the venue, which was the signal to get all the helpers into the cavern for the night. The dogs were sent out with appropriate messages, inviting the helpers to the cavern.

Lucy had provided some comfortable spaces and blankets for the extra bodies in the space she had cleared. It was quite a party atmosphere as the newcomers entered the cavern and talked excitedly about it. They were totally impressed that Robin and Lucy had made this their home, but when they saw Mickee and the 2 girls, realising that they had been rescued just in time, their respect for what was being done increased greatly, and felt honoured to be a part of it.

Lucy had some help from the girls in feeding everyone, but it was still a major action. "An army marches on its stomach," she said, smiling and recalling a quote she'd read in the library.

"That was marvellous," said Harry, "I can't recall ever eating so well." The others of course agreed.

Jane was especially reserved, with both she and Anne reluctant to be too close to the strangers on their own. Robin tried to explain how he knew the girls would be feeling, "Tom found Anne and Jane tied up and ready to be transported to the lords. They look better now, but they are still shy. I'm just so happy Tom did rescue them. The same applies to Mickee, who is a great kid."

A while later as they all started to relax, Jane came up to Robin and kissed him very gently on the cheek several times. "Thank you," she said, with all of her heart.

*

The morning came all too soon. Robin checked on his PC if anything was going on at the American building, or at their intended destination. It was all quiet, so he decided it was time to get going. "Tom, just thinking, we should go in 2 groups so that we do not get spotted too easily."

"Good idea, and we can meet up at the gates to the palace."

"Has everyone got their food parcels?" Lucy asked. They all nodded and thanked her.

Before Robin left with 3 helpers and Digga, he took Lucy by the hand, twirled her around so she was facing him, and gave her a big hug, followed by a long kiss on the lips. She went red but kissed him back happily. Tom left 5 minutes later with his 3 helpers and Whiskey. The other dogs were told to protect the cavern.

*

Tom made sure to take a slightly different path to Robin. He could see where Robin had entered the bushes by the marker left by Digga. Moving up the path some 20 yards, before wading into the deep undergrowth, he wondered what they would find inside the luxury home they were planning to raid. There was no need to check his compass just yet, he could get the general direction from the sun, but it was a nice day for a walk. He and Robin had decided that a more direct route was appropriate, cutting out the detour they had previously made via Gravesend. That way they would hopefully reach their goal before dark.

*

Robin made a habit of running wherever the ground was flat and climbing a big oak tree whenever he could find one. He was searching for any potential trouble but was also interested to keep tabs on Tom; being competitive, he wanted to make sure he arrived first. They stopped just before midday to eat and drink something, then pushed on.

"It would be nice," suggested Andy, "if there were more smooth paths going to the palace. It seems to be quite a long way, especially if we have to do this often."

Robin agreed, "The trouble is though, I'm pretty sure the lords could spot us too easily if we use a path all the time. I'd rather stay hidden wherever possible, and not give them any clues as to what we are up to."

"Will you show us how you use that PC of yours and make that light burn the chiefs?" asked Paul.

"I certainly will," said Robin. "There is no point in keeping this knowledge to myself. If I get taken that knowledge would be lost to our group. Tom and Lucy know a little of it, but there is a lot more to share. That's why I am so keen to educate everyone in the villages about how we came to be in this situation. Sometimes I wonder if the people before us were simply stupid to let it happen, but when I looked at all the deceit going on, it was easy to see that the lords were confusing them and acting in secrecy."

"How did you locate this information?" asked Paul.

"Well," Robin smiled at the recollection, "I'd read a good number of books in the library that described life before, so I had a good basic idea on what things used to be like. I came across a book that talked about PCs, which was initially confusing, until I found one hidden behind a ton of cobwebs and dust. The fortunate thing was that it had been left on and connected to the web."

"Now I'm confused," admitted Harry, with a half frown. "You found a PC under a cobweb that was still connected to the cobweb. How did that help?"

"Ah, confusing terms. A web is a bit like a cobweb. It connects to many other different PCs that hold information, all over the world."

"All over the world," gasped Harry. "That is surely a big cobweb, sorry web."

"Yes. And a cobweb is a great way to describe it actually," said Robin. "It links in to all the old knowledge that was available before the lords took over."

"That must have taken a long time to work it all out though, if you had to read so much data," said Paul.

"Weeks and weeks solid, but I was sick to my stomach when it all finally clicked into place. We must never forget what happened. I plan to get some

PCs for you soon, and I'll show you everything."

Digga had been listening intently, "Yelp," as if to say, "what about me?"

"Sorry, Digga, you need fingers to use a PC."

A disappointed dog gave a short groan then rushed ahead, leading the way as she usually did.

*

Lucy probably knew almost as much as Robin did when it came to what was possible on the PC, although she made a point of not showing off. She certainly knew how to take files from any PC to hers via the local internet. She hadn't told Robin that she could view his progress towards the palace, but she felt that she needed to keep an eye on things, and if necessary, she wouldn't delay in using that killer light beam. She was not worried by what she saw when she looked. There were no people or serious obstructions in their path, but she kept watching anyway.

*

The 2 groups met up just outside the palace gates within 15 minutes of each other, a fraction after 4pm. Robin already had his PC up and running when Tom quietly joined him. A strange thing happened as they looked at the view over the palace through the PC link. The view actually moved as though it was being controlled from somewhere else.

"That's odd," said Robin. "It moved towards the front of the building, but I swear I didn't touch it."

"Try moving it over the roof, see if anything happens."

Robin did as suggested and this time it stayed on the selected view. "Hope that wasn't a lord checking on his palace, but no time to worry about that. We have work to do."

While Robin kept a watch for any movement, 3 helpers went to each side of the building, checking for any occupancy through the windows that were at head level. Tom had them stay close to the building front, just observing, as he went back to tell Robin what the inside looked like and where people might be.

"If the way looks clear, we should check the front doors, then search inside," suggested Robin. While Tom went back to the troops, Robin moved towards the front of the building.

"We need to make sure this is empty," Tom emphasised, with a whisper. "Be very quiet, keep together as a team of 3, and be prepared to use your knives on any lords. Watch out for slaves or masters. I suspect the lords left someone of trust to look after this place."

Andy was in the lead for the team going in to the left side, with Harry going to the right at the head of that team. The first thing they both noticed was how worn everything looked. The fittings and furniture by their standards were luxurious, but not clean, nor maintained. "Not what you'd expect for a lord's palace," George whispered.

On the wall of the main room, an image that nobody could miss was displayed grandly in bright colours. A large triangle set against a red background, was seemingly meant to show the social structure of this society. It was labelled as THE TRIANGLE OF SUBSERVIENCE. The bottom of the image showed slaves, labelled as workers, servants or fodder. Above this were 3 levels of master, presumably with different levels of loyalty applicable to their title, the highest being TRUSTED MASTERS. Then came 4 levels of lord: UNDER-LORD, LORDS, HIGH LORDS, AND KING LORDS. Above all of these sat the gods. The lords and gods certainly wasted no effort in making the slaves feel anything but worthless.

Lights were on in all the rooms they went through, but there was no sign of anyone working on the ground floor. "Shall we go upstairs?" Andy whispered to Tom after they'd made a full circuit of the inside. That was when they heard a loud whirring sound coming from outside.

"Quick," said Tom, "make yourselves invisible inside. We have to capture whoever is in the flying machine. Let them come inside then grab them, attempt to knock them out cold if you can. Andy, Harry and George, you take the first guy. Johnny, Paul and David get the second guy. If there are more than 2 men we will have to split up, with David and George going for a third man. I will do what I can to back you all up."

Things became tense as they waited for the flying machine to land on the roof. Robin had seen the machine and waited anxiously to see if he needed to get involved. He was very aware that his presence was as a backup in case things went badly wrong. He decided he had better stay out of it, for now.

Hiding behind the front doors proved to be the wrong thing to do, as the people returning didn't use the doors. They stayed upstairs, meaning that Tom and his band of men would have to go up to them. Tom searched for a way to the level below, fearing that if staff were downstairs, they could be alerted to attack them as they took on the new arrivals.

There was only one obvious access to the cellar rooms below, through a door, too frequently used, that squeaked a little, and led to a gloomy space that was only partially lit. Tom slid down the stairway with Harry as backup. At first, they saw nothing that made any sense, then their eyes began to pick out shapes. Several rooms on the left had doors partially open. A quick look inside each identified 3 of them as store rooms. The 2 remaining rooms were clearly used as sleeping quarters, with rough material scattered over the floor. The aroma of stale sweat pervaded everything, but fortunately there was nobody occupying these rooms.

They proceeded down the corridor, which turned sharply to the right. Neither Tom nor Harry was prepared for the sight before them. Metal bars stretched the whole length of one wall, with metal doors at intervals. The metal bars were close together, to prevent any kind of access. The stench told them at once that these cells were only used to hold slaves that had already been tortured, with more pain and death just around the corner. They checked each cell, that could hold maybe 20 people, to see if there was any sign of life, but there was none.

As Tom looked through the glass panel of the door at the end of the corridor, he could see Robin edging closer. He waved and got his attention. The door was heavily locked from both sides. Robin undid the bolts on the outside, as Tom forced the catches open on the inside, telling Harry, "This will be our escape route if we hit problems."

"What's happening inside?" asked Robin.

"We've searched the downstairs and were just making sure we could get out this way. So far, no encounters with the 'you know who'. You're best off staying outside for now until we deal with those above." Robin nodded.

Tom had noted that there were 2 sets of stairs going upwards. A very elaborate richly decorated one was almost opposite the front door. Another one, that was probably known as the backstairs and which were rather drab, was accessed from a side door. Tom, with Harry and George, went up the glamorous stairway. The other 4 went up the back way.

*

While Tom was slowly opening the door to the first room on the first level, Robin had decided to seek out weapons in case they were needed. Holding his nose and mouth against the putrid smell, he saw what looked like pistols he'd seen pictures of on the internet. He could see no place to load bullets, but when he pressed the trigger sparks flew. He realised he had found some kind of electrical gun. "That will do," he told Digga, putting one pistol in his pack and keeping one in his hand.

Upstairs, there were 3 men in the room, 2 were sitting comfortably in what was a much more luxurious setting than downstairs. A third man of about 28 was standing with head bowed, holding a tray of drinks, his legs in chains.

The taller, smartly dressed man, most definitely a lord, addressed his slave. "Take my bag upstairs and unpack. Run my bath and hose down one of the doll-boys for my pleasure afterwards. Now move." The slave moved as quickly as he could, leaving through another door that led to another set of stairs.

The lord continued, now talking to the man sitting close by, "You'd better go and rest in a spare room. That unfree will show you and bring you some dinner later. I want you fresh for tomorrow. I have to visit several locations to make it look as though all the lords have not disappeared. They are in fact having a glorious time, while I drew the short straw and was left behind."

The man said nothing, all too aware that most lords had a short temper, and whatever he said could be misconstrued. He simply nodded, leaving his eyes looking at the ground until the lord spoke again.

"You realise of course, that if you continue to please we will have to find someone else to pilot the helicopter, and you just might become one of my junior lords."

The other man smiled, "Thank you so much for the trust you put in me, my lord. I promise I will live up to your expectations."

"You have no choice," said the lord, with not an ounce of goodwill. He arose, going to the stairs, his pilot submissively walking behind him.

The pilot returned to his seat, smiling smugly, and drinking more wine. Tom realised their chance had come. Andy came quietly into the room behind the pilot, about to grab him, as Tom approached from the front.

Seeing Tom, a strange unknown figure, the pilot initially became alarmed, then assumed him to be a master or something less, "Get me another bottle of wine from that cabinet." Tom obeyed, bringing the bottle over, for the pilot to see. "No, you simpleton, I want wine." As the man leaned forward to shout at him, Tom pushed the head of the bottle hard into his open mouth, into his throat. The man gagged and staggered back. Andy now grabbed him by the chin and held him firm.

"I'm afraid you won't be taking any more trips in flying machines," Tom said with mounting anger. "Harry, can you find a small room that would take several bodies." Harry soon found a small closet used for hanging clothes in. Tom and Andy walked the man over. He was clearly expecting to be thrown in and left there, but as Tom removed the bottle, Andy gave a very firm twist of the man's head, who slumped into the closet, dead, with a broken neck.

Tom had everyone search this level for anything or anybody of interest. Little of importance was found. As they moved up the stairs that went to the suites above, they could hear the lord shouting his orders.

"Where is my music player, damn you? Bring it in here and plug it in to the power."

Tom saw the slave walking from one room into another, carrying a small box-like device.

"Get a move on," demanded the lord, then some music started to play. The slave came out and went through another door.

Tom peeped inside. The lord was steaming in a bath tub, lying up to his neck in hot water, smoking something that smelled of old compost. With knife in hand and Andy close behind, Tom entered the room, having spotted something interesting. On the coldest of winter days, back in his village, they had been allowed inside a teaching room instead of being outside to learn the rules. At the front of the room the chief had a 2-bar heater that looked very like the one sitting over the bath. Tom also knew it was powered by energy, and energy did not mix well with water. That was something the chief had mentioned.

"My lord," Tom said, in his best sickly attempt at appeasement. The lord had just begun to relax into his bath with eyes closed, "there is something I must do for you." Without waiting for any response Tom pushed the heater into the deep water and turned around to watch the lord convulsing.

For once the lord could not manage to say anything. He gasped a few times as he tried to stand up, but that was beyond him, and he collapsed back into the tub. Tom turned off the energy to the heater that was sparking, then pulled the bath plug so that the water would drain out. Andy made sure the lord was dead by cutting his throat. They then man-handled the corpse downstairs and threw it on top of the cupboard occupant.

The suites' level contained 17 rooms, with one larger, especially luxurious room plainly belonging to the senior lord. "We'd best search all these rooms, including the cupboards," Tom said to the others. That all took about 10 minutes, which seemed like a long time considering how hyped up they all were, living in fear of being overwhelmed at any time.

"Harry, please stand at the top of the stairs in case we get visitors," Tom said. "We need to go and see what's upstairs." This was not something anybody was looking forward to, guessing that young slaves were kept upstairs for regular abuse.

It was a short flight of steps up to the attic level where they could hear the male slave they'd seen down below, talking to someone in a gentle tone. "When he comes at you, try and relax your muscles. That way it will hurt less. When he hurts you make a loud noise, or he will deliberately give you more pain to make you cry."

Tom entered the room where the slave was, noticing how a young boy was stood under a shower, with the man standing close by with a towel. "You won't have to worry about that lord abusing any more children," Tom said loudly above the noise of the water.

The slave was startled, backing off away from the intruders.

"Turn off the water," Tom ordered, "you have nothing to fear from us."

"Who are you?" asked the slave, wondering if these visitors would also be causing him more pain.

"We are neither lords nor masters," Tom stated. "We have come to free all slaves we can from their horrible lives. Let the boy get dry and find him some clothes. Are there more like him?"

"Oh yes, in those 2 rooms." He pointed.

"Thanks, my name is Tom," he offered his hand to the slave. "What is your name?"

"I am 734..."

Tom interrupted him. "What is your given name?"

The man was confused for a moment. "I can't remember, no wait, my mother called me Eric."

"Nice to meet you, Eric," said Tom. "These are my friends, and we plan to free up all slaves. You are now a free man. Will you help us to free others?"

It was all too much for Eric to take in, "Yes, but how, what if the lords come now?"

"The lord is dead. You need not fear him. Now take us to the other children."

Eric showed the way into the other rooms that consisted of large metal cages. The room was dank and smelled of fear.

"Open these cages, then get the kids cleaned up. They will all need some clothing, after which we must remove your shackles."

The man, an abused and tortured slave all his life, couldn't quite believe that this could be happening, but he was so used to being told what to do he immediately followed his orders.

"There must be secrets to this place," said Tom. "We will talk downstairs when the children are ready. I will leave George and David here to help you. Come down to the first level when you are ready."

*

Robin had been sitting out the back of the palace, frustrated at no news of what was going on. He kept the PC viewing the area, glancing at it occasionally, or glancing around. Digga was sat quietly at his feet, so he knew she would warn of anyone coming from behind. Suddenly the view from the PC changed, and instantly Robin was perplexed but worried that some lords could see what they were doing and would retaliate. The view though had moved towards the front of the grounds. There was now a watercraft beside the wooden walkway, first one then 2 more men got out of the boat and started to walk towards the front door with heavy packages.

Forgetting his concerns about the lords watching, Robin wondered what he could do to alert Tom and the others about this new danger, "Not a lot," he told himself. Holding his nose he walked in the back door, and positioned himself just behind the partially open cellar door so that he could watch the men coming in.

*

"Tom and the others relaxed for a moment on the comfortable chairs on level one, then they set about looking inside all the nooks and crevices, not to mention a host of large cupboards. There was a big kitchen that was unloved, dirty and untidy, but there was a huge selection of food in a pantry as well as a freeze box to feed 10,000.

It was Johnny who was at the top of the stairs on level one when the 3 boatmen entered through the front doors but jerked back quickly out of view. They made plenty of noise, not expecting any difficulties or excitement away from the normal routine. One shouted, "Where is that good for nothing slave?" They dumped their packages down and started to walk up the stairs, most inconveniently at the same time as Eric was leading the clothed children.

"What the hell is going on? Why do those kids have clothes on?" the burly man at the top of the stairs wanted to know.

Eric was flustered, and all he could think to say was, "For the new lords," and indicated the lounge area.

Not wanting to confront this ugly brute head on, Johnny saw an opportunity to knock him down the stairs. Grabbing hold of the door frame, he swung his legs in the direction of the lout, connected with his chest and sent him backwards and downwards. Halfway down he collided with the other 2 who hadn't seen the acrobatics from Johnny. "Hey, careful," said one man, but the first already had a lump on his head from the fall and wasn't listening. The 2 men dragged the first up the stairs and lay him down inside the lounge.

Tom and the others stood around, not willing or able to physically attack the newcomers, wary of their strength.

"Who are you guys?" asked a newcomer. "We were not expecting any new people."

Tom jumped in, knowing he had to say something. "We were told to come here by the lord. He's gone for a bath after his long journey. He promised us a treat." He indicated the children.

The 2 boatmen left standing smiled at this. "That sounds real. You must have done some good work to get such a treat," said one of them.

"Oh we did," agreed Tom. "He didn't say any others would be joining us, but nice to have company. You could show us the ropes. Are we going to have any more join us, there are only so many kids to go around."

"There won't be any more," insisted one of the brutes, "what with the lords all away, we are stretched thin, and some things must go on as usual. Perhaps that was another reason you got invited here."

The first brute started to groan but didn't quite wake up. Andy saw his opportunity, "Help me get him onto that big seat in the corner where he can be quiet." Once the man was moved, he created a distraction by asking for someone to get some cold water and a rag. While everyone was watching Paul and Harry going for the requested items, Andy sank his knife deeply into the side of the man's neck, away from where he was facing. The blood spurted out, but this was hidden by Andy's body. When the water and rag arrived, he made a bit of theatre of applying the cold water to the lump on his head. "That's a nasty bump," said Andy. "Best if we leave him to sleep and wake up when he's ready." Everyone agreed with this, and they all moved to another part of the large room.

Tom, like the others was standing around nervously, wondering how they could handle the 2 remaining problems. He looked at Eric, fearing he and the children would get caught up in any violence, "Put the butt-kids down on the floor behind that big chair, out of the way, while we decide who goes first."

This pleased the 2 men from the boat, but Eric was even more confused and didn't know what to expect. Robin was picking up some of this from downstairs and was worried that there might be other people on the boat. Thinking that he couldn't help those above if there were other boatmen to attack them, he went out the back, to see if there was any sign of life on the boat via his PC. There was. He told Digga to stay and guard the very important PC. Walking nonchalantly down the wooden path leading to the jetty, Robin kept his hand firmly on the electric gun he'd found. "Hello," he called, "who is there?"

A head appeared, bristled, with the pallid look of a long-term slave. He looked up at Robin, just recognising a well-fed healthy individual, knowing that whatever he said it would probably mean some pain for him.

"What are you doing here?"

"Just cleaning up, sir," the man mumbled. Robin saw that his feet were tied up with chains so he couldn't move far.

"Who else is on this water vessel?"

"Nobody, just me," croaked the slave, with eyes downcast.

"You look hungry," said Robin. "Is there any food down there?"

"Yes, sir, but I'm not allowed to eat until they throw the leftovers on the floor for me."

"I'm going to give you an order."

The poor man looked bewildered and frightened.

"Go inside and cook yourself a meal and eat it on the table."

The slave looked even more troubled, thinking, *They'd beat me for a week, sir if I did that.*

"I don't think so," said Robin, guessing what the slave was thinking. With supreme confidence he continued, "I'm now the high lord here and you will never be beaten again. Go and eat."

The slave couldn't force himself to comply with Robin's orders, knowing how badly he would be hurt when the others returned. But Robin had satisfied himself that he wasn't going to be ambushed from behind when the boatmen were confronted, so proceeded through the front doors of the palace. He gently whistled for Digga to join him, and they both silently made it up the stairs, with the intent of becoming a distraction for the others to tackle the 2 boatmen.

*

"We are new to all of this," said Tom, "you'd best be first." The 2 men were manoeuvred until they were separated from each other. Tom indicated they should be knocked out if possible.

"Wait a minute," said one of the masters. "There's no rush here. We need to have a few drinks, and I don't want the lord to come charging down saying we are taking all his best butt-kids. Let's relax a little."

They all sat down, and that was when they noticed the dark stain seeping from the big chair on which the first master lay. "Hey, what's happened to him?" The masters turned the first guy over and saw the stab wound in his neck. "Somebody has killed him, and I'm about to kill someone else." He approached Andy who backed away from the man who now had some sort of weapon. "Line up against that wall. I want to know what is really happening, but first I'm going to shoot the guy pretending to be a doctor."

"Hold on," pleaded Tom, walking to the left so that they were spread out.

Robin had already had his cue, walked to the top of the stairs with Digga at his heels, pointed his electric shooter at the man with the weapon and pulled the trigger slowly and gently. The next instant Digga had taken down the other man, her teeth embedded in his leg.

Andy quickly ended the struggles that followed, with his blade cutting into exposed necks.

"Ah," said Tom, "that was a little painful. Thanks, Robin for your timely entry."

Looking around, Robin quickly took command. "We can't leave these bodies lying around. If we ever come back here, we need it to be in a healthy condition. The blood must be cleaned up for a start. Somebody see if there is any disinfectant or bleach to do that. Blood can make us all ill if we are not careful." He recalled reading that online. "While that is going on can we please get these bodies outside and dumped in the sea?"

"Eric, stay where you are," said Tom. "The good guys, us, are winning."

*

Literally 15 minutes later the dead had been thrown into the sea, and everywhere smelled of something strong.

"This is some adventure," Harry noted. "Several times we could all have been killed, but it was surely worth it."

"Indeed," said Robin, "now we have other things to do. I want to see a rough summary of everything inside this place. How many lords' suits, and shoes? How much food, and anything else that might come in handy, like weapons?"

"Eric can help with that," said Tom, "he's been here forever by the sounds of it."

Robin and Tom walked to where Eric and the kids had hidden themselves away. They both smiled at Eric and the kids, who were all too traumatised to do anything but hug each other.

Robin offered his hand to Eric, who shyly took it, to be helped up. "Nice to see you, Eric. You are now a free man, and we will be taking your ankle restraints off. When we are finished here, we will be taking you somewhere safe, but there are several things we need from you. Firstly, can you tell us all about this place, you must know all of its secrets. Are there hidden cupboards or rooms? Do they have weapons somewhere? What did the lords hide from everyone else?"

Eric nodded, understanding that this was his chance to betray the beasts that had tortured him for so long. First, he showed them a secret room behind the drinks' cabinet, which housed weapons and many electrical devices. Most of the devices meant nothing to Tom or Robin, but plainly were of importance. Robin did spot the master console though, and that was something he needed.

There were several other concealed drawers and cupboards in the lounge room. Several bundles of printed papers took Robin's attention. He wasn't sure what they were but looked important, so he stuffed them into his backpack.

Upstairs on the suite level, Eric continued to identify other hidden things, from small weapons, needles and drugs, to horrendous images of kids being tortured. Eric indicated that was all.

"What about stores?" asked Tom. "Is there a big room where they kept big things?"

"Ah, yes," Eric agreed. "The cellar." They went down to the bottom of the house, but even with the end door open and a fresh wind blowing the stench was almost enough to make Robin and Tom heave. Eric was used to it. There was a door just before the cells, concealed by a length of wall. The room was huge. It stretched much further than the house on one side, and it was full of many things. Tom opened a box at random. It held clothing. Another box had electrical cables and fittings.

"This is amazing," Robin exclaimed. "We have quite a find in this alone. When the boys have finished upstairs, perhaps 2 of them can come down and hose out the cells to reduce the smell.

"Thank you," Tom said to Eric. "Now we must do something for you and get those damned shackles off."

"That would be wonderful," Eric mumbled.

"I do believe there were some metal keys in that secret room on level one," said Robin. They went up and found the right key. For the first time for well over a decade, or possibly 3, while his legs had been constrained, Eric could stretch his legs out and walk properly again. A huge smile broke out all over his face.

"There is another person we must free while we are here," said Robin. "Eric, will you come with me down to the boat and persuade another ex-slave that his freedom has come? We will need the right key."

"That key works for all shackles," said Eric.

Robin and Eric walked slowly down to the jetty. Small talk was hard to come by, but Eric was just so happy having his legs free. When they reached the boat, the spiky head popped up again. "Hello again," said Robin. "Eric here, is a free man. He has a key to untie your shackles. Will you allow us to give you your freedom?"

The man was still unsure, suspecting a trick, but nodded. Eric went onboard, unlocked the mechanism and threw the shackles into the water. The newly freed man was now unsteady on his feet as he was helped onto the wooden planks. "This way," said Robin. "My name is Robin. What did your friends use to call you?"

Overwhelmed with uncertainty, the man's memories went back to the time he had lived in a village, "Runner, they used to call me runner."

"Did your mother call you Runner?"

"No," said the man thinking hard, "she called me Roy."

"Can we call you Roy?" asked Robin. He received a short, dazed nod, for all of a sudden Roy came to realise who he had been all this time, and what he had lost. His eyes filled as his mind replayed the dire times he had been punished or abused by the lords, but the thing that sent the tears flowing was the images he hadn't looked at for so long, of his distraught mother crying as he was taken roughly away from her.

Gently holding Roy's arm to support him as they walked back to the palace, Robin said to them both, "Now we are going to cook and eat the most delicious meal, and we will eat them on the ex-lord's best plates."

*

There were so many willing hands to cook a meal to feed so many of them that it was a wonder anything happened at all, but eventually a variety of dishes was available for eating. The children were served first, sharing several large plates, and eating with their fingers as they were used to. The others with food stacked on their plates tried to become familiar with knives and forks, having at best had broken forks or bent spoons to eat with before.

While the food was being consumed Robin kept his PC open to make sure no other unwanted guests crept up on them. After the food, most people, especially the kids, dozed with comfortably full bellies, but Robin was thinking ahead. He called Andy over. "We have to make sure all of the ex-slaves die here as far as the lords are concerned. Tom mentioned your medical skills. Can you take their chips out? There is plenty of whiskey here to dull the pain and clean up the wounds."

Andy smiled at the recognition, "Of course, I'll start with Eric and Roy, as they will be the hardest."

"Better give them plenty of whiskey to drink," Robin smiled.

While Andy killed off the ex-slaves, Robin went back into the secret room to power up and use the lord's master console. It had more features than he was used to, including one called broadcasts. He hit that button which produced an image of the lords seated in a semi-circular arrangement, facing a central group. There must have been well over 3,000 lords all dressed in their fine clothing. The central group, he assumed, were the supreme lords, with a strange figure seated behind them on a raised platform so that he had a good view of the lords. Robin couldn't make out the strange figure and there was no zoom available, but he was either wearing a grotesque mask or he was fiendishly misshapen. He listened to what was being said for a few moments. It was all about squeezing bigger quotas and more production from the slaves. That soon got boring as they went into great detail about how to motivate obedience. Robin wondered how they could keep this up for several weeks.

Now was not the time to sit and listen, there was a vital task he had to carry out, and he didn't imagine the lords would have anything to say that would reveal any real information that would be useful. Calling out to Tom, he said, "I'm just going to direct the light beam where it will do a great deal of good. It would be a good idea to post guards around the building to see if any retaliation is coming our way." Tom nodded and went off to organise it.

Wasting no more time, Robin went straight into the console's view option, using the coordinates he had acquired for the large building being occupied by lords from all around the world. He zoomed in to hold the building within the range of the active area. Without hesitation or regret to come, he hit the ANNIHILATE option five times, narrowed then moved the active area against the left side perimeter of the building, hitting that 5 times. He kept repeating this, moving and firing until the building was not just rubble, but a smouldering crater.

Leaving the console open he felt his temperature rise and went outside to cool down and tell himself that as a mass murderer his actions were fully justified. He wanted to believe himself, but a nagging doubt, just out of sight of verbalisation, remained.

*

It was dark outside when Robin came back to the console. The kids had been bedded down, and everyone else apart from the sentries were relaxing or dozing. Andy had removed the chips from everyone without any real drama. There were other things Robin need to do with the console. He still wasn't aware of how the transportation system between London and the villages worked but was determined to make life easier for the 3 villages they had liberated. In the memo section this console had a feature not available from his PC. It was an approval button. Going through the requests from the 3 villages for equipment, he approved them all. He was hoping that this would mean the system automatically did what was required to get the things delivered. Thinking that he still did not know enough about the memo system, he decided he had better work harder to get it fully under his control.

Working into the night, Robin reviewed every possible feature and option he could find. There was one interesting privilege that gave authorisation to different IDs. He hadn't spotted before that his PC had an identifying number at the top of each screen. This was used to vary what powers a connection would have. The chief's consoles would have very limited access to do things, like sending a note to the lords. He naturally assigned HIGH authority to his own PC but didn't notice any immediate difference.

Tom came in to check on him. "Are you going to be there all night?"

"No," answered Robin. "It's probably time I took my turn as a sentry guard. I really could do with the fresh air after trying to find my way around all of this."

"Come on then," said Tom. "The guards are just about to change."

The air was indeed fresh as they walked around the building. Tom accompanied Robin for a while, making small talk, feeling the need for some encouragement. "It's impressive," said Robin, "how everyone works so well together. You made good choices in selecting these good people." Tom smiled, knowing that Robin was acknowledging his work.

Alone to walk about, Robin looked at the shapes around. It seemed it was a good therapy for Robin's mind, having been so focused on what he could achieve with the console.

*

"Do you think there will be repercussions from wiping out so many lords?" Tom wondered when he came to relieve Robin.

"Hard to say," said Robin. "There are bound to be changes, but we need to hang on to what we have won. We've got to do far more though. We've only just started to free people, and there is still, no doubt, plenty of lords out there that can use their system to bring us back under control."

"What do you see as our next point of attack?"

"While we use our troops to free other villages from evil chiefs, and educate them, I have to figure ways to get control of the communication and transport links. Then there are the factories. Our influence must extend within and well beyond everything we know about."

*

The morning came with some people like Eric and Roy wondering if they were still dreaming. The whole concept of being rescued from servitude was pretty unreal, and they kept expecting the heavens to fall in on them. Nonetheless they both managed a smile as hot cups of tea were consumed with a little breakfast.

"Load up your backpacks with the food you can find in the larder," said Tom to the helpers, "and take some apples and pears along for the journey."

*

Lucy was there, at the upper level of the cavern to welcome Robin and Digga back. With a happy smile on her face, and bright eyes, she planted a big kiss on his lips, and hugged him close. Not saying anything she just took him downstairs, holding his hand tightly. The groceries he'd collected were stored away, then she took him into their private quarters for the best snuggle they had ever shared.

*

The helpers all went back to their own village to surprise the chief and others with some luxuries. Tom also went back to his village, with all the ex-slaves in tow, hoping some of them might belong there. The kids never complained once about the long trek. In any case they were welcomed by the village folk as their own and soon had been adopted by a loving family. Roy and Eric found a cosy spot each to call their own, being sheltered from the weather, breathing the air of freedom with a renewed spirit.

CHAPTER 5

EXPANDING THE BUSINESS

TOM KEPT HIMSELF, AND HIS helpers, busy by visiting a new village each week and converting it to their cause. Each time he found a good substitute chief and 2 extra helpers who were able to travel and spread the news of what was going on, but more importantly they told the story of how they had all become slaves in the first place.

Robin found he now had the ability to approve requests for materials for the villages from his PC and was even more surprised when the requests were filled, and vital materials found their way to where they were badly needed. None of the village homes, except the chiefs, had ever been properly maintained, and where something was repaired it had been done with inferior replacements. It would take a long time, but conditions were slowly improving for all villagers. Robin spent a lot of time wondering what could be done next to lessen the grip of the lords on this land but was often left with far too many unknowns.

Robin had kept his promise to provide the helpers with a PC, and he did his best to educate everyone on how it all worked, but he was constantly getting bothered to fix simple things that didn't work first time.

While visiting one of the villages towards the south coast, Tom, Robin and Andy got to chatting about how Andy would pass on what healer skills he had to others. "It's almost like we need a school in each village to reteach the important things we should know about," said Tom.

"I know what we badly require," said Robin, "teachers. There are a whole lot of subjects that we need at least one person to be skilful in. We have to choose that person who has a liking of a particular subject, and really get him trained up. Then he will be the point of contact, and the educator for that thing."

"Do we have enough people to do that?" asked Andy.

"Yes, if we do it carefully," said Robin. "We of course need to make sure that all helpers have the best education we can provide from the internet, but to become exceptional in an area and capable of teaching it, we need intensive study. First, we need to identify the subjects, like medical healer, PC, English, and sums. We can make a full list of them, then as we get helpers who are interested, we get them trained up. We probably can't match the level of training people had in the old society, but we need to know how to make energy and build houses. This would be a start in relearning what has been lost to us. I'll ask Lucy to start making a list. She's pretty good at stuff like that."

As they approached Tom's village that he had moved back into, along with Mickee, he asked, "Is there any reason why we haven't taken your old village, Robin? I know the chief has been missing for 3 weeks, but it is close by."

"I was worried," said Robin, "that he would suddenly reappear with some thugs and undo everything. I can't imagine why he would go away, or where, but it was odd that it happened well after I blew up the lords, and there is no indication if he left someone in charge. I'll check through the memos again to see if they give any clue as to his absence. His home is almost rebuilt, so shall we schedule his village in for 3 weeks' time unless I find something dangerous happening?"

"Sounds good to me," smiled Tom. "We will have to approach it differently if there is no single thug in charge."

"Good point," agreed Robin. "Let me see what I can do to find out some information on that."

*

Since their visit to the palace there had been no indication at all that anything had changed, apart from a lack of notes between lords on the memo system. The only new notes were from villages requesting items. There had been no visitors to villages, except the normal cars and carts to pick up some produce or to deliver building material. It was all very worrying, but satisfying, at the same time.

*

Lucy spent a lot of time researching educational subjects from the old world. There were many variations of what was fundamentally, the same thing. "For example," she told Robin, "if you start off with sums, or more correctly mathematics, it gets more complicated as it evolves into many different branches, and eventually there should be a teacher for each of those branches. I'm making a chart for all of this, but just the introductory subjects comes down to over 20. These are just the subjects that we need some basic skills in, to move forward."

"Sounds great," said Robin. "Now we need to match up helpers to subjects. You know what we will need next?"

"Allow me to make a guess, links to appropriate study material? I'm halfway there," she said with a smile.

*

Robin invited all of the 14 current helpers to a meeting in the library. "As we slowly take back our lives, it has become plain to see that we have been deprived of skills and knowledge. I want to change that here, today. There are many basic subjects that we need to acquire knowledge in. I'm proposing that all of you become the experts in a subject, so that you can learn it well, and pass it on to others. I see you all taking on trainees, who will learn from you, so that skills are spread around. This is something we must do. We need to be able to build new homes and work out how to create energy and be able to direct it. Education is the basis of what makes a society work. Lucy has made a list of the subjects. See that chart on the wall? Don't worry about the descriptions to the right. They are subjects in their own right that evolve from the basic field of study. Look it over and write your name against the base subject you'd like to take up."

The trainees enthusiastically chose their own subject and got to work reading up on it. Nobody was expecting instant results, but it was a seed in the ground. "Don't forget," said Lucy, "there will be some unusual words when you study. Be sure you understand them fully. If you are having trouble, come and see me. I have found a way to be able to grasp the sense of new words quite easily."

*

Tom had gotten into the habit of joining Lucy and Robin in the cavern each Tuesday, to discuss progress, and to make other plans. He also enjoyed what Lucy cooked. Jane and Anne always joined them, but rarely had something to say. "Do you recall how the palace had walls of brick?" he asked, but not waiting for an answer as Robin had just taken a mouthful of rabbit stew. "Well, we now have a way to make something that looks like a brick. Soon we will be able to build real walls for the houses. It works this way, some mud is cut into the appropriate shape, then it is fired in a kiln. Those are technical terms I learned," he smiled. "It just means the mud bricks get heated up until they are very hot, the moisture is taken away, and the brick becomes hard and solid."

"That sounds like real progress," said Robin, after a good chew and swallow.

"But," said Lucy, "the bricks must be stuck together to build a wall. What are they using as the glue?"

"Johnny is working on that as well," replied Tom. "Not sure what he is using, but he hasn't had any success yet. The wall keeps falling down."

"I can do some research," suggested Lucy, "but it is probably better if Johnny did it for himself as he is the master builder."

"Indeed," said Robin. "How is Andy getting on with his medical studies?"

"Good, I think," said Tom. "Certainly he has several young followers who try to catch frogs or birds so that they can cut them up to see what is inside."

"I hope they make sure the animals are dead before they cut them up," said Lucy alarmed. "Anybody that deals with dead bodies, or cutting up live ones, should always wash themselves very clean afterwards."

"I'm sure Andy knows about that," agreed Tom.

"So that's Andy and Johnny keeping busy. Do they still manage to hold classes on the subject of our collective slavery?" asked Robin.

"Oh yes," said Tom, "we've even had Paul and David in to teach English and sums. The covered area that we erected for teaching was packed out every time. The people are really loving this freedom to learn."

They were quiet for a few minutes as they contemplated the villagers getting educated. "You know," said Robin, "I'm still wondering how we can expand our control of the other things that are going on, and this is beginning to bug me because we can't just stop as we are. For example, we know nothing about how the train or the pickup car is managed, or even their other destinations, apart from the fact that the train and car meet at that station. Then there are the factories. We don't know what they make, where they get raw material, or even where the completed products go."

"That has to be the next big operation, and I suggest we try and get a ride on the train. Can you use your PC authority to tell them to expect us, and to take us on a tour of the factories?" Tom said.

"That's an approach I hadn't considered. I will work on that, but our next action is my village. There is no sign of the chief anywhere. The memo system shows nothing, and there was no handing over of power that I can see, although it looks like one of the bigger bullies has taken charge. I sent a note to the village asking where the chief was. I got something back that was barely English. I hope when I send the usual request to assemble the villagers and recite that rhyme that it will be understood."

"If not," said Tom, "you will just have to burn all the bullies into the ground. I will be there to point them out."

*

Robin sent the usual note on the Thursday, asking additionally if the instructions were clear. A positive, but very succinct, response came back, so Tom, Andy and Johnny were primed for the Sunday.

*

The crowd had been gathered together when the 3 reached the centre of the village. The man in charge, a big beefy man with hands that moved in odd ways when he spoke, was standing there looking at the villagers. "This is Sunday," he declared, as if making a momentous assertion. Around him were 5 other bruisers, challenging the crowd of people with their eyes. Evidently nervous at receiving instructions from the lords, his words were hesitant. "Who has seen the chief? The lords are asking, so do not hide his body."

One of the braver souls in the crowd piped up, "We've searched the village 10 times. The chief must have left." One of the bruisers took offence at this, poking the brave soul in the ribs. He would have given him a painful clout to the head, but his victim ducked and dived out of the way. The bruiser started to chase the man but was called back by the big lout.

"Never mind him, I have a message from the lords that you all must hear." He took a deep breath, concentrated hard with eyes screwed up to read out, "Little Bo-Peep has lost her sheep, and doesn't know where to find them." He spaced out the words as he read and spoke them from a sheet he was holding. He didn't have his men read any, possibly because they couldn't. "Leave them alone, and they'll come home, dragging their tails behind them." He looked around as some sniggers started up. "This is serious. You must hear this. Little Bo-Peep fell fast asleep." He had struggled with the words again and was getting red due to more giggling.

Robin decided that it was time to put everyone out of their misery. His finger hovered over ANNIHILATE, then he thought, *What the heck*, and gave the louts a suntan. They loved the warmth coming down on them, for a short time, happy that the lords were pleased with them. A few moments of that and they were getting too warm. "Now," Robin told himself, and they really did fry.

Tom ran to the front and did his usual speech, after which everything went to plan. A new chief was installed, and 2 more helpers were recruited who quickly lost their chips. Nobody, not even Lucy who had been spying in on the operation, saw an old man to one side of the crowd, with a tatty hood covering his head. Where a long straggly beard used to be he now had barely one day's growth of stubble. He listened in to all that was said before stealthily making his way out of the village, unnoticed, except by Digga. As the man crept quietly out of the gate, the dog yelped quietly to get Robin's attention. That was when Robin spotted the man. By the time he was down from his tree the man had literally disappeared, and even Digga could not find his scent.

*

Paging through the list of recipients on the memo system, Robin finally worked out which were important contacts as far as distribution and manufacturing was concerned. There were plenty of individuals shown that had some variation of lord in the title, most of which had sent no notes since their conference was burned down. He made a note of the 6 lords still active in the UK, none of which were from the Southeast. They didn't seem to be doing much but consolidating their position and jostling for top-dog positions. "There seems to be a group of high masters in London that control the factories. They are the people that keep things running for the lords and are likely just as dangerous as the lords are," he told Lucy.

"So it is they you have to convince, these masters, you need to make them respect you," said Lucy. "What about using the name of a high lord to introduce you."

"Not a bad idea, not a bad idea at all," smiled Robin.

*

"We had better look like lords then if we are going to pose as them," insisted Tom.

"That means another trip to the palace then," said Robin. "I think we should go in force to take a look at what happens in London. Which of our helpers are fit and can look mean when they want to?"

"Interesting question, but you are right. No smiling allowed, never let them know we are satisfied with what they do. Only use questions that demand more capability. What about Andy and Paul? They are both pretty smart."

"Good," said Robin. "The 4 of us can visit the palace on Sunday as we are not planning to convert another village yet. While we are there, I will alert the senior masters to expect us on the Wednesday and pick us up from Crayford railway."

"Sounds like a plan," Tom agreed. "Now that we've converted all of the villages we know of in the Southeast, I'm concerned that there are other locations marked on the maps that we don't know anything about. I'd hate that we were missing something."

"Well, we can't do everything ourselves, let's send a couple of helpers to spy on these locations and find out everything they can about them. By the way, am I right in saying we now have 36 helpers?"

"Fair point, and yes we do have 36 helpers in total, all busy with learning a particular skill and passing it on," said Tom.

*

David and George were chosen as the spies to take a look at the unknown sites. "You will probably get internet access as you come close to a location, which you can use to send me a memo. Reference each one by its map reference and give as many details as you can. If you can access it, all the better. Please get into the habit of sending a note when you are outside, and a final note, with a full description, when you leave."

David and George were excited and keen to get started, but they knew the risks of being caught. They promised to take no chances.

*

Sunday came along. It was a nice fresh but sunny day for a walk, and the 5 enjoyed their trek to the palace. Digga especially liked the outings, she always went where Robin went unless told to stay, and she was smart enough to know that when Robin didn't want her to come along that there was a good reason for it. In good spirits, Andy and Paul explained how they had improved on their skill set and were actively educating others. Their villages were doing well, and the people had never looked happier.

"It really has made a huge difference to all the villagers to be free of the old system," said Paul. "We are sending slightly less produce up to wherever it goes, but now everyone has plenty to eat, they don't get beaten, and work far less. They also understand the reason why their lives have improved and what kind of treachery was involved in making us all slaves. Every single one of them would do anything to bring down the lords completely."

"That's good to hear," smiled Robin. "I never had any intention of telling anyone how they should live or what they should do, so any help we get is always appreciated. I will continue to reduce the quotas so that all villages have a good stock of food to last through the winters."

"We would see more inter-village trading going on if we had better ways to transport goods," said Andy.

"I don't have a good answer for that, not yet," said Robin, "other than to suggest that we build better hand carts. When we get the skills, we will find a way to use some form of energy to push the carts, but that's some way off yet."

"It will be interesting to see how they move things around in London. Maybe we can get some ideas there," suggested Tom.

*

They reached the palace late afternoon and found everything as they'd left it.

The boat was still at the jetty, although the smell of disinfectant had faded somewhat. There were so many brand-new lord suits in the wardrobe, in different sizes, that it didn't take long to find 2 pairs each that fitted perfectly. "We'd better find some shoes as well," said Tom. "If we appear in handmade but ragged sandals we will surely give the wrong impression."

"In that case," suggested Andy, "we should all be clean-shaven and hair combed down nicely when we go, just to make sure we do impress."

*

They made themselves something to eat, then went in search of anything else they might need for their London trip. They took an electronic pistol each which fitted neatly inside their jackets in a special pocket. After that, it was time to settle down, chat and rest, except for Robin who had the job of writing an identical note to all of the senior masters he'd identified, telling them to liaise with each other to make this a good visit. It was sent from the ID of the Southeast high lord, instructing them to receive a visit from the new high lord with 3 new lords. They were to be picked up by train and taken around the major factories. They should consider this an inspection. It was expected that a summary would be provided of what each factory produces, in what quantities and how many slaves are used as well as how many are wasted each year. The 4 lords expect to be housed and fed overnight in suitable accommodations and will return by train.

Robin had Tom and the others read over his first note. "Looks good and specific to me," said Paul. Then Robin copied the words and sent them to each master.

"I think I need a little alcohol after that," said Robin, "something that will help me sleep."

*

Wednesday morning came. The masters had all replied, stating that they would comply in their usual grovelling manner. They were dressed and ready to go by mid-morning. "It will take about 90 minutes to reach the railway," said Tom. "We really should avoid the fast route as that will mean us walking through too many thorns. We should be looking fresh and clean when we get there, but I suggest we wait at the end of the road for the train to come in. It would not be appropriate if it seemed that we were waiting for the train. We must all adopt an attitude of superiority. Look down your noses at everyone. Question what is said with malice."

"We get the idea," said Paul. "We are the nasty lords, even nastier than the lords that were."

*

Before they left, Robin checked to see if David and George had sent any messages. "They should have reached the first location by now," he said. The spies had indeed reached a building that had been marked as important on the map. The report stated that they were in front of a large structure that had once been attractive and tall, with steps leading up to the main entrance. After watching for several hours with no sign of anyone inside, they had decided to take a closer look. David went in, leaving George in reserve, just in case. That was sent minutes before they departed for the railway.

*

Standing at the end of the railway approach just before midday, the 4 brushed themselves off, while practising sneering at comments. "I hear the train," said Tom, "time we started to walk."

The train came in, 3 men got off and waited on the path, watching the 4 lords walking slowly down the path towards them. Tom made a point of stopping and pointing at a broken tree, laughing. As they got close to the 3 railway men the sneering faces were a fixed feature. "Who is in charge here?" snapped Robin.

The men had bowed as the 4 approached, now one of them raised his head, "Me, sir, 256710..."

"Yes, yes," interrupted Robin. "You will come with us. I will call you 25. Now why are we standing around here? Escort us to this train. I want to see the engine driver."

"This way," said 25, fawning. "This way, your lordships."

They went through onto the platform, Robin ignored the man, leading the way to the front of the train. The man called 25 rushed to get the engine driver, throwing him to his knees in front of Robin.

Robin looked at the poor man, abused for having skills. "Now, engine driver. I hope you are going to give us a comfortable ride?"

"Yes, sir," the man said, looking up, worried.

"Tell me, what kind of engine is this?"

"It's a diesel, sir."

"Is it clean inside?" asked Robin.

"Not clean enough for your lordships to sit in," answered the man who was trying to make himself even smaller than he was.

"In that case go back and make it cleaner. One of my lords will be riding with you to make sure you are working appropriately." Turning towards the other 2 masters he said, "You 2 go and help him. Find something to put over the seats so that my lord doesn't get filthy dirty."

The 3 men did as they were told while Robin walked 25 up the platform as if inspecting the coaches. "Which carriage are the slaves put in when you transport them?"

Robin took a look inside, scowling and holding his nose. "Get it disinfected. It stinks."

"Yes, sir, I will tell the depot people when we get in."

"And this carriage?" asked Robin. "What is its purpose?"

"This carries the produce," said 25.

"Well," exclaimed Robin with some venom creeping into his words, "it is not good enough. No wonder the produce is damaged and smelling foul when it is used. This train must be improved. In future you are personally to make sure the carriages are cleaned every day. I want some changes made. The seats are to be ripped out and replaced with appropriate containers so that the produce is stacked properly, without damage or breakages. Do you get that?"

"Yes, of course, sir. I will see to that," 25 said quivering slightly at the responsibility thrust upon him.

"I will inspect this at a later date to make sure it is done properly. Now, as for the slave compartments. Too many butt-kids are dying before they achieve their potential to provide what is required of them. They are bruised and damaged on the journey which makes them less attractive. Take better care of them. You can start by making sure there is new carpet laid that will protect them somewhat and give them some food. Some of the wretches can hardly stand up."

"Yes, sir. I fully understand your lordship's requests. I will make sure the train is changed as you specify. Thank you for showing me the wisdom of your knowledge."

Tom got into the driver's cab after it became a little cleaner, and the train moved off. The 3 lords and 25 sat in a carriage that had already been cleaned up at the depot, and made attractive, if not comfortable, the other 2 sat in the part of the train reserved for vegetables and other goods.

The 3 lords took it in turns to interrogate 25. "How often do you make this journey?"

"Normally just once a week, unless there are kids to pick up."

"What do you do the rest of the time?"

"There are 4 other routes that we pick up from, so that keeps us fully employed."

"What do you do in the evenings?"

"Distribute the collected goods, sir."

"How many places do you pick up from on each route?"

"Just 3 stations on each route. The lines are blocked mostly, so we can't go too far."

"Where do you store the goods you cream off?"

A flabbergasted, flustered face stuttered for a moment, "Sir?"

"Don't deny that you take some of the best produce for your own benefit."

"Sir, we've always been allowed to take some food to feed ourselves. We wouldn't eat otherwise," pleaded 25.

"Not a good answer. How do you propose to make amends?"

"Sir, the food we take is for ourselves, our families and those that allow us to keep our jobs."

"Bribery in other words. Anybody would think you were lords!"

"No, sir, yes, sir," sweated 25.

"What else are you doing that our high lord would not approve of?" Paul asked.

"Just doing what I've been told to do," admitted 25.

"Ah, OK, so you are saying the system is corrupt?"

"Not sure, everybody does what they have to survive, I guess."

"We are not blind to the system," said Robin, raising his voice, "who do you think put it in place? Just be a little more restrained in future and remember what we've spoken of."

Clearly confused, having expected to be thrown from the train while it was moving, 25 could only mumble and nod his head.

"You will take us to your senior when we arrive."

"Oh yes, sir, he will be there to meet you."

"Now tell us about the places you visit."

Relieved that the subject had changed, 25 went on to explain the names of the places they stopped at with the train. "On this route we stop off at Bexley then Sidcup. We pick different things up at each stop."

"So what makes Sidcup worthwhile if the villages to the south supply so much produce?"

"Sidcup is mostly extra old slaves, but also green vegetables."

"What are the other routes you drive, and what do you collect?" demanded Robin.

"Well, sir, there are wagons added to the train, for the other 3 lines. It can be broken glass, old metalwork, or gravel. Those sorts of things. The next route goes to Dartford with us stopping at Barnhurst and Eltham on the way back. Next after that is Erith, with us stopping at Plumstead and Maze Hill. Then comes Beckenham Junction, stopping for Lower Sydenham and Catford."

"And the last path?" Andy asked.

"Oh yes, that will be Averley with us taking on mostly things like cables and plastic things, also from Forest Hill and Brockley."

Paul and Andy were taking mental notes of these details.

"These are all very short journeys for a train," announced Robin. "Why don't they go further?"

"Not sure, sir. Some lines are blocked."

"It strikes me," Robin stated in his fierce voice, "that some people are not doing a good job on maintenance. Time we had a more reliable way to manage collections. I take it from the state of this train that it probably breaks down frequently?" The railway master known as 25 had no answer to that. The man was given no respite though, they kept up the questioning on a variety of subjects until they reached their destination.

*

Tom was giving the driver an easier time. "What is it like driving the train? Do you have many problems?"

"Not often," the driver replied with hesitation.

Tom pulled a chocolate bar from his pocket, that had been found at the palace, and started to eat it, with the man watching from the corner of his eye. "Here," said Tom, handing the driver a bar. "Don't tell anyone." The driver took the bar but wasn't sure what he should do with it. "You have to take the wrapper off," Tom said gently, taking the bar back and pulling back the wrapper. "I give you permission to eat this." The man finally, reluctantly obeyed, taking a small bite and feeling the chocolate melt on his tongue. Despite everything, the taste opened up his eyes wide, and a small smile appeared on his lips. He blinked his eyes, relishing a treat he had never known before. "Glad you like it."

"Oh, sir, that is the best thing I've ever eaten." The driver smiled with warmth at Tom, relishing each morsel.

"Now tell me something, what was the name your mother called you? I don't want your number. What is your name?"

"I truly don't remember," said the driver, but with more confidence, "I was only 5 when they took me to work in the depot."

"OK. Give me your ID number. I will give you a name later." The man repeated his given number laid down by so many beatings. Tom wrote it down.

"How many trains are there that run from the depot?"

"Only 2. This one which does the short trips and one that goes longer to a place called Brighton. That is the best set of rails, going south. It even crosses under the river to go north as far as St Albans."

"Fascinating," said Tom, "and I suppose that is a diesel engine?"

"It is," agreed the driver, "although we still have a working steam train from the old days. I've been pushed inside that many a time as a lad to clean out the boiler. No wonder they wanted someone small."

"What do you know about the old days?"

"Not a lot, but I do know they left us a lot of equipment that nobody can look after or make work. It must have been quite a good life back then. They must have been smart."

"Not so smart that they allowed the lords to take over," insisted Tom.

It was at that point the driver became aware that this lord sitting nearby was not acting nor sounding like any lord he'd ever seen, and he had seen too many of their evil kind. There was something different about this lord. He was pleasant. He made him feel at ease and had even given him a treat, but it was his overall demeanour that made him think that this was no lord. He would never say anything to anybody, but this lord had introduced a little brightness into his life. If things were to get better, it would be because of people like this. "Er," said the driver, "just seems like something terrible must have happened."

"Indeed," said Tom, now aware he might have mentioned too much, "but that is all in the past." Tom changed the subject, "Where are we now?"

"Just coming up to the depot now, your lordship."

*

"Get off the train and make sure your senior is there to escort us and let me know when you have swept the floor clean," demanded Robin, as the train came to a screeching halt.

They heard a certain amount of quiet but angry exchanges as 25 requisitioned a broom and started to sweep away the dust between the lords' carriage and his senior. Robin stood at the doorway and looked out with all the disdain he could summon. As 25 completed clearing a path for him Robin stepped off the train, heading directly towards a man standing on his own, who could only be the senior bully in the area. The man was stout but strong looking, his face had seen a lot of personal abuse, but his eyes showed him to be a man of the system, now able to dish out to others at least as much as he'd ever received. Robin looked down into his face, him being about 3 inches shorter, directly into his wary eyes that blinked once or twice at being so close to a lord.

"Is this place always so disgusting?"

"Er, yes, sir," the senior bully answered.

"You mean that all of this filth on the floor is there all the time? To contaminate food and everything else?"

"It's always been like that," the man stammered a little.

"Not any longer," insisted Robin, and the 3 other lords walked up behind him, eyeing everything with noses in the air. "In future this area where butt-kids and food are received must be made and kept clean. Brushed down twice a day and wet-washed every week."

"I'm very short of people to do that. If my quota could be increased, I could get it done of course, but all my men are constantly busy."

"I'll tell you what I'll do," said Robin, poking a finger into his shoulder, turning him around and walking him towards what looked like an office, "give me a list of all the men under your control, and what they do all day, and I will consider your request."

The man produced a sickly smile.

"You can give me that on my return journey, now where are the factory masters?"

"This way, your lordship. They are awaiting outside with their coach."

The lords were led out of a double door across a pavement onto a tarmac road that was fresh and pothole free. Ahead of them was a shiny metallic vehicle, a bit like the car they had seen, but much bigger, with a good dozen wide seats inside. In front of this large car stood 4 of the ugliest bruisers the would-be lords had ever seen. It was easy to sum up their feelings for each other, which was certainly not even close to friendship. Their faces were dour, their expressions wooden, bordering on hostility. They bowed as Robin approached them. No lord would ever formally recognise another individual, other than another, lord as a real person, as all knew too well. Instead, Robin went down the line looking each man in the eyes for 2 seconds, then nodding his greeting. If the depot bruiser was hard-boiled, then these 4 were additionally glazed in acid.

Tom was watching the 4 factory men closely, who were watching and estimating the high lord in front of them. *He's far too young to be a high lord*, went the communal factory thought. *His arrogance is lacking, and his eyes are too soft. Let us see how we can take advantage of this new boy.*

Tom sensed from the way their thoughts reflected on their faces what was going on in their minds, and though he was no real thought reader he could read people. He moved towards the men, stopped 2 paces away and waited for Robin to move aside. "Do not for a moment imagine that we do not know how things are here. Do not mistake the look of youth for softness. We would just as easily assign you to the mines as leave you in positions of power. Prove yourselves useful to us and you will retain your fiefdoms, but on no account should you make any assumptions."

The 4 factory masters blinked in unison, feeling found out. *Ah, that makes more sense. This older lord is the real high lord who is testing his trainees as well as us. Better be careful not to arouse his suspicions for we have a good thing going here,* went the group think.

"Today's agenda was left up to what you want to show us, so where are we going first?" asked Robin.

The shorter of the men started to speak, "Can I just ask what it is that you want to get out of this visit? I can supply lots of numbers to show how we meet quotas if that is what you want?"

Robin was ready for that question, "Numbers and quotas only tell part of the story. They do not show how efficient you are. I want to see some typical factory processes that go from raw material to completed product, even if that means we are exposed to some dirt. First off, tell me in sequence what your factories are responsible for making."

The first man said, "I take raw materials, broken glass, old metal, or plastic, melt them down into a shape and size that can be used somewhere else. Some glass window products are completed on an assembly line, as well as any special requests that come in."

Robin looked towards the second man, who said, "I burn any kind of rubbish to keep the electric generators going so that there is electricity."

The third man said, "I receive in various grains from different sources, and turn it into flour. I also bake pies and a dozen other food items made of flour."

The last man replied, "I get in different threads to weave into carpets or clothing for the lords. Usually an order comes in with the appropriate weave."

"Good," said Robin, "for the benefit of this inspection you will be known as Raw, Rubbish, Baker, and Weaver. Now let's go see what happens after you receive the raw materials."

Despite the coach being powered by electric batteries, it made a heck of a noise as they drove along, which was a welcome relief, for Robin was not so good with small talk, especially with masters.

As they stopped at the first destination, Tom asked, "Why is this bus so noisy? Electric vehicles are supposed to be silent."

"It's the lack of maintenance," said Rubbish. "Perhaps you should also be visiting transportation, but that is north of here."

"I do believe we should do that," agreed Robin.

*

Tom had been paying attention to the route they took as the coach took them along a wide, but smooth road. There seemed to be little but brick walls bordering the road, as though one were being kept secret from each other.

There were few junctions, while the scenery didn't improve any as they journeyed on for about 15 minutes.

They stopped outside a red brick building that had seen better days. Some of the masonry was showing damp patches, and in places bricks had come loose. "Looks like we don't do very much to keep our resources functional," Tom said critically.

"Raw, you can lead the way," said Robin. "The rest of you can relax for 15 minutes or so, or you can start preparing your production reports mentally."

There were several layers of rooms and corridors to go through before they reached the first working area. "This is where the glass comes in," said Raw. "First it is graded by opacity, to measure how transparent it is. That's important when we get to the final component. Over there you see the great containers where the glass is melted down." Robin stayed close to Raw, constantly questioning him, while the other 3 took a closer look at the mechanics. Dozens of slaves with no protection against the heat or equipment scurried around, with several bruisers, wearing protective jackets, making sure they worked hard.

They followed Raw as he made his way through this part of the factory, with the melting process on the right and many smaller containers on the left full of glass. Raw continued almost to the end of the building, "As the glass reaches the correct temperature it is poured into many different moulds." He pointed at the wooden and metal frames that changed the glass into the required shapes.

As they approached the final section of what was a huge building, Robin asked Raw, "I wanted to get the chance to talk with you alone, which is why I didn't invite the others along. Tell me. How much can I rely on you? How faithful are you to your job and the lords?"

"I should perhaps be offended," said Raw. "I've been a faithful servant all my life."

"Yes, yes, I've seen your record," insisted Robin. "That I accept, but would that change if you were to be directed to another role, with more responsibility?"

Raw smiled. "I would welcome the opportunity."

"There have been rumours of some disquiet going around the London area, and it seems to indicate masters just below your level. Keep your eyes open, root out any masters that are taking too much out of the system for their own purpose, and let me know. Suitable rewards will follow."

Raw smiled once again, more solidly this time. "You can rely on me, your lordship."

"Now," said Robin, "how do you evaluate the other 3 factory masters? Can they be trusted?"

"Not in the least," Raw said determinedly. "I wouldn't trust any of them as far as I could throw them. Scallywags, all 3, risen above their station."

"That was the thought I was coming to," agreed Robin, "just from their attitude. You on the other hand appear to be a professional manager."

That made Raw blush, having never expected to receive praise. "Thank you, sir."

"Now don't mention any of this to anyone. This conversation is top secret. Certainly you should not discuss it with the other 3. This is too important, and I will find out if anything is passed on. Now take us back where we came from."

"I can keep a secret," said Raw. "Your lordship can rely on me."

"Good for you," Robin said with some disdain. He didn't want Raw to feel too good about himself. "I will let you go now. Send me that production report, and keep me advised of what you find out, or if you need anything."

Raw was beside himself and bowed very low with great respect when the 4 would-be lords left the building.

"OK," said Robin after they had boarded the coach, "take us to your factory, Rubbish."

*

Again the roads were smooth, the walls close up, and the bus very loud, but there was the occasional piece of spare ground covered with sparse grass that was more black than green. "This has to be the most polluted area I've ever been in," said Paul, sniffing the foul air.

"It is the high chimneys," said Rubbish, pointing up at 3 very tall towers, black with soot rising into the sky, belching out dense black smoke, "spreads the muck all around here."

"That truly is disgusting," said Tom. "When were the filters last changed?"

Rubbish started to get flustered, "Er, we haven't had any since I've been here."

"Inspect the chimneys, personally, and work out what kind of filters are needed. I don't intend to stay a moment longer in this foul place. Get this cleaned up, and don't forget your production report!"

Rubbish was left standing on the tarmac, distressed with the result of the inspection that took far less time than expected, and with an unhappy ending too. Meanwhile the coach headed off for Baker's factory.

Close to the Baker's factory, a good 15-minute drive away, the air became rather more breathable. Over the noise of the coach, Baker shouted, "We don't have any chimneys here. We keep everything clean so that our food is good to eat," expecting a compliment. Robin looked at him briefly, giving him a half nod.

They left the coach behind with just one factory master left inside with the driver. Baker showed off his impressive entrance. Grand steps in good condition led up to an impressive colonnaded entrance. Going through 2 sets of shiny glass doors, Baker said, "Perhaps we should have started with this factory for your visit. It makes the others look old and derelict."

Robin chose to disregard that statement, "Lead on, Baker, show us what you do."

They walked up a corridor that had doors at intervals, all labelled. At each junction or entrance, an identification indicator lit up for Baker, but nothing of course happened for the 4 lords. The first door into the factory proper they entered was called, 'Wheat into flour'. They saw at some distance, huge containers, into which grains were being loaded.

"This is the start of the process for all we produce here, although we take other grains from farms, they all go through the same process," said Baker above the noise. "The grains have to be sifted to get rid of the chaff, then washed thoroughly." The floor was clean as were the various containers.

Tom in particular was making mental note of the slaves. Here they were relatively clean and didn't looked starved or beaten half to death.

Robin started to give some admiration to this man, for as his mother had always told him, "cleanliness is next to Godliness." He said, "At least you are doing better than Rubbish, but that is a very low target to compare against."

Not sure if that was a compliment or not, Baker carried on, pointing out the process of washing and grinding the raw product. Finally he took them to inspect the flour that was being packaged up for distribution or put into pots for local use.

"Where do you get the paper packets from?" Tom wanted to know.

"There is a factory in the Southwest, near where an ancient forest grew. They cut down the trees to make paper products. They send us a regular order every month of the same type of package. All we have to do is open them up, pour in the flour, then seal them up. We send our flour all over the south as well as just north of London. I'm told there are other factories, like ours, further north."

"You know a great deal about all of this," Robin said questioningly.

"Yes," said Baker with a sigh. "As a young-un, and as I grew old, I was trained on every job you see in these factories. I've been buried frequently in grains or flour for my pains. I've been sent with special packages all around the south, to palaces, farms and all manner of camps. So, yes, I have built up a lot of knowledge."

Robin nodded by way of an acknowledgement.

*

The rest of the tour demonstrated that Baker's factory was relatively efficient, clean, and as Baker admitted when they sat down for a cup of properly brewed tea to sample some of the pastries made there, "I don't personally believe that beating my workers produces the best results." The 4 lords enjoyed the afternoon tea, while telling Baker he was a good baker.

Unable to restrain himself, Robin said, "I like very much how you have organised this factory. It's head and shoulders above the others. For your ears alone, I can tell you that we are rolling out a new strategy to treat the workers better so that they will produce better. Your factory epitomises that concept. Well done."

Baker was staggered. Never had he ever received a real compliment before, now he was overwhelmed with several. "I do my best to serve," he said humbly.

"There are a few things that could possibly be improved," Robin continued, with some restraint, "so when you come for a visit make sure you bring the plans for the factory, along with full details of your suppliers and customers, location and quantities."

"You're inviting me to your palace?" asked Baker, astounded.

"Do you know how to get to the palace just to the east?"

"Oh yes, I can arrange with the transportation depot to drop me off and pick me up again, but it will need your approval."

"That won't be a problem. Make your request on the memo system for next Wednesday. Expect to stay until 5pm. Who will be in charge while you are away?"

"I have 2 masters that are vying for my position, but I will nominate one of them as being in charge."

"Bring them here so we can evaluate them, one at a time," insisted Robin.

Baker went off, somehow feeling much taller, to get the first man, "This is the flour master."

"Sit down, flour master. We have some questions for you," said Robin. "Baker, you can wait over by the doors."

The master sat down, looking white, and not just from the fact that he had flour over his face and arms. "Do you have a name?" asked Tom.

"7561023837474AR," said the white man.

"Far too hard to remember, I shall call you White," Robin insisted. "Now tell me, what do you achieve here?"

"I er, make sure we achieve the quotas," said White, hoping that would be the required answer.

"Do you have to beat the slaves to get the work done?"

"Quite often," said White. "There are some lazy people that won't work unless they are black and blue."

"So that is an important part of your job, discipline?"

"Yes."

"Does your master beat the slaves very much as well?"

"No, sir," said White, thinking he could tell a tale. "My master tells me not to hurt them too much or they won't be able to work."

"I see," said Robin, "so your master is lax. What else does he not do properly?"

Smiling inwardly, White carried on, "He gives them too many breaks, and too much food."

"That doesn't sound very efficient," suggested Tom, pushing the man to admit he was cruel. "What other ways does he treat the slaves too easy?"

"Well," said White, smiling now. "When a slave gets sick, he gets them medicine, instead of throwing them into the incinerator, and getting a replacement."

"So," said Robin, looking intently at the man, "if something happened to your master, how would you change things to make production better?"

White listed off several areas where he imagined he could make the factory more efficient.

"I don't want to see a massive slaughter going on," Robin insisted, "but when were you planning to take control, and how many lower-masters would support you?"

"Soon," said White, now smirking, "a few weeks before year end, we get a big delivery of new slaves. While he is busy sorting them out it would be easy to take over."

"I see," said Robin. "I'm not condoning this, but just do not get any blood into the flour."

The man smiled a sickly smile as he was dismissed, and Baker came back with his other second-in-command.

"Baker, wait over by the door for a few moments," Robin said firmly.

"Now," he said, looking at the man in front of them, not so tall as Baker, with a ruddy complexion, and hands, which he was twisting around each other in an anxious way, but which had seen plenty of hard work. "You look like you've been working hard?"

"Oh yes, sir, I'm never still," admitted the man. "There is always something to keep me busy."

"What do your mates here call you?"

"Haven't got any mates, sir, don't have time for idle chatter," he said, trying to impress.

"In that case I will call you Ruddy."

"Yes, sir," he said, a little puzzled.

"I want to know how well your master runs things and what you would do better if you were factory master?"

"He does well," admitted Ruddy. "He doesn't waste workers with too many beatings. He treats us all fair, sir. If I was the big master, I would do just as he does. It all works smoothly when he is around, with no trouble."

"Good to hear you are loyal to your master," put in Tom.

"How often do you need to beat the workers to get them doing their best?" asked Robin.

"Don't need to," replied Ruddy. "They know what to do, and most get on with it for an easy time."

Tom looked at Robin, their minds in agreement over this man.

"You can go back to work now, Ruddy, but I want to hear from you if things stop going smoothly, or there is trouble. Do you know how to send a memo?"

"Oh yes, sir, I know alright. Thank you, sir." He rushed off even redder than when he was called in, but more perplexed.

"Baker, we will return to the coach now."

*

The drive to the next factory took them through grubby streets and blackened buildings. Robin was considering whether he should refuse to go inside except that the area around the entrance was not only clean, the grass was very green around it, and it had been cut recently. To their backs lay the railway lines. To their left a bridge spanned the river they knew to be the Thames. In front of them was a huge, ancient, brick structure which had been hollowed out at some time, but never made into anything worthwhile.

As was normal, the computer posts registered just the factory master as they went inside the polished glass doors. The floors were clean and washed, and the inside of the building had a good smell to it.

"So, Weaver, show us what you do."

Weaver showed them around the different parts of the factory. Workers were chained to looms and knitting stations, unable to walk far. Some of the slaves' legs were raw with sores. "What happens when their sores spread over their bodies?" asked Tom.

"They're no good to me then," insisted Weaver. "I send them to the incinerator and get more slaves to replace them."

"Isn't that expensive in terms of slaves?" Robin asked. "Doesn't that also mean you constantly have to retrain them?"

"It is an overhead," admitted Weaver, "just the way it has always been done."

"Well," said Robin, "I want you to find a better way. Along with your production report I'll expect to see some indication of how you will stop wasting slaves. Are there no healers in this area?"

"Healers? No. Never heard of any around here."

"Part of the reason for our visit," interjected Tom, "was to look at ways of improving output. I don't see how you can be working efficiently, given what we have seen here. Slaves are being used up too quickly. You must find a way to look after the slaves you have, not recklessly lock them in chains until they become dysfunctional."

Not expecting the criticism Weaver shrank within himself, "I'll work on something better," he said.

"You need to," Robin said. "I won't mark you down on this assessment if you can make major improvements within a month. I will be sending another inspector, and I want those chains gone by then. You only need a master at each row to stop them running away, but where would they run to? Additionally, feed them more!"

"There are ways to do this gradually," said Tom. "For example, do one row at a time, remove shackles, keep a junior master in view. Make sure that works fine, then continue the action."

*

Weaver was left in no doubt that he was to treat the slaves better, and accepted the idea as being cost effective though he would never have understood the term.

Having seen all they wanted to the would-be lords went back with Weaver to the coach. "How far is the transportation depot?" asked Robin, seeing as how it was still light outside, and it did seem like a waste not to make more use of their time.

"The driver will know better than me," answered Weaver. "Driver, how long will it take to drive back to the depot, I believe our lords want to meet the overseer for transportation?"

The driver responded with, "About 15 minutes, sir."

"Good," Robin said. "Weaver, I'd like you to come with us. Be good for you to see how other units are operated."

Unused to not being told directly to do something, Weaver still recognised the implicit order in the statement. They got on the noisy coach and made their way down some narrow roads along the river bank. The buildings became grander and bigger, although many were showing signs of damage or age. Suddenly they saw a high clock tower in front of them. It had one face open to the elements and a long crack running vertically.

Tom and the others looked warily out of the window at the water far below.

"Is this bridge safe?" asked a worried Robin.

The driver answered, "Yes, sir, as long as we keep to the middle of the road, we will be OK."

"That's not very encouraging," Robin shouted over the noise.

Just past the bridge on the left side was another very grand building that had seen better days. It must have been an important place with such fancy brickwork and fence around it. The depot was only 2 minutes further on, much to the relief of Robin and Tom.

"Here we are," said Weaver, as the coach stopped outside a large shed. "Driver, go find the overseer. Tell him his high lord requires his presence immediately."

*

The overseer of transportation was a tall thin man with a shiny bald head, a scrunched-up face that made him look like a prune, and a sour disposition. He bowed with some difficulty when he saw the party of lords, grimacing with pain in his hips. Weaver stood to one side and introduced the new man. "This, my lord, is the man responsible for maintaining what vehicles are available. You will excuse his demeanour. He was in an accident some years back, which damaged his spine."

"You are making excuses for him?" asked Paul.

"No, my lord. I am only asking that you do not dismiss him as disrespectful. I have known him many years, and he has always been a most faithful servant."

Robin led the party over to where the man had stopped. "I prefer to measure a man by his actual worth, not his apparent worth. We come to inspect your work. Weaver, you may come and provide support for your friend."

"What is it you wish to see, my lords?"

"Take us to your office first, then you can find someone to escort my 2 junior lords around your establishment." He indicated Paul and Andy.

While the escorted tour was going on, Robin and Tom sat in the overseer's rather large office and interrogated him on what he did. "I'm also interested in what mechanical vehicles you have here and what they are used for," Robin stated.

They found out many things, apart from the fact that no worker was shackled anywhere, most of them had the ability to move around without any master being with them. There were several different types of vehicle, which were described in some detail, including the electric cars which took Robin's attention.

"How do you keep track of your people," Tom wanted to know, "if they are scattered around?"

The overseer showed an electronic screen with a map of London's roads. Every so often a red dot flashed. "That will be one of our workers. When they go outside of London the vehicle itself will light up in blue as well. I always know where everyone is."

Spy in the sky, thought Robin, looking at Tom, intending that he should pick up that thought. "I want a printed copy of each of those maps. Can you do it from that system?"

"I'll do it straight away, sir, and you can show me which maps you want in what depth."

While the printing was being done, Robin continued with the questions. "Are all the roads on your maps passable?"

"Yes, sir, these are the approved routes. There may be other roads but there's no saying how good they are."

"Do you look after watercraft or sky craft of any kind? I currently have a whirly sky craft without a driver."

"No, sir, no water and no sky vehicles, and certainly nobody that can fly."

"Show me," said Robin, "who requests a vehicle, and how it goes through the system."

The tall man shifted uneasily in his chair and straightened his legs while pushing his back into the chair. "Usually we get a request in for something immediately. That means we have to have all possible vehicles ready to go out at a moment's notice. So as soon as one comes back in it is made ready to go out again, although that may be many months away. We have to be ready. You see that map on the wall? That's the area and route we cover for the London area. The big map shows the routes we take for the south. All the requests come in from a memo and I log it in this computer on my desk." Tom and Robin browsed the log to get familiar with the process and who might make a request.

"Tell me why that old electric coach was so noisy," said Tom. "Electric vehicles are supposed to be quiet."

"That's just some old metal stuff tied to the axles. I was ordered to do that for all electric vehicles because nobody could hear them coming."

"It has been overdone with that coach certainly. I take back the previous order, and order that you cut the noise so that it is possible to talk inside," Robin demanded.

"That I can do, your lordships. Perhaps you'd like to have one for your personal use? There are several that never go out. I can even let you have a charging point for it."

"I will take you up on that," Robin smiled at the idea of driving around from village to village. "I will, however, require 2 charging points. You can remove the tracking device as I won't need to be watched. It will need big wheels for rough ground."

The man smiled readily, happy that he had been able to do something to put him in the good books of a lord. "This way, your lordship, please come and make your choice."

The weaver had to support the tall man initially as he stood up, then they went out to the garages, where they found Paul and Andy at the end of their tour. Andy attempted to be sour, "Certainly room for some improvement, so don't forget to send those statistics in," he said to the master who had shown them around.

A brief smile of conspiracy passed from Robin to Paul and Andy . "We're going to choose our vehicle," Robin said, "come along you two."

"This car," said the tall man, "has enough space for 4 people easily, and room for plenty of things to be carried. It is called a rover, and as well as being able to plug it into get charged, it is also self-charging, so in theory it should retain its charge unless it is idle for too long."

The car was dusty on the outside but had a distinct green colour that appealed to Tom, as did the huge wheels. "That will get us over most of the rough land by the palace," Tom said.

The front door was opened, and Robin jumped into the driver's seat. The inside had the look and feel of something fresh, recently made, while the smell of it was most inviting. "It doesn't look like it has been used much. How old is it? You will need to show us the controls when you deliver it to us."

"It is as old as all the other cars. This was sealed away for nobody had any use of it until now. I will leave a driver with you for as long as you want, as long as you can feed him. He will be your instructor. We will get it polished up all over as well to protect the paintwork from the rough ground. Perhaps, it is possible, that I might even have the owner's guide. You will need to send it back here every year to get it maintained, and we will keep it working like new for you. Please tell us where we should deliver it."

The overseer was rewarded with a smile from Robin. "Do you know the palace on the east coast? I'm not aware of any proper roads, but if you can get it there that will prove its worth. Will it be ready to drive by next Thursday?"

"Next Thursday, of course," said the tall man, now in a happy frame of mind. "Yes, I know exactly where the palace is. I've been there a few times. It is very close to the river and has a jetty for watercraft. Known as the Gravesend palace I believe."

"I'll be expecting your driver at midday then," said Robin, closing the deal.

Weaver and the 3 lords headed back to the coach while Robin had a last word with the overseer of ground transportation. "Your operation seems to be well run. Contact me if you have any problems, and I will come back at some time. I wanted to ask why we do not build these cars ourselves? You seem to have expertise."

"Ah, thank you a thousand times, my lord for your good words. I am here to serve. Yes, we have some expertise, but nobody has ever been interested in making new cars. There are many parts that combine to make a car such as the rover, and that technology has been lost."

"OK," Robin said, "let me ask you this. Have you the knowledge and materials to build something that would help trade between villages. Too many villages are dying out. I have the task to make them more vibrant and trading easily between themselves is a major part of that. I'm thinking about carts that are not so hard to push. Is it possible to add some mechanism, some kind of motor that will make carts less of a burden to haul around?"

"My lord asks a lot of this humble soul. I am but a servant."

"You are a mechanic. You know enough to keep old vehicles running. I am asking you to use imagination and old skills to provide what I need. Set yourself and your workers this task. Create a design, a model. If you fail, you will not suffer. But I ask you to make that attempt. If you succeed you will be rewarded. I will return within one month."

*

"May I speak freely, my lord?" asked Weaver as the coach now almost silent made its way to a villa reserved for the use of lords.

"I expect that you will always speak your mind," answered Robin.

"The lords have never been interested in what we do here. Are things going to change?"

"Yes, most definitely, things are due to change. For too long we have allowed things to degenerate. Our workers and slaves grow weak in numbers and in body. That is one thing. I have the task to reverse that, to have us relearn those things we have forgotten. To make the workers more willing to toil without the risk of being beaten or abused for no good reason. We have much to do and I will take any help from those that will help. The old ways must improve."

"I noticed while you are demanding, you are not like the lords I have met before."

"Indeed," smiled Robin, "consider us to be the new version of the lords. We will reward hard work. Nobody has to be mistreated for pleasure. I hope you will take these values and enforce them within your factory."

"I understand," said Weaver, "but it sounds to be too good to be true, that our shackles will be loosened."

"Loosened but not yet totally removed. Not yet. We must do this gradually or the world will fall in on us. First, we get the idea out to stop unnecessary cruelty. Then we get the workers happier. A happy worker will produce much more than a beaten one."

Weaver looked like he might cry. "My lord. That sounds incredible. All my life I was beaten, just as I have beaten others. I can see the good in what you say, and I will pursue the aims you mention."

Robin looked closely at Weaver, estimating if he was being truly honest, deciding that he probably was, he placed a hand on his shoulder, "Weaver, if this world improves, it will be because of decent men like you. Do your best for our combined future."

*

At last the villa came into view. It was noticeable by the number of lights on in the building, which could be seen from some distance away. The coach entered into a long winding drive. On both sides the garden was extensive, and beautiful. The trees and bushes were still green, although some leaves were beginning to turn brown. It all made for a glorious welcoming sight.

A number of slaves were standing outside the elegant front entrance to await the lords' arrival. "Driver, take this man back to his factory, and return here at 8am tomorrow."

"Yes, sir."

Getting out of the coach, Robin approached the slave standing just a pace in front of the others, making sure he didn't get too close. "Are you in charge here?" demanded Robin in as harsh a voice as he could muster.

The small, wiry man stepped forward, better clothed and fed than the others, a short leather whip in his hand. "I am the house master, your lordship. How may I serve you?"

"Is this all the slaves you have to run this house?" There were 8 young people, and 2 elders, their ages impossible to guess. They all had ankle shackles and wore rags.

"These are the waiting slaves, your lordship. They keep the villa clean. The cook and others are preparing your meals inside, plus there are 10 butt-kids locked upstairs awaiting your pleasure."

"Who looks after the grounds?" Robin wanted to know.

"The resident lordship, when he returns, sir. He arranges for some labour from the prison camp."

"Seems I will have to take on that responsibility as well, because he will not be returning here," Robin snapped. "Show us around," having taken an instant dislike to the man.

Tom and the others restrained their disgust at seeing the sorry state of the slaves, knowing all too well that this was how all slaves were treated.

The entrance hall they passed into was sparkling and bright. Marble pillars lined the walls. Many artistic busts and decorative items, vases, figures and pictures, were on display either on shelves or in alcoves. This villa was clearly kept in good condition for the highest of London lords. "This way, your lordships," said the whip man, leading them into a sitting room with a large video unit, extensive bar and several comfortable lounge seats.

The man went down on his knees to grovel, "May I serve you some drinks?"

"Beers will suffice, for now," Tom answered for them all, not really wishing to engage with this man, even if he had some sympathy for his situation, for it was the system that had made him what he was. He watched the man closely as the beers were poured from bottles into long slim shiny glasses. "You may sit in the corner while we relax."

The man sat very close to something that was a prominent part of the palace they were now familiar with, clearly, he had no objection to it. They all frowned when they saw the TRIANGLE OF SUBSERVIENCE.

With half an eye on this man that he had come to despise so quickly, Tom sat down next to Robin who had taken out some of the maps. "There," said Robin, "this villa is even marked on this map."

"There are another 5," counted Andy , "just on the south side of the river. We really ought to inspect them."

"Agreed," said Robin, "but this one is the best located for our immediate needs, being close to the factories, and on a direct link to the road to the south." They finished their drinks and stood up. "We will eat now, what has been prepared?"

"If it pleases your lordships, the first course is beef barley soup. The main course is Salt-Baked Leg of Lamb with Olive Oil Potatoes. The dining room is this way." The man walked to the end of the room, opening a set of double doors to expose a table laden with fruit, and plates of different sizes that all glinted with golden artwork. They sat down, with Robin at the head of the table. "May I get the meal served, your highnesses?" He seemed to anticipate a positive response, walking quickly to a side wall and pulling a cord.

A moment later 4 of what must be the women kitchen staff, who were slightly better dressed than the waiting slaves, walked in, each with a tray holding a bowl of soup and crusty bread. This was gracefully served to each would-be lord, and they left.

Robin and the others found the array of cutlery very confusing, but dared not ask their slave what was what, instead they chose the biggest spoon and tucked in to the soup. "Hmm, very nice," said Robin, as the man served red wine, after which he went and sat in the far corner.

Andy spluttered over a mouthful of hot soup, a combination of breathing and swallowing at the same time, but the house master looked across with alarm all over his face. Andy quickly recovered after drinking some water and continued to enjoy his starter. Meanwhile, the uneasy master had gone into the kitchen, small whip in hand. He came back, smiling, "I've punished the person responsible for that," he said.

Tom looked up, furious, but a glance from Robin calmed him enough to carry on eating.

When the main course came out, the woman serving Andy was seen to limp, causing Tom to see red again, but he restrained himself once more, diverting his attention to the food which was exceptional.

"We have a superior kitchen here," Tom said, after the meal was eaten and everything cleared away. "We must inspect it and see what it is capable of."

The master didn't like that idea. No lords had ever wanted to see anything beyond the luxurious rooms they inhabited, and he was beginning to have doubts about these lords. They were surely not used to high luxury, and they ate like common villagers.

Tom led the way into the kitchen area, anxious to stop any more abuse of the slaves. The 4 women and 2 other helpers were stood at work surfaces either washing, cleaning or preparing some food. A big woman, in addition, stood at the end of the row, watching and giving orders. The master went and stood next to this woman. With the lords' attention elsewhere, the master whispered several things to this woman. She looked up with sad, hard eyes at the lords, initially in fear, then whispered something back.

Robin had noticed the interchange, "So you are the amazing cook?" he said, looking her up and down. Physically she was nothing to admire. She was better fed than the rest, but older and somehow more broken, yet still fighting for something.

"We wanted to come and thank you for a most excellent meal," said Tom, looking at the 6 slaves and master cook in turn. "Now you must all eat, for you look tired. House master, obtain 8 bowls for the workers here, yourself and your good woman."

The house master was perplexed, "but, your lordships, slaves are not allowed to eat the same food as your lordships."

"I insist," stated Tom, with some venom showing in his eyes. "I'm in a good mood tonight. I want to see you rewarded for your good work."

The house master did as he was told, and the master cook ladled out some of the soup into each bowl. Tom passed a bowl to each slave in turn, telling them to eat it. They did so reluctantly, wondering how they would be punished for this. Tom watched as the bowls were emptied, satisfied that 6 slaves had eaten well for a change.

"Show me," said Robin to the cook, while Tom started to inspect the slaves for damage, "the larder and deep freeze." The larder was as big as the dining room, stocked with every possible commodity and then some. A gigantic walk-in freezer was almost as big, and this was full of animal carcasses and food items that needed to be kept very cold. "Impressive, but how do you keep it so full? Where do you get your supplies from?"

The woman pointed at the house master, "He. He sends an order."

Robin could see that Tom was becoming heated, having looked the 6 slaves over, he found bruises and cuts by the score. Addressing the cook, "You and these slaves will now go to your rest. Tomorrow morning we will eat breakfast at 7am. Be ready."

"Yes, sir, a full breakfast will be waiting for you," she said, confused.

Cook directed the 6 out of a back door, but before she left, she glanced briefly at the house master as if asking permission, but his face was blank.

"Now, house master, there are some things you need to relearn," Robin said, urging him and Tom into the lounge area. He quietly asked Andy and Paul to follow the cook to see where they slept. Back to the house master, he said, "You have been taught to abuse slaves for any slight fault. You may sit down on the floor if you wish." The man reluctantly sat down, staring at Robin with mixed emotions. "It is no longer permissible to punish slaves without a very good reason." Disagreement mixed with confusion in his facial expressions reflected his inner turmoil. "Do you understand this?"

"Yes, sir, no, sir, how will I keep them in line? They won't work if I don't hit them."

"Other ways must be found," insisted Robin. The man was nodding but clearly having an internal discussion.

"Sir, what happened to the other lords?" he said with confusion. "I understood the old ways. Now I don't know."

"Can you not show some kindness, some compassion?" demanded Tom.

"I'm too worried, when the real lords come back, I will be in trouble. You're not like them. Are you from the villages?"

"The old lords will not be coming back," insisted Robin. "We are the new lords, and we are bringing in new ways. You don't need to know where we came from."

"Yes, sir. Can I get on and do my work now, sir, lock up the house and order supplies?"

"OK," said Robin, exasperated, "but first show us to our sleeping quarters."

They followed the house master upstairs, where a dozen or so luxury bedrooms with en-suite were situated. Each room had a full wardrobe of clothing. The man excused himself to complete his chores, with Tom following him unnoticed.

Andy and Paul passed Tom on the stairs as he was going down, and found Robin searching through cupboards. "Well," said Andy , "the conditions are not so bad. The cook has her own tiny room. Looks like our house master sleeps there as well, but that's better than him abusing the kids."

"Please check where the butt-kids are and see if we can do anything to relieve their suffering without giving ourselves away." They went on another search.

Tom had watched the house master as he took the waiting slaves into a room in the basement, slapping and tripping them as he locked them up. After closing the main door and 3 open windows, he went downstairs again to another room. Peeping around the door, Tom realised that this was a memo station, assuming that the man was going to put an order in for some food. It was hard to see what the kitchen could possibly need, so Tom quietly moved close enough to see what was being typed.

The house master was not just slow on the keyboard, he was uncertain where each letter was, so there was a gap of several seconds between each letter. The to address was the one that Robin used, that would have been generated automatically, which was strange for Tom had never seen requests for supplies. He thought it should have gone to a supply group. Slowly, the sentences were formed, causing Tom to see a very deep shade of red, 'MY LORDS, PLEASE HELP. FROM VILLA BECKHAM. 4 PEOPLE ARE HERE PRETENDING TO BE LORDS. THEY ARE S.'

Tom had seen enough. He yanked the man out of his chair before he could do anything else and threw him into the corridor. "You really do not have any compassion for anyone, do you?"

"I serve the real lords," the man shouted. "Not the likes of you pretenders. You could never be lords. Too soft. I know how to be a lord. You will always be ignorant villagers."

"Thank you for that," said Tom, "that helps me to justify what I am about to do so much easier." He poked the man with his knife, made him stand up, marched him out the front door, then around to the back. An extensive lawned garden made their passage easy as they walked to the end of a very long yard, Tom's knife now drawing blood.

The man began to squeal, not really forming sentences, trying to express some hateful thoughts.

"You die as the worst example of what the old lords could create. You're the product of hate and deceit, and there is no longer any room for you in this world." The knife dug deeper, the man struggled, tried to shout, but the knife went further in pinning the man against a wire fence. Blood squirted against Tom's arms as he pushed the knife into the hilt and cut across towards his spine. The man was still alive, groaning and cursing. Too many bones were getting in the way of a good clean cut through to the heart. Tom removed the knife, turned his victim around, slicing into his neck as he came level. The body drooped, and the man was almost silent save for air escaping his lungs. For being so short the man was heavy and it took all of Tom's strength to lift the body over the wire fence and throw it into the brambles beyond.

The effort had drained Tom, not just the physical element, but the sordid task of taking a life, even with the many justifications he had ready to explain to Robin. He went back upstairs, his face a picture of regret and loathing. He looked Robin in the eye once. There was in the end no need for an explanation. Robin knew. He simply said, "You'd better take a look at the memo console in the basement," after which he went into a spare room, closed and locked the door, then spent the next 30 minutes under a hot shower, trying to wash away his hate for the old system, and his disgust at his own crimes.

Andy and Paul had found the butt-kids upstairs, frightened as hell, wondering if their time had come, but otherwise in a reasonable state, save for a few bruises. Paul found some food in the kitchen and passed it through to the kids. The room was warm enough, so that was about all that they could do for those that had been under a sentence of death.

*

The morning brought a refreshed Tom, in a better mood, having thought out the implications of his actions the night before. He found a fresh suit to wear, made himself smart and entered the kitchen where the cook was only halfway ready.

"Sorry, sir," said the cook, all perturbed, "the high lord told me 7am to be ready."

"Keep to that time," Tom smiled. "I wanted to tell you something. The house master has left us. We will need you to take charge of the villa for a short time. Can you do that?"

Before she could answer, Robin who had entered just behind Tom, came and stood the other side of her, realising what Tom had in mind. "You are the most senior worker here now."

"I am," she said, "I don't know everything that the house master used to do, but I can try if it pleases your lordships."

"Did you once live in a village?" asked Tom, "and would you like to go back to living in a small house in a rural village where the master doesn't beat or abuse you?"

The woman looked surprised then delighted. "That sounds like heaven, but who will do the work here?"

"We can talk about that, but we just want you to know that things are changing for the better," said Tom. "No person should have to be beaten. We are reshaping our world, and with your help we can make it better."

"After we leave today," Robin said, "I want you to make sure all the slaves here are well fed, each day. Find them some clothes to wear and make them clean. In about 10 days' time I will send for you, and we can talk about your future. If you decide you want to come back and live here that will be fine. It will be your choice."

"I don't know what to say," said the cook. "I will keep everyone well fed, close the villa down in 10 days' time, and wait to be collected." Her smile was so genuine she suddenly looked 10 years younger.

*

Eschewing the idea that they should take some slaves back with them, Tom, Robin, Paul and Andy ate a most enjoyable breakfast, sampling what they considered delicacies, before getting into the coach that took them to the railway. Everyone was very polite, propitious even, while the platform and train were somewhat cleaner. Even the carriages were looking better, now altered as directed by Robin. When they reached Crayford station, they headed straight back to the cavern to share their news with Lucy and whoever might be there. Andy and Paul soon left them to head for their own villages.

The news from the 2 spies was interesting. David and George were still visiting the establishments that Robin had suggested. Their reports which they sent back via the memo system were concise if a little short on detail, but they did confirm that they had identified the purposes of the establishments and that they had not run into a major problem.

Tom, Robin, Jane and Anne were sat around in the cavern, on some comfy seating arrangement that Lucy had set up, drinking tea and taking snacks. Lucy was wrapped around her man in a most loving pose.

"We are making some kind of progress," admitted Tom, "but are we going too fast? Apart from any actions resulting from what George and David find, we have several other things going on. Baker will be meeting us at the palace on Wednesday, and we need to work out what we want to say to him. The next day we get the car delivered, and that will mean several days at or around the palace getting to know how to use it. Our promise was made to collect Cook and the kids from the villa, but we haven't decided yet where they will live, and if we are moving them then they will need their chips removing, which in turn will require an overnight stay at the villa for 2 healers."

"That's a pretty tall list," admitted Robin. "I see it as spreading our seed, as much as anything else. We did make some useful contacts and understand so much more about how the system works. I agree though, please rein me in if I am going too far, too fast."

"So you don't think I was reckless for disposing of that house master?" asked Tom.

"I can see why you did it, and if you hadn't, we could have been in trouble from some direction, so no," said Robin, "we are on the same track when it comes to ex-slaves or masters that fight against us."

Tom nodded in acknowledgement. "We probably need time to digest what we've learned. I suggest you spend a few days curled up with Lucy, relax, mull things over and we can all meet up here on Tuesday, ready for our trek to the palace."

"Who shall we take with us?" asked Robin. "Adam and Paul are quite experienced but maybe we should introduce others to the luxuries of the lords?"

"I would suggest that we use Andy and one of his assistants, Larry, to handle removal of the chips for those at the villa. Then Paul and perhaps Marty can come with us to the palace."

"Hmm, OK," agreed Robin, "you know these people better than I do. But just thinking about Wednesday. We could do with some slaves around to make things look natural to Baker, and to the car driver."

Lucy stood up with a cheeky smile on her face, and bowed low to Robin, "I am forever your slave, oh lord."

"You want to go on that long trek, get your legs scratched and keep us fed as well. An interesting idea," said Robin, "but you'd have to wear something with a few holes in to make you look like a worker rather than a princess."

"I've saved my old dress," Lucy responded. "The one you first saw me in. That would be perfect, and we must take Anne and Jane. They would also love to get away from the cavern for a change."

"What about it?" Robin looked at the 2 younger girls. "It is a long walk."

Jane smiled at the invitation while Anne said, "I want to see the palace, please."

"Sounds like that is settled then," said Tom. "We even have our own slaves to beat."

"Don't you dare even think about that," declared Lucy, smiling, and pointing a severe finger at Tom.

"I hope the weather isn't going to turn just yet," said Robin, changing the subject.

"Agreed," said Tom. "We've had some pretty stable weather since we escaped. Let's hope that will continue."

"We could always go and live in the palace or even the villa," suggested

Robin, smiling. "Something to think about, perhaps."

"Perhaps," agreed Tom, a little negatively.

"What I'd like to know," said Lucy, "if we have got rid of so many of the lords, what is our final aim?"

"As it's always been," said Tom, "total freedom."

"We continue as we started," said Robin. "We eliminate the oppression, educate ourselves on what happened, as well as getting better fed and stronger in every possible way. Fundamentally we must get to completely understand the system that has been put in place and use it to our advantage."

*

David and George arrived at the cavern on the third evening after the adventure to London had been fully discussed. They had plenty of news to add to the general feeling of high spirits that things were going in their favour. Tumbling over each other, verbally, they outlined what they had discovered from the first 3 locations, which they considered vital to tell in person.

"Let me make sure I fully get this," Robin interrupted, "the first place you looked over was a formal building of some kind. Did it have books like our library, or was it more the sort of place where important matters were decided?"

"A little of both," agreed David. "There were books certainly, that seemed to be about the way the lords ran things."

"That was only part of it though," interrupted George. "There were shiny benches where people could sit in opposition to each other, so it could be where law was talked about or settled on."

"Yes," David continued, "we couldn't get right inside to the inner rooms because there was a dozen or so lords walking about the place with their noses in books. If we'd stayed any longer, we would have been found out."

"Interesting," said Robin. "Now what is your estimation of how that could be useful to us? Was there anything that would help us?"

"It probably wouldn't take much to capture the lords. They are mainly old ones, but without being able to hear and see what was going on behind closed doors, it was impossible to find out more."

"OK," said Robin. "I'll put that one on my list to visit dressed up as a lord. That uniform works wonders."

They looked at him with the thought he was a little mad but nodded anyway.

"Oh, I'll be taking you 2 along with me just in case of trouble, but not just yet, there are plenty of other things I have to do. What about the second property you visited?"

"That was a wire compound holding about 300 people. I'd call it a prison camp, as they all looked more miserable than we used to look in the villages," said George. "They took people inside this single-storey building every so often, but when they came out, they could hardly stand. So some sort of torture going on as well."

"The interesting thing I noticed," said David, "was that the gate to the compound was not locked, just like village gates. The masters could pass through easily, but when a prisoner tried the same thing, meaning to attempt to escape, the little lights came on at the security post, and the guy was blasted with something until he collapsed. All automatic. After that he was dragged back inside, unconscious."

"Sounds painful," said Robin. "That must have been some kind of electrical field he triggered when the thing recognised the chip in his head. Very nasty. We must find a way to get them released."

"Strange that these were only grown men," offered George, "no kids, and no women that we could see."

"They must have been special problems for reasons known only to the lords," said Robin. "Better make sure we don't end up there."

They all thought that consideration over in their minds, increasing the intention to be very careful in what they did.

"You will like the third place even more," said David, interrupting the moment of quiet. "It took us a long time to work out what it was all about, and I do admit we were less than careful."

"It is quite a place," admitted George. "The grounds were beautiful, with great trees and bushes, with beautiful fields of manicured grass beds." Robin got the idea, but would have called the grass beds lawns, now that he knew how keen the lords were on fine gardens. "There were several big houses in a similar style to the first one we investigated, but even grander. The biggest we found when we crept inside was used as luxury sleeping rooms for the lords. Dozens of fantastic looking rooms."

"There seems to be a specific routine," said David. "We were able to sneak in there because the young lords were all taken out to walk around the grounds, while the slaves tended to the garden. We were unable to get inside the other buildings for a while because there were lots of people going in and out of them. Quite a few older lords, along with plenty of slaves."

"We finally got in well after midnight when all activities had stopped," George said. "The doors were unlocked, they didn't have security devices on, so we were reasonably safe. It was a shock what we saw though. Each section of the room had a great many tubes, they were blue with liquid bubbles, and something was growing inside. The ones closest to the door were very small, and we couldn't recognise what they were. It was only when we looked at some other tubes in a different row where the thing inside was bigger, that we came to understand what was going on."

"Can you believe," said David, "they were growing bodies of lords in those blue tubes. We saw them, from small baby sizes to teenagers. It was a total shock."

"Growing bodies for lords. That is too incredible," said Robin.

"We were totally dazed with the idea," admitted George, "which was why we hung around. We found a place to hide, to learn more. We saw how they moved the tubes from close to the door to the next frame. They talked about adding things, chemicals I think, but even over one night the things had got visibly bigger."

"We were just getting ready to make our escape when an old lord came into the building and told everyone to speed up the process," said George. "He told them that since so many lords had died it was up to them to get new lords ready in the shortest possible time, and they should skip some steps."

"We wondered if we should smash the place up, but that would have taken us all night, and we'd have been found for sure. We sneaked out as soon as we could to come back and let you know," said David apologetically.

"You did the right thing," Robin said. "Your role was to spy and report what you'd found, which was done with great merit. Well done to both of you. I have a better way to handle this body factory. It's still a little before midnight. A little early for what I have in mind. Let's relax and talk about something else."

Lucy had gone to her bed, alone, which allowed Robin and the others to snack on some ginger biscuits she had made. "I've been thinking," said Robin to George and David. "We really could do with more clever guys like you 2, who can go observe things that are going on, so that we can make plans and react accordingly. How would you like to start a school for spies?"

They both smiled, thinking it was a great idea. "A spy class in every village. I can just see it," said George.

"Why not?" smiled Robin. "Every army, every movement in history, and I've read about a lot, was only successful because they knew their enemies, and what they were doing, how they operated. We still have a heck of a lot to learn about how this oppressive society works. You'd have to set out guidelines for how spies should operate. How to be successful. That does, however, mean that you 2 would have to learn your trade very well. Get on the internet and find out how to be secretive, how to avoid capture, what tools you can use. Don't take it all too literally. In the past they made spies look romantic. It is a deadly game. You would need to concentrate on the basic points of survival in hostile territory. Here," he said, giving each a book with 007 in the title. "Do not take these novels to heart. They tell exactly how you should not operate. Remember the rules: observe, be invisible, stay alive, get out safely, report back what has been found, do not make up a new plan while on a mission."

George and David stared at the books for a moment, digesting what Robin had said. "It is beginning to sound very serious," said David, realising what they were taking on.

"Don't ever consider it serious, because then you will fail. Keep it light, inject some fun into it, but if it becomes serious then something is wrong. We are playing an important game here to strip away the power from the lords. We can win this by holding on to what we have achieved. That can only happen if we keep pushing against the boundaries in a safe way so as not to expose ourselves. Now don't worry, we can go over all of this before you start teaching others."

Both smiled back, content, but still a little worried. "Seems like we have a lot to learn."

Fetching and opening his PC, Robin activated the browse function, "What are the coordinates for that last place you spied on?" He was told and he pinpointed the exact location. The villa wasn't so easy to spot as it was mostly dark, meaning it took a while until David and George could accurately identify the buildings concerned. All told there were 4 buildings, close together, but each would require several shots of the beam to wipe out. Robin practised moving around the area.

"You know what I'm going to do, don't you?" asked Robin. "You are probably wondering about the slaves, and yes, I hate the fact that they will be hurt, but sometimes there are things you must do. Thanks to your intelligence work, we have the opportunity to strike a big blow against tyranny, and at the same time reduce the number of lords being in our country."

Strangely things started to happen around the grand house. Lights came on, and people started to move around, some went into the low building containing the blue tubes, with some being brought outside. "We've been found out!"

Hitting the strike beam as fast as he could, Robin manipulated the view and direction of beam to reduce the birth incubation chamber to rubble very quickly, but by this time the young lords were piling out of the bigger house and scattering. He now had more targets than he could easily deal with. "It is vital we take out every possible lord," he said, keeping the beam wide and targeting those now walking away across the lawn.

"They won't like that," said George, "the grass is going to be very far from green when they see it after you are done, if they get to see it."

Robin worked at finding and eliminating the moving targets. He searched all around but couldn't be certain that he had removed these threats to humanity. Now he concentrated on hitting the other buildings, putting ash and broken materials where once had stood fine accommodations.

"Were there any other places they might run to in the area?" Robin asked.

"I'm afraid some have escaped."

"Just the trees all around the estate," suggested David.

Robin searched some more but all he found was ashes. "I'll look again when it gets light."

The 3 of them dozed restlessly until the morning broke through. Robin was the first to stretch and immediately turned to his PC. There was some movement on the ground, to which he zoomed in. An older lord was walking amongst the wreckage, making attempts to salvage some things, although little was recognisable as being useful. The man's face was turned upwards as he scanned the empty blue sky, clearly yelling something into the breeze that was more anger than real sentences.

Zooming the view closer to the ground, the man became large, his pasty face visible, his unshaven chin tilted up in arrogance. He lifted his arm, waving his fist at the gods, seemingly, but to Robin it was a direct confrontation, as though the man could perceive him watching. More angry words followed, as Robin's memory started to work. This face he knew. It belonged to a lord from that party they had watched at the palace. No longer was Robin feeling sympathy for the destruction he had caused at this estate. It took but a split second of remembering the shocked and hopeless faces of those kids lined up to give pleasure to the lords. "Rot in hell," he cried aloud as he hit the button to fry one evil creature and to annihilate this satanic manifestation.

Closing the PC, Robin told David and George to make themselves comfortable, and stay as long as they wanted to. He headed for the warmth of Lucy's bed. Still half asleep, as Robin crawled under the covers to hug her closely, she knew he had done something horrible. This was his way to seek redemption, and some relief.

CHAPTER 6

CONSOLIDATION

"WE HAVE A LOT GOING on this week, and we must get it right. So much hangs on what we do in the next few days," Robin reiterated as he made sure his backpack had everything in it that he might possibly need in the coming days.

"Will we do as your slaves?" Lucy asked, smiling, dressed in an old rag of a dress. Anne and Jane had similar attire.

"Far too clean I'm afraid," Robin answered. "Besides, I don't see any cuts and bruises. We'll have to do something about that." He grabbed Lucy, lifting her up to make her giggle. "I hope all of your legs are ready for a good walk. You will need to wear something heavier and more protective until we get to the palace."

"Oh, we can manage," said Anne, with a cheeky smile. "We are tougher than we look."

"Where are Tom and the others?" said an impatient Robin. "I want to make an early start."

"Yelp," went Digga, announcing that the visitors had arrived: Tom, Paul, Marty, Andy and Larry. They all had their own personal equipment with them, including a small PC each that Robin had acquired for them.

*

They went the direct route to the palace, arriving mid-afternoon after a stop to rest weary legs and to eat. The dogs ran on ahead to sniff out if anybody had been around except for them. Digga came back to Robin as he was going through the gate, wagging her tail to say that all was OK.

"It is getting a bit rundown here. It really looks neglected," Tom mentioned, "it could do with a woman's touch." Lucy gave him a frown, not being very keen on the idea of getting such a large place cleaned up. "Perhaps I meant a decorator's touch," admitted Tom smiling.

"It has seen better days for sure, but do you think we should get some labour to renovate it? Indeed, should we keep it permanently occupied," asked Robin, "to keep up appearances?"

"Something we should consider," said Tom.

While Tom and Paul went inside to make sure nobody was lurking, Lucy insisted on walking completely around the grounds outside of the property, admiring it and appraising it, but also noting where repairs were needed, especially the garden that was overgrown.

"It looks in places like it has seen a lot of misery," Jane insisted.

"You are not wrong there," Robin agreed. "It is a beautiful old house though, and we should try to improve its image."

Having seen the palace from the outside and completed her evaluation, Lucy then wanted to see the inside. She turned her nose up at the scruffy lounge area but took note of the big graphic on the wall showing the triangle of subservience. "Now that is something I would love to change," she said. "Maybe I will bury it somewhere."

"This is the kitchen area," said Robin, pulling his woman by the hand to look at the well-stocked cupboards to distract her from anything drastic.

She broke away, saying, "I didn't come here to just dwell in the kitchen like some poor fodder slave. After all, you've told me of the sleeping rooms and the comfortable beds that high lords sleep in, I want to see some of the luxury this palace has to offer."

"This way, my lady," Tom obliged, taking her hand and showing her the way upstairs, having completed his inspection to make sure it was safe. The 2 girls followed, and soon there were appreciative, "oohs," and "aahs," coming from upstairs.

"Looks like they prefer the sleeping quarters to the kitchen," said Larry. "Maybe we should see what they are getting excited about. I've never seen a real bed."

"By all means, but don't let the girls go up any more levels," said Robin. "It's not very nice up there, and neither is the cellar."

*

The girls did tire of the bedrooms, deciding they would take stock of what the kitchen had to offer. The boys retired to the hidden study to go over what was happening in the next few days, and what goals they were setting.

Robin introduced the first challenge, "Baker will be here tomorrow. Of the 4 masters he seemed to treat his workers best. I want to get him more used to the idea that he doesn't have to beat or ill-treat anybody. He is a good source of general knowledge, so we should get anything out of him regarding what he knows about how the lords did things, especially where they did specific functions. I asked him to bring the plans for the factory, along with full details of suppliers and customers, location and quantities of materials used or created. We can use those details to get him talking about anything to our advantage. My view is that information is key to whatever we will be doing, how we progress and so on."

"Makes a lot of sense," said Andy. "The more we know about what we are up against, the easier, I hope, things will get."

Tom wanted to know, "Who will be playing slaves for the purpose of the next few days?"

"I don't mind," said Andy. "It will save me having to make myself all smart and lordly."

Marty agreed, "I still haven't gotten used to nice clothes with hardly any holes in, so that would suit me as well. Just don't go abusing me too much."

"You'll be safe here," Tom replied seriously to Marty. "The people we take offence at are the snotty masters that stay loyal to the lords and gods. Probably best if you 2 stay mainly in the kitchen while visitors are here. Take the occasional walk through the lounge to make it look like you are working."

*

As they were all sitting down to eat dinner Tom voiced a thought that most of them had, "In a way it would be nice to live here. Make it our headquarters, perhaps. It might be more realistic when we do invite visitors here. If we are going to be using this palace regularly, we really should keep people here all the time to maintain it and keep it ready for whatever usage we put it to."

"Yes," agreed Robin, "it is a shame it has been allowed to get shabby. I'm sure we can entice some people to come and live in a bit of luxury. What do you think, Lucy, would you like to live here?"

"Maybe. I will have to consider that question. Apart from anything else, everything could do with a good wash. Especially the bed sheets," announced Lucy. "That is something that badly needs to be organised."

"We should have brought Eric along," said Tom. "He would know how they kept everything working."

"Perhaps we can get him here sometime soon," said Robin. "I'm considering inviting all village chiefs for a bit of a conference."

*

Baker arrived well after a luxury breakfast had been consumed by those in the palace, and even though the treats he had brought along were tempting, they put them aside for later.

"We've taken over this palace," Robin stated, "but I'm afraid it was left in an awful state by the last owner. For now it will do, until we can get the labour to improve on it."

To Baker's eyes, the lounge was a little worn, but still far better than what he was used to. "So much of where we live, and work has not been looked after. It is a good thing you are now putting some attention on such things, or it could happen that we are unable to produce goods in future," Baker said.

He received an affirmative nod from Robin.

Maps and plans of Baker's factory were spread around the room on different tables. "This is a good map of London, but can you identify some of the places marked?" asked Robin. "I still don't have a good perspective on how the systems flowed. You will of course be aware that a good number of lords were recently killed, which is why we are trying to pick up the pieces, even though this was not our area."

Baker was plainly shocked, "Killed? No I didn't know about that. That is awful. I'm glad you were around to keep things together."

"Yes," said Robin, a little impatience creeping into his tone. "Now what about these locations?"

Baker went on to tell what he knew about the smaller offices around, where lords had worked from, or where some technology existed. Anything that Robin didn't scribble down on the map was noted down on a PC by Paul.

"Are those old roads marked faintly on your map?"

"Yes," agreed Baker. "A lot of them are overgrown, and hard to find."

"Hmm," said Robin. "That is something I want to improve as well."

After this Baker went on to explain in some detail the process flow in his factory and where he had problems.

"I noticed a lot of the metalwork was tarnished," Robin interjected. "Think about what needs to be done to bring everything up to a high standard. Also, I'd like to see more rye loafs baked each day and distributed initially to villages in the south. Check out if there is enough space to increase the savoury pies you produce also. Make plans for how you can do these things."

Baker looked rather perplexed, but didn't complain, "I'll have to make myself a note of this." He took a small notepad from his top pocket, writing in it what he recalled, "more rye loafs, to south villages, more savoury pies, improve metalwork, make plans for more production. OK I've got that."

"It must be time to take a tea break," said Tom, who had been eyeing the luscious looking pastries that Baker had brought with him. "Shall I order a brew?"

"Please do, I'm parched," said Robin. "Give that cord a pull."

*

A few minutes later they were enjoying the tea the female slaves had brought in, along with several sweet pieces each which Baker had delivered. "Delicious," they all agreed, causing Baker's face to smile happily. The girls had made an effort to look dirty for the guest but had definitely overdone the blue marks on their arms meant to emulate bruises, for even Baker could see the fruit pips. Lucy managed to look guilty as she went back to the kitchen.

Robin left Tom, Paul and Larry to get further details from Baker, while he checked for any new memos on the console in the private office. There were the usual village requests for goods requiring approval, which he didn't hesitate to approve. He was more interested though in taking a fresh look at the location he had incinerated. When he had it on the viewer, he didn't see anything fresh, nor any sign of anybody that might have escaped. He still felt guilty about the casual murdering of so many though.

He switched the viewer to the prison camp to get a better idea of the layout, and was able to see how much land was used. Apart from a series of huts there were no guards, just the electronic gate, which was bigger than most. A good number of prisoners were just walking aimlessly around. He could feel their despair, wondering what they might have done to get extra punishment. He was interrupted in his thoughts by the arrival of the car to pick up Baker.

He walked the master out to the car, saying, "There was one other thing I need to tell you. Please be careful about one of your assistants. The guy who was covered in flour. I called him White if you recall? Do you know who I mean?"

"Yes, I know who you mean. That man has always been a pain, but I've managed to keep him under control so far. What has he done?"

"It is more a case of what he will do. I understand you are due to get extra workers at some point. Make sure you have handled him well before that time, I will leave it to you what you do with him and his buddies, but they are no friends of yours. Do not let him take over."

Baker was shocked. "So he's planning something is he? I'll teach him. I won't ask how you found out, your lordship, but I thank you humbly for the information."

"We look after those that help us," said Robin. "If there is anything you need, let me know, otherwise I will expect to see your improvement plans in about one month's time."

*

Leaving Lucy to gently doze and luxuriate in the soft fabrics of a comfortable, huge bed, Robin needed to be up and busy the next morning, with something, anything. For some strange reason he was fascinated with the idea of having a car to drive around in. It would certainly make it easier to get about, but then he worried about how he would manage to control it. The idea of driving something mechanical was still very alien, even if rather appealing.

Impatience drove him up to the top of the building, where the slaves had been held. It still had an odd smell when he looked around but saw nothing that would take his attention away or even hold it temporarily. The stairs to the roof tempted him, and he soon found himself standing close to the whirly flyer. He pulled the door open, touched the seats, but simply could not imagine how the controls could relate to moving the thing through the air.

Moving away from the mysterious machine, towards the wall that surrounded the rooftop, he saw how much of the land had been reclaimed by nature. Looking out across the great abandoned wasteland, his eyes sought any movement, without success. The occasional trail of smoke from fires met his gaze, but these were quite far away and mostly in the direction of London. He'd never spent time looking over the layout of the land, now he did, plotting it in his mind, imagining where the old roads might be, and where they could be salvaged. He visualised a pattern of wide pathways linking up the important locations, at least important for the people, the ex-slaves.

Turning towards the water, the mist was still clinging to the great river in places, even where the water was moving, he again sought movement by people, lords, or even gods, but all was still. The birds sang, the trees rustled, while the sun tried hard to warm the cold air that had been left behind by the night. He rarely noticed the cold, for some curious reason, he was aware though that there were many other things he could be concerned about. He worried mostly that the complete message of how their slavery had been created with many great deceptions in the last century had not been fully understood by enough villagers. Most people were aware of how vicious the lords and masters could be, but failed to understand that the situation they were in didn't happen naturally. It came about because of a concerted effort to destroy the old society so that a golden elite could live off the backs of slaves, while abusing the young and drinking their blood. He felt his blood pressure rise with these thoughts.

Turning his head towards the London area Robin concentrated on the shapes and the vague outline of the skyline. He knew it was very different from what it had been, but from images he had seen, he knew it used to be spectacular compared to what it had become. He wished he had brought his binocular glasses up with him, but was distracted by a gentle nudge to the leg. "Hello, Digga," he said, stroking her raised head.

"Yelp," went Digga, as if to say, "what are you doing up here so early?" Followed by a slow, "Yelp," meaning, "isn't it time for breakfast yet?"

Robin laughed, knowing only too well when Digga wanted something. He went back down to the kitchen to seek an early breakfast for them both. For Digga there was some sliced meat, but as soon as that was available, several other little dogs appeared to be fed as well. Robin made himself some hot buttered toast, as the freezer was packed with frozen bread, which took only minutes to defrost and get toasted inside a special device.

Relaxing in the lounge, he told Digga, who had eaten enough by now and had joined him on the couch, all about the difficulties of life that were piling up on him. "I feel like I'm living a fantasy," he told her. "So many things have changed, not just for me, but for all the people we have touched, yet I'm so afraid. I'm afraid that it will all unravel, and the lords will crush us in an instant."

Hearing noises downstairs, Paul had walked quietly down, and stood listening to the outpouring.

"If you hadn't been there for me, Digga, none of this would have happened. I will always love you for helping me to become free." He looked Digga in the eye, "You know, sometimes I feel I'm imagining all of this that has happened, and I will awake once more, back in the village, in the nightmare life we had before."

Digga, lying next to Robin, nudged his arm, as if to say, "you were the first human I could trust. You have given me plenty, so anything I gave you was well earned. Thank you." She licked his face gently, as he rubbed her belly and held her close.

Robin continued, "How can I tell if I'm leading things in the right direction? How will I know if we are going wrong? I wish I had certainty."

Digga had spotted 2 others quietly joining Paul at the bottom of the stairs but kept quiet. They listened also, interested that Robin was talking so openly about his concerns.

"So what are we going to do with the villa, and this place? I don't want to be alone making the important decisions, but just like me, everyone is feeling their way. Nothing is predetermined. We've made a good start, I feel, but I shudder, and worry at how it might all go wrong, how it could end badly." Digga pushed her nose into his neck and whined gently. "It's alright for you," he said, "but if I do something wrong it will have an impact on many others."

Digga yelped again, looking him right in the eyes without blinking, then gently bit his nose.

"Thanks. Well, OK," Robin continued. "We have plenty to do and even more to think about. I can't sit around all day being idle, even if you can." He sighed heartily, "But damn it, Digga," he said with explosive frustration, "this is all well above my capability level. I'm in way over my head, and I'm scared to hell that I will let everyone down. There are no ready-made plans for getting out of serfdom, and if we ever do, how do we create a new, decent society where everyone can thrive and live well? I seem to be driven in trying to make things better that I don't fully understand."

Digga rolled over onto her back, encouraging Robin to stroke her belly some more.

"Come on, let's go back on the roof. Looking out over the land helps to settle my nerves somewhat." He grabbed his glasses while the 3 listeners disappeared back up the stairs, embarrassed for listening in, but also feeling sympathy for what rested on Robin's shoulders, for he was the visionary amongst them, and without him, they knew, there would be no concerted effort to achieve something better.

*

The coolness of the morning had faded a little as Robin walked around the roof. It was big, but it was likely that the whirly machine needed plenty of space. *I wouldn't like to be in its way*, he thought. He changed his attention, and focused his field glasses towards London. He could see so much more than with his naked eyes. There were even a few cars travelling along the pathways that were once roads. Digga quickly became bored and left him to his observations. In the direction of the great river, on the far bank, many buildings were visible, some glass structures, some of stone, but all fascinating to his mind. He felt an urgent need to go and explore, but he knew he was restrained by what was really important. "Having personal transportation was vital," he told himself. "It would make a difference."

As the sun rose higher it glinted against metallic constructions, making viewing a little tiresome. He decided it was time to get back to work and respond to the large number of memos he received these days.

*

It seemed like almost the middle of the day when the car turned up. Robin had been concentrating so much on getting through a list of approvals that he had even missed the big breakfast Lucy had prepared. The horn from the car told him it was time to think about other things, beckoning him outside, joined by the other would-be lords.

The driver was known to them, and he stood smartly outside the car with a smile of welcome. The car was shining having been richly waxed and polished. They walked around the rover, admiring it, touching it, then Robin made a decision. "Let's go inside and discuss the theory before we try to jump in it and crash it. Come with us, driver and bring the instructions."

The driver, with 4 smartly dressed lords, sat around the dining table, and the driver was told to explain how the car worked. He did so with the 2 male slaves looking on and paying great attention. Lucy brought in the tea, and a bun for Robin left over from Baker's visit.

The driver was thorough, really knowing his subject. He showed illustrations from the manual, as well as making sketches to show the finer points of what he was explaining.

"So," said Tom, "we must keep the roof surface clean so that the sun can warm the car up to give it energy?"

"Not quite," said the driver. "Keep the roof clean, so that the sun's rays can hit the receptors." He pointed these out again. "They collect the light energy from the sun, which goes down wires inside the car to the batteries. If the batteries run out of power the car will not run, but there is a gauge in the car that will tell you if the charge is low. When you are driving there is a mechanism that feeds charge directly to the batteries from the motion of the car itself. This is in addition to the receptors."

"Oh," said Tom, "that means we have to use it to keep it charged?"

"Correct, and if all else fails then plug in the car to the electricity supply. I think we've covered the main points about how the car functions. The controls are complex, with a great deal of options, but if you stick to the basic ones that will work best."

They all sighed, except the driver, wondering what they were taking on. The driver continued, "It is worth making a note of this, for each time you get into the car." They all started to scribble as he spoke. "Select the seat position for you comfort. You should be able to easily push the pedals to the floor without being too close or too far away, while having a good view through the front window and the little mirror that points backward. Sitting comfortably without knees squashed is very important." So it went on, the driver, with great patience, explained all of the controls that would allow the car to be moved or stopped. With that over, they went outside.

"I will drive it to the nearest road, then you can each try it out. Please pay attention to what I do." Tom got in next to the driver, while Robin, Paul and Larry watched as well as they could from the back seat.

It was a good 10 minutes' driving across muddy or overgrown fields before they reached a good stretch of road. The rover took everything in its stride, although it was assumed by most in the car that this was due to the driver's skill.

Tom was the first to get behind the wheel. He nervously touched the accelerator to move forward and didn't do too badly just going forwards. The others tried that in turn, until they each could control the car enough to stay on the road, after which the driver gave them slightly more complex things to do. They stayed at it until the light started to fade. "Who is going to take us back?" asked the driver.

Recalling the obstacles there were no initial volunteers, then Larry put his hand up. "I was watching how you controlled the acceleration on the way here, I'd like to have a try."

"OK," said the driver as Larry put his foot to the pedal, "but as the darkness is creeping up on us, you'd better put the headlights on." Larry did so with no fuss and continued to the palace with no problems at all, going over hills that those in the back seats partially closed their eyes to. "Well done," said the driver, "you all did well, but the current driver gets a gold star today for his excellence."

*

The driver stayed with them for the next 2 nights, eating with them and sleeping on a couch. When not driving they all spoke constantly about driving. They all improved to the point that when the driver was due to leave, that they could get across the rough terrain and do most functions reasonably. It was Larry that excelled though in the way he controlled the vehicle and understood the controls. The driver told Larry, "You are a natural driver."

On the last morning Tom and Paul watched from the back seat as Larry drove the driver back to the vehicle depot, without incident but with further praise. The car arrived back at the palace a while after midday, in good shape, if a little muddy. Larry immediately volunteered to clean the car, following directions left by the depot driver.

Robin had spent the morning mulling things over with Lucy and searching through the console options for anything he may have missed. He was pleased to see that Larry was taking good care of their car, now they just had to work out how to make best use of it. That evening over dinner, they discussed their next move. "I don't see any point in delaying us picking up the kids from the villa," said Tom.

"Fair enough," agreed Robin. "I suggest that if we can find our way back to the villa in the rover, we go there tomorrow to prepare the kids, then I'll arrange for a coach the next day. That will require Andy and Larry to do the operations, and either Tom or me so that they recognise us."

"I'll go," volunteered Tom. "I'm sure you can find something better to do with your time."

"Well," smiled Robin, "there were a couple of things I wanted to organise. I want to get all the chiefs up here so that we can keep track of the general progress we are making regarding education and improving the way villages operate. How we can expand that and make us more resilient. We will need all the helpers as well, so that will be quite a party."

"There are more chairs in the stock room," confided Lucy. "I can rearrange the lounge area so that we can get a good number in, and there is a board you can use to write things up on."

"Brilliant," Robin smiled his love smile at Lucy, who blushed quite happily.

"It seems like your mind is never still," said Paul with admiration. "I think we'd be lost without you pulling all these things together."

It was Robin's turn to blush. "Thanks, Paul. It's not that I want to do things my way, but I suppose I do seem to have a grasp of where we should be going. I will never call myself a leader, even if most of you accept my suggestions willingly, but I feel a desperate need to keep pushing our survival potential in all directions."

"We understand that," said Tom, patting his shoulder, "so do not ever stop having ideas. We are with you, even if we can't always keep up with where you are going."

"Alright, we are picking the kids up day after tomorrow, where are we going to take them, to any particular village?" asked Andy.

"The closest village would probably be better," said Tom, "which makes it Robin's old village, now run by chief Bruno." They all nodded in agreement.

"Let's make sure that we install the cook from the villa as a teacher for everything to do with good nutritional meals," added Robin. "That concept really applies in so many other cases. Where people have a natural skill or ability let's make use of them to spread that knowledge and know-how around."

"Good point, but you have that look on your face, Robin. There was plainly something else on your mind," said Tom, "what else are you planning?"

"Ah," said Robin, smiling, "it was just that now we have transport, it would be a good idea to improve the roads we need to use. We know there are some prisoners being held that need to be rescued, so I was going to find tasks for them, and get them freed so many at a time. Haven't got everything fixed in my mind yet, but I will start off by sending a memo to the prison for 50 of their prisoners. After which a way needs to be found for them to disappear."

"Great idea. Kills 2 birds with 1 stone," said Marty, getting poetic.

*

Larry, driving the rover, found his way without any problems to the villa, while Robin sent Bruno a memo to expect the extra mouths. Andy and Larry did their job very well in removing the unwanted chips without alarming the cook or the kids. The coach picked them up and delivered them to Bruno's village as expected.

The next thing on Robin's list was to invite the chiefs and helpers to the palace for a get-together. He also asked for Eric, the old slave that had previously been in the palace, to come to help with the catering. For this he ordered several coaches, suggesting they take the long way round in getting to the villa. "That will happen on Monday," he told Lucy. While he was waiting for the chiefs to respond, Robin located the memo ID for the prison camp, and told them they should supply 50 prisoners and guards for a job of work that needed to be done.

"I assume you want the fit ones?" came the reply. "When, and where, do you want them and what do they need to bring?"

Robin's reply told them it would be next Thursday, for about a week. They should bring some food rations, as well as implements to clear scrub, emphasising, "They will be locked away in the palace overnight, but should have appropriate clothes for working outside in the cold." He also provided the grid reference of where the roads to the palace started to fade away into scrubland, which was where he wanted them to start.

*

With some time to spare before the guests were due Robin commenced his own clean up, starting with the cells in the basement. They certainly smelled better than before, but if the prisoners were going to occupy them, he was determined they would hold no filth and be as comfortable as possible. He swept them out, then used bleach to wash away any filth. The others joined in when they realised what he was up to. After that they cleaned the cells upstairs. A good number of warm blankets were made ready for the slaves.

Lucy and the girls started on the bedrooms, replacing all the bed clothes with fresh ones from a store cupboard. Having become familiar with the kitchen she used a big boiler to wash everything.

Despite a chill in the air, they opened all doors and windows to allow the breeze to take away the chemical smell that had pervaded the building.

Rearranging the lounge to Lucy's design took longer than expected as she kept finding places or things that needed a good wash. It was all done to Lucy's satisfaction just before she needed to start on the dinner.

*

Joining Robin on the couch when the food had been eaten, Lucy gave a contented sigh, "So, me lord, how did the slaves perform today? Was everything to your satisfaction?" She squeezed close to him, prompting a smile or a compliment.

"It was touch and go," admitted Robin seriously, "I'm just wondering whether you all deserve a good beating before we cage you up."

Lucy's frown was enough to make everyone laugh, while Tom said, "That may have been the wrong answer."

"Damn," said Robin, "I'm getting to think too much like a lord these days," as he grabbed for his woman and gave her a good tickling.

Jane and Anne, while not as placid as they had been, had begun to come out of themselves, with Jane in particular taking an interest in the new boys. She sat quietly, but purposefully next to Larry.

"You know something," Marty started up, "I get the idea that the way we live now is very different from how things were in the early part of the last century, but I'm still vague on the exact steps that were taken to ruin what had been a good life for most people?"

"There's a host of stuff on the internet if you look in the right places," Tom stated. "You have to avoid the normal news media because they were full of propaganda, and just lied to people, which of course was part of the problem. I can send you some links, because I had similar questions to you when Robin first told me."

"I would recommend that approach also," said Robin. "I keep a few specific dates in my notebook though and add details when I get them. The treachery really started in the year 2019, for the UK. By this time a virus said to be created in China, aided by America, was rampant. The government insisted on a total lockdown for about 4 months. This started to destroy many people's ability to earn money. Stores and places of employment were closed. They had things called restaurants where nice meals were made to order and served at tables. These were closed down and of course were badly affected by the loss of trade. This went on through 2020 every so often."

"You mean," interrupted Marty, "that people were forced to do no work, and stay in their homes while everything crashed around them?"

"Pretty much," admitted Robin. "Of course, they allowed some things to carry on, hospitals, police authorities, food supply chains and so on. It was the things that made life more worthwhile that were closed down, putting a big strain on the economy and way of life as well as happiness."

Marty began to look confused, "Too many concepts I do not understand."

Tom jumped in, "You probably need to go back earlier and study how the society operated. For example, they used something called money as a means of barter, except that the costs were the same. It was a way to use paper money and coins where we might use fruit or rabbits."

"Oh, OK," said Marty. "There's a lot to get my head around, no wonder I didn't realise what it was all about."

"Indeed," agreed Robin. "Do go and check out all the links Tom will give you. It will provide a full picture. You could do a full write up of what you find, spare no definitions, because a lot of people are like you in that they will miss some data, and it would help you to explain it to others."

"That sounds like a worthwhile thing to do," agreed Marty.

Robin continued, "Just to complete what I was saying, we had the virus with the first lockdown which was supposed to cure everything. All was looking better over the summer months of 2020, then the medical elite started to make noises about it getting worse in winter. They were more concerned with fake sick numbers and not using up all hospital beds than the health and livelihood of the nation. So another lockdown came about. Oh, they said, this will last until at least April 2021. By this time they were talking about a vaccine that was supposed to cure everything, but most people suspected it was a way to reduce the population."

"Careful, everyone," smiled Tom, "Robin gets pretty worked up about all of this, and quite rightly too."

With real anger straining his voice, Robin went on, "The next thing was health passports. A means to disallow people from doing things if they had not been vaccinated. People were excluded from using a great many things including travel by train or coach. That's when other aspects of the plan by the new world order came into play."

"Whoa," insisted Marty, "new world order. What is that?"

"For years it had been in the planning stage. It was a project started by the United Nations, a world organisation that was supposed to encourage peaceful interaction, to usher in a single oppressive world government. Their tools included lies associated with the weather, which was another way to control what people could do. Electric vehicles were something they insisted on, so, being obedient, the UK government banned all cars from using petrol from the year 2030. People were supposed to use electric cars and so on. The technology was far from being capable by this time, which meant that the economy suffered further hits as people were unable to travel. By 2035 the economy had crashed heavily and destructively, far worse than before."

"So did people recover from the lockdown of 2021?" asked Marty.

"Not exactly. It went on for 3 years even though the vaccines were out, but ineffective. The economy and people limped along, then got hit by the ban in 2030, which was a total disaster for everyone. Food became scarce, and opportunities worse. Violent gangs roamed the streets, which were somehow permitted by the authorities. When it came to ordinary people protesting about vaccines killing people or a lack of food, the police beat them into the ground and took them away to slave camps. The country became a nightmare, but still ruled over by the same oppressive government and prime minister that had allowed it all to happen. Somehow, they had bypassed elections. People got chipped out of fear, as the virus mutated and got worse, but it was the vaccinations that killed so many people, which is how it had been planned."

"You mean they used the virus as an excuse to use a poisoned vaccine to kill huge numbers of people, and those left were totally under the control of the new world order, slaves, like we were?" said Marty.

"That's the basic story, but that only happened because of a series of gross deceptions played against the human population for many decades before that. Brainwashing was a crucial element, as was political correctness along with other socialist dogma. They could arrest people for having the wrong thoughts," insisted Robin. "Too many people were affected by the constant propaganda from the media. They were brainwashed constantly with false statistics and ideology, and that's how they became malleable. They were so frightened that they did everything the government told them to do. Most of the population didn't have the education or the brain power to work out that they were being lied to constantly. That's the main reason the NWO was able to win so easily. So many people were stupid beyond imagination because they couldn't, perhaps that should be wouldn't, believe that what was happening was a series of suppressive acts by a government that was supposed to serve them. Looking back, their ignorance was astounding."

Marty sat there with his mouth open, some of the others knew some of the detail, but most were also shocked.

"You mean," said Larry, "that we'd all have had much happier and fulfilling lives before 2018, even if most of us were mostly unable to understand what was going on with the oppression?"

"Who knows," said Robin, "in an earlier life you could have well been a famous car driver."

"Gee thanks," said Larry. "That concept will fuel my dreams tonight!" Jane gave him a warm smile, hoping she might feature as well.

*

The lounge filled up rapidly as the village chiefs and other guests arrived. It was the first time that everyone had been together who understood the fundamentals of what was going on. Most villagers were happy that life had become easier and tried not to think about the bad times before, or what the future might be like.

Tom and Robin, dressed as lords, welcomed everyone at the door. Eric and Cook came along to help with the food, and they both looked so much better than they had before. Eric was wearing clothes that fitted, for his frame had filled out. His face was no longer gaunt, but had a healthy glow, while Cook seemed to have a ready smile on her face always. Eric grabbed the hands of Tom and Robin enthusiastically, expressing his thanks for his freedom and new lease of life.

The crowd settled down in chairs where available, while Tom and Robin went to the side of the room where an improvised platform had been put in place to stand on, to give them a better chance to be seen by everyone.

"I don't know if we should have a name to describe what we are trying to do here," Robin started off with. "I do know that in the past history of this land, when anarchy was in play by the elites, that groups like ours did come forward to fight it. Sometimes they were called revolutionaries or even terrorists, other times they had fancy names. Not all of them were what they said they were, but let's just say that there has never been any group quite like ours fighting against a world-wide conspiracy to enslave all of mankind, so we are pretty unique, with an almost impossible goal." He paused briefly as some eyes opened widely. "There was a figure from the twelfth century that I sometimes feel akin to, even though he may have been a made-up figure from folklore, but what he allegedly stood for impressed and guided me. He dealt in reversing the crimes against ordinary people, with individuals taking some control of their own lives. He operated in a chivalrous way, not with hate, but with purpose and targeted attacks, which is what we need to do. I fear most of you will not know what I am talking about, but I would urge you to investigate Robin Hood for yourselves."

"What does chivalrous mean?" asked Larry.

"It means," said Tom, jumping in, "that we always behave with integrity, honesty, consideration to our own. We are heroic and big-hearted, courageous and bold, but not spiteful."

"Nice definition," agreed Robin. "I do believe I will get a plaque made with those words on to remind me, to remind us, what we stand for. There is someone else from history I want to mention. A king who was certainly very real, and what he accomplished, with his descendants is very much like the task we have in front of us. He came a lot earlier than Robin Hood, well before real civilisation had started to take a hold."

"Tell us his name. Let's see if we know him," said Paul.

"His name was King Alfred the Great. His country was our country, England, which had been overrun by invaders, who were brutal and hard. He initially had to hide away from these invaders for they had appeared very suddenly. Gradually he built up an army, uniting the separate groups of people. Amazingly he fought against the stronger enemy, forcing them back, freeing his lands and his people, driving the intruders into a much smaller area of the country. It fell to Athelstan, grandson of Alfred to complete the full conquest of occupied lands, and he became the first king of Britain. Yet it was Alfred who set the course for all to follow. He encouraged learning, reading and writing, establishing the concept that wisdom, or knowledge, was something vital for all to have. It was King Alfred's wisdom that set the path for a better life for all." Robin paused for a moment to let that sink in. "We have to emulate that wisdom, with real learning for everyone. Foremost we must ensure everyone knows of how our forefathers were defeated by knavery, subjugated and turned into slaves. Then we must all acquire more knowledge, and more knowledge of how things work in this world. We have to know how to build good homes, how to create the energy that gives us lights, and a million other things. There is so much wisdom that we must gather unto ourselves. If we are to save ourselves, we must get away from the idea that we are slaves, a sub-human species. We are the descendants of King Alfred the Great and we will eventually depose the cruel invaders of our lands."

Several cheered Robin's words, which had evoked a refreshed spirit within the room.

Tom realised that they were throwing a lot of terms around that few had ever heard before, for some of the smiling faces were also a little blank. "We don't mean to confuse you with words you've never heard before. What we should do is get the teachers to tell the tales of heroes from the past when they come around the villages. All that we were trying to say, here today, is that while there have been great men in history that we can be like, there has never been a cause like ours, and we intend to create a better life for ourselves. A land where we live that we can be proud of, that very much includes justice, and not anarchy." This the rest of the crowd got and smiled encouragingly.

Robin went on, "If we are to win against the lords and the gods, we have to get bigger and stronger. That means we must educate ourselves, learn all possible skills, and take more things away from those that enslaved us. From what I hear conditions in the villages are improving with better homes, more food, less work, and certainly no beatings. Do the village chiefs agree? Do you need something specifically to make things work better?" He looked at the chiefs in turn, encouraging them to talk openly.

"I fear," said Bruno, smiling, "that with a contented people, we will soon be growing our population, especially as the women are producing more young, more often, and of course we are not sending our young away to be abused and killed."

"Plus we are seeing slaves returned," said another voice.

"Good comments," agreed Benny, chief of another village. "We do have plenty of space, but perhaps we need to plan our expansion better, rather than just building anywhere."

"Interesting points," said Tom. "Perhaps what we need is a way to make a plan for expanding the number of village homes. That would need to be investigated so that any village could adopt similar ideas."

"Excellent idea," said Robin, "that's an example of why we all need to talk together from time to time. We have lots of helpers, but maybe we need to expand their numbers. In the meantime, if any helpers who are not fully engaged would like to volunteer for roles as village home planners that would be most useful." Several hands shot up. "Lucy, please take their names and locations. We need to provide them with information and internet links to appropriate subjects."

*

They went on to talk about a variety of things affecting the villages. Robin wrapped that section up with, "We have been in contact with some of the

London factories. I hope that within a couple of months that we can see more distribution of food items to villages. Also, there is no reason why we cannot get trading going between villages, where one village, for example, has too many turnips, they could barter them for something another village has." There was general agreement as Robin continued, "I've already asked a factory to look at producing handcarts so that goods can more easily be moved around. Specifically I asked them to make carts that could be easily pushed, perhaps with some mechanics. When available I will get them delivered, but that may be some time."

"It doesn't sound like you've been twiddling your fingers, Robin," said Richard, the first of the new style chiefs. "I won't ask how you've managed all of this, but I thank the one true god, not the gods of the lords for they are surely evil, for the day that Tom walked into our village and started us on the path to salvation. Each thing you speak about hits me like a small miracle, yet you keep coming out with things that improve our lives. How can we thank you?"

"I appreciate your comments," said Robin, going a little red. "I won't bore you with the details. I have always sought for us all to be free, and what you are doing is enough for me, improving the way villages are run, and giving people back control of their lives is fundamental to us taking back our country. We still have a huge way to go though."

Richard and most of the others stood up and clapped, while Robin held up his hand for quiet, but also acknowledging the applause, glancing at each person in turn.

"We are getting stronger," Robin continued. "It all started when Lucy and Tom came on board. They were very much a part of my inspiration, but then others joined us to pass the word, to explain and to educate others about what had been done to us. We had great helpers like Andy, Johnny, Paul, David, George and Harry, to mention but a few, as well as every village chief here. I thank you all for your support."

"Don't forget Digga," said Tom when quiet resumed. "Without her so much would not have been possible." The dog, having heard her name spoken with love, looked up at all the people. She studied the faces watching her, gave them a loving yelp, then lay down, relaxed that she was amongst friends, wondering when the next meal would be.

"Too true," agreed Robin, bending down to stroke his dog warmly.

Tom continued, "We must emphasise some things. We have been careful not to stop things that need to happen. For example, we need to provide food for the people in London that give us the power to make the lights or the cookers to work. Which raises another point about us learning about how everything works. Electrical power is but one thing we must come to understand. How it is created, what the technology is all about, yet this is but a single thing requiring many skills to implement and maintain. Other than that we intend to gradually remove all trace of the lords, which means not doing things that draw attention to us. Anybody that needs to go outside the village should have chips removed, but if we suddenly do this to everyone the lords will come to find out why so many have apparently died. We must, however, grow stronger, be better fed, more knowledgeable, and fundamentally better able to withstand anything the lords will throw at us, for that is inevitable. I am not going to hide anything, for there are dangerous times ahead. We must prepare for all possible futures, even a violent one. We have certainly hurt the lords and reduced some of their number, so when they hit back it will not be easy to confront them. We must do that, however, for we would be better off dead than what we had before." This produced several frowns. "Simply, we have to prepare ourselves in every way."

Robin jumped back in, "How do we prepare? We do it by getting stronger in terms of numbers, but most vitally we must make sure that everyone knows how our forefathers were deceived, tricked and then forced into becoming slaves. That is the most important thing we need to do, to spread that message." He paused for a moment. "We will need more helpers; chiefs can identify bright, competent people to add to the existing helpers who can get them trained in the things that everyone needs to be able to do or know something about. New skills are something we must learn in order to survive and function better."

"We can do that," agreed Bruno. "I also suggest that we village chiefs get together and share our problems and successes. A way needs to be found for us all to meet, say twice a year."

"Great suggestion," said Tom. "Something we all need to do is to keep in touch and be informed of any issues. Let us know when and we will organise coaches."

"I also want to raise some other things," said Robin. "We know of a prison camp to the south that holds maybe 300 people. We are working on ways to free them, again without attracting too much attention. If it all works out, a number of these abused prisoners will need somewhere to live, and I'm sure you would welcome them to your villages. Their mental state will be unknown, meaning that they might become violent. Please be prepared to deal with that if it happens. It probably won't be a problem, but we should be aware of how effectively the lords have hurt so many of us over the years."

"We will need to put them somewhere quiet initially," suggested Richard, "then slowly introduce them back to village life."

"That sounds like a way forward," agreed Robin. "That should be happening in about a month's time." He spoke quietly to Digga, "Go fetch Eric and Cook in here please."

There was an extended period of silence, with many wondering if the discussion was finished, with only a dog's yelp heard to suggest otherwise, then Eric came and stood next to Robin with Cook just behind him, both smiling and happy, watching each other like newly-weds.

"This is Eric and Cook," Robin said. "They are very talented in making tasty meals, and they have been working hard on some dinner for us all which will be ready soon I expect. They both know how places like this lord's palace work, which is knowledge we need to have. As we take over places like this we will need to staff and maintain such buildings to a high standard, not for the lords but for our use when we need them. I am looking for volunteers from the villages to come and work here. They will of course require their chips removing, but if I can ask the chiefs to find gardeners and others that can keep these places well looked after, please do let me know. Cook and Eric can give more data on how such places need to be taken care of."

During the pause that followed, Eric raised his hands, "Dinner is ready, please form a queue into the kitchen." He took Cook by the hand, and they led the way towards the kitchen door where bowls had been stacked ready to receive a thick beef stew.

*

After dinner Robin and Tom individually went around to speak with the recently recruited helpers and all the chiefs, to get to know them a little better. Robin was often asked why he wore the hated uniform of the lords. He admitted, "It is for purposes of deception. If drivers and others see no lords here, they will start to make rumours, which will not be good, for that would prompt others to investigate. I will also interact with some lords, like at the prison camp, so I always need to look the part."

*

There were not beds to go around for everyone. Robin and the others slept on the lounge floor, allowing the chiefs to enjoy the extravagance of real beds. They were all woken, but not too early, by being licked on the face by a bunch of excited semi-mature dogs, who had been locked away downstairs for the previous day.

Everybody got a good breakfast before they left in the morning. While munching a bacon sandwich, Robin announced, "In just over 3 weeks' time it will be a special day. The old society before us used to celebrate December 25 as a holiday and a feast day. At my old village there was a special meal for the first day of the new year. Does everyone agree that we should keep these dates, celebrate them and make them winter feast days?"

Benny, who had really enjoyed his food, stood up. "I second that. Now that we are producing excess food, and our store rooms are full, the only thing we need to do is fatten up the pigs."

"Well," said Robin smiling, "traditionally, December 25 was a day for the birds. Mostly turkeys or chicken, but also geese."

"That's a shame," said Benny, "it's only Martin's village, the southernmost village, that has any turkeys."

"I feel a trading option coming on," said Martin. "It is true that we have the big birds, but for a real feast every village would have to raise their own. We can start them off, for a suitable exchange of course."

"Fair enough," said Benny, "we can stick with pigs this year, but let's plan to have a real big turkey festival next year."

Everyone agreed with that.

"It will," added Tom, "be a time of celebration, for story-telling, as well as a reminder of what we have to be thankful for." There was nobody that could disagree with that.

*

The horns from the coaches alerted everyone to the transportation arriving. Many hands grabbed at what was left of the breakfast to eat on the way back to the villages, and very soon the coaches were boarded. Suddenly the palace was so very quiet with the visitors gone.

*

Before Cook and Eric had left, Robin asked them if they'd like to manage the palace, with others. "Not any more," admitted Eric, and Cook nodded agreement. "We'd be happy to come and help out at special occasions, but to be honest, I've wasted too many years in this house, and I would rather keep well away from it in future."

"I totally understand," Robin said, "but would you be willing to train others for say a couple of days at a time? That would also apply to the villa, Cook. It would help our cause if we could keep these places running well."

"That would not be a problem," Cook replied with a big smile, feeling important for once in her life.

*

"That was a good meet-up," exclaimed Tom. "How do we all think it went, did we get our messages across?"

"Very good," Paul said. "It's nice to see that we are all going in the same direction. It's easy to get giddy when you think of everything going on as well as what's in Robin's mind."

"Right now my mind is blank, totally empty, except for thinking about taking a walk in the morning sunshine," smiled Robin.

"Maybe we should review what is coming up that needs some form of management?" suggested Tom. "We've set in motion some things with the London factories, which should carry on without our direct intervention. The chiefs have several things to do which will help them run things better and be more in control of their environments, but we don't have to watch too closely over that. Do you agree, Robin?"

"Agreed, except that we need to keep half an eye on progress all round."

"OK," said Tom. "Aside from that while we set about emptying prison camps, I feel we badly need to have a lot more helpers in the near future. Also, it's probably about time we expanded to the west to get more village chiefs under our banner."

"Agreed. Identify the villages and I'll show you how to work that beam."

"That should keep us all busy," said Andy, "which is good for morale, but what else is on the horizon?"

"Nothing from me, except more of the same," replied Robin to a shocked audience. "As I said my mind is a bit of a blank when I try to plot the future. Maybe a walk will give me some ideas. Let us consider this a time of consolidation. A time to think and consider what the future should look like, to make what we have somewhat better."

"Isn't that what we just decided?" asked Paul.

"Yes," said Robin. "I'm not trying to be obtuse. We've achieved as much as I ever thought possible, but where we go from here will be hard to plot. I'd prefer it if the amalgamation of villages, trading, increased helpers and education was self-perpetuating, so that we grow organically."

"You've lost some of us with those big words you keep finding in your studies there, Robin, but for the benefit of us all, what I think you mean," said Tom, "is that we keep all current plans and ideas rolling along."

"That about sums it up," agreed Robin, and taking his woman's hand he called for Digga as he went off into the fresh air.

*

Larry drove Tom and Robin to meet the prison work crew that had arrived at the point where the roads needed to be cleared. Larry, as was appropriate, was dressed as a slave.

As they arrived, the prison master in charge of the 50 men stood up to greet them, while the slaves remained seated on the cold ground, some grumbling about being cold. Although it was December, the weather was still mild. The grumbling visibly ceased when the 2 men dressed as lords got out of the car. Most faces turned towards the ground, not wanting to attract any attention to themselves. There were 2 other masters with the group as well as the 2 drivers of the coaches that had collected the prisoners.

Robin walked over to the drivers, "I want you back here at 5pm exactly to take everyone to the east palace. Tomorrow you can pick them up from there at 8am," not caring what they did in between times.

Tom meanwhile addressed the 3 guards, "This road has become overgrown and hard to drive along. You can see what used to be road, the tarmac is still visible. Have your men clear the brambles and other weeds away from the path. Without making holes or damaging the tarmac further," he insisted. He was always wary about making contact with others that assumed him to be a lord just because he was tall and dressed like a lord, but he had steeled himself to the role anyway.

Robin came over, looking like he was inspecting the sorry bunch of men still sat on the ground. "Was this the best you have? These wretches look like they have no strength to hold any implements, never mind do any work."

"They were the least damaged, me lordship. We had trouble finding enough men who were strong enough to do this work," the prison master said with a sour look in his eyes. "These are stronger than they look. It won't take them long to clear the jungle away. In any case we have our whips to make them work faster."

"Not on this job," Robin insisted immediately. "If these men are damaged, I will hold you 3 masters responsible. I want these men in best possible shape to get things done smoothly without any trouble. So no whipping and no punishment, unless I agree to it, then I shall see to it personally. I don't want any complaints from the prison lords about the state of these prisoners." As these words reached the ears of the prisoners several looked up, suddenly interested.

"Yes, sir, me lord," the master said, utterly confused.

"Get the men to work then, Master. We will observe the way they work directly for a short time, but never forget we can watch you from the sky."

"The sky, me lord?" said the man now getting worried, having heard but rumours of things in the sky. "Of course, immediately." He shouted to the prisoners to get moving, who complied in the usual fashion associated with the oppressed, slowly with deliberate motions.

Tom and Robin watched the workers closely as they hacked away at the over-growth, specifically noting those that reacted first to commands, the ones that the others followed. These would be the primary targets for what Robin had in mind. Once satisfied, they took each master aside for an evaluation, as to whether they could be trusted, or would sound the alarm if they spotted something odd.

"I like to attach a name to those I have to deal with," admitted Robin to the senior master. "Where did you come from before you worked at the prison?"

"I was in a village till I was about 7 years, then I was pressed into service," the man said clearly with memories flashing by his mind's eye. "My old mum, I never saw her again, she used to call me Pip."

"Well, Pip, how would you like to go back and visit your old village?"

"Oh no, sir, I couldn't do that. Everybody would be gone that I knew as a boy. Besides, it doesn't hold the best memories for me."

"I can see that," said Robin, "but if all goes well with this work, I will see that you get some reward."

"Very kind, sir, the only thing I really want is to be on my own, away from the bad memories. I've always wanted to be by the sea."

"Keep that dream alive, without a goal to think about we are lost, and you look like a man with purpose."

A confused Pip frowned, wondering where this was going and if he was being set up for something or just being tricked. "Yes, me lordship. We'll do a good job here and perhaps you can tell my lords at the prison so that they will give us some privileges."

"That sounds like a deal, as long as you mention this conversation to nobody," Robin smiled. "Tell me though, what did these men do to end up in that wretched prison?"

"They misbehaved too many times. Some fought against their masters or refused to work, so they got sent to the prison for 5 years. That's the standard term. After that they usually work better, those that survive."

"I see. Alright, Pip, let's see how much progress you can make today."

*

They had similar discussions with the 2 other masters separately and in confidence. Max was the name of one, and Jeremy was the other. Of the 2, Jeremy seemed to be the most belligerent, the least easy to work with. Jeremy was the master that would need to be watched most. He was also the master the prisoners cringed away from.

Satisfied that progress was already underway, Larry drove the 2 lords back to the palace, where Robin kept an eye on activities using the spy in the sky.

*

Just after 5pm that day, the coaches delivered the prisoners to the palace. "Be back at 8am tomorrow morning," Tom told the drivers.

"We don't have spare rooms for masters, but you may use the top floor to rest in," Robin told the masters after the prisoners were taken downstairs and locked in their cells. "The rooms upstairs were designed for butt-kids, currently empty, but they have been well cleaned up. They should be adequate enough for you. Come down for dinner at 7pm. While you are here you will eat well." The masters seemed to like this. He showed them up to the top level then set Whiskey to watch over them, to make sure they didn't wander about too much.

With the masters upstairs, Robin and Tom, with Digga, went down to the cells in the basement, to look over the alpha prisoners they wanted to get on their side. Through the bars of the cell holding one of the targets they saw a tough looking belligerent man that had more scars than most, some of which were fresh. As the cells had been made warm the men were able to get comfortable and remove their top layers of clothing.

Robin and Tom had agreed that it was crucial they got certain men to warm to the idea of freedom, and that they could give it to them. Considering how best to approach it was another matter. Opening the cell of this man they tried a direct approach to get him talking, "Do you like dogs?" Tom asked. "I used to have 3 beauties until some bitch of a chief hacked them to death."

The man was confused at this approach, and very suspicious. Lords didn't usually bother to talk with prisoners, they only issued orders or condemnations. He backed further into his cell, fearing something bad was going to happen.

"Don't worry about this dog here," said Robin. "She is used to much better steaks for dinner than you present. You are very thin. She would easily rip at your throat though should you do anything silly. Do you have a given name?"

Frightened but also wary, the prisoner managed, "Arry, me big sister called me Arry."

"Don't worry, Arry. We are not here to harm you. Somebody has already done that," said Tom. "When was the last time you were whipped?"

Reluctant to answer, but fearing the worst if he didn't, Arry replied, "Last week, I trod on a master's foot."

"OK, Arry," said Robin. "While you are here there will be no whippings or beatings as long as you cooperate. If I see any fresh marks on you while you are here somebody will be punished." He opened a small container of medicated ointment, and held it out towards the man, "Use that to heal your scars. Take a small amount on your finger and rub it into the open scars."

Arry gingerly pushed his finger into the ointment, extracting a little, then rubbed it against a painful open scab. The ointment clearly gave him some relief for he immediately used it elsewhere. "Share it with those that need it," Robin told him, laying the container on the floor between them.

They moved on to the next alpha prisoner, opening his cell door, and asking for his name. "Joe," he said. Tom nodded and also gave him some ointment.

After that they identified Ricky, Jan, Mike and Steve. Each received the ointment and used it. "Share it amongst your fellow prisoners," Tom said. "Make sure you do not have any on your hands when you eat. You will be getting some food shortly, but wash your hands properly first, that stuff doesn't mix well with food."

With that done, they closed the last cell door, and went back upstairs, leaving a group of bewildered prisoners to wonder what was going on. They were not used to being treated with consideration.

*

"You know," Robin said to Tom when they were back upstairs in the lord's office, sat around the opulent desk overflowing with gadgets they still did not understand, watching over the console and answering memos, "I don't have any real plan in my head for how we should proceed. Up to this point I have just been lucky at exploiting opportunities."

"I do get that," replied Tom, "but when you say your mind is blank, we all get worried."

"I'd be quite happy for a real leader to show up and tell us how we should proceed. I certainly feel I am not him, for I lack vision."

"You are so hard on yourself. Without your ability to exploit opportunities, and the leadership you have shown we'd all be still suffering as slaves, or worse, we could be dead. If I hadn't had you and Lucy outside my village to come to, I would have certainly done something bad enough to get myself killed or sent to that damned prison."

"I'm really glad we were there for you, but actually it felt like you were there for us." This produced a bright smile from them both. A shared moment of affection and empathy.

"Increasing the influence of our group is going well, and if we can establish more villas and palaces as strongholds that has to be the way forward. More villages will come into the fold next year as we move west. Perhaps we can get the prisoners downstairs to join with us, and then we must consider what to do about the remaining prisoners in the camp?"

"Yes," agreed Robin. "I'm wondering, considering the poor state of these prisoners downstairs, whether the remaining ones will be in any kind of condition to make the transition back to village life. It might be a blessing to obliterate the whole prison camp?"

"We must try and find that out from our alpha prisoners, if we can get them talking. From the clearing progress we saw today I'd say it will take them 2 weeks to get the roads into a reasonable condition, which means less than 14 evenings and nights to sweet talk them."

*

With so many to feed in the morning, the kitchen staff wrapped up bacon sandwiches for all prisoners and the 3 guards to eat during their journey. Lucy also made sure the drivers got theirs as well. Everybody else had a more relaxed breakfast until Paul raised the subject of how the basement cells were going to be kept clean. "Already they smell disgusting."

"I don't think we should have to clean up after them," said Tom. "We have to show them how to keep their living quarters in a reasonable state."

"Agreed," said Robin. "Is that something you can organise when they get back?"

Paul wasn't so happy at that but allowed himself to be chosen for the job.

"It probably seems to everyone that it's only me and Tom that lead the activities. We should spread this out more so that everyone takes all of us for lords, as we are all pretty capable of seeing what needs to be done and then getting it done. Let's all of us start acting like stroppy lords, to others that is."

"I don't intend to get my hands dirty," said Paul, still a little bitter.

"Apart from anything else, if these people are going to live in our villages, they have to start changing their ways. We have to start them on the right path."

"Yes, we must do that," said Robin with a hopeful smile on his face, "but to change the subject, I was looking over that watercraft at the end of the jetty. Do any of you fancy trying it out?"

He got nods from Larry and Tom. "You mean, shall we try not to crash or sink it? I'll skip it," said Paul.

"Time we learned how to swim like the fish," said Robin, leading the way. "At least we can see if it is usable. It might come in handy someday."

"Is this another one of your big ideas?" asked Larry, trailing behind, following Digga who sensed adventure.

*

The boat was bobbing up and down against the jetty, a warning that the water was choppy. They jumped aboard, taking note of its features. A plate above the steerage announced that they were aboard a class 5 cruiser with 5 berths. Having included boats in his recent studies, Robin was able to show off his knowledge by turning on the ignition key and firing the engines up.

"That's good, we have just less than a half tank of fuel," Robin said, tapping on the gauge as he had seen other sailors do from his PC. "You see those orange jacket things? We each need to put them on in case we fall into the water." Tom and Larry complied. Tom threw Robin his own safety jacket. "Cast off then." Digga slipped between Robin's feet as he tied the luminous jacket about himself.

"What?" said Tom.

"Untie the rope from the jetty so that we can leave," said Robin.

Free of the shore, the boat slipped away from the land and slowly headed in the direction of the far shoreline. "Where are we going then?" asked Tom.

"I wanted to take a look at what is over there. It's all part of the London area, but we don't have any details of what the buildings are for or if they are of any use."

"Aren't they derelict?" suggested Tom. "When I looked at them with my glasses, I saw no sign of life."

"Let's investigate, we may find something to our benefit."

"Darn, I forgot to bring my explorer hat along," Larry said.

*

The tide wasn't too strong as they struggled to make the boat respond but it took a while before they got the hang of giving the engine enough power to go in a straight line, after that they went more or less where intended.

"That looks like another jetty right in front of us," said Tom. "Yes, I can read the sign, this is the Nustar Grays jetty 2." It seemed to be in a reasonable condition, with only a few visible holes. "Let's get as close as we can to solid ground though, no telling how strong this thing is to walk on."

Robin adjusted the speed of the boat to a crawl, bumping the side of the boat against the splintered side of the walkway, then turned the power down to neutral, while Larry took a rope and jumped across the small gap to the jetty. He wrapped the thick rope around a post standing as tall as he was, which had seen better days. This slowed the boat that was still heading for the shore but didn't stop it. Larry jumped aside as the rotten post collapsed. He made a grab for the rope, just saving it from sliding into the water.

"Find something stronger," suggested Tom with a smile, doubting that he could have done better.

A smooth looking pole, painted red and white, looked more substantial, which it was, for it helped to reduce the boat speed to zero when the rope was wound around it. Robin and Tom joined Larry on the jetty, looking closely at it, wondering if it was stable.

"It will have to do," said Tom, "there is nothing else to tie it up to, and it is far too big a craft to drag it onto the shore."

"Yelp," went Digga, requesting some help to get off the boat. Robin did as requested.

Tom was still dubious about the structure. Every few feet, of what was left of the jetty, he dug a heel in hard. At the third attempt his heel broke through, splintering a plank. "No telling how long this has been here, but it won't be here for much longer by the looks of it," he said prophetically. "Are we going to keep these jackets on?"

"Might as well. It is unlikely this structure will just fall apart in the short time we will be ashore," said Robin, ensuring it was cursed to collapse. "I only want a quick walk about, so we'll be back soon."

The real ground was a few steps away, and nothing happened to the jetty even when they were 15 paces onto solid land. Robin led the way across a tarmacked road to stare at an open space. Wrecks of old vehicles lay around. "That's not of importance to us," said Larry, "unless we want to land a large flying craft on it."

To the left the road seemed to end abruptly at a wall. To the right looked more interesting, which was the way they trod. As they came to a bend in the road a sign caught their eye, likely indicating the name of the road. "Interesting name," said Tom, "Wouldham road, wonder if it means anything." Further to the right was a cluster of houses. "Those are not in bad condition. Perhaps they could be used to hold some of our people when we expand."

They clambered over the remnants of fences that were in their way, to rummage in some of the houses they found. "It's a very long time since these were lived in," Robin pointed out. The floor and ceilings were still firm though, although anything of value had long since either rotted away or been taken by someone. After leaving one house it started to rain lightly. The wind also picked up.

"These would be great examples of the new homes we need to build. We must bring the design team here to look these over. Not sure why they had so many rooms though?"

"Maybe they were to house several families."

"Not from what I saw of some old moving pictures," answered Robin.

"Every family member seemed to have a large room for themselves, to sleep in and study. There was even a separate room in which to eat in, like our dining room at the palace."

Digga was enjoying the old smells that lingered in the dusty corners of the houses and came away covered in cobwebs. "Nothing more to learn here, for the time being," suggested Robin. "Let's get back to the road."

The road led them to further buildings on the left, which looked like factories. A quick investigation showed them to be but shells held up by rotting metal frames, with little of any significance inside. After this, the road led them to a bridge that spanned a railway line.

"Look at how shiny those rails are," announced Robin, ducking down as the wind nearly blew him over. "They must be in use quite often." No sooner had he said this than a train appeared, from the left, but not the same type they had used before. This looked clean with 6 carriages in a smart condition. "I wonder where that is going?"

"We may find out one day," suggested Tom, "but I'm worried about our watercraft. There doesn't seem to be much we can see here in a short visit. There must be many places like this in and around London."

"You're right," said Robin, "we should head back."

As they retraced their steps back to the jetty the weather became fiercer. They had to struggle to walk against the strength of the stormy wet wind.

"I wonder how the prisoners are getting on with this foul rain?" asked Larry.

"I'm wondering how we will get back across that stretch of water," complained Tom.

At last they reached the edge of the jetty, or at least they reached the place where the jetty should have been. There was no sign of any boat, not only that, there was no walkway, except the planks which had broken off and were now several feet under water.

"Oops," said Robin, suddenly alarmed. "Now what are we going to do?"

"Yelp," agreed Digga.

"Swimming is probably not an option," suggested Tom angrily.

They walked up and down the shore several times, wondering, and looking for the boat. "Which way is the tide going?" asked Robin.

"That way," said Larry, pointing out towards the sea. "At least I can see some small things floating that way. Perhaps that is what is left of the boat."

"That's certainly where our craft will be going then, heading out to the open waters," grumbled Tom. "I don't suppose the tide will ever bring it back?"

"Pretty unlikely," Robin agreed. "Our only option, it seems is to make our way back through London, but that will be a long walk. Better get moving along the rail track."

"Why don't we halt the train when it comes back?" Tom suggested hopefully. "Do you imagine it would stop for us, 3 half-drowned scruffy lords?"

"The big question," said Robin, "is, would whoever is on board accept us as lords and give us a lift?"

"With our cheek how could they fail not to?" joked Larry.

"We will need to find a long straight piece of track to give the train plenty of time to slow," said Robin. "We will need to wave something colourful, and hope they spot us from the cab. Maybe these orange jackets will do the trick."

*

An old rusty, metal ringed fence initially barred their way onto the track, but not for long. A degree of anger drove them easily through the obstacle, and on to the track. They searched up the line for the train coming back, yet all was quiet.

By the time they had gone about a mile down the track, the sun had come out and their clothes were a lot dryer, although their hair was still plastered to their heads, which made them look very mean and serious. The track itself was in good order, which made walking easier. To their left, as they walked and got closer, they saw a huge structure. Robin suddenly realised what it was. "I know that thing. It is a bridge. A very big river crossing. It used to carry 4 streams of traffic across the water."

"Will it help us get back?" asked Tom.

"It certainly will. It's not so old. There should be a clear solid path across it. Otherwise, as I recall, there are also tunnels going under the river."

They clambered off the rail track, which was just as well for mere seconds later the train came hurtling back along the line at what seemed like an incredible speed. There had been no warning of its approach, and if they had been still on the track, they would have been reduced to mangled flesh and bones. "Yelp," Digga went.

"Oops," said Robin, "that was almost fatal."

"That makes 2 lessons we should have learned today." Tom stretched his leg up and over a small fence, just above the incline they had climbed up from the track.

"Don't walk blindly along rail tracks," suggested Larry. "What's the other?"

With a certain annoyance in his voice, Tom answered, "Don't tie your watercraft to something that could get washed away."

"Oh," said Larry. "Yes, must remember that."

*

The road leading to the bridge was not easy to reach on foot. It either meant going some way until the road was level with them, or somehow getting onto the road in front of them, which meant a climb without decent places to grasp with hands. They decided to walk the extra half mile.

The bridge was certainly immense, with metal girders going up very high, and thick cables that stretched great distances. The road itself was pitted, but still safe to walk on, although small amounts of metal debris suggested the bridge had once had cars on it even after the last great lockdown. They felt very small walking up this wide roadway, imagining how many strange vehicles must have travelled it, and for what purposes. It was hard to imagine what so many people would have been doing that required them to travel across the river. At the highest point they were still some distance from the end, where some small huts had once stood, now damaged, but their shape was intact. Towards the bottom of the road a pair of trucks had seemingly crashed into each other and burned out. They must have been of a superior construction for despite the many small round holes in the sides of them they were still a solid shape. The rubber wheels of the trucks had long since perished. The small holes were caused by projectiles of some kind, which got the 3 explorers wondering again what had occurred.

They wanted to turn immediately left to follow the coast, but that was not possible due to a marshy but overgrown area that way. They walked on a little way until they found a road that went in their general direction and followed that.

"Will this take us all the way to our palace?" asked Larry.

"Close enough," said Robin. "If we find ourselves getting too far away from the river we may have to cut across country. I estimate it will be a nice leisurely one-hour walk."

*

"Here come the coaches," Adam announced, "but where are Robin and Tom? They've been gone all day."

"Not to worry," said Paul with confidence. "We know what needs to be done. To be honest I suspect this may be a little test, so we can show we can handle things on our own."

"Hmm, possibly," agreed Adam.

"I've got to get the prisoners to clean up their cells. Will you back me up, please?"

"Of course, always," smiled Adam. "Have we got together the cleaning materials?"

"Yes, there's something to soak up the pee, several extra buckets to collect the solids or do the mopping, and I've 3 of those spray bottles to disinfect with. I plan to position a master at either end of the cell corridor. The master called Pip can walk around with me."

*

The 3 masters led the prisoners into the palace and down to the basement where the men were locked in. As the masters started to leave Paul stood in their way. "Before we settle down there is something we need to get done." He addressed the prisoners, "The state of some of these cells is unacceptable. You may live like dirty buggers normally, but not here. Your aroma is already enough to attract flies that were hibernating. Each cell has to be cleaned before dinner." He asked Jeremy and Max to observe the prisoners while the cleaning was going on. Paul was still wary that they could be violent.

"Now some of you," Paul continued, "have made your cells wet or just spread your waste too far. In future you will use the buckets, which will be emptied daily. Is that understood? There will be extra portions for those that keep their cells clean and smelling acceptable."

Everything went well for a while. Prisoners did the job of cleaning up their own mess, cells were opened to allow prisoners to pour their waste down a toilet situated towards the end of the corridor. Paul then went in and sprayed everywhere.

Just as Paul was coming out of one cell, a prisoner, that had taken offence at having to clean up his mess, threw his half full bucket in the direction of Pip, then made a dash for the far door, knocking over Max as he did so. He was almost through the exit when he was stopped by a figure in front of him. Digga growled viciously forcing the man to retreat. He was caught by Max who was about to give him a good hiding when Robin appeared.

Looking over the scene it was easy to see what had happened. "Find something to tie his hands." That was quickly done, with several wondering what the high lord was going to do about this incident.

"If anybody was going to play the clown it would have to be him, wouldn't it?" Jeremy the master snarled. "This time you will not get off lightly, you little skunk."

"That was a disgusting thing to do," Robin said to the prisoner, taking control, "and there was me thinking you were all relatively civilised. Pip, throw that top away and go get a good shower. Can't have you walking around like that, it's not your colour at all. Lock all the cells until I have dealt with this scoundrel, but before I take him outside for the last time, are there any other prisoners that would like to join him?" He indicated the slops thrower. All prisoners immediately backed further into their cells. "Good. That is more like it. We will not tolerate a filthy rabble here. After your cells are spotless, you will all be hosed down."

Robin looked towards Paul who was a bit embarrassed by what had gone on. "After the cells are cleaned and the men are dry, burn their clothing. Talk about filthy!"

The cleaning went on, a little slower this time, but with more purpose, then as required prisoners threw the rags they called clothes out through the bars, and their blankets were put somewhere safe. A hose was turned on each prisoner in turn, and they all stood there shivering waiting for the water to drain away. Meanwhile Digga escorted the offender outside, towards the sea wall, well away from the palace.

"You are Steve if I recall," Robin stated, remembering him as an alpha prisoner. Tom joined him while Larry went in to help Paul. "Tell Paul," Robin whispered to Larry, "to give them fresh outfits from the store cupboard once they are dry.

"I'm not going to mess with you," Robin continued, tying his wrists to a tree. "If I gave you over to the masters, you'd be black and blue for weeks, but I've got a better proposition for you. It all depends on how smart you are."

Steve frowned, wondering what torture was going to be inflicted on him. "I'm used to being mistreated, so that won't do you any good. I'll still attack you damned lords and masters whenever I can, after all you've done to me."

"What makes you think you have had a worse life than any of us? None of us have had it easy growing up," Robin said with real anger. "What makes you special?"

Normally unwilling to talk, Steve opened up, probably for the first time in his life. His anger was nonetheless very real. "When I was 6, they wanted to send me off to a lord's palace. My mum and me dad tried to stop them.

They beat my dad up, 3 of them, then they wedged him up a tree, unconscious. I never knew what happened to him, but they slapped my mother away, bleeding and crying."

"That's normal process for butt-kids," Robin continued, playing with his anger.

"I was raped that night, for the first time, for the pleasure of me lords. I saw other kids bleed to death, their blood collected in silver cups, drank by several lords. I wished many times to have my blood taken, to die and be free of that misery, but for some reason they preferred to bugger me. Day after day, year after year," he screamed.

Robin sighed quietly to himself, feeling the pain for Steve, who just kept on relating details of abuse he had suffered.

"They kept us in small cells, hardly any rags between us butt-kids, cold and hungry, we cried ourselves to sleep when they had done with us. We lived in constant fear of being beaten or punished some way." He gulped, as a memory came back to him. "For a change they also brought young women to abuse, and like all the entertainment we were made to stand there and take it all in. My mum was brought there one day. I tried to call out to her, but she didn't see me. They abused her good. A lord at her back and another at the front. Time and again they forced themselves on her, as she screamed in pain, until she collapsed, bleeding." His tears started to roll as the pain came back. "She was dead," he screamed with great venom, "and I've never been able to avenge that." His head dropped as the memories ripped him apart, his chest heaved, and the tears dropped soundlessly to the ground as he sobbed away.

Robin untied Steve's wrists, had him sit down. Robin rested Steve's head on his shoulder, holding it there with his hand to give Steve some comfort.

As the sobbing stopped, Robin said, "I can see that we both hate the lords a great deal."

This confused Steve, now too weak to move, he just sat there in apathy. "Stop playing with me for God's sake. Put me out of my misery if that's what you plan to do."

"Let me tell you my tale, or at least part of it," said Robin. "I was fortunate not to be abused, but my early life was a nightmare. When I was small, I saw the village chief take my sister to his house. I saw through a crack how he raped her several times until she fell down. She died a few days later. My father was dragged away for disagreeing with the chief. We never saw him again. My mother was so angry she took a knife to the chief. We found her body the next morning in a ditch."

Steve looked at him in amazement, as Robin getting more upset over his own issues continued. "I had a home, of sorts, with an uncle who seemed to despise me. I worked hard, got fed little, but every day was an effort, and I felt my anger growing by the day."

"But you're a lord," gasped Steve.

"Only on the outside," Robin managed. "My misery ended when the chief's sons picked on me. They hurt me bad, and cut a small piece of my head away, but that was my lucky day. They cut out by accident a tiny device. Without that device in my head I was able to move anywhere. The gates that monitored my movements ignored me. They thought me dead."

Steve's eyes were opening wider in wonder, his mouth dropped open, perplexed but somehow hopeful that this story was going somewhere good. "What happened?"

"I found a way to survive. I found friends, and we removed their devices. We were all dead to the lords' system. We started to fight back against the lords and the more evil masters. We have come a long way, but we still need to be very careful in what we do. When I found out about the prison camp, I came up with a plan to get you all free, but as I keep saying, it has to be secret. We cannot move too fast. A little at a time is our approach. There are still not many of us, but all the village chiefs in the south are our friends."

Shaking his head, Steve said, "I don't know what to make of all of this. You make me want to believe you, but how can I?"

"What if," said Tom, speaking for the first time, "your device could be removed? That would make you a free man. You could join us, make your own way in life, or we could take you to live in a village?"

"I took an awful risk telling you all of this, so I'm hoping you will trust us," said Robin. "By the way my given name is Robin." Robin offered his hand, which Steve took, smiling a weak acceptance, still fearing the worst.

"It seems I am a dead man walking, so what worse things can happen?"

"OK, as far as everybody else is concerned, for the time being, you are dead. We will need your help to convince the other prisoners to join with us, not for our benefit although we always need more friends, but because they will become free. First off, we need to get you inside the palace, without you being seen. By the way this is my great friend Tom, and this is Digga," Robin said, encouraging his dog to say hello to a new friend. She came and licked Steve's hand to know him better. Tom and Steve then shook hands.

"Tom, please make sure the way is clear, and we need Andy or Larry to do their thing. Let's aim for the external bathroom on the first floor."

A few minutes later they were ready to follow Tom. "Just a little something I have to do to convince everyone that you won't be going back," said Robin, taking his bullet pistol out of his pocket. He fired it into the air twice, with Digga wincing as much at the loud noise as Steve did. "Let's go. They should all have heard that."

When Robin and Steve reached the bathroom, Tom and Andy were already there with a suitable bottle of whiskey. "This is going to hurt," promised Andy. "You will need to get your head under that shower head to wash it clean. The whiskey here will be used to clean the area, and you can drink a certain amount. Whiskey by the way is an old-fashioned alcoholic drink our ancestors loved. Drinking it will help to ease the pain."

Steve did what was requested of him, and his scream was nowhere near as loud as the gunshots in the garden that everyone had heard. Adam showed the chip to Steve, "They won't know where you are from now on. I suggest you have a long soak in that tub so that we can recognise who you are." They filled the bath with hot soapy water and Steve wallowed in the luxury of something never before experienced.

"If this is a dream or something I don't care," said Steve, "but if it's real then I'm happy to die now."

"Enjoy your soak, but don't die on us now, please," said Robin. "Don't leave this room. We will bring some food up later. In the meantime, Tom will keep you company. Feel free to ask any immediate questions you might have." Then to his dog, "Digga, stay."

*

When Robin made it down to the cells all was quiet and smelling good. "I've dealt with that prisoner," he announced to the masters. "He won't be throwing any more vile slops around here."

Pip looked at him with some disdain, but Jeremy had a satisfied smile all over his face. Max was clearly perplexed, thinking the punishment was harsh even against prison standards.

After a further silence, Max said, "Looks like he made you dirty as well, sir," looking at Robin's, stained jacket.

"Yes," agreed Robin, noticing the marks. "That is ruined now." Looking around he asked, "Are we all done here? If so, we'll go straight into dinner." He made sure to put on a clean jacket first.

Over dinner, Robin was determined to get Pip on his side, asking him, "Why were you unhappy at what happened to that prisoner? Surely you are used to them being killed or heavily punished?"

"Oh indeed, yes, sir," replied Pip. "Only we don't usually kill them all the way. We let em live to feel the pain again and again." Jeremy laughed loudly, very much in agreement.

"What would have been a suitable punishment in your prison?" Tom asked.

Jeremy was keen to add his comments, "After a good beating he'd have been hung upside down from a pole, and he would get kicked every time we passed him by. We might let him get over that then he would be buried up to his neck in dung for 2 days. That would make em quiet for a few weeks."

Robin was watching Pip and Max, their eyes held grief and disdain. He realised they were not as vindictive as they might appear to be, certainly not in the same way that Jeremy was. He felt his original gut feeling that he could trust these 2 was still correct.

"Shooting a man is a little final," Pip said. "I've never known that happen before."

"I don't do that very often," Robin said. "I usually only kill someone when there is no logical reason left within that person, and no way to reason with them."

"Would that dog really have gone for him?" asked Max. "It looked really fierce."

"Oh yes," Tom said, "that dog would be quite prepared to get itself killed protecting us or taking out a dangerous man."

"Tell us more about the prison. If the men downstairs were your best, what state are the rest in?" asked Robin.

"Most prisoners go nutty after 3 years, or sooner," said Pip. "They lose the ability to relate to anything or anybody. Normally they sink deep into themselves, and they are lost, not worth anything as a slave even. They just fade away and often die where they sleep."

"That sounds worse than being shot," claimed Tom.

"We don't make the rules," said Pip, suddenly defensive. "We have to do as we are told."

"Indeed," said Robin sternly. "Give me some numbers, I'm interested in how many men this all ties up."

"Well," Pip went on. "Around 240 prisoners at any one time. 30 masters, and 3 lords. They bring in new prisoners, from all over, every month, and a few die, when they've had enough."

"What do the prisoners get to do during the day?" asked Robin.

"Mostly walk around the compound," admitted Max. "They do all get some kind of corrective activity about once a week or when directed by the lords."

"What form does this correction take?" asked Tom.

"They get told to do something, and if they do it straight away, they don't get any punishment, but usually after an hour they get slow or start to resist," said Pip. "I'd rather not say any more than that, it might spoil our dinner."

"Don't worry, I get the idea," said Robin, who knew only too well how brutal a chief's masters could be.

*

Before the masters went upstairs to their sleeping quarters Robin asked them to linger in the lounge. They sat with the men dressed as lords and were given watered down drinks, meanwhile Robin invited Jeremy to take a brief walk with him and Digga.

"Jeremy," said Robin. "I can't help but notice that you are very much like a lord with your contempt for slaves."

Jeremy took that as a compliment, "Thank you, sir. I always do my bit to help the lords out and to do what they tell me."

"Indeed, but have you ever considered being able to do something else, being free to follow your own life in some way?"

"Oh no, sir," Jeremy guessed he was being tested. "I wouldn't know what to do unless it was to keep prisoners in order."

"I can see that, Jeremy. I only say that because I'm looking for masters with a given talent to look after this house and gardens. Do you like plants?"

"Oh no, sir, I wouldn't be any good with that. I only know prison work."

Or helping to make prisoners go insane, Robin thought to himself.

"I'm keen to know more about the methods used at the prison, perhaps we can chat further some time, but do not mention to anybody what I have said?"

"You have my word, sir."

As Master Jeremy slid back into the lounge, Robin indicated that he wanted Pip to join him. They walked towards the back of the garden before Robin spoke, "I sense something is troubling you Master Pip, and it's not just what happened with the prisoner. It seems to be your role in life. Are you not happy helping prisoners go nutty?"

The reflected light from the house was enough that Robin could read the anguish on the man's face. Feeling that he could be more than frank with this lord, Pip spoke about the things sitting heavily on his heart. "If I can be open with you, me lord, keeping a prison was never what I wanted to do, but it seems my destiny is not mine to decide."

"Yes, life, or a higher authority, often decides for us, but tell me, do you have any skills or talents, other than those related to prisons?"

Surprised at the question, Pip hesitated a moment. "I was always going to be a healer, but because I was big, I was told I would have to become a master, and the lords had me train for my job there at the prison. I know how to stop a runaway, or cripple someone, but I'm not sure that's what you mean."

"I'm interested in your healer skills. How good are you with taking things out of people, bullets or whatever?"

"Never had to do that, sir. My mum taught me about remedies, herbs and so on. She did show me how to cut puss from wounds, and I often do that for some of the prisoners when they get beaten or whipped too bad, so I'm not bad with a knife."

"I fear you are a good man underneath that rough looking face," said Robin.

"Thank you, sir," Pip responded, not wanting to share anything more of himself.

Robin took Pip back to the lounge, telling him to keep quiet about this conversation. "Tomorrow night there is something I want to show you."

Max next joined Robin for a brief chat. "Max, I sense you are a man of hidden talent. What do you like to do when you have some spare time at the prison?"

"I like to make things grow, sir. There's a patch of ground near the fence where I've been growing a hedge. It's a way for me to forget where I am. I know it's important for prisoners to learn their lesson, but I don't like hurting others. I do it because I must. Others could be more spiteful, like a certain master that you spoke to earlier."

"Jeremy? The master who laughed?"

"Yes, him, sir, he can be very spiteful."

"I gathered that," said Robin. "Now I'm looking for people to look after and maintain this house and grounds. If I can swing it, how would you like to become the gardener here?"

Robin had never seen a man's face so suddenly and so dramatically shift from a gloomy open disposition to something entirely different. Max's face lit up with hope and brightness, a twinkle of light was in his eyes that showed him to have a bright soul.

"You don't have to say anything, Max, your face has told me everything I need to know."

*

That night Steve slept in the same room as Larry and Adam, it having 4 beds. Steve still felt like he was dreaming.

*

The prisoners went off as usual the next morning, then Robin spent most of the day talking to Steve, explaining what had happened, and giving his education a major boost, especially on how the old society had been pulled apart. "I have a double anger," Robin stated, "first there is the abuse and awful treatment of those I have known, including myself, but more fundamentally, I despise the way the political elite of the last century set up all the deceit and lies to force us to become slaves. No doubt about it they were patient and planned very well, but their evil deed has had many repercussions. They will never be forgiven, and for that reason I will show them no mercy."

"Oh my god," exclaimed Steve, who was so overwhelmed by everything, especially his new freedom, that he was only taking in part of what he was told, but he certainly got more than the bare bones. He shook his head to try and clear it. "You do know that I'm not the most reliable of people. Many have called me crazy, and yesterday I just felt so mad at everything, I had to do something that I knew would get me hurt."

"The system did that to you, Steve, but now you're getting better. If you ever feel like going crazy just think about what I've told you and how we are trying to free the human race from the worst kind of evil."

"I'll try," smiled Steve, "but you'd best keep an eye on me."

"Now, about tonight," said Robin. "We need to start convincing the other prisoners that we are on their side. I badly need your help with that. I could give you some words to say but it would be better if you used your own.

Let's practice some ideas to see which sounds best. We will be in the garden, and you will be just outside the sentry gate. The first prisoner to come out will be Arry. What do you say to him?"

"Hello, Arry. Bet you don't know who I am? You probably thought I was dead."

"Good start. Tell him about the chip in your head."

They carried on using different opening lines with more information, until Steve could think with what he was trying to get across. They spent a good hour on getting Steve's story straight.

"If Arry gets troublesome we will be around," said Robin.

*

After the evening meal the masters went upstairs with Whiskey to look over them. Robin positioned himself with Digga close to the exit gate. Steve waited just beyond the entrance gate at the back of the garden that registered ID chips. Fortunately it was a dry night and a warm one for December. Tom and Adam took Arry out of his cell for a little chat.

"Where are we going?" asked Arry, getting more concerned as it was a long walk to the end of the garden.

"There is someone we want you to meet. It's not far now," said Tom, as they reached the gate.

A smiling face greeted them, "Hello, Arry. You know me. I didn't get shot after all."

"What!" shouted Arry. "What's going on? I don't know you!"

"Come now, Arry," said Tom, "you must remember a fellow prisoner? A fellow prisoner who is now free. Steve walk through that gate to show Arry what happens."

As requested, Steve walked through to show that the gate no longer registered him.

"You try, Arry, and see the difference," said Tom.

The light flashed as Arry came near the gate.

"What ave you done to im?" demanded Arry.

"Explain for Arry please, Steve."

"I'm a free man," said Steve. "I can go anywhere I want now. These people ain't lords, but they did take something out of me head that makes me a free man." He leaned forward to show off his scar.

Arry was confused, which had been the expected result.

"Look," said Steve, "I've even ad a barf. I'm as clean as a newborn. If you open yer ears, I've got a tale to tell that will warm yer art."

"Not lords?" managed Arry.

"They're slaves, just like us," Steve continued. "They came up with a plan to rescue us from that vile prison. First, they get some of us here to do some work. Then they will take our chips outs. The things that tell the lords where we are."

"What kind of gimmick is this?" Arry gasped.

"It ain't no trick, Arry. It's for real. These blokes lived in villages and they've all ad their chips cut out. They are saving our lives for God's sake, Arry. Listen to me. We can go back to a village and av a normal life. They have to be very careful though. It all has to be done in secret so that the masters don't get wind of it, and the lords don't crush us, so we av to keep our mouths shut."

"It's all true what he says," Robin said, coming forward from the shadows. "I'm pretty sure you want your freedom as the rest of us did. We have achieved it, and we want to help you all as well."

"It's all a bit sudden," admitted Arry. "Ain't never seen anyone but a lord dress like you do."

"That is part of our disguise," Robin said. "It is amazing what we have gotten away with dressed like this. Our purpose is to free as many people in villages, prisons and factories from the control of the lords. If you agree to join us you can help in that and get some satisfaction, some revenge, in hurting the lords, even if it is only to keep kids safe and away from abuse."

"I think I believe you," said Arry. "When you gave me that cream, I knew you were different. What do I need to do?"

"Just make sure that the masters know nothing of this. Then spread the word to your fellow prisoners. We will take them one at a time to remove their chips over the coming nights. Warn the prisoners to keep their mouths shut. We cannot afford for the plans to leak out to the wrong people. We have to make everything seem normal."

"OK," Arry smiled weakly, anticipating a better life, and perhaps some vengeance taking.

"Remember that you have to complete the job of clearing the roads," said Robin. "After which we take you back to the prison, because there will be hell to pay if we don't deliver the same number of prisoners back. It will only be a temporary stay. If we get you back just in time to settle down for the night, when it's all gone quiet you can simply walk out of the prison camp, leaving your chips behind, if that is what you wish. We will give you the chips back, and you just need to keep them close to your skin until you are inside the prison. I had planned to have you just walk out, but I know there are a lot more prisoners there. We need to find a way to take over the camp, kill any lords and the masters that are bad, and free everyone."

"Sounds too fantastic to be true," gasped Arry.

"I know," agreed Robin. "We must plan that properly, later, but for now we will start with your chip. Are you ready to start walking to freedom?"

Arry looked at Steve. They exchanged a glorious smile of relief and hope, and probably for the first time ever, friendship. "Ready I am."

*

The road clearing took less time than anticipated due to the new-found interest in getting back to the prison camp and settling a few scores. The masters began to wonder what was going on because the prisoners were smiling and working hard.

"I've never seen anything like it," Max told Tom one day. "Prisoners that smile and whistle. It must be the fresh air and the food you are giving them. It will be quite a change to get back to what passes for normality and miserable faces."

"Maybe not," suggested Tom. "We plan to come back with you to find out how the lords running the camp can turn good men into such broken wrecks."

"That will be interesting to see," Max smiled. "Can I watch?"

"Make sure you and Pip stay close to us lords. I want your support in talking with the other masters."

"Sounds like it will be quite a confrontation," said Max.

*

On the eighth day the roads had been cleared and everyone got back to the palace for an early meal. Robin had already booked the coaches for a long day, so the food was fed to all inside the coaches to save time. Larry drove the rover, with Tom, Paul, Adam and Marty as passengers, to the camp, all dressed as lords, with the coaches following.

The transport stopped close to the road. The prisoners and masters got off and walked across an overgrown path that didn't see much use, towards the gate of the prison. The masters watched each prisoner light up the sentry light, and also counted the men in.

"You are one man short," said a stroppy looking master.

Pip nodded at the man, "He misbehaved. Got himself shot."

"That's one painful moron less then," said Stroppy.

After watching the prisoners trail into camp, Tom led the others in, ignoring the contemptuous look of Stroppy and other masters. The prisoners, each with a scar on the side of their heads, walked slowly, apparently aimlessly, but waiting for a signal.

The villa was where Tom was heading. It was important they dealt with the lords quickly, to keep confusion down to a minimum. As the lords relied on the masters to keep order within the camp it was fairly certain that the lords would be safely inside, probably a little drunk.

"Take us through the front entrance," Tom said to Pip and Max who were their guides. Pip hit a button on the side of the door which was locked.

"This is master 377456619834 reporting back from work assignment. The lords from the palace came to meet with your lordships."

Something clicked on the heavy door, enabling Pip to push it open. They found themselves in a semi-lit hallway, with doors either side. "Stay close, and do not be surprised at what happens. Remember your dreams of freedom," Tom whispered to Max and Pip. Knowing his way around Pip went to the left door where he normally received orders. This room was small and bright, but comfortable looking. At a table facing them sat 5 lords with a haughty look of contempt on their faces.

While the 2 masters went down on their knees, as was the custom when talking to prison lords, Tom strode into the middle of the room, facing the lords, with his hands resting on his hips, his face expressing a good example of scorn, looking around as if evaluating everything. "I wanted to return your prison scum personally, and to commiserate for your lousy posting," he said, looking over at each lord. Knowing how combative they were, he gave no sign of weakness, despite the butterflies in his stomach.

"Do I know you?" the tall lord at the end asked.

"I doubt it," replied Tom with great derision. "We were brought in after that accident reduced our fellows to dust a while back in that conference. I don't imagine there will be another big one like that for some time. We've been cleaning up some of the mess they left behind as well as completing projects they should have done way back."

"You'll probably know why the supply of butt-kids has dried up then. We haven't had a supply for weeks now, and the prisoners are so much more difficult to bugger," said the same tall lord.

"There's been an excessive demand from the north. Something special going on I understand," Tom lied like a professional. "We haven't seen any for a very long time."

"So what's this I hear about you killing one of our more senior patients?" said the tall lord with half a sickly smile.

"Oh that," said Tom. "Damned idiot was beyond working with. He threw his slops over his master there," he pointed to Max. "No amount of threats would control him. He tried to jump a fence, which he couldn't of course, but he was far too gone to be of any use to us, but I hear you have plenty more like him to work with."

"Yes, plenty of crazies. Sometimes it feels like we are the prisoners, with so much mayhem all around us."

Tom laughed loudly. "I don't envy you at all. Now then, aren't you going to show us around this madhouse before we have to leave?"

The tall lord laughed this time. "Ah, you want to see how we handle the worst of the lunatics. Come with me."

Before they could get outside another lord who had been keeping half an eye on a screen suddenly shouted, "Something is happening. A total of 10 prisoners have just died."

"Nothing to do with us," said Tom. "The prisoners we brought back were in good condition." He was very keen to get the lords outside so that Robin, on his console back in the palace, could help if required. "Where are these dead men? We need to take a close look in case your prisoners are infected with something."

"Hut 16," answered the second lord.

The whole party of 12 started to walk in the direction indicated. Paul happened to glance back at the villa. There was a light on in a top floor window. A hooded figure was watching them. "Who is that?" demanded Paul.

There was no time nor inclination for anybody to answer, for the ex-prisoners without chips had become tired of waiting. They had started their fight for freedom. The more unsympathetic masters were jumped on and died quickly. Jeremy found himself cornered by 4 men, and his lights were quickly extinguished, permanently. The lords watched in great confusion, having never seen such chaos nor allegedly beaten human beings able to work together.

"Is this the way you keep order?" demanded Tom.

"What's happened here?" asked the tall lord. "Is this your doing?" He looked harshly at Tom, still wondering but it was too late for him and the other lords.

"Yes," Tom said as he shot and killed the tall lord, while the others pulled pistols on the remaining lords. They were quickly shot through their heads.

"Come with me," Paul said to Marty, "there is someone upstairs." They raced into the house to find a way up to the top level, to search it.

The noise of the gunshots meanwhile had signalled a pause in the fighting. "Bring all the masters here," Tom shouted. He had to repeat it several times until they all took notice and complied, with the remaining masters herded back towards the small villa where Tom and the others now stood. There were just 15 masters left standing, plus Max and Pip.

In turn, he stood next to the kneeling masters, asking, "Who can vouch for this man, was he truly evil?" There was only one man the crowd decided was truly evil, and he was quickly put out of his misery by Adam, with a bullet through the temples.

"OK," said Tom, as more lights came on. "These men are all our brothers now. Rescue your fellow prisoners that have been in punishment and bring them out here so that we can tell them they are free men."

Paul and Marty had searched the villa but there was no sign of the hooded man. That worried Paul, who told Tom, "I have a strange feeling I've seen that figure out of the corner of my eye several times. I would like to know who he is, and what he is doing."

"We may never find out, but I'll get Pip to organise a search of the camp as well. In the meantime we need to start getting these ex-prisoners cleaned up so their chips can be removed."

By this time there was a big crowd around Tom, all of them wondering what would happen next in the most exciting day of their lives. Having seen lords killed and nasty masters get their just reward, they were keen to just get out of the camp.

Tom addressed them all, shouting loudly, "There is something we have to do before we can leave here." He called for Arry and a few others to stand beside him. "If you look at these men you will see a small scar on their heads. We removed a tiny electrical device that the lords used to track you with and kept you unable to escape through the gate. We must now remove the chips from all of you or you will never be free. It will happen inside the villa, and we will move as quickly as we can, so please be patient. Form a line by the front door and we will get started."

The men complied while Tom looked around for Andy and Larry. "Can you 2 set up inside the villa. I'm sure you will find plenty of whiskey." They went away to get ready, but that didn't take long, and ex-prisoners were soon getting their own personal scar.

Tom watched for a few moments then recalled that they had an outstanding problem of the hooded man. "Pip and Max, can you help me find someone? It might be another lord, or a spy, but there is a man in the camp wearing a hood. Can you organise a search party to find him, starting at the back of the villa?"

The 2 ex-masters were happy to be doing something. They persuaded most of the prisoners that had already had their chips out to help them, and they all went off in search of the mystery man, first attacking the cultivated grounds of the villa, then diverging off in different directions.

Not one of the men complained about the operation, but some did enjoy the swig of whiskey. Whenever there was enough to fill a coach, the men were sent off to one of the villages that had agreed to take them. The chiefs had all been warned to expect traumatised men, to be ready to feed them well, and bed them down for the night. Tom decided that the chip removal queue was going too slow, so he set up an area for himself to do some removals, and things went faster. Even so, it was a good 2 hours before everyone had been done. Nobody caught another sight of the hooded stranger.

*

Robin had been paying close attention to what had been going on at the camp, although the fading light meant he didn't see everything that was going on. He tried to set the beam at a low level, which worked for a few minutes at a time then faded out. It took a further 3 minutes before he could use it again, which he found rather annoying. He did see Adam point towards the villa and then run inside. Suspecting it might be hidden lords ready to counter-strike, he focused the beam's bright light towards the side of the building. He just caught sight of a dark shape moving between the bushes, somehow familiar as he pulled down his hood, to look up to scan the sky.

For a second it seemed that the man was looking directly at him, at his face. Robin cursed as the light went out once more and he lost the figure in the darkness.

*

It was much later when Tom and the others got back to the palace, all greatly relieved that none of them had gotten hurt and that they had freed so many happy but damaged souls. Tom voiced his hopes that the prisoners would settle into village life without causing problems. Thanks to the way the village chiefs welcomed the men in and provided them with more comfort than they'd ever known, plus the fact that the ex-prisoners were simply overwhelmed with joy at being freed, meant a very cosy relationship soon developed with all concerned.

CHAPTER 7

SOMETHING MORE TO CELEBRATE

RICHARD, THE FIRST OF THE new chiefs, now firmly in charge of the village where Tom had once lived, stood at the entrance to the newly erected covered area, welcoming everyone to their first freedom celebration. The area was now holding far more people than ever intended, but far less than the entire village population. Some form of seating and chairs had been set up outside, which stretched for some way up the wide paths.

Obtaining enough spits for the freshly slaughtered pigs to be cooked on had been the main problem, although in the end, villagers had supplemented their slices of meat with their own vegetables, so nobody would lack a full stomach. Mead was in short supply, so that was saved for the guests of honour and as many others that could bring a cup up for half filling.

Richard had even found someone that could play the old piano that had been retrieved after being dumped out of sight by the old chief. Several of the children had watched images of past celebrations where carols had been sung and wanted to do the same.

At last the guest of honours arrived, Robin, Lucy and Tom, driven down by Larry. As they entered the village centre, the people stood up and cheered, but allowed their chief to welcome them with a little speech of his own. "A big welcome to the best friends we ever had," said Richard. "You all know who these good people are," he said, addressing his people.

A great roaring cheer went up.

Almost deafened, Lucy stood her ground and smiled beautifully, looking around at the so happy faces, with tears in her eyes, so glad to be part of this new life.

"We all know," Richard carried on, "that we owe these people a great debt. Let us start this end of year celebration by wishing them well and wishing them and ourselves great prosperity. We, in this village are already rich with great friends around us, and as the next year comes along, we will see even greater riches as we grow more food and improve our village. Happy year end to all of us." Everyone cheered again with many waving their arms in joy.

Robin, Lucy and the others were sat just inside the shelter and served their food by the recognisable figure of Roy, the ex-boat-slave, who gave them a beautiful smile and an extra portion of everything.

"Next year we will have turkey," Richard promised them all halfway through the meal. He went quickly quiet as the piano started to play.

They all looked towards the small stage holding the piano as a group of angelic voices started to sing, "Noel, Noel... The First Noel, the Angels did say..."

Everybody had a great time, even when some old crooners started to sing vaguely remembered songs from the old days, and where they didn't know the words, they made it up, and everyone loved it.

*

"It's a new year," said Lucy, cuddled up with Robin in their cavern, a few days after the big celebration. "We are supposed to make our intentions known for the coming year. How we want to be better, and what we will do to make things more harmonious."

"I'm going to need some help with that," Robin replied. "I already have everything I could possibly dream of. If I had to make a wish it would be that all of this, you and me, the happiness in the villages and so on, could last forever."

"Nobody or situation lasts forever," insisted Lucy, "they either get better or worse. Equilibrium is hard to achieve. Besides, you will grow tired of me especially when I grow old and wrinkly."

"Never, even if you become the greatest ever philosopher," insisted Robin, grabbing his common-law wife and tickling her until she laughed out loud, causing Digga to check in on them. "Yelp, I thought we were being invaded."

"Ask me again in the morning, because you are right, we do need to make plans, but for now there is only one thing on my mind, you." Lucy gave a satisfied sigh and sank deep into Robin's arms.

*

"Let's make a list of the outstanding issues, then put some sort of plan or resolution around them," suggested Tom. Larry, Marty, Paul and Adam had joined Lucy, Robin and Digga, in a new year's planning session. Robin then sent Larry to collect David and George, their chief spies. They carried on with the other things that didn't involve secret activities.

Robin started off with his own list, "Expand number of villages, increase number of helpers, free more prisoners, staff for buildings we've taken over, keep in touch with London factories, plans for better homes in villages, find out who that hooded figure is, we know very little about what goes on in the rest of the country and how the lords are organised, find out where the car that delivers things to the train comes from, more conferences with chiefs and most experienced helpers, and we need to get more people understanding the use of consoles and other online information the lords set up."

"Well that's about all the usual stuff that always comes up," said Paul. "I don't see anything new that will make sure we win this war against the lords. Not that I'm being critical. I can't think of anything new."

"It's not that we need something new," Tom interjected, "it is more a case of being thorough on the things we need to do. Yes, we keep talking about the same things, but these are the important items we must get right if we are to secure a real future."

"Fair enough," said Paul, a little put out. "I just thought we'd be talking about what could be happening. We are expecting the lords to do something to us at some point. Shouldn't we be thinking and planning for that?"

"Good point," admitted Robin. "I personally cannot judge on that question. We don't know really how the lords think or operate. But, yes, we do need to be ready. What do you suggest, Paul?"

"There are probably about 300 men in different camps that could become our fighters, the tough ones, the ones we rescued from prison," said Paul. "They need coordinating, maybe some training, with a structure, like the old-time armies had with different levels of command."

"Sounds reasonable," agreed Robin. "Let's add that along with the idea that we need to learn more about the lords." The rest nodded in agreement.

They talked on for a while, considering the things that had gone well for them were down to them taking chances. "That's probably the attitude we need to instil into our helpers, plan ahead as much as you can, but take advantage of ignorance," Tom stated.

"Should we invite more helpers to our inner circle?" asked Paul.

"Yes," agreed Robin, "but only as and when they stand out for doing a very good job with something."

"OK," said Tom, "that was it for the list, now what about priorities? I want to keep at number one as an ongoing task to get more villages under our banner. Extra helpers will automatically follow from that."

Nobody disagreed with that, except Adam said, "I will get more helpers trained up to remove chips, because I feel I'm going to be busy elsewhere."

"Let me know as soon as you've done some as I want to move forward with that personally, and convert one village every week, if possible, to be chip free."

"OK," said Robin, "that will keep you pretty busy given the distance you will have to travel from here. As soon as you have more helpers, I will show more people how to use the consoles. We should go and pay a visit to the factories and train depot. Who wants to come along?" Marty and Adam volunteered.

"I'd like to start organising our army," said Paul, "initially just to get them used to the idea that they are part of a team. I have some ideas on how we can use them to make the villages secure. I think it would be a good idea if they also patrolled the buildings, we now control."

Robin looked hard at Paul. He had noticed a steely determination in him of late and was wondering if he would eventually become the leader, he felt the group needed. He decided to encourage Paul's ability to do things on his own while keeping everyone in the loop. "Let us know how the ex-prisoners take to all of that, sounds like it could be useful. You will need a couple of helpers though, which is something we should all keep in mind when we make new moves. Never be alone in what you do."

Robin continued, "On a different subject, I guess the people who would know most about the lords would be the slaves that worked as masters and workers under them. I've had some names for people to maintain and keep a presence at the buildings, but we also need to keep it staffed with some of us as lords. We need names for that, but I think if we get all those ex-masters and personal slaves together, we can find out more intimate details about the lords. I propose that for next Wednesday, and I will organise the transport."

"Don't forget," said Lucy to Robin, "that you were also going to lead the small team looking at better village homes."

"Oh yes, thanks for reminding me of that. Who is in that team so far?"

"Adrian, Alex and Albert," answered Lucy. "They are all from our old village."

"On the subject of the lords and territories beyond London," Paul said, "should we think about sending people to spy it out, to travel around and map the various places the lords control?"

"It wouldn't hurt," agreed Tom, "but we'd need more than just 2 spies. Additionally, we need to keep track of who is doing what and where they are."

"I'm keeping a spreadsheet of all the helpers and what they are assigned to," Lucy added, "although that needs expanding. I can work on that as long as we can make sure all helpers let me know if they start new activities or move location."

"So clearly a requirement for more spies as well," said Adam.

As Robin made notes of the discussion so far, as well as listing names and purposes of those he needed to meet up with, Larry arrived back with David and George.

"Good timing," said Tom, "we were just talking about you."

David beamed, while George looked a little worried. "Hope it was not too unfavourable," said George.

"Not at all," said Tom, "Paul was just suggesting that we need to extend your activities beyond London. One thing seems certain, we need more of you."

"Good to hear," said David. "We have been far from idle, working towards a school for spies. There is now an area in 3 villages, so far, where we can teach the basics and recruit others to do the dirty work."

"Excellent," said Robin. "As you recruit people get their chips removed, but please let Lucy have the names of them, what they get assigned to, and where. There are quite a few things going on, what with expanding the villages and so on, we need to understand what's happening with all helpers, so we don't do something silly."

"That we can do," agreed George, "but it sounds like we missed the earlier discussion." Robin read out from his notes to bring the 2 spies up to date with what else was planned.

"I'm still interested in your spying activities on the various installations used by the lords," said Robin. "Did you find any more?"

David pulled a folded piece of paper from his backpack, unfolded it gently to cover most of the desk, then said with a big smile, "Again we have not been idle. We have scoured every part of the country to the south. As you can see, villages have been marked, as well as any location we found inhabited. See the blue spots?"

"There are a lot of those," said Tom, "but what are the numbers next to them showing?"

"Blue numbers are estimates of lords, red are the slave numbers."

"Gosh," said Paul, "that means there are literally thousands of people we didn't know existed, nor their purpose."

"We can fill in some of the detail as regards purpose," said David. "George and I did extensive observations of most of these places, with some interesting results. Robin, we did send our location data to you, so you will have the exact physical locations in the memos."

"Good work," replied Robin. "Let's have some more detail on which of these could be a threat to us, and which ones hold our people. Lucy, will you take a note of these, please? We need to keep a record of the type of building, whatever, its purpose, its threat potential as well as exact location, plus any other details David and George can supply."

"I feel a very big spreadsheet coming on," Lucy smiled. "It is so nice that the lords allowed us to use the old technology even if it is starting to break down at times."

"That is another task for the future," laughed Robin, "to work out what is behind all of this technology we use, how it works, and how we can build it ourselves, but we'll save that for another day. George and David, please take us through what you found."

The 2 spies had found camps of various kinds, where slaves were used either to mine material or lift heavy things and fill rail trucks. Sometimes the slaves were in long sheds working machinery, other times they poured some kind of runny liquid into containers bolted together. "We did find one camp where they seem to breed geese and other birds, under a vast wire roof which stops the birds escaping," David announced.

"Altogether, there were 8 of what we termed production centres," said George, "with 2 more prisons, each with around 300 prisoners. Additionally, there were around 6 large fancy villas occupied by lords, who used the slaves as servants, all in beautiful grounds and a large degree of luxury."

"You have done amazingly well to get all of that data. My head is going dizzy at trying to figure out how we will handle them all," said Robin.

"We will take them one at a time, with planning and cheek," Tom smiled, quoting Robin's concept back at him.

"Do you think we'd get away with the same trick of using the prisoners for some work?" Robin asked.

"Why not?" said Paul. "Successful actions should be repeated. It will just mean we will need another base further south."

George jumped in with an answer, "If you see the most southerly village, just below it is a big villa. It has some nice grounds, as well as a host of small houses. The main building is not so grand, more functional than attractive, but it does seem to get plenty of usage, with lords coming and going. It is possible the lords who sleep here might just administer some of the other interesting places we have identified. If we could take over that it would make a perfect location to manage attacks on other objectives."

"Yes," agreed Tom, "but we need far more information on it before we go charging in. Like what purpose does it serve and is it just to accommodate lords? You 2 may have to dress as lords and pay a visit to see what is going on there." George and David smiled at this idea, welcoming real spying activity.

"Let's shift any real action to the end of February," said Robin, "that will give you 2 time to get in there and find out all you can. We can get a real planning meeting together when we know more."

The discussion went on for some time, looking at different angles of the plans made so far, after which Robin summarised the bare bones, with the intention of making more detailed plans as time permitted.

*

Robin acquired some people to look after the mansion and the villa, which satisfied a few people including Max. By the second week of January he had invited those ex-slaves to the mansion who knew the lords best. Now that there were security men, cooks, housekeepers and maintenance men, the 2 locations ran themselves, but more importantly gave the impression of normality. Additionally, it allowed for somewhere to rest up for those on missions.

Larry was now recognised as the primary rover driver. He brought Baker, Eric, Cook, Roy, and Pip for an overnight stay, to tell all they knew about how the lords worked together, and what they did. The man in charge of making wonderful pastries came first, giving Robin some time to enlighten him.

"Baker," said Robin, once they were inside the mansion ground office. "I have a confession to make. Not all is as it might appear."

Baker laughed cheerily, "Let me guess. You are not really a lord, and you have no authority over any factories?"

Robin's jaw dropped open and he was silent for several moments. "How ..." he managed.

"I suspected it from the start. You were too nice, too reasonable. You made me feel human. You were all pleasant to be with, totally unthreatening. In short you could never be mistaken for real lords."

"Oh my goodness, and there was me thinking we were such good actors."

"Not bad, but it was your kindness that gave you away, and the way you wanted the slaves treated better."

"Did you discuss this with the other 3 factory masters? Do they know?"

"No," said Baker, "I never spoke to them about you, but I could tell they thought you a soft lord."

Robin decided to tell Baker everything. "Look, I realise that you could be monitored from different sets of lords, so it was important to make things appear normal. I hope you can understand my point here. We have made progress in establishing a safe place for us and our friends, but I want to avoid making ourselves too obvious. Where possible we must produce as before."

"I can totally understand all that, and I have eased up on the slaves since your visit, but to be free we have to do a lot more."

"You are not wrong," agreed Robin. "What would you say if I told you that we had already taken over all of the villages in the Southeast with people in them running their own affairs?"

"I'd say that was close to amazing, but how?"

"With a lot of luck and a certain amount of cheek," Robin said, smiling. "We go in, and take out the bully boys and existing chief, find someone sensible to lead the villagers, then help them to get used to their new-found freedom. We naturally tell them to go on as before with regards to what they produce and send away, with the exception that no more kids are sent away. Although we have found that being free people they produce more because they are happier."

"Now that sounds like you haven't been sat around eating cakes. All of the south east you say, now I know that is a big area."

"Only the villages are with us, but we did manage to empty a prison not so long ago and freed a lot of abused prisoners who now reside in villages. There are other places still controlled by lords that we still need to handle, which brings me on to why I asked you to come here."

"Oh," Baker frowned, "what becomes of the lords when you free prisoners and so on?"

"They always die pretty quickly. I have no time for anyone that perpetuates the crimes against our people. In my book they are all equally guilty and deserve no special treatment," Robin stated with determination. "On the other hand, those slaves that have become masters do deserve sympathy, but woe betide those that mistreat other slaves."

"My goodness, the lords won't like that you know, when they find out what you've been doing."

"It's the only option we have," Robin insisted. "If we don't take control of as much land as possible, and grow strong, we will never be free from being slaves. We know they will come for us at some time, but even if we fail utterly and they turn us back into slaves, we will have tasted freedom for a while. More than that, we will not be ignorant of their crimes which will become part of our culture."

Baker sighed, taking that in, thinking it a recipe for disaster, but admiring Robin's spirit. "I wouldn't be any good as a fighter," he managed.

"You don't need to do any fighting. You only need to keep on doing what you are doing. You will be safe that way. Just treat the slaves well. You do, however, have information that can help our cause."

"What do you mean?"

"I mean that you've been around lords a lot more than I have. You spotted traits that gave us away as non-lords. Perhaps you could show me how they are different to how we behave? That would be a start."

"Oh," giggled Baker, "to sort of train you to be nasty and brutal. Yes, I can pass on a few tips, certainly."

"That will help, but I need much more. I'm bringing in a few other people so that I can learn more about the ways of the lords. More importantly, we still do not know exactly how they are organised. Where they are mainly located and what they do, what is happening elsewhere. We have stumbled on a few of their activities, but that won't do for the future. We badly need to be better informed."

"Oh, OK, I get it. I might have a few snippets."

"I strongly suspect that," smiled Robin, "but before the others arrive, give me some pointers on what makes a lord look like he is evil incarnate."

*

They worked away for an hour or so, improving the way Robin snarled, increasing his ability to look at Baker with enough hate in his eyes to make him flinch and turn away in fear. It was the change in the timbre of his voice that made a real difference. Robin could now turn any sentence into a condemnation to make the strongest feel guilty and worried. "That may all come in handy," Robin said, thanking Baker.

The others arrived soon enough, with everybody quickly becoming friends with Baker, which may have had nothing to do with the pastries and pies he had supplied. They were joined by the usual helpers as well as Digga.

"I want to know how the lords are organised," Robin started off with. "Also, what plans they might have, and if possible, how do they think. We know very little about them, so anything you can tell us will be useful. Things like the purpose they have for the different places they run, in fact anything."

Roy started off with, "I was taken often on trips in the little boat you found me in. I can tell you about them if you want?"

"That will make a good start," said Robin.

"Has anybody got a map, then I can point out the locations?"

"There's a nice big map on the inside of the door to the study," said Eric.

"Now that is a good one," Robin said. "Never knew it was there because the door was never closed when we were in here. Please continue, Roy."

"We paid a visit to most of the places with a blue pin. There are lots of lords at each place with plenty of activities going on. I didn't often see much because I was always on the boat, but you can tell some things from just looking across at the people moving about or the type of buildings."

"Why don't you work around the coast, starting from the most northern place you've been to?" suggested Tom.

"That will be Great Yarmouth then. We entered a river and moved some way up before stopping overnight near a large house that sat on the river bank, close to a bridge. During the day they all sat outside in the sunshine drinking beer and laughing, mostly at me. The next day we started early and went up a rather narrow river, north, towards the main part of Great Yarmouth. We stopped at some sort of place that has lots of different types of clothing, trinkets, and other things what looked like luxury to me, furs and soft fabrics. Each establishment had their own workshops, employing dozens of slaves each. The lords would all came back to the boat with a lot of parcels as well as new gold trinkets on their wrists and round their necks."

"So that was like a store house?"

"Yes, but much fancier, and they made clothing as well as other things. There were a great many little houses, each with a big glass window so you could see what they had inside. There were other boats, bigger than ours being loaded up with these things, so perhaps this was a centre for luxury items. We only journeyed that way when the lords were authorised from above for something they'd done well."

"Any idea where the raw materials might have come from?"

"From boats I suppose, but I didn't see any."

Robin scratched his chin, trying to get his head around what this place of luxury items was all about. "Did the lords have to exchange anything, money, credit notes, or any authorisation to take these goods away?"

"Not that I saw," said Roy, "all I ever saw, from a distance was that they offered the store people those little plastic cards. The master there would take the card away into the store and return it a few moments later."

"Interesting," said Robin, "like they were checking identity. I wonder if they had to make an appointment to go there?"

"The master that greeted them when they got off the boat was expecting them, certainly."

"Interesting. We will pay them a visit in the warmer spring weather. That will give me time to investigate how they were notified. Do you fancy a trip with us, Roy?"

"Could be interesting," Roy said with a smile.

Robin made notes of everything Roy was telling him, then they went on to discuss other locations visited in the boat.

"There was Woodbridge. We went up the River Deben for a good 8 miles to reach it. It was a place where the lords played with their sail boats on the wide river, and where boats were built or repaired. Harwich was a coastal place we stopped at several times. It was strange because there were a lot of big boats there with huge guns. Plus, large boats would come in from other countries with many different types of things on board."

"Big boats with large guns," Robin said excitedly. "Now that is of interest. We may need to steal such a boat at some time."

"That won't be easy. There are many guards on each boat, and around the area, day and night. I've never seen such disciplined people. There were many masters amongst the lords, hundreds of both in fact. There was also a training school I walked by carrying some papers to an office there with one of my lords. Even though it was lords being trained they treated them like slaves, brutally hitting them. You know how vicious they can be."

"I do indeed. That sounds like another interesting place when we are ready to go to war. Do go on, where else did you travel to?"

"Oh, OK, well many times we travelled up the Thames to different locations, mostly factories within London. I'd have to show you because their names were not clear."

"Another trip in the spring then," Robin smiled.

Roy then described trips to a variety of locations on the east coast, then the south coast as far as Southampton, with Robin making notes.

"There is an island near there, have you ever been there?"

"No. They didn't like to use the boat for sea crossings, even short ones, but I did hear that was a place of pleasure. They all wanted to go there for some fun and enjoyment, but you can guess what they meant by that."

By the time Robin had secured as much information from Roy that came easily, the others had started to remember little things that added to the big picture. Every last piece of data helped Robin to build an analysis of the overall jigsaw that they had to confront.

Pip was able to add a good amount of information on how the lords received orders from above, and their organisational structure. There were more ranks than they'd ever thought possible, from trainee, which was a slave state, effectively, to other ranks that mirrored the old army designations, with colonels and generals almost at the top. Even the structure of generals was further defined by the number of stars on their suit.

Pip had seen a one-star general once, "A vile looking man with hate etched into his eyes. Nobody would dare to look him in the eyes. His body looked and smelled most unhealthy, and just during the period of a one-hour meeting, an aide was sent out to bleed a butt-kid to give this monster a boost."

"Sounds disgusting, but how do we get our uniforms to show a high rank?"

"All the ranks up to major wear the same suits as you have. Colonels wear blue, while generals wear brown."

"So how can I become a colonel?" Robin asked.

"You will have to go to Great Yarmouth, but you will need a special certificate. They won't just make it for you without an official piece of paper."

"I feel a spying mission is called for," said Robin. "Must get all the authority we can. It would only help." While the thought was fresh in his memory, he sent a memo to David and George to come for a meeting at the palace.

The chatting went on well into the night, only interrupted by food, with Robin gaining a lot of interesting but useful information. When the others had gone, he wrote it all up in the diary he'd been keeping. Every scrap of useful information acquired was now part of this diary. He felt it vital to make sure that no matter what became of him, that he had to prepare for the others that would follow on, and eventually free their souls from the lords.

He had no concept of he himself achieving it, for they were just so weak compared to how the lords were organised, even if he had managed to kill off a few lords. Information would be key to taking things forward. After bringing the diary up to date he printed 30 copies and left them out for Larry to deposit with key individuals, as well as every village chief. They could be read by any helper or chief, or indeed any villager.

*

It was 2 days later when the spies arrived at the palace, to find Robin, Tom and Lucy fully engaged in talking tactics. Robin explained about the need to obtain high ranking uniforms, as well as the likely locations where information could be obtained. "Harwich will be a tricky place but be sure to look important and snarl at everyone. It will be full of lords all ready to show their superiority, never their companionship."

David and George accepted their new assignment easily, now feeling confident in their role. They'd already trained others who would keep the training and spying activities going wherever they were. Then they mentioned all they knew about the last objectives they had been sent on. "You'd have been proud of us, for our cheek," David said. "We had the garage in London deliver us to the grand villa just south of the last village. We were given a suite each, which was nice, as it seems our borrowed uniforms showed a higher rank than most of the lords staying there. They called us a 5, although I'm not sure still what it was that gave our rank away."

"We were able to explore the whole site," inserted George. "It would take a fair few people to assault it and kill the lords there unless we were clever about it. We noticed that there are fire alarms in every room, so if we were able to trigger them the lords would all go outside to a location nearby, ready for you to zap them with that light beam."

"Now that sounds like a plan," Tom said.

"I'll say," agreed Robin. "With the lords out of the way, we can get a good group of us down there to take up residence briefly. From there we can travel to each location our spies have identified to take over. Most places will have only masters left to run things I suspect, and if we go in force, we should be able to free quite a few people. Some we might leave in place because they may be making things we need, but that will be a decision to make when we get down there."

*

While the spies were away, Robin concentrated on forward planning. Larry became an extra for Tom's team. He would drive Tom, Marty, Adam and Reg, the new boy who could remove chips. Larry would be sitting in the rover, out of sight, and in control of the light beam to roast village nasties. Tom planned to use the same process he'd always used to get everyone in the village together, as it had worked so well so far. Every week Tom had the old chief recite the nursery rhyme just before he and his bullies were zapped. This way he added a new village to those already rescued from anarchy.

If they were to visit some of the places Roy had told them about, they would surely need a boat. It took Robin a good while sifting through indexes to locate the memo address for a boatyard that provided boats, then he found two. They looked identical from the description, but using the spy in the sky to view the actual locations, Robin was able to see the difference. The first one appeared to be where bookings could be made to use sail boats to enjoy the wide river. The second was more promising, with a series of wooden yards, with slipways, lining a side of the river.

Psyching himself up to be as unpleasant in demeanour as possible, Robin started the memo with, "I want a replacement for my cruiser that was lost due to a design fault in rough seas. Fortunately it didn't kill any lords, or I would be taking this further." He went on to demand a 4-berth motorised cruiser that could cross open sea if required.

A reply was received within the hour, saying that a boat was being sought. Next day a subsequent memo reported that a boat was being made ready, due for delivery the next day. Robin was on hand to take delivery and take the keys from the delivery master. It was a very shiny craft, even the wood gleamed. Robin almost forgot himself, starting to say something pleasant about speed of delivery, but he caught himself in time, giving the man a snarl instead, cutting off the man's efforts to explain some of the features below deck.

"We're not stupid here, man. Just make sure the user guide is where it can be found."

The master cringed, "It is in the locker next to the wheel."

"You've requested a lift back, haven't you?" demanded Robin with eyes narrowed, turning a question into a statement.

"Yes, me lord, it won't be long behind."

The lift turned up as Robin was about to wander back inside. The small wooden vessel looked like it would have a hard time making headway, for the small engine at the back was low in the water and appeared to be rather ineffective. "Make sure you don't drown yourselves going back in that pathetic craft, or I will get the blame."

"Oh it will get us there," said the master with a tight smile as he boarded the wooden dinghy. "I've travelled much farther in it than this before now."

Robin relaxed his demeanour and nodded the men off, hoping their confidence was well placed. He went into the house to tell Lucy and Digga to come look over his new cruiser. It was indeed quite luxurious down below, with a galley fully stocked with food and very adequate facilities. Digga especially appreciated that there was a space for her to lie down close to the table and tried it out. They left Digga to enjoy the feel of her cosy corner then stopped by the largest cabin where a large double bed enticed them to lie on it. They cuddled closer. "We really should take it for a little trip," said Robin. "I should get Roy back to help us navigate. Perhaps, though, it would be best when Tom gets back."

"Yes, you should have a trip out. The sea air will be good for you," agreed Lucy, "but I'm not sure I should go in my condition. That water looks far too violent for my liking."

Suddenly alarmed, Robin raised himself on his elbow, looking hard at his beloved. "What's wrong with you? Are you ill?"

Lucy smiled a wicked smile, eyes bright, "Not at all, but I am growing a little." She took his hand to her abdomen and held it there. He maintained his look of confusion for a whole minute, with Lucy looking at him, her eyes glowing with love. The penny finally dropped.

"You're going to... We're going to be parents," he spluttered, taking her face in his hands and kissing her all over. "We have been truly blessed. That is much better news even than the new cruiser," he smiled brightly.

*

They did get to take the cruiser out for a short trip when Tom got back, but they were very nervous about finding their way back again, so didn't go far. A message was sent to Roy to ask for his help whenever he felt like it to help them explore with their new craft. In the end they settled on late March when the weather would be warmer and the wind less biting.

*

Robin continued to add to his plans while the weather was too cold to invite much activity. He also took the opportunity to look at how homes in the villages could be improved. He knew any new homes could not match the ones from the earlier centuries, but he wanted to take the best features and somehow incorporate some of them. Water was an interesting issue. Obtaining the correct metal to store water was one thing but then that had to be filled, and easily available for use. He decided he needed someone with knowledge of metal. Perhaps a factory to the south would provide that expertise? That thought made him switch back to planning mode for taking over the southern villa, and how the slaves in the various locations run from the villa would be made free.

*

Spring came with Lucy and Robin spending most of their time in the palace, where they received regular visitors. Digga stayed with them, while the young dogs, all 4 of them, trailing after Tom on whatever adventures he was involved in. Robin was very keen to get the new uniforms that would demonstrate him and Tom, and several others, as holding a high rank as a lord. The spies had done a great job in making this possible. Bold as brass they'd walked up to the depot that issued the required documents to certify lords of high status and demanded some. It would seem that since so many lords never came back from a conference security was rather lax, which didn't hurt the mission. Using methods they kept a secret, they had first scouted around to find out how these certificates were obtained, all the time making new contacts with junior lords, and even drinking with them. Now it was up to Robin to go and get those uniforms from Great Yarmouth.

*

With the certificates in his hand Robin sent a memo to the uniform makers, quoting references and key physical measurements. In typical style, he told them they should be ready in 3 days' time. Almost immediately the order was confirmed. Robin printed off this confirmation and made ready to leave, with Tom, Larry and of course Roy. Spies David and George had even obtained new plastic cards for the newly promoted lords with a huge spending budget.

The sea was welcomingly calm as they made the trip up to Great Yarmouth, but it was getting dark by the time they had entered the estuary leading to their destination, making it hard to find a suitable place to tie up the boat for an overnight rest, but Roy's memory helped them well.

With things going so well, Robin was more than a little nervous when they reached the service area the next morning. They'd arrived at the small dock too early and had to wait impatiently for the shops to open. They dressed Roy in a junior lord's suit which made him giggle and admire himself in the mirror in his cabin. Having been so used to curling up on deck in all weathers, Roy was as pleased as punch and relished his new-found status with a big smile. Having a whole luxury cabin to himself for the trip was one thing, but the luxury of it almost overwhelmed him. In his wildest dreams, while being abused as a slave, he had never imagined he would ever see such a thing.

Several small cruisers and one large one joined them at the dock while they were having a last cup of tea impatiently, so they decided it was time to venture into the arcade. Larry had agreed to be the slave today and waited with the ship, in watching distance of his friends. He noticed a lord and his entourage of 3 juniors leaving the big cruiser and was a little horrified as he made his way towards Robin to strike up a conversation with an equal.

Robin appeared to snarl in an appropriate manner and the 2 seemed to become friends almost at once.

After a few minutes banter, the lord asked, "You say you are in charge of most of the Southeast quarter? That's a big area, but I'd heard that the palace just off the Thames estuary had been sacked and ruined by some escaped scum."

"All too true," admitted Robin. "That was really the first place we had to clean up. Damned scum were everywhere, but they didn't last long when we went in. I think there may still be a corpse or 2 in the garden." They both laughed heartily at this.

The 2 lords chatted further as their assistants ran around and collected the required uniforms and matching accompaniments. The lord noticed the style of the uniforms being carried now to the boat, "Congratulations on your promotions. You must be doing well, and I'd appreciate any hints you might have," passing an evil smile to Robin who wanted to just spit it into the ground but retained it long enough to pass it back.

"I control the area north of the Fenlands," the lord continued, "but the lazy scum are getting hardened to the whip. If I hang any more of them there won't be enough of them to do the work. How do you motivate your workers?"

Robin allowed one of his deranged smiles to creep across his face and gave out a noise between a laugh and a grunt. He wasn't sure why; it had just seemed appropriate to go with his snarling lips. "You won't believe how easily they take things in; they are born believers of any old rubbish. I had some of the more vicious camp chiefs replaced, you know, the really violent ones, because they were creating the same situation as you described. I had the new chiefs go easier on the village slaves, and even suggested to them that they were free men who would be working for themselves but would still need to supply a certain quota to me. You could not believe the difference. They produced more, they sent in more, and they actually started to make their villages more functional without me enforcing anything on them. They even smile at me when I make an inspection." They both laughed loudly at that.

"That sounds too amazing, so being kind you got more out of them?"

"A little correction there," Robin smiled his evil look, "to be kind is to be weak. I just gave them a little lie to make them feel better and stopped them getting whipped and beaten for no good reason. It was done mainly with subtle indoctrination to make them think they were no longer slaves."

"I do like the sound of that," said the lord, making ready to go back to his boat. "Thanks, you've given me something to think about."

"Good luck," said Robin. "Now I have some browsing to do." With that he collected his 2 assistants and went from store to store, picking up whatever took his fancy, as well as several sets of decent shoes for himself, as well as some for Lucy. Then he sought gifts for everyone he knew. One store specialised in perfumes, and he thought such a gift would help the women in his life smell nicer. There were scarves and coats in another store that really took his fancy, and so it went on. The storage on the cruiser was overflowing by the time Tom had selected items for himself and Larry. Roy took his time, and quietly purchased some luxury items that would remind him for a very long time of the day he became a lord, even if it was for a very short time.

*

There were several visitors at the palace when they got back, and Robin was glad he'd purchased some extra smelly liquids which he gave to Anne and Jane, as well as special ones to Lucy. The girls also received a coloured scarf each. The men received leather wallets, even if they had nothing special to put in them, but they did look impressive. Most of his parcels and boxes he deposited in his bedroom for later inspection.

"Now that we are colonel lords," Tom stated, "we really must get on with freeing up our kinsfolk down south, and that's why I invited everyone here."

"Ah, OK, that all makes sense now then," said Robin, smiling, happy that someone else was making decisions.

*

Robin brought out his sketches and ideas for taking over the large country mansion that housed the lords who appeared to manage various groups and activities in the far south of the country. "It will be necessary for us to dispose of unnecessary lords and masters, because otherwise they will just cause trouble, and I don't know what else we could do with them."

"That means then that we will all have to carry guns and not be afraid to use them," Paul added.

"We can make use of the plan suggested by David and George to get everyone outside so we can make toast of them, but there are bound to be some that escape. We may be able to make use of them, so we could capture and interrogate any that remain. Having the colonel uniforms will allow us to walk in and simply take over, and that's what I want to do initially."

*

When it came to the day, everyone was collected from their village by coaches, or driven down by Larry in the rover. All told there were 10 of them, which Robin had decided was an optimum number. "Rather too many than too few troops," he had said.

The rover arrived ahead of the coach by about 10 minutes, giving the colonels time to get a good look of the outside. They walked up and down, across lawns, until eventually they were noticed, and a master came out to fawn and greet them.

Tom and Robin stood together, their noses in the air, ignoring the intrusion, pointing out things they chose to criticise. Robin looked down at the man as he sank to his knees, sneering with his eyes. "What is it, man?" Tom demanded.

"Your lordships. Nobody told me you were coming."

"Nonsense," exclaimed Robin. "My number 3 sent a memo personally, telling you to expect an inspection. Who the hell is in charge here during the day?"

"That will lord 17."

"Go and fetch him, now," screamed Tom.

It was clear the lord in question had been interrupted in the middle of something. His trousers were roughly pulled up, and a little blood was evident on his top lip. The man himself was not very tall but made up for it in attitude. When he saw the uniforms, he became less belligerent in his manner as he hurried across to where Tom and Robin stood. He became more clearly nervous, slowing slightly, as he approached the high-ranking lords, his mind working overtime trying to figure out why they were visiting.

To add to the man's torment the coach pulled in with extra lords for the cause of freedom.

"Your forgiveness, my lords," begged number 17. "Your memo didn't reach me. How may I serve you?"

"Wipe your pleasure from your face and get dressed properly," Tom scorned with a real bitterness. "Then you can show us around these premises, and explain why your general area productivity is so low."

The man swallowed hard and corrected his looks. He pointed at the mansion, trying very hard to work out how he could get on the good side of these high lords. "Of course, my lordships. This is the main building we use to accommodate the lords and juniors who look after the slaves in the general area and the various production factories. I am responsible for the running of this establishment."

*

"Are there any other lords here?" Robin asked.

"Yes, sire, there are 3 others taking a brief respite from an arduous schedule."

"Resting?" demanded Tom. "No wonder your production figures are slipping."

"Get them here immediately so that we don't have to keep repeating ourselves," Robin spat.

The man was happy to get away from the close scrutiny and ran to comply. He returned a few minutes later with 3 other lords, again, who were surely interrupted in some savage game. They stood in a line facing their superiors, who urged them to provide what identification they could and what they did to compensate for living in such a beautiful location. They were simply known as lords 22, 31 and 38.

Tom addressed them, "We are here to inspect your working activities so that we can see why your quotas are static. If a factory is doing well, we should see a gradual increase. Now, after you 4 show us everything in these grounds, we will want to see inside. After which we will see all of the production figures you keep."

"Yes, my lord," the 4 said in unison.

"We will be staying overnight," Robin insisted. "There will be adequate appropriate sleeping rooms available for me and my assistants." He indicated the lords with him as well as those standing some distance away, admiring the lawns, that had recently left the coach and sent it on its way.

"Of course," said number 17, "I will personally ensure the rooms are to the standard to match your status. I will also make sure you have an adequate supply of butt-kids for your pleasures." He grinned wickedly, thinking most lords, especially high ones, would be calmer and less aggressive if they could take the fresh blood of a youngster or three.

"This is a work trip," Tom shouted, almost in a rage, but controlling himself, just. "This is not a pleasure trip. We all have important work to do here, and we can tolerate no distractions."

Number 3 blushed crimson at the short tirade, "Oh, I see, my lord. Of course, of course."

"Now," shouted Robin. "You 4 will escort us around the external area and explain what the buildings are used for." He signalled his troops to follow on.

The tour lasted a little less than an hour and gave everybody ample time and information to be able to come up with a plan of action to dispose of this as a centre for the foul lords. Apart from the main house there were 3 outbuildings, 2 used for sleeping quarters and one long hut for storage. Robin made a mental note to avoid blowing up the hut, for there was a vast array of tools and electronic devices that would come in handy.

The main house comprised of over 30 sleeping rooms, most of them, save for the few shared ones, maintained too luxuriously. A group of 20 butt-kids were caged in the basement, supervised by 2 masters. "This place smells disgusting," Tom screamed at both masters. "How could anyone touch any of these butt-kids when they lie in such squalor? Take each one out. Give them a hot shower, and make sure the cells are disinfected before putting the kids back there."

"I don't want to see any more marks and bruises on them," Robin added. "They will be our entertainment once we have completed our task in a few days' time. They look too feeble to have any blood in them. Do you actually feed these scarecrows?"

The first master started to stammer, while the second was a little bolder, "Yes, my lord, twice a week as directed."

"Well give them some extra food. I can't stand scrawny, filthy butt-kids," Tom insisted.

As they were leaving that room, Robin asked, "How many slaves and masters are housed here?"

"There are 5 masters and 14 slaves altogether, that sleep in the basement, milord," 17 responded.

Robin and the others took over the top floor and attic. The 4 lords were kept close by all the time, with either Robin or Tom throwing questions at them to make them uncomfortable.

"I shall want to interview everyone as they come back," insisted Robin. "Tell them to get cleaned up then queue up until they are called. We will start with you 4 so that we can understand what functions everyone performs. The lounge looks private enough, so that is where we will be." Tom and Robin settled themselves in the lounge while the others went out to explore the whole grounds and more of the buildings. They looked in cupboards and other places not covered in the tour. Very specifically they were taking any weapons they could find, leaving them in Tom's room, to limit the options if the lords should fight back. Every room was searched for anything that might get a lord into trouble, but it was small guns and fighting knives that were the target. The searchers went everywhere. Larry made a note of all items found in each room to provide Tom and Robin with useful information.

The 4 resident lords waited patiently in the corridor while Robin set up his laptop. They came in one at a time, with Tom asking the questions, making them intrusive and biting, starting with, "Name if any, number, rank, age, room number, current function, place of origin, history of service." The questions went on and on, leading into how many butt-kids they had had, and frequency, as well as perversions. After Tom had drained each lord in turn of personal data he asked questions about the others, and how relations were between everyone. This gradually evolved into matters of trust and who wasn't working hard enough to get the quotas done. Even with just 4 contributions, Robin soon had several pages of jealousies and incriminating actions to throw at certain other individuals.

When the other lords came back, they gathered even more important information. Each factory and location maintained from this mansion was described in detail. What they produced or their reason for being there, as well as where the raw materials were sourced from was extracted in great detail. By the time all of the lords had been interrogated it was approaching midnight. The residents went to their sleeping quarters, still alarmed at the sudden inspection and cross-examinations, fearing for their positions. Robin and the others relaxed for a short time before executing the next part of the plan.

At 2am, having given the lords just enough time to get into a deep sleep, and awake in a daze, the fire alarms were set off, sending the sleepy lords scurrying towards a patch of safe ground outside the mansion. Tom and the others made a point of standing some distance to the lords, while number 4 and 2 masters were sent inside to locate where the fire might be.

"Our high lord is missing," declared Tom, rushing back into the house, with the real intention of distracting attention away from Robin who was getting ready to activate the satellite beam.

All the lords were perfectly lined up. Robin made sure his friends were situated safely away before hitting the destruct beam to turn 50 or so spoiled brats into charcoal and watched as the victims looked up towards the brightness before they were incinerated.

Larry and the others started to move back into the house, almost colliding with number 4 as he came out to give the all-clear. "The others have already gone back to their beds," Larry lied, preventing 4 from seeing the dark patch on the lawn. The masters were locked away.

Everyone went upstairs where Tom was there to confront 4, "This disruption is appalling. You will be held responsible."

The lord spluttered, whined, then accepted his fate as he was led up to the cells holding the butt-kids and put inside a spare one.

*

The slaves and masters were allowed out of their sleeping quarters in the morning. Tom told them, "Do what you normally do. Prepare yourselves for a different way of working. The lords that previously ran things here have been removed because they were not doing a good job." Addressing the masters, "From now on we will not allow you to beat or abuse any slaves. If you are having a problem with anyone report the situation to me. Is that understood? If we are to get the best out of slaves, then they must be treated better and fed well." The masters looked baffled but nodded in compliance.

The masters and slaves were fed at the same time as Robin and the others, after which the butt-kid masters were told to find the kids some clothes and feed them, but keep them in another room. "They're going to mess all over the place," the braver of the 2 butt-kid masters insisted.

"It will be then," Tom raised his voice, "your job to train them not to, and if I see any extra bruises on them you will suffer." The man cringed, muttering something under his breath, then sank backwards.

Number 4 was left alone in his cage in the room at the top of the house, for now. "Who is the senior master?" Robin wanted to know. A gruff, well-built, but short man stepped forward. His face showed signs of many conflicts. A cheekbone was larger than it should have been, several old cuts across his neck and forehead stood out, and it appeared that his left eye was lower than the other. Before taking him to one side Robin told the others, "There will be big changes from today. If you do your work, you will not be mistreated. You masters know what is required, get on with organising it." The masters selected their slaves and set about ordering the various actions that needed to be done to maintain the house.

Robin and Tom now sat down and spoke with the senior master. "Do you have a given name?"

Through his confusion the man answered, "They just call me You."

"Do you recall where you were born, or what your family called you?"

"No, sir, all I've ever known is being in service to my lords and betters."

Robin looked the man in the eyes, saw that he was becoming troubled. "We are not trying to make you uncomfortable. I like to give good people names, and you look like a decent man underneath your years of abuse." The master saw a real kindness in Robin's eyes but remained quiet until he was asked a question. He'd received too much pain over the years for not holding his tongue.

"Do you have a colour you like best?"

"Oh yes," he insisted, "the blackness, when I close my eyes at night, it's so welcome to me."

"OK," said Robin. "Can we call you Blackie?"

"If it pleases your lordships, but I might not always remember it."

"Don't worry, Blackie, you are with us now, and we treat people like human beings. There are many things you can help us with, for too many like yourself have seen nothing but beatings and abuse. Will you help us to change things?"

Blackie's eyes brightened with wonder, hoping this could be true. "Oh yes, sir. We all wish for a better life."

"That better life starts now," Tom interjected.

"Part of our mission here is to give a better life to all the people that were controlled by the lords that have now gone away. We are now in control," Robin added. "We will be visiting the camps and factories. You can tell us all you know about them. The people, the masters that feel like you do. We will have no encouragement for bad masters that treat slaves badly. We need to know who the good ones are, the ones who still have a soul."

Blackie thought for a moment digesting what had been said, wondering if this was some kind of spiteful trick to get him to mark some people as working against the lords. It was the memory of the openness in Robin's kindness that convinced him to do as requested. "I know all the masters, and a lot of the slaves. There are some who can still talk friendly, but there are some that would put a sharp knife inside you as soon as look at you."

"There will be those that cannot be rescued from the past, for they are too much in the nature of abusive lords. We will only collect the good ones for our purpose," Robin said. "Tell me about them."

By camp and factory Blackie went through the masters he knew at each location, listing and counting them by some system of identification he had worked out. "What will happen to the ones that cannot be saved?"

"We will see," said Tom, "who wants to come over to our way of thinking."

*

With a clear understanding of what went on at each location, who the bad guys were that might cause trouble and what each site produced, they were ready to attack the first camp. All of them were within 10 miles of the house with most being just 2 or 3 miles away. Tom went to find the drivers who had brought the lords back, while Robin had a final word with Blackie. "I hope you will be able to restrain some of the masters and convince them we are earnest in what we are doing, to avoid trouble."

"I'll do what I can, but I'm not sure they will listen to me."

"OK. We set off with good intentions. Let's see if we can give some good people some freedom."

Paul and Marty were left behind to retain a presence at the mansion, as well as making sure things functioned in a normal manner. An important task they also had was to determine who, if any, of the masters could be trusted enough to help. This was no easy thing to do, to evaluate how a person would react to sudden freedom. It meant they had to dig down into the person to reignite their real personality. They started this by asking about each master's history. Sometimes this brought anguish, but that was a good sign.

So while Robin and Tom, with the others heading off to the first factory, Paul and Marty took the first master into a small lounge. "How long have you been a master?" Paul started.

"Oh about 10 years," said a tall man, thin of structure, whose twinkle had died many years ago.

"You may not have realised it yet," Paul continued, "but we are making some changes around here. Will you help us to improve the way things have been, or are you going to fight it?"

"I will help of course," the man smiled unconvincingly.

"The one thing we have to get across to people like you who have been abused for so long is that we are serious about making improvements. We have to stop the cycle of abuse and punishment."

The man looked even more bewildered, unable to comprehend the scope of what was being offered.

"We know you have a number because it's on your arm, but do you have a name?" Marty asked. "Do you recall a time before you were put into service? Did you know your mother?"

The man was suddenly terrified as images of scenes long since buried in his mind were replayed. His parents held back by several men then beaten as he was dragged away screaming. Tears filled his eyes then rolled down his cheeks.

Choking back sobs of anguish, he called out, "Mummy…where are you?" The full horror of his abduction and loss suddenly hit him hard. His head sank, he sobbed uncontrollably for several seconds until the bad memories faded and he remembered where he was and who he was talking to. He looked up at the 2 men before him dressed as lords with anguish in his eyes. He wanted to kill someone.

"Too many people have suffered in the same way as you have. We must stop it happening ever again to anyone else," Paul insisted.

"I remembered my parents," said the thin man, wiping his wet face with a sleeve. "I haven't thought of them for so long. They used to call me Macky." His face went red suddenly embarrassed at his emotional overflow.

"Do not be concerned about the tears, Macky," said Marty. "It is good to get these things off our chest, and as we said there have been so many like you who suffered in this way. We will start changing things today by treating the slaves as human beings. Can you do that?"

A smile, with long since absent eye twinkle greeted the 2 men. "I certainly can. No longer will I tolerate spite or harm to any others. We have all suffered enough."

"Good," replied Paul. "We are all human beings and deserve to be treated as such. Are there any question you have for us?"

"Many," said Macky, "but I cannot form the words. Perhaps I can ask them later?"

"Not a problem," said Paul smiling widely at the master. "When you go out, please send the next master in."

"Please," Macky almost shouted. "Nobody has ever used that word to me. That shows me that you are not the lords we have known."

"Correct," Marty and Paul replied together.

As the man stood up to leave, Marty added, "We are part of the new movement that promotes decency and a trust in our combined humanity. Welcome to it."

Macky smiled back brightly as he headed out the door.

The next man came in, warily, looking at Macky as he walked away, his shiny wet red face a sign that something significant had occurred.

The new master was a little more belligerent than Macky, but they finally broke through his tough exteriors to reach the man inside, who eventually agreed that there was a better way to get things done than by using violence on the unprotected. Most of the day was taken up by getting the masters on their side. Only one man failed to understand. No matter what they said he opposed a softening of treatment for slaves. The master started to become difficult.

"How do I know you are lords? No true lord would tell me what you did. This all stinks."

"If you are not going to be with us then you are against us," Paul said, pulling out a taser. They marched him to the top of the house and put him in a cell opposite lord number 4.

*

Robin and Tom meanwhile had a much more complicated task on their hands. Having arrived at the factory, their first requirement was to understand how the masters would take to them. Macky did his bit, he smoothed the path to stop the masters getting worried at a new set of lords. He simply told the group of 5 other masters that had come out to meet them, "Meet your new lords. The others were found wanting." The 5, immediately on seeing the high lords' status from their uniforms, went down on their knees, and dipped their heads in respect.

Robin stepped forward, examining each man as they stood up. "I always wonder why we need so many masters when the slaves do all the work. Tell me what extra benefit you bring to these production lines?" He indicated the first man.

"Well milords, it is true the slaves do the heavy work, but each of us knows how to keep the machinery running. Slaves come and go, but we are always here to keep the production lines running."

"A good answer, however, you touched on something that concerns us. You use the slave up too quickly. You must find a way to make your slaves last longer."

The first master, slightly emboldened, "We are not getting replacements so quickly like we used to. Already this year 4 slaves have been lost."

"That is a problem you will need to focus on," Robin continued, "and part of the reason we are here. Let's just say that there is a bit of a hold up with getting new slaves. Their labour has been diverted elsewhere."

The 5 masters frowned at this, expecting some kind of punishment to come their way. A second one interjected with, "If it pleases your lordships, we all work hard to keep up the quotas, but if we run low on slaves there is only so much we can do."

"Yes, yes, yes, I get that," Robin replied with some bite, "for now we have to make sure that the processes are much safer so that we do not lose any more slaves. Your expertise will be called upon in that respect. I'm sure such experienced masters as you have your own ideas about how to improve things. We will listen to your ideas and provide what is required." The men liked the sound of this, nodded encouragingly.

They walked across to the first brick structure that had hot steam escaping from all sides. "That surely is not economic, losing so much heat that way?" Tom insisted. "That's the first thing we need to address."

"The bricks are old," said a third master, "the linings from the ovens badly need to be replaced to keep the heat contained."

"From the outside it looks like it needs a total rebuild," said Tom. "Let's see how it looks on the inside."

They went through heavy double doors, followed by another set, before they were able to catch any sign of activity, although the heat came to meet them immediately. Male slaves dressed just in tight shorts were manhandling a machine, pushing it in one direction while it spewed out molten metal. Above the machine a large pot was being heated, to turn ore into liquid. From the side of a furnace heat visibly escaped through a small crack, which the slaves tried to avoid even though they had to get close to manually feed in more raw material. Slaves were all around this activity, supplying native minerals or guiding it. Others were spraying water on the still very hot metal to cool it.

"They cannot stop this process, or the sheet of steel will be ruined," said the first of the 5, no doubt worried that the lords through ignorance would ruin their morning's production. They all watched for some minutes as the metal slowly formed into a long length. As well as the pushers, manacled slaves stood too close to where the strip was being laid out, ready to adjust what it rested on if it were to shift position.

"This is a thoroughly antiquated process," Robin stated, although the masters looked blank at this description. "This process was done far more easily by our ancestors. It needs more mechanising. I can see why you have trouble missing quotas. It doesn't help that the slaves are manacled. No wonder they have accidents. I want all those manacles removed instantly."

The masters looked shocked. "But they will run away," said the short, fat master.

"Where will they run to? They are trapped," Tom insisted.

"Don't let me have to repeat myself," Robin warned. The masters immediately complied, and the slaves had a much easier job.

"See how much better they control things now?" Tom insisted. "From now on we treat slaves better, and you can throw away their chains." The slaves were not blind to what had been said and took notice of the lords that had given them some freedom of movement. The slaves moved better together, although it was clear that an older man was doing much of the coordinating. Tom indicated the man, "I like him. He has experience and knows what is needed. That is what we need to encourage."

Turning to the first master, Robin asked, "Are all the sheds like this?"

"Yes, milord, the only differences are the size and shape of the product."

"This will not do at all. I'm authorising you to take one shed out of production at a time to totally redesign it. Make it a safe process, that requires less workers. We will go and sit down to make some plans. Lead the way, masters." They went back out into the brightening day, towards a small hut. Tom and Robin went inside with the masters and sat at a long wooden table, while the other lords surveyed the whole site, keeping an eye on how it operated, looking out for any potential trouble. The first master used a small knife to sketch out some ideas on the table top which had seen many scratches previously.

"Tell us what you are drawing."

The master described the components needed to create the steel from ores, and the general process. "To do this properly we'd have to measure the components exactly, but to make it as automatic as possible may take some trial and error."

"Let me see if I can find something to help us," Robin said, taking out his laptop and checking for a wireless connection. "Yes, we can connect." The masters looked on in awe at the computer screen, never having seen anything like it. The browser came up, and after a couple of attempts at searching for ways to make steel Robin came across a very clear guide. "There, that's what we need."

"That's amazing," a master said, with the others agreeing. "It's like magic."

"Not magic," Tom said, "it is however a technology from before, and we can make use of it to find out important things."

"Before what?"

"Before, when the world was free, and there were no lords," Tom answered, a little blindly.

Robin jumped in to ensure they got the right concept,"There was a major civilisation that existed before, some 100 years ago. They had many things and great freedoms. We want to recreate that to some small degree." The bafflement in the eyes of the 5 masters told its own story, but he felt enough had been said on the subject. "I will make some prints of this so that we can review it further." He had the images sent to the printer residing at the mansion they had recently occupied. Then he went out to find Macky. "Macky, do you know where the printer is within the mansion?"

After some discussion, Macky agreed that he did, then was sent off to collect the prints. While they were waiting, Tom, eager to get back to practical things raised further the question of safety, "What do we need to do to make these sheds safer and the work easier, more efficient?"

Robin looked at Tom to stop him proceeding too far, "For that we really need another expert view. One who is closely involved on a daily basis. Will someone go and fetch that older slave that was clearly directing the process." With great uncertainty one of the masters stood up slowly.

Robin continued, looking hard at the masters, "I understand your reluctance to include a slave in this, but if we are going to make things work better, we will need views from all sides. I'm not doubting your own expertise, but consider this as a way to make it all better. We no longer beat slaves; we reward them when they work well. It will be to our advantage, as well as theirs to make this all work better, so let's see what gems we can glean from this man."

The slave came into the room, reluctant to look anyone in the eye, nervous, and not at all bold. He was sat at the end of the table so that the masters didn't have to look directly at him. "Do you have a given name, or a nickname?" Robin asked.

"279376374883, your lordship," the man mumbled back.

"OK, I will call you 83 for now. Stop fretting. You are not here to be punished. You are here because you have knowledge." The man continued to keep his eyes down, staring at the wooden table surface as though his life depended on it. "I've briefly seen the conditions you work in and the process you have to use. I ordered your shackles removed so that you could work more easily. It is in all of our interests to make what you produce easier and less dangerous, so I want to hear your views. Tell us what can be done to make what you do safer?"

The man was dumbstruck. He'd never had a lord talk directly to him, and this was a high lord. He had long since learned to not look a master in the eye, so was petrified of doing that with a high lord. Robin tried again, but still was unable to get anything out of the man. He was interrupted in this with Macky bringing back the printouts. "It seems that 83 is unable to share his views yet, so let's get back to your proposals to repair what we have," he now addressed the masters.

"Well," said the first master, "I would add in a request for bricks that can stand very high temperatures. Then we could get the fires properly contained. To properly line the furnaces we really need ceramics. I've seen these in London, and they really make a difference to the plaster we use for ongoing repairs." They talked some more about materials needed, and what quantities. Robin noted it all down on his PC.

"That's a good list," said Tom, glancing at the man at the end of the table who was still silent. "What about safety improvements. That clearly needs to be a high priority." This brought a flicker of interest from the silent man.

"Some of the worst accidents happen because of poor lighting," said a master. Robin added high powered lighting and the means of suspending it from the ceiling.

Other ideas came from the masters causing Robin to keep on typing, then the slave let out a small grunt, still unable to speak freely, there was something the others had missed. "Out with it, 83," Robin urged gently.

The slave raised his head a little, but it was only when he raised his arms to show fresh burns on his arms that he spoke in a weak voice they had to strain to hear, "Every day, more burns. Need something to protect us."

"Hmm," said Robin. "That looks nasty. Do you masters have protective clothing?"

"No, it's seen as part of the job that slaves, and sometimes us, get burned."

"That's very poor. We have to do something about that, but don't you have any balm or medicines to treat burns?" The masters shook their heads with a look that said, "who cares?"

"That's an attitude we must improve on," Robin said sternly. "Our workers are our resources. If we misuse them, we lose them. Anything else, 83?"

The man glanced up at Robin quickly, then his eyes darted down again. A small no was visible in his nod.

"We are doing well here," Tom interjected, "but it's time we looked at the printouts of steel-making from a bygone age to see if there is anything that will help improve the sheds that we have. We still have other things to do today." The images and text were passed around. "These will give us a goal to aim for in building new sheds with improved equipment. The question now is, does any of this give us ideas on making the current process any better?"

"Oh yes," one master agreed. "The way the molten metal is poured and then directed, is something we could incorporate into our process." Several other conclusions came up, which Robin added to his list. When there were no more ideas floated Robin typed up the memo to the supplies yard in

London to deliver the requirements immediately. He approved it as well.

*

The old slave 83 went back to work, while the masters walked across to speak with the remaining 5 masters, to explain what had been discussed. The other men could be seen nodding their heads in welcome agreement. Robin gave them a couple of moments, then walked over to meet them. "Gentlemen, we are here on inspection. Our aim is to make sure things run more smoothly, which means taking care of our resources. We have made a good start on that today, but there are other aspects of factory life that we probably also need to make work better."

A master that hadn't been involved in discussions smiled broadly, "Thank you, your lordship, this all sounds like very good news to us."

"Indeed," Robin agreed, "and when the materials arrive, we will be around to make sure repairs and new features are done to the best standard. Now, as well as improving working conditions, I want to see some improvements in food and clothing. So many here look like scarecrows, and some of you, even, look like you've not had a good meal for years."

"We only have what we get sent," said the smiling master. "We don't have any choice, and sometimes the stuff isn't fresh at all."

"I get that message, which is why we are going to make a deal with the nearest village. All local villages perhaps. I know they could do with some help in making metal things for themselves. I'm going to suggest a barter. You set up a workshop with a small furnace where small knives, wheels and so forth can be shaped, and we will get them to supply you with food. That would mean either creating that workshop and teaching someone how to use the equipment, or one of you taking a position in a village." The masters all considered this. The prospect of living in a village again appealed to most of them.

"That good food needs to be shared with the slaves of course, and I suspect you will need a real cook here."

"Oh," said another master. "That would be very nice. We rarely get anything good to eat."

Robin turned to helper Wilf, "Can you get hold of Cook, and bring her here, she needs to set up a canteen and create healthy menus for these good people." Wilf went off at a sprint.

Turning back to the masters, Robin said, "I hope that everything we've talked about here today will all make things easier for all concerned. I need to add that the slaves must also benefit. There will be no beatings for any reason. Shackles are to be removed for good. Now go and carry out my orders then return to your normal schedules."

*

"Do you think that was all appropriate?" Tom asked Robin. "I'm concerned there will be some problems."

"Let's see. The masters took it all well. The promise of better food really pleased them. Can you take a master to the closest village and make that barter work? I will need a list of materials required at the village to build the blacksmiths yard."

*

Tom went off with the smiling master to negotiate a trade of food for expertise just as Cook arrived. She was dressed in a flowery dress, smiling at the prospect of doing something important for Robin who she appeared to worship. She gave him a kiss on the cheek and smiled expectantly at him. Robin took her aside to explain how they were freeing the slaves a little at a time, removing the chains while gradually improving their lives. Food was a very important part of that.

"Their cooking facilities are very basic," Robin told her.

"Oh yes, I can see that. We are going to need a new building and plenty of equipment to make a proper kitchen and storage for all the required raw food and cooking implements. Then we have to work out for how many we need to cater for."

Robin called over a master and told him to assist Cook in working out where the new kitchen and canteen could go and to help her with any questions. He asked one of his helpers to watch over them. Then Robin spoke with Johnny, "Your brick building skills will be useful here. A brand-new building is required to serve as a kitchen and a place to eat. I envisage a kind of self-service set of trays, but a fully fitted kitchen with fridges and cookers. Please talk to Cook when she is done and work out exactly what building materials are required. I will order them." Johnny did better than that. Before the day was out, he'd marked off a patch of ground that would house the new building. He got as far as digging the foundations, then had to locate the source of the energy supply. Phil was the electrical guy, so he was on the list to talk to. Johnny was going to create space on the roof for a water storage tank but would need copper pipes to bring the water to where it was needed from where it came into the camp, as well as taps. He knew these items could be taken from London stores, so could see no delays to getting it all up and running quickly.

*

Tom had a successful trip back to the village, where it was all arranged for the blacksmiths quarters to be installed. The chief thought it a great idea to have someone who could fashion implements and was only too willing to trade meat and whatever they grew. Tom would, over the next few weeks, sell this idea to other villages.

*

Back at the factory everyone was just a little excited at the prospect of good things to come. Masters were walking around with half smiles on their faces, and even the slaves were more animated. Before leaving Robin told the masters to keep up the good work. "Expect us all back when the materials arrive."

The next day they paid a visit to another factory, that turned out finished products, large and small from the steel sheets the first factory produced. Here there were 2 long sheds full of cowed slaves. The shed and equipment were in good order compared to the previous factory, but the slaves less so. Whenever a master even came close the slaves would shrink away from them while still working with their hands.

Robin used the same approach as before, but it didn't go down so well. The 8 masters were more hardened, and thick skinned. They didn't refuse commands from the lords, but they did delay things by deliberately not doing things as directed. When told to remove shackles, they removed only those of the slaves closest then stopped. Tom in particular started to get angry at this attitude. He indicated to the belligerent senior master, the others were imitating, to join him outside. Robin walked out also while the others continued the inspection of the first shed.

"I can see why it needed so many lords to keep things running here, and why the quotas were often missed," said Tom. "I've never seen so many slaves in such a poor condition, bruised, beaten and crushed. This place needs a total shake up, and we are going to see that it happens. Are you going to help the process or are we to dismiss you?"

The master snarled back, seemingly threatening violence, "Our quotas are good. It's the fault of the slaves. Lazy they are. Don't need a shake up, just more slaves."

"More slaves to beat and work to death to show your power over them? I don't think so. You have wasted all the slaves you ever will. When I give a command, I expect it obeyed immediately. There will be no second chances. There will be no more beating of slaves, and you will see that all shackles are permanently removed so that the slaves can be more effective."

They went back inside to where the focus was now on a slave that had somehow dropped a piece of metal into a lathe that was stopping it from working. Ignoring the lords, the senior master, now very angry, walked over and demanded to know what had happened. The slave immediately sunk to his knees, not expecting any mercy. "Let me see what happened here," Tom demanded, interrupting the master before he reached the slave. "This was a mistake waiting to happen. If the shackles had been removed this wouldn't have happened. This slave was stretching across dangerous machinery while locked into position."

"No," said the senior master, "this useless slave has done this before. He is going to spend the night in the hole with no food. That's how we keep our quotas up," he snarled to nobody in particular. Taking a strap attached to his waistband, he raised his hand to whip the slave.

"I told you no more beatings," Tom screamed at the man who was intent on demonstrating his authority, and angry that a lord would dare to question what he was doing as they had trained him in this way. Tom's words fell on deaf ears and the strap hit hard against the slave's shoulder. Tom was infuriated, went very red in the face, and pulled his pistol out. The master saw this but continued to raise his arm to beat the slave again. The shot rang out throughout the shed, disturbing all the slave workers, making them all aware of what had just happened. A lord had killed a master for disobeying his commands.

"Now," said Tom, aggravated beyond reason, addressing the other masters, "is anyone else going to challenge my commands?" There was no fight or challenge visible from the masters. "Let me be very clear. You will not mistreat or beat slaves from now on. That has been going on for too long and stops now." These words rang out clear and loud, hitting the ears of every single slave there, which left them wondering what was happening. "Make sure all shackles are removed, and then we will look at the other reasons why this factory has been so badly run." The slaves returned to their work while keeping one eye and their hearing tuned to what was going on.

It took some minutes before the masters had removed the metal chains from the workforce, who were now rubbing their ankles. "Throw them away," Robin shouted. "We don't need them any more." The masters looked forlorn but did as instructed. The junior lords started to hand out ointment to the slaves and told them to rub it into their cuts and bruises.

The inspection continued, with nothing more to worry about except that the slaves were very thin, badly under-nourished and worked too hard. A visit to the sleeping quarters then took place. It was a squalid hovel, the worst Tom had ever seen, and his hackles rose again. "Robin, this needs all throwing out. It smells horribly. It must be infested with every last possible bug and disease."

"Agreed, you could see from 10 paces that it is full of fleas." They sent someone back to the mansion to collect new blankets, brooms. plenty of disinfectant, some food, as well as some clothing. While they were waiting for this the masters were instructed to dig out the vile mess and burn it. Some of the slaves watched from the shed, and some even cheered to see the masters doing some work. The goods arrived, the slave quarters were cleaned up, then the slaves were washed down in the showers. Their heads were full of lice, which Robin promised a special soap for. After they were clean the 50 or so slaves sat down on the grassy hillock and were given food.

"What about our quotas for today, this will put us well behind?" complained a master who resembled the now dead senior master.

"I will sign it off," said Robin, "consider today a refresh day, from here on out we treat all people like human beings, who with good food, will produce more. We are not leaving you out of that equation, masters, because we do understand that you all have been equally abused in your time. Take a seat and help yourselves to the food provided."

Things went a lot better from that point onwards. The food supply and cooking were also improved, and it was noted that the masters started to work with the slaves instead of bullying them. Despite the progress there was more to be done for both factories before they became bastions of free enterprise. That would still require weeks of a steady freeing of the mental ropes that held the structure in place.

*

There was still work to be done with the slaves and masters at the mansion, so Robin decided to be blunt, and gathered them all together in the lounge. "I'm going to give you all your freedom," he announced to no reaction. After a pause he continued, "By that I mean that none of you, slaves or masters will be anything but free men. There are 2 options I can offer. A third would be to rely on your skills to survive in the countryside but trust me that is not a viable choice. For those that wish to stay in the mansion, paying for your board and lodging by keeping it running, there is that option. This will need housekeepers, cooks and gardeners. This will be a place where we will come on a regular basis and will expect everything to be maintained to a high standard. In contrast to that you may return to a village of your choice, take a small home there and contribute to the wealth of that village, working as all villagers now work. There is no longer forced labour, no beatings and I hope no injustices. All the village chiefs are good, rational men, and you will be treated well there. Think about your future, because now you have one. There are many roles we are encouraging people to learn and practice, from barbers to builders. Let me know your choice. The assembled looked around, thinking this very strange, until Cook spoke up.

"I was once a slave at a villa close to London. These people gave me my freedom, and now it is your turn, please come and join us."

Robin hadn't expected tears of joy, but the lacklustre response was certainly underwhelming, "Still they needed time to get used to the idea," he conceded to Tom later.

"The kids that were previously abused by the perverted will be going to villages. Those of you that have made up their minds may go along. If there is not space on the buses, we will do another trip tomorrow." Some people shifted to one side, closer to Cook. "Oh," said Robin, "one other thing. You are all no longer just a number, from now on you will answer to your given names. So find some way to display that name on you somewhere." That produced a smile.

*

The days slipped by as progress was made in adjusting the way the slaves and masters behaved and thought. Food supplies improved to both factories, and the materials turned up quickly that were required to improve the manufacturing of steel. Before this, Robin had sat down with the masters with the expertise to design on paper the revised layout. "We will close down each shed in turn totally," he said, "then you masters will be in charge of getting everything installed to our satisfaction. We will provide extra labour, but we will expect the slaves to join in too."

On the day, the slaves and masters were almost struck dumb when they saw lords stripped to the waist, doing manual labour and humping materials around to the directions of the masters. Slowly this encouraged the slaves to join in, and very soon there was such a great atmosphere, there were even displays of friendship and cooperation. It was a most successful day that not only produced a much better factory shed, but it broke the old bonds. Slaves, masters and lords all joining in, working together. This new relationship was further cemented when they all sat down together to eat, with even the slaves talking excitedly about having a brand-new factory process. During all of this they had to be a little careful, for it was assumed that most slaves would still love to knife a lord in the back, which was truly understandable.

*

The next day, at the first factory, renovations continued. The weekly supply of iron ore arrived on a lorry, which then transported the steel produced to other factories, including the local one. After it had left, Robin told the masters, "In future we should hold some steel in reserve, especially the smaller sizes, because when the village blacksmiths are fully functional, we will want to send more to the villages." He got several nods in agreement.

The work continued on until day by day, they made progress in equipping the sheds out with better, easier and safer, processes. The kitchen and canteen went up very quickly, and within 2 weeks Cook was training ex slaves on how to create tasty and nutritious meals and run the canteen. At the end of all of this, as everyone was eating, Robin told them that he wanted a big sign erected to show that this factory was a collective, where only free men worked and lived. This went down very well. Once this was all complete, Tom made sure that someone from the villages would visit regularly with fresh foods, while at the same time the factory workers would visit the villages and help to progress new implementations to work the steel and any other metal work that was required. This was helped as the London car factory had produced enough easy-push carts for all villages to have several.

The bigger problem was still the second factory that produced finished metal goods. While the focus had been the first factory, Robin had made sure there had been a lord's presence there on a daily basis to let everyone know they were still there. Now they were able to go back in force and work out a way to convert them from slaves to free men.

*

"I'm going to try an experiment," Robin addressed the masters of the second factory. "To show you how a factory can operate without cruelty, I will take 2 or 3 of you at a time, to another factory. My men will be monitoring what happens here while we are gone. I will start with you 2. He indicated 2 masters, then asked Larry to drive the 4 of them over in the rover.

In the car, approaching the first factory, Robin said, "I'm tired of not knowing what to call you masters. Numbers do not do it for me. Do you have given names? Do you recall if your family had a name for you?"

The master to the left smiled and said, "My old mum used to call me a little sod, will that do?"

"I'd rather not have to call you that," Robin smiled back. "Can you do better?"

"OK, I call him," he indicated his colleague, "Smudge, because he always has a sooty nose, and he calls me Boots because I'm always losing my boots."

"That will do nicely, Smudge and Boots, welcome to the factory collective of free men." The 2 men raised their eyebrows at that description but took it onboard as something new and a lesson to learn about. It was a successful day. Smudge found it hard to believe that slaves and masters could now talk to each other without any whips involved, yet it finally did sink in that this was the way forward. The other second-factory masters received the same education.

Things kept on improving at both factories, but there were still concerns that masters at the second factory could slip into their old ways without constant supervision. Robin decided on another experiment. "Today we are going to try a role reversal." He selected one of the older slaves, "You look like you know the work backwards, come here and tell Boots how to operate this machine. Boots, you stand there and let's see if you can produce as many indented metal plates as this man."

Boots moved into position, with great reluctance. Addressing the slave, Robin said, "Now explain what has to be done here."

The slave slowly found his voice, a bit croaky and quiet at first, "... the metal goes into that stamp. Must make it tight with green vice lever. Foot goes down on hammer." Boots did as he was told, was still not happy, and did 4 pressings then stopped, hoping the experiment was over.

"Very good," said Robin. "Now I timed this man earlier. He can do 100 in 5 minutes. Let's see how many you can do." The big clock on the wall showed the second hand going past the 12. "Start," Robin shouted, with all lords, masters and slaves watching. At the end of 5 minutes they counted the items pressed by Boots. "Not bad, you did 79, but clearly you need more practice." The slave smiled with glee, seeing a master embarrassed in this way. "Keep on going, Boots, we will be back shortly to see how you are doing." Leaving a lord to watch over Boots, Robin proceeded to switch all masters with slaves, to give them a lesson in production.

This all went on for over 30 minutes. Robin or Tom watched each master in turn, smiled encouragement at them, and even received a smile back from most of them. By this time the rate of production had increased, and the masters had a better appreciation of what it meant to be on a production line. "Enough, enough," Tom shouted. "You've all done very well. I recommend that all masters spend some time on the machines, for they need to understand how it feels to stand there all day, besides, it is good for the heart and mind to concentrate on a repetitive task for a while. This will make you better managers, for we are disposing of the term of master."

"Excellent," said Robin, "now it's our turn. Smudge please time us 5 minutes to see if we are any good." He and Tom went to different machines. The workers laughed loudly at this, having never expected to see lords doing their dirty work.

"Your time is up," Smudge shouted, and counted the pieces done. "I'm afraid neither of you achieved your targets."

"Oh dear, in that case," said Robin smiling, "we'd best hand over to the professionals who really know what they are doing." The workers went back to their machines smiling and motivated, the managers joked amongst themselves, and even with some of the workers about their own limitations or expertise.

"Things are getting better," Tom whispered to Robin, as they walked out of the shed.

"That was almost fun," agreed Robin, "not sure I want to do that all day though." Looking towards the end of the shed he said, "I've noticed these things before, like windmills on poles. What are they?" Tom had no answer, but a manager called Flint, who had followed them out, did.

"They give us electrical power to light those bulbs you see everywhere. They don't give us much power, but it helps, along with the sunlight we collect from the panels on the roof." Robin asked to be shown. "There's a windmill at the end of each shed which collects electrical charge from wind friction and holds it in batteries. We get most of our power from these underground cables, but there have been times when that got turned off. Without the batteries getting some charge we wouldn't be able to do much on those occasions."

"Fascinating," Robin stated. "I've seen these things at other places but always ignored them for some reason. Thanks for that explanation, Flint." Turning to Tom he said, "That's just what we need for the villages to light the dark paths. I'll put orders in at once."

"Robin," said the familiar voice of Phil, a new trainee pretend lord, "there is something you need to know. You remember that black hooded figure who was lurking at other places we have been, well I saw him again just now. When I approached, he just disappeared."

Looking up angrily, "Damn that man. I do not like being spied on. Keep a lookout for him at all times. Anybody that captures him gets to ride the cruiser."

*

They left some temporary lords to watch over the factories to make sure all was going well. The trade and communication between factories and villages soon picked up, and there were even some who asked to return to the villages, while some villagers wanted to learn skills in the factories. The butt-kids from the mansion had settled in to their new life in the villages, claimed by mothers who had long since stopped weeping for their loss. Several of the mansion ex-masters and ex-slaves also moved back to their old villages, hoping to find someone still alive that they had known. Robin was now keen to investigate the state of the prison camp. This was a little further out, but not too far from the mansion they were staying at.

Robin admitted to himself each night as he fell into a lonely bed just how much he was missing Lucy, Digga as well. This was all taking a lot of time, but it had all been worthwhile, so far. He decided that he would have to start to make real preparations for a real home in his old village for Lucy and the new baby. That would be a priority once he got back.

Macky was with them when they drove to the prison, 2 coaches and one rover of pretend lords, come to free prisoners. Macky was a good intermediary. He knew the other masters and how to prepare them for what was to come, "Don't expect these new lords to be anything like the old ones," he told them. "They have their own way but have certainly made things better in many ways. Just do not be surprised at anything." This caused a few glum faces, for they were not used to change, or doing things differently, for that usually meant some form of pain.

After getting inside the fenced area that included the prison and some grounds, Robin called the masters to him. "I want to see every prisoner here in front of this main building within 5 minutes." Most of the prisoners were led out of huts, although several had been in punishment cells. They were brought out also. "What about the ones buried up to their necks for bad behaviour?"

Reluctantly the buried prisoners were dug up and brought in front of the lords. Robin walked along the line of some 70 withered, gaunt and wretched human beings, their eyes full of hate and despair, wondering what bestiality was about to be inflicted upon them now. Most of the prisoners had chains around their legs, but some were clearly too feeble to even walk with such constraints.

"Before the chains are removed," Robin said with a penetrating voice that stirred even the hardened masters, "I want to ask for your patience and your self-restraint. I'm aware that if you had the opportunity you would like to kill as many lords and masters as you could before dying a martyr's death. I really hope that won't happen because I have some good news for you."

The camp was deathly quiet. News or any kind of change was always bad. The masters had no clue what was to follow but knowing how the lords operated suspected it wasn't anything that would make their lives better either. The slaves just stared ahead indignantly.

"Before we go any further," Robin continued, "you will be separated out into groups depending on which village you originally came from." Lords went down the line of slaves, who were then were walked over to a holding area for each village. There were plenty that didn't know which village they came from, so they were split up equally with all of the village groups.

Robin stood in front of them once more. "I have good news for all of those from village one Southeast. You are all pardoned for your crimes. You are now free men, and we will shortly take you back to your old village." Some men cried with hope that this could be true, but most saw it as a trick. Robin repeated the same message to all the other groups in turn.

Addressing the masters who still couldn't work out what was going on, Robin went on, "I want to see one master in front of each group to unlock the chains as the men walk towards them. I must insist that this is not a time for violence. You prisoners are being given your freedom. I am not playing a trick on you, so please behave." Everyone did as they were told, assembling back in their groups just as extra buses arrived to take them home. The now pardoned inmates entered the coaches, still worried, but behaving. They found a package of food on each seat as they sat down.

Each coach had 2 lords to accompany them. "There is water and food on each seat. You look like you need it," they said. The starved wretches said nothing but ripped open the packets and ate with a passion.

After all the coaches were on their way, Robin turned back to the front gate, took out his taser, and setting it to high, he zapped the controls that had kept so many men locked up in misery. "That is no longer required."

"What about us?" several prison masters called out.

"You are all going to be reassigned," Robin informed them. "You will be picked up tomorrow. In the meantime close this place down for now, store things away and turn off anything that uses power. Be ready to leave at 10am."

*

As each coach full of ex-prisoners approached a once familiar village where they had grown up there were several with watery eyes. The coaches parked to allow everyone to march through the gates, past the now flourishing fields of plenty, along the smart tidy paths that had once been overgrown with weeds and stinging nettles, and further into a smart, refreshed village centre, where people had come from the fields to greet them and receive them. Some prisoners found family members waiting to take them in, while the others were made welcome by people they didn't know, yet they would come to love. Typically, a man who had left the village over 30 years previously, who was creased and worn with age and beatings would fall to his knees, tears pouring down his face, just so glad to be home. "It's over," the lord would say, "your lives start afresh, here and now. Welcome home."

*

Back at the mansion the next day, Robin, Tom and the other lords were discussing what to do next. "There seems to be 2 more factories of specialist items that get assembled, no doubt we will find out what they are used for. Then there is that strange building. Be interesting to find out what it is housing," Robin said. They took on each factory next, making similar deals as with factory 1. All went smoothly, and no more masters had to be shot. They even found out what their products were, but 2 more weeks had passed, and they were all keen to complete this extended mission.

The noble building gave them some rather interesting surprises though. They marched in as usual in their smart high lord uniforms to demand attention from those inside and an immediate tour of all rooms and facilities.

"This is very disturbing," a lesser lord complained, "our work here is vital to our plans to continue to create a haven of fruitfulness and prosperity for all."

"That's why we are here," Tom insisted. "Where are the fruits of your labours?"

The craggy lord had no answer save for some bluster, but he wasn't about to cross a high lord, no matter how important he thought he was. "The ground floor contains our work rooms and our debating room we use to discuss directions or conflicts." They inspected the small room with shiny wooden benches in. That was of little interest except that there were a good number of heavy books. Robin decided that whatever they were about they would make a grand addition to his library.

"The first floor is set aside for meals and recreation, while the second floor holds the lords' bedroom suites," the irritated master continued.

"I shall want to see all of that, and no I cannot assure you there will be no disruptions. We have yet to see anything fundamentally worthwhile from here that could be put to great use."

The man spluttered again but could find few words to adequately express his disgust at such words, "But... this is what the gods commanded."

"Now what about the roof level? How many butt-kids do you keep up there?" Tom demanded.

"We've only got 20 left. We've had to be somewhat careful as we haven't had any new ones for over a year," the prickly lord replied.

"You will probably find out," said Robin, "that there was probably a good reason for that."

"Oh?" the man questioned but got no reply.

"Tell us now," challenged Tom, "how many lords work and reside here, how many masters, and how many slaves you work to death?"

Tom made a note of the details in his notebook as the lord counted off the personnel, "17 lords including myself, 4 masters and about a dozen useless slaves that have to be whipped constantly before they will do anything." This last comment caused Tom's left eyebrow to rise.

"I will want to know how closely you are following your mission statement," Robin stated, making this up on the spur of the moment. He thought it sounded good though.

"Let me show you," said a heavily disgruntled lord now reaching a point where he might explode, leading them through a deeply polished ornate door into a wide corridor. A prominent plaque met their eyes immediately. "There you see what our goal is." He read it out in full, in a grand manner, ' *"By the authority of the Gods of Earth and this sector of the galaxy, the establishment known as FYF5 has been assigned the following important task. Subject: analysis, preparation and planning to create concealed, safe, warm and self-sustaining homelands for the elite of Sarandach, who will be moving to Earth'."*

Tom and Robin gasped quietly, just about restraining their tongues from asking obvious questions. Robin managed, "Do continue."

The lord continued, feeling as though he'd scored against these high lords, ' *"A total of 26 homelands will be required, each with living pods to accommodate 20,000 elites in total convenience, as well as an adequate number of slaves to serve their needs'."*

Tom had recovered his composure somewhat but was still shocked at what this meant. The Earth was going to be occupied by some kind of aliens. He couldn't get his head around this, with too many questions coming to mind. He made a concerted effort to act normally, "Time to show us how much progress you have made." The lord led the way, while the other pretend lords followed on. Robin turned to them, putting his finger to his lips to ask them not to say anything on this subject, yet.

The room they entered next was full of quiet concentration. Flat video screens sat in front of 12 lesser lords, who only slowly raised their heads to look at, acknowledge, and bow their head to the high lords, as the building's senior lord explained what was happening here. "These lords act as analysts to the higher lords who each have their own area of expertise. Here they search out data from the net as well as making calculations for scenarios proposed by the same higher lords." Robin glanced at what the lords were keeping record of, then indicated that they had seen enough.

Back in the corridor there were doors to small studies each occupied by a lord. A description was posted on each door, it was assumed this was intended to describe what was being formulated within. "In this room our expert studies aspects of which are the best materials to build with, while the next concentrates on the most suitable land masses, as well as geothermal provision of heat. We are currently reviewing the islands to the south of this landmass as they are generally warmer than this larger island."

"I assume this all comes together at some point?" asked Robin.

"Oh yes, that all comes to my second-in-command, and we make the plans for each area."

Robin nodded, "This confounded inspection doesn't have to take long then. I shall require that my lords interview each of these senior lords, and I will speak with your second-in-command."

The lord almost smiled, "Very well, I shall alert them to this." He went from door to door telling those inside to expect a lord in to question them on the project. Robin took this time to give directions to his lords, to get what was happening in each room, and any contact points that were dealt with by that lord. They were told it was a 2-man job.

Tom and Robin took the final planning man. Going into that office Robin dismissed the head lord, "We will not need you for the time being. Where will you be when we are finished here?"

"In my office, labelled senior lord." Robin nodded, closing the door after he and Tom had gotten inside.

This lord was well past his prime with a feverish glow that clearly came from drinking too much preadolescent blood. He stood up awkwardly as they came in. "How may I help you, my lords?"

"Tell us what you do and how you do it. That will do for a start," said Robin. "There have been concerns raised by the gods themselves regarding the progress of this project. If you are suffering problems we will make them go away."

The lord smiled, "Oh you know, we always hit some silly problems, but that's mainly down to lazy slaves not working hard enough. That's really out of my control at the various depots we use."

"Let's have a complete list of those, and their locations, as well as what materials you order from them."

"That's an easy one, I have a complete list of over 30 of them." He printed the list off and handed it to Robin.

"We understand that you pull all the planning together," Tom entered himself into the conversation. "Can you tell us the process?"

The lord described in some detail how schematics, detailed building lists, architectural designs, details of physical locations, and many other things about the build and proposed site as well as how to supply an indefinite supply of energy and heat, were accumulated and made into specifically complete drawings.

Robin took copious notes. "What about the physical locations of these 26 homelands?" Again the man quickly provided a printed list showing graph references. "Very efficient."

"If you look at that list, you will see that plans are complete for 19 homelands. These have been registered with the local lords planning centres and at the end of each row is the grid reference where all the required materials are now stored." The man couldn't help but smile at his own effectiveness.

"You are well advanced," said Robin. "I must admit when we came down here, I was expecting to see many holes in all of this, but I'm impressed that there doesn't seem to be any, so far." A further sickly smile passed the lips of the lord at his desk, feeling much more confident.

"How do you know that we have got all the details right for the future residents? What do you know of conditions on Sarandach?"

The man smiled even wider now, knowing for sure that their grasp of the project was limited, and anything he said need not be so accurate, but still he couldn't help boasting, "I've been there."

Tom's mouth almost fell open, "You have been there?"

"Oh yes. I've met with all the important elites there. I know their requirements very well, from the most enjoyable night time temperature, to the minimum it should be during the day. As cold bloodied creatures they really have to prepare their environments correctly."

"Yes indeed," Robin managed, still just able to keep a straight face even at this news.

The lord couldn't help but tell more to boost his own importance. "I was on the planet for 3 of their months. Very impressive it was too. The elite have created a superb, tiered society, and even the slaves do everything so willingly. Their control system might be implemented here, except that we already have our slaves so well under control."

"I don't think we need any further means of making slaves do our bidding here," said Tom, "but do go on, what were the other conditions like?"

"Fascinating. Where we conquered this world so many years ago on the back of carbon usage and other deceit, there they needed no such excuse, for the slaves are bred to be just smart enough to do as they are told. A great example to us all, but of course planets are not plentiful, and their elites' population grows quickly. The gods of course rule them, as they rule us."

Robin wanted to delve in and ask for more details about these gods, but he could see that Tom was getting agitated, and just might say something they'd both regret. He looked down at his notes by way of an excuse not to answer the lord in front of him. "I do believe you have furnished us with what we need to know. I can't see any issues here. We will of course speak again some time." With that they left the office to find their colleagues waiting in the corridor.

They next found the senior lord in his office. "We are about complete here. I will be reporting on very adequate progress." More smiles. "Given that we have disrupted your day, I'd like to invite you all over to the mansion for a celebration on your splendid development. I take it you have transport?

Do you know where the mansion is?"

The lord could hardly contain his enthusiasm, "Oh yes, I know where that is, and we have our own coach."

"Great," said Robin, "it takes about 30 minutes from here, so we'll expect you at 7pm. Do bring all of your lords, I'd hate any of them to be left out. I feel like celebrating after your good news, which to be honest was a great relief to us. Plan to stay overnight." He winked casually.

*

"The coaches are just leaving the grounds of the house," Robin informed Tom. "I'll let them get some distance, ideally where they will get blown off the road."

"Good idea," agreed Tom. "It wouldn't do to have twisted metal all over the tarmac."

Using the eye in the sky satellite, they followed the coaches' progress. Robin was aiming the beam at a wheel, which was not easy given that the view was directly down. He still had no idea that there were multiple satellites up there, and he could have chosen to view at an angle, if only he had known how.

Robin saw his opportunity as the coach slowed to take a steep bend in the road. He focused the instrument just in front of the coach, direct at the point when it would hit the bend. Without a second's delay he hit the destruct switch, hitting the left front part of the vehicle. Skidding out of control the coach ploughed into the thick bushes just off to the left side of the road. There was not much apparent damage, although it did seem that a tyre had burst. The second coach pulled up next to the first one, well off the road.

Tom nodded, "Good hit," as Robin lined the beam up once again. "No point in letting them get out of the coach." The next beam, still a narrow one, lasted longer, cutting into the metal at the front then zigzagging down the middle of both coaches. Back and forth went the beam of radioactive light until most of the wreckage was wafer thin and smouldering, with everything as well as everybody, that had been inside evaporated. Robin made one more full circuit to make sure.

Now Robin keyed in a physical grid reference of the first store holding the components for the first alien homeland. "I'm damned if I am going to allow any more elites to our world. We have enough trouble with the scum lords we already have." The building was huge, and it took a good 10 minutes to reduce it to rubble even with a wide, powerful beam. That was ticked off the list, then the next one was dealt with, and the next, until they had all been made rubble.

"We are going to need to go back to that house tomorrow and wipe out the data on those computers," Tom added. "We can't blast that house with it still full of kids and slaves."

"There are probably backups of the data as well," agreed Robin. "Those must be destroyed as well."

Searching through memos sent from the grand house to various suppliers, Robin was able to locate the ones to suppliers. He sent additional notes either cancelling the request or putting things on hold. Feeling mischievous, he altered the specifications of some strategic items and gave a different location grid reference for where they should be sent. He chose beaches or remote cliff tops.

"What are you smiling for?" asked Tom.

"Just my odd sense of humour. I've amended the delivery addresses on some vital items to be dumped very far from originally intended." Tom shared a smile.

"Will tomorrow be soon enough to handle the computers?" Robin wondered aloud. "All of that accumulated data and years of work must be totally gone."

"Let's make a very early start at first light," suggested Tom. "The house should be safe for a few days I would have thought."

"OK. I will leave my PC monitoring the house, and it will wake me if anybody comes or goes."

*

Just before daylight the PC woke Robin to tell him of an intruder approaching the house. When he looked the figure seemed to be very familiar. He was dressed in black, with his head covered in a hood. "Damn you, you are the one that has been prowling around everywhere. Time we put an end to whatever mischief you are up to." He had no doubt that whatever the man was doing it was not for their benefit. The figure had entered the house by this time, so Robin could only wait for his reappearance, and get the beam ready for action.

It was a long 10 minutes before the man came out, carrying a small satchel. "That must be important," Robin muttered to himself. He aimed the narrow beam directly at the man who was now running into the darkness. It glanced his shoulder holding the satchel, without seriously harming him, although that was enough to make him scurry away faster, dropping the package as he did so. Robin widened the beam and incinerated the satchel, but by this time the man was nowhere to be seen. Despite browsing the whole area with the beam on the light setting, there was no trail to be followed, no footmarks. It almost looked like the man had vanished into thin air. Robin kept watch on the house until the sun crept out to show for sure that nobody was hiding in wait, then it was time for a quick breakfast.

Tom and Robin jumped into the rover with Larry driving as usual. They would get to the house well before the coaches could get their friends there, and Robin was in a hurry to find out what had been stolen. They passed the burned-out tiny skeletons of what was left of the buses, giving them only a quick glance. When the rover arrived, they were met by the house master, who kneeled at their presence, shaking with fear. "My lords, we have been attacked during the night. The master on night duty has been killed, and some things have been taken from the computer suite."

"Yes," Tom said, "we know. Far worse. Your lords never made it over to the mansion last night. There was some kind of accident in the bus. They are all dead."

"Oh," groaned the master, now fearing for his life. They would surely find him complicit in some way. "What can I do?"

"For a start," Robin jumped in, "get a search done of these grounds. Look for any footprints, and find where an intruder came from, for we know there was just one man. While that is going on, go and make a list of anything disturbed or stolen. We will also join that search."

Going into the old senior lord's office, Robin found the master memo terminal. He placed an immediate order for 2 large coaches. The office was a treasure trove of bric-a-brac, as well as records going back more than 60 years, which it appeared was when the homeland project had kicked off. There was nothing in the cabinets that gave any real information that might be useful. Everything he touched was about the project. This will all have to be burned," he said.

By this time the 2 search groups had completed their tasks. There were no signs of anything related to the intruder except for some melted plastic outside the front door. The house master reported that only some computer disks had been stolen, that some computers had been turned on, but everything else looked OK.

"Where are the computer backups kept?" Robin asked.

"Locked away in the basement, milord."

"Go and retrieve them, see if any are missing." Robin nodded to Tom who got the message that he should follow the house master.

The other masters stood around awaiting orders, Robin gave some. "Go and get breakfast made for everyone. I want all slaves and masters to eat a good breakfast, as well as the butt-kids upstairs. Keep everyone in the lord's dining room." Not quite sure what was meant by a good breakfast the master got the kitchen slaves working while everyone else was made to stay in the designated room.

The house master came back with 3 boxes of backup disks. "We found just one set missing."

"Those need to go into the back of the rover, and someone needs to guard them." What Robin meant was that when there were no witnesses the backups would be melted.

Addressing the house master again, Robin indicated the files in the cabinets, "Take all of these outside on to the lawn. They must be destroyed." When the master looked at him in anguished surprise, Robin continued,

"This project has been compromised. Who knows what damage has been done already. We must protect this data by making sure nobody else can get to it. This house is being closed down on my order." This time the master thought he understood and started to carry out the papers to build the bonfire outside.

*

When he was alone with Tom, Robin asked him to accompany the slaves and butt-kids back to their villages as he had done before to unite them up with any relatives they might still have. Tom smiled at the prospect. He took Paul and Marty with him. Meanwhile Robin worked on every computer. There was nothing special about them and indeed they accessed the same internet he used, but he needed to delete all possible data, even if stored across the internet. After the computers had seen their data deleted, their data disks were formatted, and just to make sure Robin created multiple logical disks from the existing data partition. He removed anything that looked like a lord's program, leaving just the basic operating system, thinking that they might be able to make use of this hardware collection at a later time, which was as powerful as anything he'd seen.

Robin made sure that the heavy books he'd found in the debating room would go back to their mansion for studying. They had the feel of importance.

They had their bonfire, then all the masters and pretend lords piled into coaches and rover, to go back to the mansion. Before that the house was sealed, all devices turned off and everything was made secure. Robin took hold of the keys.

*

On the journey back to the mansion Robin wondered what they were going to do with so many masters. In the end, he asked for volunteers for who would like to go and live in a village and become farmers, and who could maintain their mansion, which meant keeping it in good order, grounds as well, without any slaves, for when lords visited. It ended up as an equal split, for it was clear that so many were tired of the old life. Robin reminded the masters staying with the mansion that they could be tracked wherever they went. He didn't need to elaborate on that, but he did want to avoid a mass exodus to the countryside.

CHAPTER 8

REVERSAL OF PROSPECTS

BACK AT THE MANSION ON the coast Robin spent some time luxuriating in Lucy's company. She had brought along Digga and Whiskey. For some reason the other dogs hadn't quite grasped the idea of not doing their business inside, so for now they were excluded. Whiskey was so much more mature than his siblings. Lucy spent a lot of time explaining how much better their village looked now, but Robin was more interested in how her bump was doing.

"I've found the ideal place where we can build our house," Lucy hinted. "Have you had time to work out those plans yet for new homes?"

"I will need to talk with the builders when they get back from the factories. Did I tell you about the exquisite furniture in that last grand house? I will go and collect it when we are ready. It will look so nice in our tiny house." They cuddled some more.

"There is a lovely lady who will be my midwife when the time comes. I'm so looking forward to having our baby."

"Me too," grinned Robin.

*

It was 5 days after the last incident where they had nearly caught the hooded man. Tom and Larry had joined the love pair at the mansion while the others spent time in their adopted homes. Realising that they were probably being spied on constantly, Tom and Robin devised security schedules for around each premises they had taken over. Ex-masters in most instances made excellent security guards.

In addition they were considering what they should do to exploit their gains. "We now have full control of the Southeast," Tom said. "We will continue to move west to include more villages under our influence. The villages are absolutely wonderful, blooming with growth, they are amazing to see compared to how they used to be, and the fresh blood that now lives there is also helping. We have plenty of space to more than treble the populations, which will be good on several levels."

"Yes," agreed Robin, "totally amazing what happens when you remove the threat of suppression." Robin was still worried though. "I don't like it that we cannot capture this hooded man we keep seeing, because I feel something is going on, something worrying. I keep expecting some payback after we ruined their plans for their homelands on our world."

"Perhaps we should also increase security in and around the villages?" suggested Tom.

"That wouldn't hurt, but we should keep it as a low-profile thing, that the village chief organises. With so much traffic between the factories and villages we should just make those moving things aware that not everyone is a friend."

"Indeed," said Tom, "with everything else going so well, it seems there is always a shadow hanging over us. I still can't quite get over what that senior lord said about that alien world. I'm beginning to wonder if the whole sorry history of the human race was manipulated by aliens that just wanted to steal our planet and make us slaves to them."

"That's certainly the way it looks," agreed Robin. "From everything I've read there seems to have been influences for hundreds of years for us to advance in certain directions, which many would say were illogical, but which led to situations where people were controlled to a very large degree by governments that were supposed to serve them. Treachery was rife, but well hidden, and not clear enough for the average person to spot. It was hard to know who was pulling the strings, which could have so easily been these damned aliens."

"Have you ever looked up into space with your spy in the sky?" asked Tom. "You wonder if they are out there in some kind of vessel."

"Interesting thought, let's try it." Robin used the manual controls to point the satellites away from Earth, but all they could see was the moon. "Nothing out there that looks like a space boat of any kind."

"They could have invaded us, and fought for the planet, but they might have lost, even with superior weapons. That would at least have been more honest, maybe less easy than what they actually did."

"Perhaps that alone tells us everything we need to know about them. Their deceitful ways define them."

"In other words if we ever meet them, trust them as far as you can throw them," Tom concluded.

*

Robin and Lucy did get to spend a few days in the village, which was more like a holiday than anything else. It gave them both time together. Tom had gone back to the factories to make sure all was working out. Lucy had chosen a piece of ground just a few minutes' walk from the village centre, mostly surrounded by trees, with a grassy front. A bubbling stream was close by. Robin wondered if he could make use of the fast-flowing water to grind corn, like he'd seen pictures of. They stayed with the village chief Bruno. He had extended the original one-storey building with extra rooms for visiting chiefs or VIPs to use. It was also where the village internet was located.

"Good morning, Robin," Bruno said. "I have a message from Tom. He wants to have a mini-conference day after tomorrow at the mansion by the Thames estuary."

"Morning, Bruno. Yes, that will be fine. Please ask him to bring a cook if there are going to be many of us because we don't have one there currently."

"In that case, I will come along and make your meals," Lucy insisted.

Robin knew it best not to disagree with his woman, instead went off to find Larry, to ask him to drive them. They found Paul with Larry, so they all made the trip together. They'd just settled in when Lucy started to feel unwell. Morning sickness had been a problem for a few days, but now it felt as though something was happening inside of her. "You'd best go back and talk with your midwife," Robin insisted. Lucy did as she was told. Larry drove her back, telling Robin he'd pick up anyone else that had arrived at the village and drive over in the morning. "No problem, me and Paul will have plenty to talk about," he said as he kissed his wife goodbye. The mansion was suddenly quiet except for Whiskey digging up some flowers. He had a strange feeling of always saying goodbye to Lucy and being separated. It played on his mood.

It was coming up to lunch time, which encouraged Paul and Robin to seek out something easy to cook from the pantry. They were disturbed by Digga who was barking ferociously. Robin rushed outside, knowing that this tone from Digga meant trouble of some sort.

Coming around the side of the house were 4 men dressed from head to foot in dark green. Their gait was odd, as though the knees bent outwards, other than that they were very slim. A woollen mask covered their facial features, although their green eyes seemed to be luminous. They didn't say anything but behind them was the hated figure of the hooded man. This time with his hood down. Despite his head being shaved he was immediately recognisable as the old chief of Robin's village. That large purple growth on the side of his nose was a dead giveaway. This was the vile man responsible for killing his parents. The man who had raped his small sister, killing her. Robin saw red, in fact his brain almost exploded with the colour. Never had he felt more like ripping a man apart with his bare hands.

"That's him," shouted the old chief, as Robin rushed towards him, trying desperately to get between the 4 other figures to have the chance to give his arch enemy a great deal of pain. He heard a loud bang behind him, repeated, but was concentrating on pushing through the figures that stood in his way. Digga went for the ankle of one man, while Whiskey went straight for the ex-chief, burying his teeth deeply into his arm. The ex-chief screamed and Digga snapped and bit wherever she could. Robin almost slipped away from the grasping arms of the 4 men. Just as he felt like he was almost through a sudden sharp pain on the back of the head caused him to stumble, with darkness overwhelming him a half second later.

"I'm still not feeling well," Lucy admitted to Larry when he came to drive her back to the mansion.

"Not to worry," said Larry, "the motion of the car won't help if you are not feeling well, so best if you don't travel. I've got almost a full load anyway, as Tom has brought 2 helpers with him. We'll see you back here in a couple of days." Larry went off to the rover while Lucy went back for a lie down.

Larry and the others arrived at the mansion just after 10am, expecting to be greeted by the dogs, but everything was deadly quiet. The first body they found was Paul's. He'd been shot through the head as he had been walking out of the door towards the left side of the house. He was completely cold and stiff. That didn't stop Tom pulling his gun out and looking for intruders. "Where's Robin, and where are the dogs?" Larry cried out.

They quickly found the dogs when they turned around the corner of the house. Digga had been slammed against a brick wall and was still breathing, but barely. Whiskey, who had been shot, lay where he had fallen, on the black path which his blood had stained completely red.

Tom stooped to stroke Digga who opened her eyes to look deeply at her friend, trying to tell him what had happened. A tear dropped from her left eye as she remembered that she had failed to save Robin. Somehow Tom understood this, "Good dog. Stay there while we search for Robin. I will be back soon to make you better." Digga yelped a sorry sounding thanks.

Tom led the search all through the grounds, looking in the boat and even the water for some sign of Robin. Every single room in the mansion was opened and examined, but they saw no sign of anybody nor any sign of any additional spilled blood. Tom shouted loudly for his friend, fearing the worst, "Robin, where are you?" After walking all around the grounds a further 3 times, Tom's mood took on a very sombre feel, fearing that Lucy had lost her man, and he a great friend who had brought hope to so many. "We should have had security people here to protect Robin," he mumbled to nobody in particular.

Gently picking up Digga, who was trying hard not to groan with pain,

Tom took Robin's dog into the house to clean up her wounds caused by rough boots, and to examine the bruises. Expecting that Digga had lain there for a whole day at least, Tom gave the dog some water, dripping it from his hands into her open mouth. "You must be very thirsty and hungry," he said, feeding her small pieces of rabbit. He treated what damage he could by washing congealed blood away, then made Digga as comfortable as possible. She would have to wait for one of the healers to arrive. They would know better what to do with the dog's injuries.

They had just buried Paul and Whiskey, with due ceremony, when the coach carrying helpers and pretend lords arrived. They immediately saw the graves, noting that Robin was not here, and their hearts sank.

"We've just buried Paul and one of the dogs," Tom informed everyone. "There is another badly damaged dog inside if one of you healers could take a look, please? As for Robin, we just can't find any trace of him, so this looks very much like a personal attack on him for the work we did at the grand mansion. It seems we finally crossed the line, and now they are going to hurt us back. From now on we should all be armed at all times, and wary of any strangers, especially that hooded man." Tom felt he had to remain strong and resolute, although all he felt like was crawling into a warm bed and cutting the world out.

Various people did their own searching for Robin, then someone asked, "Is it worth extending the search further, perhaps Robin escaped just outside?"

"By all means, keep looking," Tom agreed, "we haven't got anything better to do until we get over this tragedy. I have no idea how I will break this to Lucy."

They kept looking and talking about possible things that might have happened. The day passed quickly and many took some alcohol to help them sleep. Some woke in the morning with some hope that maybe Robin may have turned up overnight, but more fruitless searching and wishing left everyone more depressed as they sat glumly in the lounge watching the day brighten, just waiting. The hardest part was not knowing.

*

As the darkness of unnatural sleep faded into greyness the pain became ever more real with Robin's senses waking with a jolt. His legs ached. His head hurt like hell, reminiscent of the time the Mo brothers cut his head open. It seemed like one side of his head had grown double in size, or at least that's how it felt. Worse than all of that was the crippling agony that ran the length of his spine. Not since he first escaped the village with a large, painful scar that kept him awake for many nights had he known such a throbbing misery.

He listened for any noises as his senses slowly became more acute. He was lying on his back, agonising as that was, on a firm surface. All around was quiet except for a background low-pitched buzzing sound. The memories came flooding back to him all at once, of what had happened. He had found the hated hooded ex-chief outside the mansion. That memory alone raised his blood pressure to the point that the crucifying pain in his head threatened to black him out. He didn't want to think any more, and especially didn't want to think about any repercussions he didn't know about yet. Slowly he regained his composure, and his pain eased a little. He didn't even want to think of what had been done to him.

"I'm still alive, for surely being dead wouldn't hurt so much," he told himself. "That means there must have been a purpose for my abduction. Where have they taken me though?"

There had been no sound that his sensitive ears could pick up, and he wondered if he had been put in a coffin, or wooden box, as dead. His arms or legs couldn't find any restraints either side of his body, but he had only tensed his muscles a little. If there was anyone watching over him, he'd rather not give any clues that he was awake. He waited another minute before opening his eyes a tiny crack. Neither darkness nor blinding light assaulted him, all he could make out was a dull grey lightness against a dark coloured ceiling.

Still sensing no other presence he fully opened his eyes to look around at a small room. There was a door to his right, a small window to his left, and yes, he was on some sort of bed with wheels on the bottom. He had to raise his head and look down to the floor to find that out, which was a mistake as the pain engulfed him once more. The window showed blackness and some very bright stars of red and yellow. "It must be the middle of the night," he told himself.

It was a strange feeling as he tried to move his body, despite the pain his body seemed lighter, as though the ground was not exerting as much pull as it normally did. That's when he raised his head to take a better look through the window. Perhaps he could see where he was. At first the sight made no sense at all, and he thought that perhaps this was a picture after all, but then he noticed a slight drift to one side of the whiteness that seemed to float above the circular object that filled most of his view. He raised himself higher on his elbows, trying to forget his physical discomforts, unwilling to think the thought that came crashing into his mind. "No, that would be impossible," he murmured. His head was bursting with pain as he fell back to the bed with a bit of a thump, the agony reverberating through his body once more.

Breathing deeply, he calmed his mind. He looked again, staring at this thing for several moments. There could be no doubt. He was in a space boat of some kind, and that was his world down below. Several irrational thoughts hit him all at once, from, *They're taking me to Sarandach*, to *How will I ever get home?* He calmed himself once again, deciding that, *While I am here, I'll do as much damage as humanly possible.*

Fighting back the nausea he raised himself up and swinging his legs towards the floor, he inched his body down until his feet rested easily on the warm floor. Balancing himself there for a moment, he stood still, intending the pain to dissipate. Looking again around the room he saw nothing of note, and certainly nothing he could use as a weapon. Noting that he was dressed only in some light shorts, he took a few short steps, which made him feel that he was almost floating rather than walking, edging towards the door. There was no door handle as such. He moved his fingers to prise the door open using the small crack between it and the wall but could get no purchase. There was a button on the wall that his arm must have triggered somehow, for the door pushed itself open of its own accord.

The corridor outside his room was lit only by a red unit that ran the length of it, giving off a pleasant warmth. Listening intently, Robin moved his aching body, one step at a time, seeking some mischief he could cause. Passing one door which was ajar, he glanced inside to see 2 tall beings, that he could only describe as looking like human style reptiles. They were drinking red blood from a small, battered corpse. He wanted to go in and hurt them, but didn't have the strength, so he backed away to continue up the narrow passageway. An odd symbol on the panel of a door reminded him of something he had seen at the grand mansion. Listening for a moment to see if anyone was inside, he plucked up courage to press the button, and dragged his heavy body inside. This room was smaller than the one he'd woken up in. There was a terminal, a printer and a small table with printed reports on. He glanced at some, realising that one note was providing certain detail about homelands. Sitting down at the terminal, he located the electronic version of the memo he'd just read. He wrote and told them to immediately destroy all data and software relating to project homelands, with a brief explanation to say it had been compromised badly by a rebel element. Emphasising urgency the memo demanded that all plans, backups and materials relating to this project also be destroyed at once. He smiled a wicked smile, hoping the receiver would do as they were told without question.

Feeling it would be useful to let his friends know what became of him, he sent a memo to the mansion explaining very briefly that he'd been abducted by the hooded man who was his old chief. 'Currently on a space boat. Love to all.' He had no idea if he would see them again but would rather die than end up on a strange planet.

There was an extra option on this terminal he hadn't seen before. It allowed copies of all memos sent or received to be sent to other specific terminals. Naturally, he added in the address of the terminal in the mansion as well as that of the one in his village.

Picking up the pile of reports again he picked out some interesting topics and sent back contrary commands. One report talked about a quantity of gold. They received a memo back telling them to send it to the mansion on the Thames. Crumpling up the messages he'd replied to and throwing them in a bin, he placed the others back where they had been, then stood up to leave. His ears picked up the noise of someone coming down the corridor. Quickly he heaved his aching body behind the door as it opened. One of the creatures he'd seen earlier came in, standing with the door open, reviewing the top few printed reports. Happily he didn't want to send a memo, but he did start sniffing the air.

He's noticed my sweat, Robin thought, realising he was sweating with exertion, not just from the strain of moving his body around in this warm place, but also with the tension of being an active spy, telling himself he would retire from this role should he ever get back to Earth.

Looking towards the terminal, the creature took a loud sniff. A noise up the corridor probably saved Robin from being found, for the reptile turned around to respond to the noise and moved back up the corridor away from the terminal room.

Creeping out of that room when all was quiet, Robin edged further up towards the end of the corridor. A noise coming his way caused him to listen at the nearest door for occupants then enter that room, which was fortunately empty. He stood hard against a wall, breathing heavily, pushing away the pain he still felt all over his body. His spine felt like holes had been drilled in at least 2 places, each one screaming out for some healing attention. When he touched the places, the holes were evident. It seemed like they had been sealed by melting the skin over them. *No wonder they hurt like hell*, he thought, wondering what had been done to him.

This room he found himself in contained several tables and many cupboards. There were several small silver dishes that the lords used to drain the blood of butt-kids into, as well as some short sharp knives. He felt like smashing them to the floor, but held his temper fearing that an angry reaction would certainly alert them to his presence. He did grab one of the knives which he decided he would indeed use to defend himself.

A heavy curtain to his left caught his eye. It was a thick weave with many deep colours running through it. *Very attractive*, he thought. *Just the sort of thing I would need in my village home to keep out the draughts of winter.*

Voices were coming from the other side of this heavy partition, attracting his attention, for they were speaking English. Parting the curtain very slowly, he was able to see the side view of 2 figures, from their right side. One was sitting on a generously upholstered solid, ornate, high chair. It had all the characteristics of a king's throne that he'd read about. The other figure was prostrating himself in front of the kingly figure dressed in a red satin robe.

He immediately recognised the human on the floor as the hated village chief. His right arm was hanging limp from when Robin had almost zapped him at the grand mansion. The other creature was huge, with a large reptilian looking head. A narrow, split tongue darted from the mouth of this large creature, no doubt anticipating something good. *Perhaps he is going to drain my blood?* Robin thought to himself, determined that he would extract a very high price for such a foul deed.

The chief was now on his knees before the reptile, head bent.

"You have done well," exclaimed the huge reptile, in an artificial growl.

The chief raised his head and smirked, "Thank you, my God, as I worship you, so I will serve you."

Robin felt sick at this display. This was the same chief that had treated his own people as less than worms, and here he was, with his straggly beard gone, venerating this overgrown lizard from another world.

Knowing that he would have only a single chance to kill the kneeling snake Robin started to plan his move. He was certain this would be his last act but was more than willing for that to happen if he could kill that man and perhaps do some damage to the alleged god. *I bet even gods bleed*, he thought.

The reptile was still talking, something about fixing up the chief's arm so badly damaged recently. "Enough tittle-tattle," he growled, "from now on we will be able to track wherever your pipsqueak goes. That will be your full-time job. Devices have been planted in his back where they can never be removed from. In future you will be able to know where he is at all times to prevent him making any more, big problems. He overreached his puny self when he destroyed the homelands project. But no worries. We gods are patient. We will wear him and his followers down."

"Let me cut his vile throat and give his remains to you, my God, so that you can drain his life force to make him die in great agony."

Something like a smile passed over the lips of the big creature, "A tempting idea, but no. I have other plans for him. He has done so well in reinvigorating the growing fields and making the people fat in the small area where he resides. Everywhere else the people die off too quickly, their blood is thin and tasteless. We will let them flourish for a while before we take it all back under our control, to fully enslave them and drink the blood of their babies."

The ex-chief grinned widely, "How will I watch this puny creature?"

"You will live in a room on this ship. That way I won't have to send you a message to go hunting. You will act on your own authority, watching his movements on a special electronic map, like that one on the wall. That shows where the important locations are, where vital work is done. Should he approach any of them you will go down and sabotage whatever he is doing. You will be able to call on the 5 assistants you used before. It is a good idea to keep the small ship invisible on the ground, because they will waste time looking for you."

Robin took a good look at the map. There were 2 points of interest in the Southeast he'd not been aware of, although he had seen them many times.

The large creature growled on, "Once you have confused your human and his friends you will immediately come back up to the ship and from here alert the location to fight him off."

Robin had heard enough, now he was ready for his painful death. The lust was upon him, and he had to satisfy his dire need to kill this most vile human being in the next room now. Gripping the knife in his right hand, he pushed off the agony once more and prepared to part the curtain and leap at his enemy.

Before his hand even reached the curtain edge a single reptilian hand closed over his mouth and other hands held his arms in a tight grip as he was pulled backwards away from his grave desire. The last thing he felt before slipping into a new blackness was a sharp lingering pain in the top of his left arm.

Not knowing what had happened behind the curtain, the reptile continued, "He is an example for others to follow, and we will allow his methods to take effect elsewhere. It is to our advantage to see the fields grow more fruitful and the people fatten up. As I say, we are patient, and when the time comes, we will crucify those that lead any rebellion, and then we will harvest our human prize. His efforts will mean that we will live well for years to come on their fresher healthy blood."

*

He came back to a state of awareness very slowly, dropping back to blackness each time he tried to move. His mouth was full of grass that lay underneath his face, but his head was too heavy. The pain in his back was crippling, causing him to moan, plus there were several extra points of pain that hadn't been there the last time he was awake. "Feels like a donkey kicked me in the kidneys," he told the grass. His eyes stayed open for a minute, realising he was no longer in a space boat. The sun was shining strongly on his naked back and that helped. He tried to turn over until his muscles screamed out that his spine was too tight, too rigid from reacting to some damage done to him, against the ligaments no longer as supple as they were. He lay there to catch his breath hoping he was now on Earth for sure. He tried to call out, his voice croaky, his mouth dry. "Hey, anybody." There was no immediate response.

Inside the mansion, Digga had been bandaged up and treated with some herbs and was receiving plenty of loving attention from all there. Everyone was preferring to put their attention anywhere except on the reality that Robin was gone. Suddenly Digga's ears went up. She yelped the loudest noise she could make, "go and look outside." She tried to stand up but was too weak. Tom knew what this yelp meant, and charged out of the door, gun in hand. The others followed straight after Tom, aware that this could be another attack against them.

Tom saw the body first, recognising it immediately, "Robin, oh my goodness, what has happened to you?"

Robin could barely speak, just able to move his head, and weakly he said, "Help me up." There was no lack of strong arms for that. He was lifted up groaning with pain still, and gently moved inside. They sat him in a reclining chair. "Water please." Phil helped him to sip some water until his throat was less raw, and he could breathe more easily.

"What happened?" asked Tom, as Digga once again tried to get up to greet him. All he could manage was to stretch out a hand to stroke her muzzle. She whined happily.

Robin managed a brief, happy smile towards his great friends Tom and Digga, "I've been curtailed, Tom." His voice was husky and low. "Hard to talk. See my memo. Terminal." Tom rushed to the terminal that had automatically printed out Robin's message. Tom read it then handed it to Larry.

"What does it say?" several asked.

Larry read it out loudly for all to hear, "...abducted by the hooded man. He is old chief. Currently on a space boat. Love to all." They all looked at Robin, beginning to understand something of what had happened.

"I didn't think I would ever see you again," Robin blurted out, his eyes moist.

"Well don't worry about that for now, you can tell us the whole story when you are feeling better. The healers need to take a good look at you," Tom said.

Henry just wanted to know, "How did you escape?"

"I didn't," Robin said weakly, "back so painful..." Then he passed out.

The healers leaned him forward to investigate his back. "My heck," said Andy, "his body is black and blue with beatings, but look at those holes. They've punctured his back very close to his spine, too close. No wonder he is in agony. It looks like they inserted some things at the top and lower part of the spine then sealed the hole with extreme heat. Let's get some kind of bed set up in the office, and we can start making some ointments and other treatments for him. Poor Robin, he has really suffered."

"Yes," agreed Tom solemnly, "I'm just glad we have him back with us.

His loss would have been a disaster for our cause."

*

His friends took it in turns to stay with him even when the healers were getting him to take herbal remedies. He ate little, drank a little, but it was like his body was on automatic, for there was no sign of him there, as he lay on his makeshift bed, for a good 2 days. The areas around his spine where objects had been literally pushed in were massaged to loosen the tightness.

"Whatever they inserted," said Adam, "it is unlikely that they will ever come out. They are very close to the side of his spine, meaning he could lose all mobility if we tried to dig them out."

Rousing himself, but still aching all over, Robin looked around him, so happy that his memory of being back with his friends was a correct one.

"Nice to see you awake," David smiled at him. "I won't ask how you feel, because you still look pretty pale." Robin tried to smile back but needed some water before his dry mouth would respond to his will.

"Take it very easy," Adam said. "I've never seen such vicious bruising like what's over you. What did they do?"

Robin eased himself up with a little help, "When I woke up aboard that craft, I only noticed the pain in my head and the spine. They must have kicked and beaten me after."

"OK," said Tom, who had just arrived in the room. "You can tell us all about your adventures, but for now the healer has prescribed rest and plenty of food. You've hardly eaten for days."

Robin groaned, "Oh my poor stomach, I think I've been kicked by a horse." They smiled, nobody laughed, for it was all too clear that he might well have been kicked by a horse. "Where's my Lucy? Where's Paul and my dogs?"

"Lucy is still in the village," Tom answered. "I hadn't planned on sending for her until you were at least awake. Perhaps now would be a good time to get her here."

"Give it another day so that I can get my strength back somewhat."

"I have bad news about Paul and Whiskey," Tom responded. "When we all arrived back here, we found their bodies. Both had been shot with a gun. Digga somehow survived the beating she suffered long enough for us to get back. She had also been kicked by a host of donkeys."

"I remember," said Robin vaguely. "When you brought me into the lounge, I wondered why she wasn't running all around. Will she be alright?"

"She is much better now, but like you she will need time for her body to repair itself. There were no broken bones, but some damage to her internal organs. We are doing what we can for her."

Robin's eyes started to mist over as he took hold of Adam's hand, "Thank you." Adam could only nod in response.

*

The next day, in the afternoon, Larry headed back to the village to collect Lucy and bring her to the mansion the next morning. By this time Robin was sitting up and walking almost normally if with some difficulty, but he was keen to share with everyone what he had experienced.

They all gathered around with their cups of tea while Robin sipped his herbal drink. "It all started with Digga barking outside. There were 4 figures fully dressed in dark green coming around the corner. The dogs were already nipping and biting them, then I saw that man behind the 4 figures, the rotten ex-chief of our village. He was wearing a hood which he removed to taunt me, and I really saw red. His head was shaven, as was his awful beard, but he knew me, and he was smirking. I raced towards him and was within a few feet of him despite being held back by his 4 thugs. That's when they must have hit me on the head, for I knew nothing more for some time. No way of knowing how long I'd been dead to the world, impossible to know when you are asleep, but I had a great shock when I did finally wake."

"So you are really sure about who this hooded man is?" asked Tom. "Good. That's one thing we can now be certain of, but how did he go from being a chief to being a kidnapper?"

"I'm not certain," replied Robin. "I clearly saw that mole he had on the side of his nose, and I wouldn't confuse his wicked smile with any other barbaric soul, evil barely describes him in my eyes. It would appear that he went up in the world, now reporting directly to a god."

There were several gasps and Adam said, "What was that? Did you really say he is in league with a god?"

"Not just in league, he worships the floor this god walks on and would do anything he asked of him."

"You saw this god?" David asked. "Seriously? That must have been some bump on the head."

"We're jumping ahead, but yes, I really did see someone that our enemy called a god. I was just about to attack the weasel when some reptiles caught me."

"Wow, hang on, Robin, listen to what you are saying. You saw a god and some reptiles? In space? This is really beginning to sound like a fairy tale," Phil said.

"Hang on before you make a liar out of Robin," Tom said, irritated. "He couldn't disappear and then reappear so easily without some advanced technology or spiritual powers behind it. We all know about the homelands designed for aliens who could very well be different to humans, especially as they needed a warm environment. Reptiles makes perfect sense to me."

"Sorry, Robin," Phil said quietly. "Please carry on."

Robin described the reptile people, "The god himself was sitting on a huge throne. He was twice the size of the others, dressed in a huge robe. I heard the ex-chief and the god talking. He kept calling this creature God, so he really believed it, and here is the interesting bit. Our enemy asked if he could cut my throat and feed my blood to the god. The god declined, saying that he had a better purpose for me. It seems they are impressed with the improvements in the villages. Our produce is so much greater than it used to be, and the people are so much healthier. This god wants us to keep going on in this fashion."

"That doesn't sound so terrible," said Marty.

"He has a distinctly evil reason for this. Lulling us into a false idea that we are truly free, for he plans to take back control of this Southeast area when we least expect it. Then he will slaughter and kill as they always have. We will become slaves once more and our babies will serve as butt-kids."

"So," said Tom, "is this why they kidnapped you?"

"Not at all. I overheard this all by accident. I was supposed to be in a small room, unable to move after they operated on me to put tracking devices in my back. Devices that can never be removed, so that they will know where I am at all times, and our hooded friend can intervene to stop me doing damage to their installations."

"Ah, now it all begins to make sense, except that they hadn't planned on your will power in being able to shift around a bit despite the pain," Adam said. "Well done, Robin. One good tiny thing came out of this, we know what their plans are even if we do not know when."

"Yes," agreed Robin, "what's a bit of debilitating pain when you can learn so much?" That caused a few sad smiles. "I was so ready to kill that man and suffer the consequences. I would have loved to see a god bleed."

"Wouldn't we all," agreed Tom with a big smile for his best friend.

"You know," said Marty, "that terminal is getting a lot more messages than it used to, but I'm not sure what they are all about."

"Ah, that will be my fault," admitted Robin. "They will be useful for our spies to analyse."

"What do you mean?" asked David, spymaster number one.

"After I sent my message, so you'd at least know what became of me, I found some interesting functions on the terminal on the space boat. I had duplicates of all memos sent to or received by that terminal copied here, so that we would know what they were doing. I did this by making our terminal a member of the senior terminal group, of which there were 5 others. That I hope means that all messages are shared. That does of course mean we have to be careful what we send from here."

"Bloody amazing," said David. "Having access to priority messages will be a great help to us in knowing what is being planned."

"How could I ever have doubted you, Robin, you are a genius," said Phil.

"That was a touch of brilliance," Tom smiled. "We will need someone full-time on tracking and understanding those messages now though. David and George, looks like this will become your spying headquarters."

"Fantastic, we can bring some of our trainees here as well," said David happily.

*

After a little rest Robin decided he could walk around a little, which he did. "Now that it's dark, there's something I've been aching to do." Seating himself at the terminal he went into the viewer. "I want to see if the space boat is visible from here."

Everyone looked on as Robin used the manual control to look up into the dark sky, seeking out the alien shape. It took some minutes of scanning back and forth before an object was spotted. Part of it gleamed in reflected light. "It looks bigger than the moon," Phil volunteered.

"It's a monster alright, so long and fat," Tom said. "You wonder how anybody could live up there, never mind get up there. They must have great machines."

"Machines that have been developed over many hundreds of years," Robin replied. "Can someone take a note of the exact location readings. I want to see how clever they are." He turned on the tight light beam, hoping it might rip a hole in the fabric of the long boat, but nothing happened. It seemed that the light just got absorbed. "Darn, looks like it is made of some material that can resist the light beam. They probably haven't even noticed it." Robin continued to scan the ship looking for possible weak spots. As he and the others watched they saw a small ship depart from it. Tracing the path of the small ship backwards, Robin noticed an open hatchway that slowly closed. "That's how they get off and on to the big boat." Still with the hooded man on his mind, he said, "Hmm, that gives me an idea."

*

Aboard the long spaceship, Robin's act of sabotage had not gone unnoticed. "Ha ha ha! How pathetic. Did that puny human imagine we would allow our ship to be unprepared against our own weapons? Ha ha, this ship is much stronger than that," one fat god was saying, laughing so loud that the blood he was drinking began to spill from the golden goblet.

*

Lucy arrived to find her beloved resting in an armchair. Digga was close by him but still unable to do much but half wag a friendly tail and moan gently at Lucy, although she did manage a small yelp.

"What has happened?" she cried, dreading to hear the news.

"Something bad, I'm afraid," he said, trying to gently prepare Lucy. "We were attacked by our old chief and some reptiles. He is the hooded man. They hurt Digga badly. They killed Paul and Whiskey. I was kidnapped. Then they brought me back, black and blue."

"Oh my poor love, I will make you feel better." She tried to hug him but gave up as she could see any pressure was painful for him. "What are you going to do?"

"I'm going to rest for a few days." In a voice so full of anger and resentment he continued, "Then I am going to make sure our chief never venerates any god ever again."

She squeezed in between Robin and Digga, and gently taking hold of their paws, she leaned her head towards Robin's shoulder. "Do be careful," she said.

"I will," he promised, "but what I've learned is scary. The gods are happy to let us carry on. They want people well fed and fat as their blood tastes better, and they plan to make slaves of us again at some point."

"Oh," Lucy cried in despair.

"We have no choice, we have to prepare for the worst, but we must also attack and reduce our vile enemies."

*

Gradually Robin got back on his feet. His back was troubling him less after a week of taking it easy. Now he was ready to take on the world again and do something about the prospects they all faced. With most of the crew and helpers already at the mansion, the chiefs of all villages got invited as well. There were things that had to be stressed so that they all knew the extent of the problems they all faced. As the last guest arrived to an already full lounge Tom kicked things off. "I suspect you will all know of how Robin was abducted. As a result of that he learned some disturbing things that changes our situation and what we must prepare for. Knowledge has been bought at a very high price, which makes it invaluable as it will allow us to prepare for the worst. While Robin was abducted and in the gods' space vessel, he learned primarily that the gods are allowing us to enjoy our freedom for a short time so that we can get back to health. As the gods see it, we are there to be harvested at some future time, as though we were nothing more than fodder. This whole thing just got a lot more serious, and Robin is going to outline some measures we need to coordinate."

Walking to the tiny platform, a little stiffly, Robin started to speak to all concerned. "I won't go into all of the details about my abduction. I will say this though. The so-called gods are nothing but reptilians in humanoid form. In other words they look human from a distance but are evolved from low-life reptilian creatures. They don't cope too well with the cold, so are usually dressed in heavy green clothing when on Earth. We know they come from another planet, so yes, they are aliens, who think of us only as slaves, entertainment and a supply of fresh blood that they can consume."

Some in the crowd couldn't get their heads around this information, some were shaking their heads not wanting to hear it.

"We have been told so many lies about gods and lords. The gods have used the lords to subjugate us, just like the lords use masters to beat us. I'm not trying to worry anyone, and you will have to accept what I say as true, although I can show you the space boat they live in, that sits above our world if any doubt what I'm saying."

Some nodding erupted from the chiefs that still hadn't grasped the significance of what was being said. "All of this talk of aliens is a bit scary," said Bruno. "Are you saying that we have been ruled over by a reptilian race from the stars all this time?"

"That's my understanding," replied Robin. "It is very likely that they inspired people on this planet to create a situation where our population would be reduced and made into slaves. Those that cooperated with the scheme became lords. Their purpose, I believe was to steal our planet and our lives so that they could create home lands for their own race on Earth."

"That's all history," Tom said, steering Robin back to the main point. "We must now prepare for what the gods do next."

"Let's stop calling them gods," Robin said, "for I'm certain they would bleed and die like any of us, but yes, we need to prepare. Every man has to be able to fight. Every village has to be prepared to be defended. I'm talking about putting metal and wooden spikes around every village, to stand behind and to fight from. We know the enemy, lords or reptiles will have better weapons than us. We must be able to slow them down from getting inside. We must find ways to hurt them when we attack them, and we must find all the weapons we can to help us with this task. They may not come tomorrow, but they will come at some time. We have to set up village patrols and ways to alert every one of us if something bad is happening. If a village is being attacked, we must get our own soldiers to help fight them off."

Robin looked at Lucy who came to stand by him, "I have been researching ways to defend our land," she said. "The internet is still a great tool showing many things. We can still use the tools that the lords were too lazy to take away from us to create some control on our future. In centuries past there were great castles built of stone where people could live without easily being attacked. We don't have castles, but we can find ways to make villages secure, using ditches, metal or wooden walls or even impassable brambles. We need to get inventive."

"Yes indeed," agreed Robin, "each village must get inventive. I will be asking the steel factories to provide strong metal for this purpose. We just have to find ways to plant it into the ground for best effect."

"What if they come in from the sky with some of their flying vehicles?" Toby, a new helper, asked.

"Good question," said Tom. "Perhaps we can make it impossible for them to land in the centre, but we do need to consider things like that. Toby, why don't you take on that project of how we protect ourselves from a sky attack? When you have some ideas discuss with the chiefs to make a practical solution." Toby smiled at having something important to do.

"OK," Robin jumped in, wishing to keep this briefing simple. "We all know the problem. We have to find ways to defend our villages with any weapons we can, and any barriers we can construct."

"What about big guns?" Adrian interrupted. "I've seen pictures of these huge metal objects with hollow barrels that can launch all sorts of things against an enemy."

"Nice idea, Adrian, I've seen them too, but I don't know how they work or anything about the powder that is used. Would you like to investigate that further? A minimum of 2 such guns at the entrance of each village would make me feel safer." Adrian nodded in agreement.

"This is good," said Tom, "we are getting useful ideas. We need to keep talking together though and share ideas."

"We should remember the stories of old King Alfred," Robin said, coming back to a familiar theme. "After his country was overrun by foreigners an army was built from scratch. They made all of their own weapons, swords, shields and so on. I can see the factories are going to be very busy. I shall make sure they know what to do."

"I think not," said Tom determinedly. "You are being tracked. I will inform the factories of the new designs we need from them."

Robin smiled, "As you wish, my liege. Training will be required in fighting with swords and pikes, and perhaps we can even have competitions between villages to make us better prepared."

"Great idea," Tom agreed. "We might even be able to devise other weapons that Robin Hood of ages past had to fight the ruling corrupt elite, for example, bows and arrows." He smiled at Robin. "Now we know where we want to go, I think these things will develop nicely. We have a vision. Do we all agree with it and that it's the right way to go?" Everyone agreed, even Digga gave a happy yelp. "Just a final thing before we all depart. With so many people moving around, we need to make sure our people are not tracked as slaves any more. We need a mass chip removal as a matter of priority."

"That will keep Andy, me and Larry busy for some time then," smirked Marty.

"It will be a full-time job, unless you can train some others up adequately."

"Something else to work on," muttered Marty.

*

The house was quiet after it had previously been so full. The chiefs had gone back to their villages, of which there were now a dozen, as Tom worked ever more westwards. "I need a spying activity," Robin mentioned to David and George. "There are 2 locations, here and here," he indicated the exact positions on the map. "Something is going on there which we don't know about. Now that you have this house almost full of assistant and trainee spies, I'm hoping you can find out what is there. Please confirm that you can make use of the internet within say, a 5-mile radius of each." David agreed to stay and monitor the terminal traffic, while George enthusiastically grabbed 2 assistants to go on the mission.

A day and a half later George had answers. "Both locations are mostly underground, save for some surface equipment. They are both rather large, with a lot of tunnels and hidden pathways, so it was not so hard to get access. The first of these, the closest to us, has a lot of electronic equipment, screens and so forth. They appear to be monitoring what goes on in the skies. I heard a mention of something called radar if that means anything to you?"

"I will find out more about that," Robin said. "Are there a lot of lords there?"

"Maybe a dozen or so, but no slaves that I could see."

"OK, and the second location?"

"A vile place," answered George. "Full of loud music and female slaves who are made to dance with skimpy outfits on. They get groped and abused by visiting lords. I saw about 50 lords, drunk or drugged."

"I will need a layout of both locations as well as details of entrance points," Robin added, trying to keep his emotions away from business. "What about the internet?"

"I checked that. The signal was strong for 6 miles out for the electronics underground offices, and about 5 miles for the den of animalism."

*

David came running into where Robin was sat over his PC, "There's a huge truck outside with 5 ton of metal bars."

"Ah, that will be the gold I ordered. They can load it into the basement cells."

It took the delivery men most of the afternoon to offload the approximately 400 gold bars. "It looks very nice sat behind bars, but what are we going to do with it?" David asked.

"Not decided yet, but when I was on the space boat, I saw it being discussed. It's a valuable metal. I just do not know what we would use it for except jewellery. It will come in handy at some stage, even if it's only to bribe some lords to do our bidding."

"Wouldn't a pistol in the ribs have the same effect?"

*

A whole month had passed since his abduction and now he was restless, having been at the mansion all the time. June had blossomed, and Digga was much recovered, except that he wouldn't be taking her on any more adventures just yet. It was, however, time to put his new plan into action. He'd requested a minimum of 10 helpers including Tom to back him up. They would all meet up on the road that took them to the radar place. Now he knew what that word meant he realised how important it was to the lords and reptiles.

Larry drove Robin and Tom to the meeting place in the rover. The others were waiting. Knowing that the hooded man would be watching his sudden departure from the mansion at night, Robin warned everyone to be on the lookout. "If you see him by all means take a shot at him, but I want him to escape. Don't kill him just yet. I have another fate in mind for this monster."

"So we are all here to make it look like we are going to raid this place," Tom mentioned, "but really it is to entice our man to show himself?"

"That's about it," agreed Robin. "If we all spread out as we walk towards the radar place, we'll have a better chance of seeing him." They walked on in silence with Robin checking every so often that he had a good internet signal. He decided to halt on a hill that overlooked the chosen installation, where the reception was better. There they waited for a certain figure to show himself, talking amongst themselves in spread out small groups.

It was just after midnight when a rustle in the trees nearby alerted them to the possibility that they had company. They continued to talk together as though they were waiting for a signal of some sort. It was Tom that spotted the dark figure first. "Look out, everyone, we have an intruder," he shouted, then took a shot at their enemy as he ran to one side.

"Find that man," Robin shouted. "Everybody keep looking." Nobody of course found him, but everyone made a fuss of running around, extending the search time and area to make it look as though they were reacting as expected. Having plenty of time to evade the searchers the hooded man and his assistant reptiles could easily escape in the small boat, which Robin could now to track as it moved upwards, back towards the giant space boat above them.

Tom and Robin were alone now, the PC sitting comfortably on Robin's knees, although his palms were getting a little moist at the anticipation he felt. "The small craft can really move fast," said Tom, "it's going to take him less than 20 minutes all told."

The small craft was now very close to the big ship. Increasing the size of the viewpoint, Robin made the target indicator hover over where he thought the big door opened up. He was spot on. The door opened up slowly as the small boat got closer, revealing something of the inside of the big ship, mainly light. Maintaining his patience he waited until the boat was partially inside the hold of the big ship, then hit the high intensity beam at full power, jerking it slightly left and right, to ensure the beam got as fully as possible inside the ship at slightly different angles. "There must be something inside there that the beam can damage." He lifted his fingers from the firing mechanism as the hatch closed completely.

"What happened?" queried Tom.

"Nothing," Robin said disappointed, adjusting the view for a longer image, searching for any sign that he'd done some damage, any damage. They stared at the screen for long moments.

"Darn," said Tom. "It was such a good plan."

"Ah well, we can't win every time. They must have been expecting such an attack."

They stared at the laptop for a further 2 minutes, then annoyed, Robin shut it. "We'll have to come back another time and take out the radar place," he said. "We might as well go back home." They moved slowly back to the rover, the others trailing behind them.

Larry was sitting in the driver's seat waiting for them but gazing upwards. "The stars are suddenly very bright. Look, that bright star, it seems to be getting brighter by the second." Robin immediately whipped out his PC to tune in the scene above from the angle of the spy in the sky.

"That is some sparkle," Tom shouted, overjoyed. The sky was now filled with a bright explosive colour, reds mixed with yellow and white.

"Amazing," Robin shouted. "That's what you call a delayed reaction." A small ship was shown against the brightness of the exploding space boat. "Someone is trying to escape. That is not allowed." Adjusting the view he focused on the small boat, now well away from the danger coming from the increasingly brilliant big boat. Moving the hit spot to where the small boat would be to allow for a time delay, he hit the destructive beam key once more, with determination.

"Look over there, some distance from the big explosion. There's a smaller one," Larry cried out as the escaping ship exploded.

"Good shot, Robin," Tom shouted. "Is that the end of our evil gods?"

"I wish," answered Robin, "no way to tell, but I suspect there are a lot more of them, somewhere, sitting comfortably, still thinking of us as their fodder."

The heavenly colourful fire display went on and on, as different parts of the long boat burst into flames or exploded. "A lot of people will be watching this and wondering what happened," Tom gloated.

"We can just tell them that the gods fell foul, of their own evil ways. At least one of them anyway, for who knows where the rest are. It should help to rally our people though, as we have shown them that we can fight back against oppression even against amazing technology, and that gods are not immortal."

"Well said, Robin."

Searching the sky for other black dots, Robin was keen to seek out any others that thought they had escaped. He found no more but had a thought. While they were not inclined to storm the underground radar building, that didn't mean that they couldn't do something else. Finding their current location, shifting the focus of the viewer west a little, he located the mound underneath which sat the electronics monitoring the radar. A series of metal aerials were sticking up high which gave it away. Previously he would have dismissed the sight of such things as old debris from damaged buildings from the previous era. Now he knew what they were. A short, medium powered beam, not too narrow, from the spy in the sky quickly melted the metal dishes and aerials, leaving nothing to see from ground level but smouldering metal.

The fiery display in the sky was still going on. The complete length of the boat had either broken up, exploded or was shining brilliantly as flames had taken hold from within it. They watched until finally what was left of it slipped closer into the atmosphere, towards them, and fell to Earth in smaller pieces. "Let's go home, the party is over."

*

Nobody at the mansion got any sleep that night, worrying. "They must have known it was us that destroyed the reptile's boat," Robin insisted. "I'd expected some chatter on the terminals to that effect, but there's been nothing. It's looking likely that they have another way to send messages to each other."

"Quite likely," said Larry, "just as we use the internet, so they could send verbal messages on radio waves. Time we started to investigate that because I was reading that the use of radio was in common use before the great reset."

"You mean they speak directly with each other? Interesting idea, but that will surely keep you busy?" Tom suggested. "A very worthwhile investigation though. If we could listen into what they were saying we could learn more of their potential actions."

"Nice thinking, Larry," Robin added. "I'm still worried that they will try to punish us somehow."

"There was something that came through on the terminal from the space boat," David informed them. "A very brief message but it didn't incriminate us. It just said that they were under attack. No word to suggest it was us."

"Interesting," said Tom, "you would imagine that only another space boat could attack or damage such a large vessel."

"I do believe that is what the lords' base on the mainland figured out, for all they replied was to ask if it was the Mercantiles that did it."

"That does suggest that the reptiles have enemies out there in space, which is good for us." Robin smiled at the prospect.

"Does that make the Mercantiles our friends, as in the enemy of our enemy is a friend?"

"Let's not assume too much, for this other race might be just as violent as the reptiles and just as greedy for our planet and us as their slaves."

*

The mild summer rolled on with no sign of retaliation from the lords or any so-called gods. Robin, Lucy and Digga moved back to their village permanently so that he could work with builders Adrian, Alex and Albert. They reviewed old style housing to see what practical homes could be erected easily that would incorporate useful features from before. They worked with different styles of brick and paste to make sound walls. One innovation they borrowed was building proper foundations with cellars for storage. The blacksmith helped them to create efficient stoves for heating and cooking.

The securing of all villages against attack progressed as did the creation of underground retreats in case of an overwhelming assault, but it was the metal sheets supplied from the factories that gave villages a shine and a special look. Inter-village trade and movement of people and goods to and from factories was booming. Use was made of windmills, electric panels and gushing water to provide heat, light and energy. The villages were now looking more like smart advanced settlements than the rundown wrecks they had been.

Robin still worried constantly about reprisals, even while Lucy was giving birth to their first child. He had walked out to the very edge of the village, now extended 2 miles outside the original boundary. Defensive plates were in place, which had been highly polished to blind attackers. For now, they were covered up by large sheets of rough fabric. "Now what am I missing?" he asked the sky but received no reply from that quarter. "I wish I could move out more freely," now speaking to a great oak tree that sat just this side of the boundary, "but I'm afraid. I'm afraid they will attack if I go out there again."

"Yelp, yelp, yelp," came the news from Digga, now back to health, "it's a boy. Yelp, yelp." He got the message and ran back to meet and hold his new son while Lucy, sweaty, but undamaged, lay back to recover from her ordeal.

Smiling happily at his common-law wife, he couldn't help saying, "Wasn't she a good girl, Digga, producing such a fine child?" Lucy smiled contentedly, knowing this for the compliment it was intended to be.

Digga just agreed, excited with the happy mood that had filled their home recently, "Yelp yelp yelp yelp, and you did a pretty good job yourself, even if it took you a while."

*

By the time Tommy had reached his third birthday, the villages had grown even more bountiful and the villagers even more industrious. Where there had once been squalor and misery there was now a joy for life. The old muddy paths had been replaced with tarmac, and at night the stored electricity was used to light those paths. Large silos had been erected to store the grain surplus from any year, while the growing fields saw ever more diverse food being encouraged to grow. In 2 of the most southern villages they had discovered some grapes growing wild, and with a little cultivation it had led to some sparse wine making, with more promised as they set about extending the growing areas and the expertise required was gradually acquired.

Robin liked to take time to admire the 2 great cannons that stood close to the village boundary. They were glorious shiny beasts, as long as he was tall. "Aren't they beautiful, Digga? They are a bit of insurance. I hope we will never have to use them, but we are all ready to fight and die if the lords and any aliens attack. They will not find us a walkover."

"Yelp," agreed Digga, "me too."

He threw the heavy covers back over the weapons of war, then glanced happily at the shed which had been specially built to contain the explosive powder the guns would need, as well as the metal balls and pieces that would rip into attackers. For old time's sake he surveyed the big oak tree and clambered up it. A small platform had been built towards the top which would make a great place to watch for trouble.

As he walked back to the village centre Robin realised something. It was a strange thing that nobody had ever caused trouble or been dishonest in what they did. It seemed that the threat of the lords and reptiles still out there kept people concentrating on doing what they could to strengthen the community. Even the ex-prisoners and ex-masters had lost their hatred of life to become valuable occupants of their villages. It was no longer just the Southeast that had been rescued from the lords. Tom had kept to a schedule of replacing a nasty village chief every week, and he had been very successful. This had also kept the growing numbers of helpers busy, providing basic education and many other services.

The influence of the Free People as they called themselves extended well into London, although there had been no more adventures in that area, just a gentle consolidation.

Robin had not pushed his luck in that he hadn't gone too far away from the village. He had just about everything he needed right there, always having visitors and helpers coming to say hello or looking for some advice. He had taken a hike one day, with Lucy and Digga, to the old, ruined house where they had first met Tom. It was still as they had left it except that the vegetable patch had become overgrown once more. The old smells were still there which excited Digga no end, as she ran around looking for the fathers of her brood.

Their little village house had been extended to take in all the books that Robin had found in the old library, and he used that as a study area, although it was also open to the villagers. "Books are pretty important, aren't they?" claimed Lucy on seeing her man admiring the collection. "Without them we'd have not gotten anywhere."

"That's a very good point. I just wish I could find more. I've read all of these now."

"There must be more libraries," insisted Lucy. "I know you can't go very far, but if I found locations for old libraries could we persuade someone like Larry to dig them out?"

"It's worth a try."

"Oh good," replied Lucy. "I've found 7 libraries within 10 miles of here."

"Well," laughed Robin, "that was well planned. I'll ask Larry next time I see him. If he's successful, that will mean another extension to our little house."

"You are so right," Lucy agreed, "I mean it is getting a bit small for us already. It would be great to have one of those big new houses getting built. I would really love to have some running water. Now that would be a luxury. As well as another bedroom for Tommy's sister."

"But Tommy doesn't have a sister..."

"He will before his next birthday," admitted Lucy, looking coy.

"Ah," said Robin with delight, grabbing his woman tenderly and kissing her excitedly. "You always were full of surprises."

"Yelp," Digga agreed.

*

Somewhere in between Tommy's third and fourth birthdays, Tom had come for an extended visit. He'd been working so hard on village chiefs for so long, he'd decided to find someone to hand it all over to, now that they were progressing northwards.

"In fact," suggested Robin, "let's have several teams. You've got it all so well established. Anyway, it's time you took a wife and enjoyed some of the fruits of your labours. Nobody has done as much for our cause as you. You deserve a little rest and peace, not to mention a good time."

"Yes, that would be nice. Seems ages since I took the dogs up on the heath. Let's go together some time."

"Agreed," Robin smiled. "Where are the dogs anyway?"

"They have a couple of minders back in my village who look after them for me when I'm away. Yes, OK let's aim for midweek. I'll show you how well-trained dogs can catch rabbits. So much better than that bow and arrow you used to have." They both laughed at the memory of the feeble distance the arrows had gone when Robin had put his first bow together. It seemed so long ago now.

"You wouldn't laugh at the bows they have now," Robin stated. "Talk about bowmen of England. Robin Hood would have been proud of them."

They talked on into the night, but the things that were worrying them both just didn't go away.

"It doesn't seem to matter how successful we are with all of this," said Tom, "you just can't get away from the feeling that it could all be stolen away from us in a moment."

"We've done as much as we can, I believe," Robin said. "There are more than enough strong men to defend the villages, with real weapons. At a pinch we might even be able to use the lasers against anyone attacking us. David and George provide regular information on any movements by the lords. I don't know how they managed to get spies so deeply into several lord's residences north of London, but they are doing an amazing job. They also monitor the verbal radio waves after Larry so brilliantly built them a receiver."

"So far they've picked up no evidence of any planning being done to take us back to the dark days," agreed Tom, "even though they still watch the messaging from the gods' terminal. It could be that it is only the reptiles that are in control of that sort of thing, and are letting us flourish for now, or have forgotten about us."

"You could be right, which is more worrying. Whichever reptile god has taken over from the last one must realise at some point that no lords control this area. There would be no statistics which would be a dead giveaway."

"Also of course," added Tom, "they must be wondering how so many of us died in the Southeast so quickly. Maybe they imagine there is nobody here now." Tom laughed with a wild idea, "It could be that they will think we were hit with the virus they used to deceive our people with last century. Although they would surely never believe that considering it was no worse than the flu."

Robin laughed out loud, "Now that might be an interesting rumour to start. Perhaps we can get our spies to start putting out misinformation to deceive the lords. That would be some form of justice. Especially if they were warned that the virus had mutated and was especially dangerous to the high born."

"I like that," said Tom.

"The trouble is they'd only have to take a look through the spy in the sky to see that there are plenty of people down here, and the villages are thriving."

"I imagine our spies could do something useful with that information though," Tom smiled.

Robin smiled then frowned heavily, "You know, it is still a great worry to me that they could be planning some action, so I don't want to personally trigger something by attracting attention to myself."

"I do know what you mean," said Tom, having heard this argument several times. "You've still got your computer to dig into anything you want, the expanding library of books, as well as the spy in the sky, so nobody thinks you are being idle. Talking of such things, a few chiefs are now devoting a section of their village green as a tribute to you."

Not comfortable with that last comment Robin ignored it. "I've searched the dark sky on many a night but have seen no more space boats."

"Have you tried looking from other parts of the world?" Tom asked. "I mean the spies in the sky must look at just one part of the Earth each. When you blew up that lords' conference you must have switched over to a different device for which you just provided the location."

"Nice thought," agreed Robin. "I could use the other sky-spies to search different parts of the space sky. I will certainly give that a try. Also, there must be villages like this in different parts of Earth. I wonder if we can somehow send them a message. Wouldn't it be great if we could help them to break free as well?"

"I'll think on that one," Tom smiled. "There must be a way to help other groups though. I'm sure you will think of a way to be able to send them a message, even if you have to burn it into the ground with that light beam."

"Yes," smiled Robin again, "there has to be other ways that we can make contact with people like us around the world. All it will take is a little seed of information to get them moving towards freedom. I must scan other countries and see where their villages are."

"Will they understand our language though? From what I read each country has a different way of expressing itself, through its own language."

"Good point," Robin agreed. "I know our nearest neighbours to the east speak something called French, so perhaps we try to contact any that speak something similar to our language."

"So you need to search for English speakers. From what I understand much of the world spoke it at some time in the past, while it became dominant in Australia and America, probably other places too. Did you know this country once ruled the world?"

"You have been busy reading up on all of that," Robin smiled. "I did know we had a great empire at one time."

"On a different matter, closer to now, something we didn't get to finalise, just to change the subject completely," Tom laughed. "I was watching Jane the other day. She is so bright and happy these days. So much more alive than when we found her. It's such a treat to see her like that, Anne too. The thing is, we never did find out anything about that car that delivered Anne and Jane to the railway at Crayford. It slipped under our radar."

"Just as well that it no longer seems to be operating or we'd have to go and blow it up," laughed Robin.

*

...and so it went on, always new ideas to exploit, always hope for a better future, yet coupled with the dread of what the reptile gods and lords were capable of. Wherever they gained a village, or released prisoners, the messages to their new friends were always bold and sharp about how everyone had become slaves because of a great deal of deception in the past. Education in all forms, writing, reading, plus many other skills were made available to all, so that nobody would be living in ignorance.

The future had not yet arrived, but they were well on their way to something better. It all depended on not overplaying their hand to provoke a harsh response before they were big enough, strong enough and wise enough to survive and win against a clampdown by those that would rule, enslave and harvest them so easily without a moment's hesitation or consideration. If they could keep a steady path Robin was sure the human race would eventually win. While Digga rarely disagreed with Robin, she had the final say quite often, now reminding him, "Yelp yelp. Just be careful and don't stick your neck out too far."

Printed in Great Britain
by Amazon